PRAISE FOR *1837: LOVE AMONG STRANGERS*

"Kleidon's storytelling is masterful. Her vivid depiction of a pioneer family's migration and settlement, of choices made and luck gone wrong, is quilted into the realities of America's expansion into what was then the West."
—Steve Vogel, NYT Bestselling Author, *Reasonable Doubt, The Unforgiven*

"What a wonderful story…with some of my now-favorite characters…I loved reading about the perils of travel and how careful one had to be about what could be said in public and how difficult—and thrilling—it was to choose a new home. Historical events and people are skillfully woven into the kind of experience most of our ancestors had when coming to America. I can't wait for the author's next book." — Joan Marie Oltman

"*1837: Love Among Strangers* continues the page-turning adventures of the Kästner family as they tackle the immense challenges of establishing a new home in frontier America. The author's grasp of history, her powerful imagination, and her scenes—fast-moving and stunningly beautiful—create an amazing historical fiction series set in an era she makes come alive."
—Linda Marie Smith

"Kleidon's riveting sequel, *1837: Love Among Strangers,* will surely place her in the ranks of leading authors of historical fiction. It brings you a family to cheer for as they work out how to become American, including a sensitive treatment of youngsters coming of age in a very different era. Its fealty to historical accuracy will give you new insights into America when the mighty Mississippi was the frontier. I recommend this book unreservedly."
—William Zucker, translator, Carl Ewald stories

"A wonderful story! *1837: Love Among Strangers* isn't only about excitement and romance but also about the family's love for one another and for their new country. Like the first book in the series, *1837* helps you appreciate those who embraced immense changes with courage and contributed so much to our developing nation." —Judith Mikrut

PRAISE FOR *1836: YEAR OF ESCAPE*

"*1836: Year of Escape* pulls off a literary magic trick, weaving the sweeping movements of history around the gripping account of a single family's desperate emigration into America. Kleidon vividly recreates 19th century life right down to the sights, smells, and sensations."

—Pete Beatty, author of *Cuyahoga*

"*1836* is as much an engaging chronicle as it is a novel. The tightly packed narrative unfolds like leaves on a family tree: opening, fading, growing, renewing with the passing of time. It feels as if the reader walks as a witness to a real family's journey through its generations."

—Nancy E. Turner, NYT Bestselling Author; finalist, Willa Literary Awards; Arizona Author of the Year; *These Is My Words, The Water and the Blood, My Name Is Resolute,* and the Prine Family Series

"Engrossing story, glowing prose, stunning imagery. Kleidon reminds us how history repeats itself. Or echoes."

—Steve Vogel, NYT Bestselling Author, *Reasonable Doubt, The Unforgiven*

"A compelling storyline...wonderful characters and writing...fascinating historic detail. This book stands as a towering example of what a good writer can accomplish." —William Zucker, translator, Carl Ewald stories

"Brilliant! I can feel the ocean waves, see the distant horizon. I am sitting on a little sofa on the top floor of an old brownstone in Brooklyn with my tea, reading beautiful writing. Could it get any better than this?"

—Barbara Ellis, Unicorn for Writers

"What a wonderful story! This novel introduces you to an adventurous and delightful family's harrowing experience in traveling to America in 1836... an excellent historical novel, thoroughly researched and well written. This is a read I can highly recommend." —Judi Sanna

1837

LOVE AMONG STRANGERS

1837

LOVE AMONG STRANGERS

a novel

Rose Osterman Kleidon

RIVER GROVE
BOOKS

Published by River Grove Books
Austin, Texas
www.rivergrovebooks.com

This is a work of historical fiction. Names, characters, places, and incidents are the product of the author's imagination and are not to be construed as real. Where real-life historical or public figures appear, the situations, incidents, and dialogues concerning those people are entirely fictional. In all other respects, any resemblance to persons, living or dead, events, or locales is entirely coincidental.

Please note that some language may be culturally insensitive or offensive to some readers. The material reflects the culture and context of the era and/or of the fictional characters and not the views of the author.

Distributed by River Grove Books

Cover image: *Rendezvous,* watercolor on paper, Alfred Jacob Miller, The Walters Art Museum. Creative Commons License.

An excerpt from Miller's notes, titled "The West of Alfred Jacob Miller" (1837): "The scene represented is the broad prairie; the whole plain is dotted with lodges and tents, with groups of Indians surrounding them. In the river near the foreground Indians are bathing; to the left rises a bluff overlooking the plain whereon are stationed some Braves and Indian women. In the midst of them is Capt. Bridger in a full suit of steel armor. This gentleman was a famous mountain man, and we venture to say that no one has travelled here within the last 30 years without seeing or hearing of him. The suit of armor was imported from England and presented to Capt. B. by our commander; it was a fac-simile of that worn by the English life-guards and created a sensation when worn by him on stated occasions."

For historical notes and study questions, see www.rosekleidon.com.

Publisher's Cataloging-in-Publication data is available.

Print ISBN: 978-1-63299-938-2
eBook ISBN: 978-1-63299-939-9

First Edition

TO DENNIS

whose love makes everything possible.

CONTENTS

CHARACTERS

THE KÄSTNER FAMILY
Niklas Kästner, 46, veteran, merchant, member of the underground German Democracy Movement (GDM)
Hans, 24, Niklas's son by his first wife, Angelika
Katrina Beckmann Kästner, 40, Niklas's second wife
Niklas and Katrina's children: Will, 16; Amalie, 15;
Lisette, 8; and Jakob, 5

BERLEBURG, WITTGENSTEIN, PRUSSIA
Ernst Zimmermann, town constable, served with Niklas Kästner
in Napoleon's Grande Armée
Günter Erlinger, GDM member, and Addie, his wife
Elizabet Beckmann Mueller, Katrina's cousin

CAPTAIN, CREW, AND PASSENGERS OF *ENIGMA*
Izak Peterssen, Captain of *Enigma*
Mr. Groves, First Mate
Francesca Lenzini and her daughter, Franci, steerage passengers
Thomas Segrave, owner of *Enigma*, once a shipmate of Izak's
Giovanni, a rigger on *Enigma*'s crew
Erik Thorvald, Master Gunner, friend of Izak Peterssen
Mr. Stephens, Master

NEW ORLEANS
Marguerite Robichaux and her daughter, Yvette
Karl Schneider, banker
Ivan Ivanovitch, Russian involved in the Napoleonic Wars
Luka Ivanovitch, his brother
*Jean François Girod, admirer of Napoleon
*James Caldwell, New Orleans Gas Light and Banking Company
*Louis Dufilho, first licensed pharmacist of New Orleans
Jacques, Marie, and Antoine Huber, plantation owners

ABOARD *YELLOW STONE* AND *OTTAWA*
Robin LeMoyne, Ship's Purser, *YS*
Big Mike, Captain of the Aft Crew, *YS*
Doc Marshall, Pilot, *YS*
YS passengers: John Ewing, Josiah Bedford, Mathias Cunningham,
Bert and Chester Harms, Jeremiah Brown, Mrs. Rogers, Mrs. Green
Ottawa passengers: *Ossian Ross, Havana, Illinois; *Dr. Rudolphus
Rouse, president of Peoria; *John Detweiller, Peoria, Louisa Grady
James O'Keefe, Captain, *Ottawa*

IN ILLINOIS AND MISSOURI
Gordon McArthur, hotelier, Illinoistown
*Sister Rose Duchesne, *Father Pierre Jean de Smet, St. Louis
Mr. Grafton, shopkeeper, his daughter, Lottie, Illinoistown
Lewis and Eddie Peel, Havana, Illinois
Hennepin: Oskar and Ula Miller, inn owners; Augustus
Guttmann, mill owner, his daughter, Dora; *Antonie Bourbouvis,
fur trapper; **Gus Shepard, first White child born in Hennepin;
Michael Taylor, farmer; Lars Peterssen
Chicago: Lemuel Drake, stagecoach passenger; Adam Schwartz,
land speculator; **Granville Sproat; **Chicago Germans on page
206; **William Ogden, first mayor of Chicago
Benji Wolfe, Hoosier boy
Albert Hesselberth, Illinoistown and St. Louis
Sister Ignatius (Maggie Lynch), St. Louis

HISTORIC PERSONS *portrayed or ** mentioned
**Abraham Lincoln
**Elijah Lovejoy, murdered abolitionist, St. Louis and Alton
**Will Tallmadge, Thomas Hartzell, Gurdon Hubbard, Hennepin
**Christoph Sauer, printer, Schwarzenau and Pennsylvania
**everyone except Hans at the 1837 Rendezvous, Chapter 45
**Adolph Wislizenus, Theodor Engelmann

HISTORIC STEAMBOATS (paddle vessels or P.V. steamers)
*Yellow Stone P.V., *Ottawa P.V., ** Zebulon Pike

ENIGMA BROACHED

"You asked me," said Will Kästner, "what was the most frightening moment of the voyage. There were many, including the first time I climbed the rigging, but..." He looked off into the distance. "But none compared to the moment *Enigma* broached. We were almost all the way here, just off New Orleans, when a hurricane hit. We thought we were done for."

Dora Guttmann nodded and looked down at her feet, waiting for Will to continue. They were sitting in the shade by one of the new Kästner fields, taking a break during a morning of hoeing. The newly broken field was full of weeds, and the first year's crop of corn struggled to out-compete them. She would listen all day if it meant she could sit in the shade.

"In heavy seas, in the black of night," Will said, "*Enigma* heaved to one side, and the cabin door slammed open. Papa scrambled to his feet and was flung out of the cabin.

"'Niklas!' Mama screamed over the roar of the sea. Papa was gone.

"Hans and I grabbed her before she could be thrown out, too, surrounded her, and held her tight to the post in the middle of the cabin.

"A towering wall of water hung above *Enigma* for an instant and then smashed down, shaking her to her core.

"'We are sunk,' Hans shouted.

"In that breathless moment, all of us aboard, man or woman, sailor or landsman, knew what was at stake. Would *Enigma* rise with the rising swell? Or was she sunk?

"We waited, waited, waited. After a long, terrifying moment *Enigma* rose. She surged forward, dropped into the trough between the waves, and rose again in a horribly exaggerated pitching motion.

"On deck, Papa fought to get to the wheel, Captain Izak Peterssen crawled back to it through fallen spars and snarled rigging, and Ship's Master Stephens rose from where he had been knocked down, shook the blood off his face, and grabbed the wheel. Together they took the wheel in their hands and struggled to bring the barque up to the wind. These three men, against all odds, saved all on board and gave us a second chance to make a life for ourselves, a good life with children and grandchildren to come."

Will took Dora's hand as he said this, looking at her with adoring eyes.

She gently removed her hand from his and laid it modestly on her lap. *He wouldn't dare,* she thought, *except that we are out here in a field all by ourselves.*

"What happened next?" she asked.

Will sighed and continued. "The hull groaned like a sick animal. All around, wind and waves raged. Hans and I were on deck by now, fighting our way toward the men at the wheel. First Mate Groves was, too. We saw Mr. Stephens falter, slipping in his own blood, the blood pouring from his head.

"'Go below,' Izak roared to Stephens. Mr. Groves took the injured man by the arm and led him below. Hans and I leapt into the breach, grabbing the wheel. It took the strength of us all to keep the wheel in position. Sailors streamed out of every hatch. It looked like bedlam, but it wasn't. They all knew what to do.

"'Aft to the spanker sheets!' said one man. 'Heave away!'

"'Hang on now, or we're all goners!'

"'Lay forward and check the hatches!'

"In our cabin, Mama pulled herself hand over hand to the children's hammock, where Amalie threw a loose end of line around her waist and managed to tie it. Lisette and Jakob wailed in fear or pain, Mama did not know which.

"She told me later that she felt a great wave of panic and guilt. *If we go down with the ship,* she thought, *where Niklas and I willingly brought our children, God will take us into account for our stupidity, our pride, our sin.*

"Above the howling wind, she heard Jakob sobbing. She swore aloud: 'Never again will I put you in danger such as this.' She told Papa this later. I think it was a warning to him that she had really been stretched to her limit."

"But you did get through it," said Dora.

"Ah, yes," said Will. "But we were badly damaged and nowhere near safe. Days later, *Enigma* was still taking on water despite the tireless work of the crew and carpenters. I was in the crow's nest on seas not yet smooth, under a bright, hot sun, on duty as a lookout when I sighted land and called down to the deck. Soon, Izak and Mr. Groves were in tight consultation. Papa came up on deck, and Izak motioned to him to join them.

"'Herr Kästner,' Izak said, 'We have to make port.'

"'Papa looked around, seeing nothing but sea. 'Where?'

"'Will sees land,' said Izak.

"'Papa glanced up at me. He hesitated, but with his old training as a soldier, he was unwilling to question the captain. 'Have we been blown back to Cuba?' Where are we?'

"'Mr. Groves answered him, 'It took us west, not east, far from Havana and far past New Orleans. We are off Texas.' His voice was grim.

"'Texas!' said Papa.

"'In Havana we had all had been told about Texas, a province of Mexico now at war with her. 'Don't go anywhere near Texas,' we had been told.

"'You must marshal your marines again,' said Izak."

Dora looked confused, and Will explained.

"Before the hurricane and before *Enigma* made an emergency landing at Havana, we faced an attack at sea, and Papa recruited the men of the big German family in steerage, gave them the briefest of trainings, and shaped them into a fighting force. To tell the truth, only the most generous would have called them 'marines.'

He continued. "Now Papa could not refuse the captain's request to do it again. 'I am at your command,' he told Izak.

"As it happened," Will went on, "Texas had won the war just days before *Enigma* appeared on its shores, and the fear of landing in the midst of war evaporated. A week later, the barque had been repaired, and we were sailing again, this time to New Orleans, our original destination. The steerage family had disembarked, lured into staying in Texas by an offer of free land in a German colony. In their place, *Enigma* took on men of the army of the new

Republic of Texas, brave men from New Orleans who had come to fight for independence.

"Once at sea again, in glorious Caribbean sunshine, I saw Mama laugh as she and the girls sat on deck and sewed. Dolphins played in bright turquoise waves, and the crew was in such good spirits as could hardly be contained. The delights of New Orleans shimmered in our future.

"And that's the story of how we were almost lost at sea forever."

"I am so glad you were not," said Dora, and this time it was she who reached for his hand.

BOOK ONE

WOMEN OF LE VIEUX CARRE

"I can think of nothing more American than an immigrant."
— Maajid Usman Nawaz

CHAPTER 1

THE WICKEDLY RICH, HORRIBLE ENGLISHMAN

New Orleans, June 1836

"Is she here?" Amalie Kästner whispered to her brother Will.

They were upstairs in a New Orleans boarding house so new to them that neither knew how far their voices might carry. Amalie stared down at the landing and the bright spot on it. Sunshine poured through the beveled panes of a small, round window, caught the light, and split it into a rainbow. *It's beautiful,* thought Amalie.

"That round window looks like a porthole," she said aloud. "Which reminds me of what a relief to be on land, in any house at all."

"Nonsense," said Will. "I liked sailing, and I liked *Enigma.*"

She looked at him as if he were crazy.

"I'll admit to hard times on our crossing," her brother said. "But I liked being up in the rigging, and you liked *Enigma,* too, at least when Tom was saying sweet nothings to you."

At sixteen, Will was only a year older than Amalie, and they had always been a team, the pair of them feeling much younger than their half-brother, Hans, and much older than the two laggards, the little doll-child Lisette with her blonde curls and china-blue eyes, and the baby of the family, five-year-old Jakob.

To Will, Amalie didn't look quite like herself. She, who was never pretty like Lisette, was suddenly possessed of a perfect figure and lustrous hair, which had darkened to a rich auburn instead of trying vainly to be blonde. Suddenly Amalie was attracting more attention than her little sister, and for the whole family, this took some getting used to.

Only when Thomas Segrave, the ship's owner, noticed Amalie had the family begun to grasp this new reality. Perhaps it was to be expected that a relative stranger would see it first. After the hurricane, Tom had saved Amalie from a nasty fall on *Enigma,* and at that moment, she told Will, when their hands touched, they both (she was sure it was both) felt a lightning-like electricity. She laughed as she told Will about it, saying Tom suddenly went from the wickedly rich, horrible Englishman to her personal hero.

What Amalie did not tell Will was that in Texas, Tom talked frankly with her, telling her that as the owner of a ship, he could always sail to wherever she was. He could always find her. This was something she repeated to herself each night before she fell asleep.

Will had fallen in love on their long journey, too, during the stopover in Havana after *Enigma* was damaged in an attack by pirates. It was a case of love at first sight with Will and fifteen-year-old Ezmeralda, an exquisitely dressed girl from Havana's high society. She was the most beautiful girl he had ever seen, with ravishing dark hair, sparkling green eyes, and a perfectly womanly shape. She carried a ruffled parasol and peeking out from her skirts were the most delicate high-heeled shoes. Will was determined to make their first, magical meeting the beginning of a lifetime together, and he believed it possible until the very day he sailed away from Cuba on *Enigma.*

Instead, their first, magical meeting was their last. Will did not know that Ezmeralda's family was as determined as he was. They were horrified that their beautiful hijita would give an unknown foreigner (a German Lutheran heretic!) so much as a second glance.

They took away her ruffled parasol and her fine shoes and her exquisite dress, locked her in the house, and arranged for her immediate marriage. The reading of banns was dispensed with, and a good man found, a well-established man, settled and older, an appropriate, limpieza de sangre man of pure Spanish blood, a man whose linage they could trust. Her uncle.

Ezmeralda was kept on bread and water to impress upon her the necessity of obedience. She stood before the priest so lightheaded she could barely say "Sí." A week to the day after she met Will, Ezmeralda was a married woman.

Now, on this morning when both Havana and New Orleans were bathed in the same sunshine, while Will still dreamed of her, Ezmeralda had been properly married for weeks and every morning since then, she had been properly chastised. Today, she was crouched with her head over a bucket, experiencing the result her family had intended: morning sickness. Her uncle-husband was to be congratulated.

In New Orleans, Will was blessedly innocent of the fate of his true love. He smiled at the thought of her, vowed silently to go back to Cuba for her, and turned his attention to Amalie's original question: "Is she here?"

"Francesca arrived a few minutes ago," said Will, "and Franci is with her. You'd better go down and make your salutations."

"What about you?"

"I'll be along shortly." Will's tousled blond hair fell around his face as he put the finishing touches on a drawing of a steam engine, one of his many "enthusiasms." The model he built at home had been left behind in the rush to leave Berleburg. These drawings were his new design.

He spoke without looking up. "The next one will be a working model. Able to do real work."

"Real work? Like what?"

"I don't know yet. But enough to convince Papa. 'Tis the future, Amy!"

Amalie raised one delicate eyebrow. Their papa was not an easy man to convince. "I won't stay long, but it will give you a little time," she said. "Remind me, how did Mama and Francesca become such fast friends?"

"Over cabbage and potatoes," said Will. "Really, you could forget that?"

"Oh, yes, I remember now," said Amalie. She left Will to his design, hopping down the stairs and pausing on the landing to swish her skirts and admire how the prism of rainbow light danced on them.

She thought of that happy day aboard *Enigma* when her mother and Francesca Lenzini set up a kettle on the deck and cooked something that amazed everyone aboard. In 1836, passengers were required to bring their own food for an ocean crossing that generally lasted six weeks, though that could not be assured. The Kästners' voyage had taken longer, and the fare was routinely awful until these two good cooks shared their onboard supplies to turn out a delicious meal from the humblest of ingredients: potatoes, cabbage, and cheese. There was even some for the crew. On a voyage with more than its share of shock, tribulation, and death, cabbage and potatoes were enough for a meeting of the minds.

Two more images from their voyage followed in rapid succession: the corpse of the beautiful, lost Hannah sliding down the plank into the sea, and little Jakob standing wet and shivering on the deck after Will saved him. She had wrapped him in blankets, crying and laughing and still in a panic at his near drowning.

She shook her head free of memories, skipped down the last steps and went the wrong way in the first-floor hallway. She stopped and turned around. It had been only a few days that the Kästner family of seven had been off *Enigma* and settled at the Robichaux House in the center of New Orleans' Le Vieux Carre, so she could not blame herself for not knowing the way.

CHAPTER 2

A CHARMER AT SEA

The sound of a woman sobbing brought him up sharp.

The front door opened, and Katrina Kästner embraced Francesca Lenzini. Lisette dived around the women to grab Franci's hands. The girls wanted to jump up and down in glee, but they were now eight and must act like young ladies. So they clasped hands and fell into a fit of giggles.

Madame Robichaux had prepared two tea tables, the usual one and another for the girls. It was in the parlor's bow window, set with old china, and supplied with mayhaw berry scones and tea. Soon everyone was sipping and nibbling, and the room was filled with laughter and smiles.

Lisette dusted the crumbs off her skirt and asked, "May we go outside to play, Mama?"

"Yes, but you must take Jakob and stay on the porch or in the garden," Katrina said with some severity. To Francesca, she explained, "The garden is well fenced, bounded by the porch on this end and on the other by the slave quarters. They will be perfectly safe."

Francesca nodded her approval, Katrina smiled, and the two girls disappeared into the hallway.

It was the perfect moment for Amalie to appear. She made a smiling welcome to Francesca, inquired politely about where she and Franci were staying—a place called the White Rooster—and listened to the women talk for a few minutes. Then she excused herself.

Francesca watched her go, this plain child who had transformed on their long journey into a pretty young woman. She leaned in to accept more tea from Katrina. "Has Thomas Segrave called on her yet?"

"Not yet," said Katrina, "but I am watching closely."

"Surely you would not mind such a match."

"Of course not. But she is too young." Katrina had seen the "le coup de foudre" moment on the ship, and she knew the two had had at least one serious conversation in Texas, even though Amalie had not confided in her about it.

Katrina changed the subject. "Now, tell me all about Giovanni. Will you two marry? Or have you already?"

Francesca had been born near Bonn but had married an Italian traveling merchant and lived her adult life in Italy. She was now widowed. This unusual personal history made Francesca more sophisticated and more adventurous than anyone Katrina had known in Berleburg. Francesca had helped her cousins from Bonn make the journey and that way, had not had to travel alone.

She had been enchanted by the one Italian sailor aboard, a strong, handsome rigger who was made modestly wealthy by his share in the pirate booty the Enigmas had fallen heir to. Katrina assumed that Francesca and Giovanni had married—or were to be married—in the most modest of private ceremonies.

There was an awkward pause, and then Francesca replied: "He is perfectly happy to act married."

Katrina gasped. "Oh! I am so sorry!"

"He said it would be better for us not to marry. He must sign onto a ship again; he knows nothing else. He says I would be better off without legal entanglements, should he not return."

"I know nothing of the law," Katrina said slowly.

"Neither do I, but I made certain inquiries. Mr. Groves helped me." Mr. Groves, *Enigma*'s first mate, was a Cornishman, a devoted family man who often spoke of his dear wife and children.

"Oh, I must tell you," said Francesca, "of that poor man's tragedy. His entire family was stricken by the cholera. Gone, all of them. He is beside himself with grief."

Katrina sighed. "First Gideon lost at sea, and now Mr. Groves's whole family." Mr. Groves had pulled strings to get a place aboard for his nephew, Gideon. The boy was just fourteen when he went overboard during a storm. Neither woman had seen Gideon's horrible fall from high in the rigging, but

Katrina had heard the boy scream, and both knew how deeply Mr. Groves had felt the loss.

"Yes, how suddenly things change," said Francesca. She was thinking of her own losses, husband and children dead, all but Franci.

"How did Mr. Groves learn of the tragedy?" Katrina's voice trembled.

"A letter was waiting for him here in New Orleans. It happened not long after we sailed. Months ago, almost a year."

"What a horrible shock for him." Katrina dabbed at the tears that had sprung to her eyes.

They sat in respectful silence until Katrina asked, "But tell me, was Giovanni right about the law?"

"To be blunt, no."

"Ah," said Katrina.

"I should have stayed in Texas with my cousins. Now, because of my foolishness, I have destroyed all that is left of my family. I myself am disgraced and Franci is as well."

"My dear, let's not talk of disgrace."

"What would you call it?" Francesca stood and turned away to hide her tears.

By this time, Will was downstairs in the hallway, on his way to greet their visitors. His mind was elsewhere, deep in the complexities of steam engine design, when the sound of a woman sobbing brought him up sharp. He heard a shuddered half-sentence: "He's gone—"

He stopped and leaned against the doorframe, glad not to have burst in at that awkward moment, hoping they had not heard his footfalls.

"He's gone almost all the time." Francesca was sobbing. "He comes up from the White Rooster, drunk and angry, as if I caused his troubles!"

"You are not to think any of this is your fault," his mother urged her friend. "We must find a way out for you and Franci." There was a pause, and when his mother spoke, it was in a low voice: "Does he hit you?"

Will could not hear Francesca's murmured reply.

"Does he hit Franci?" His mother's voice was thick with anger.

"No! Mein Gott, no!"

Will heard this, but not whatever Francesca whispered next.

When Katrina spoke again, she sounded even more determined. "Have you hidden any money? Any valuables?"

"Not nearly as much as I should have. If only I had known! I loved him, you know. Sometimes I think I love him still."

"Giovanni was a charmer at sea," Katrina said, "an Italian charmer, like your first husband."

"Oh, they were nothing alike," said Francesca. "My Luciano was smart, clever, and kind. Though Giovanni does look like him a bit," she admitted.

"I always assumed Giovanni reminded you of him."

"Yes, he did, while we were aboard, and there was no liquor beyond the daily grog," Francesca said bitterly. "He's completely different now. Now I don't love him at all—I hate him!"

The sobbing began again, and Will guessed from the rustle of skirts that his mother had gotten up and gone to comfort Francesca. "Stop that," he heard his mother say. "You'll make me cry too."

Francesca's sobs subsided, and Katrina said, "I'll talk to Niklas. But now, come to the kitchen. Let's call the girls. We could use a decent meal."

Will slipped into a side room and backed against the wall as the two women passed by. He understood his mother's anger, but he also knew her to be helpless. Women were not to have opinions, and if they were so foolish as to have them, certainly not to take action. The whole fabric of society depended on this: women forbidden to act. Any woman who did so was considered either loose or insane. And yet, that anyone would threaten an innocent like Franci was outrageous. He had heard enough to know he had to save this woman and child, and this conviction rapidly became a plan.

When their voices faded, he ran upstairs and grabbed his silver-topped walking stick, his one extravagance at the tailor's shop. He hesitated, studying the walking stick, and considering what his father would advise. He wished Hans and his father were home. But Giovanni was sure to be alone, and he understood Giovanni in ways that none of the others in the family ever would. Only he had been high above the decks of *Enigma*, working with Giovanni, sharing the particular thrill and danger of being a rigger.

Moments later, coat and hat and cane in hand, Will closed the front door behind himself, quiet but firm in his purpose. At the corner, he hailed a hansom cab. "Coq Blanc," he told the driver. "White Rooster."

CHAPTER 3

AS IF THE SEA SWALLOWED HIM

"If you had missed, he'd have killed you."

At a particularly bad jolt, Will lifted the leather window curtain of the hansom cab to stare at the surroundings. *Decidedly wretched.* He recognized it as a sailor town, one of those scandalous neighborhoods found wherever ships disgorged their crews into saloons, brothels, opium dens, and gambling houses built with the especial purpose of stripping said crews of dignity, sobriety, and ready cash.

"Coq Blanc," he had heard Francesca say. He saw the sign and tapped the roof of the cab with his walking stick. The driver pulled the reins and called out: "Whoa." The cab rolled to a stop. Will jumped out, paid the driver, and the cab rattled off. Will was left to stare at the sign of the White Rooster. Upstairs, above the tavern, would be the lodgings where Giovanni housed Francesca and Franci. Will decided to try the tavern first.

He opened the door and was blinded by the sudden absence of the sun. He heard two men, drunk before noon.

"A sad story indeed, mon ami," said one.

"Aye, a story such as would make Medusa weep." The second man fell into a fit of coughing.

Will's eyesight came back gradually, enough to make out a third man in the room, seated alone at a table with his back to Will. When he raised his head to drink, Will recognized him.

"Giovanni?"

Giovanni's hand went to the dagger at his waist, but the fast movement almost tipped him off his chair. The table shook, and his beer glass fell, shattering.

Will held up his hands in dismay. "Aw, Giovanni! Mate, it's me, Will."

Giovanni stared at the spilled beer. "Look what you did, you stupid bastard." He put both hands on the edge of the table to steady it, and there were the tattoos Will had so admired: HOLD across the knuckles of one hand, FAST across the other, the proud tattoo of a rigger.

When *Enigma* was under repair in Havana, Will had begged his father for these same tattoos in solidarity with those who work high above the deck. His father had had no truck with such an idea, and now Will was glad to have been forbidden it. He no longer aspired to the life of a sailor, not even a rigger, the strongest and most fearless of all sailors. Instead, he wanted to become the owner of a fine, ocean-going barque like *Enigma*. It was not the ship's crew but the ship's owner, Thomas Segrave, he most admired now. Oddly enough, it was Tom's attentions to Amalie that made Will himself think he might someday own a ship. It was arrogant, he knew, but now that he had thought it, the idea was irresistible.

"I'm sorry, mate," said Will. "I'll get you another." He raised one hand to signal the barkeep.

"It ain't the same," said Giovanni.

"What?" Will laid his silver-handled walking stick on the table and took a seat across from Giovanni, moving slowly so as not to startle him, and spoke again. "Francesca…" he began.

"She sent you?"

"No, no! I came on my own." Francesca was still a good-looking woman, and Will couldn't help but blush at the thought of being somehow involved with her.

Giovanni sneered. "Into this hell hole on your own. Hah! She's picking up boys now, is that it?"

"I said no, Giovanni." *This is ridiculous,* Will thought, *but how do you make a drunk see sense?*

Giovanni's face darkened. "The slut. She'll pay for this, you can be sure. That whelp of hers will, too."

With a flash of light, the tavern door opened.

"Look, Giovanni—"

"I'll teach you not to come between a man and his woman." Giovanni stood, looking much steadier on his feet. He drew his dagger with a slow, clearly intentional movement.

The blade caught the light, and Will saw that it was wickedly sharp. Mr. Groves, *Enigma*'s first mate, blunted any knife a sailor brought aboard, the better to keep fights from becoming deadly, but this one was new and had its original sharp point.

Will grabbed his stick, scrambled off his chair, backing up, watching Giovanni. Behind the Italian, three men were fast approaching. At the bar, the two drunks staggered to their feet and stumbled toward the door.

Will had a moment of panic. *More Italians?*

Then he recognized the men approaching. *Enigmas!* The recognition went through him with a shiver. *Whose side are they on?* He turned his attention to the immediate need: avoiding that new dagger.

"Listen, mate," said Will, "you'll laugh when you hear what she said—"

Giovanni lunged toward Will, who stepped deftly aside, dropping suddenly into the breathing and focus instilled by years of training in swordsmanship. Will used his walking stick like a sword, and more quickly than the eye could see, he brought it upward in a classic Unterhau blow against Giovanni's wrist. The knife went spinning toward the ceiling, but the blow shattered Will's walking stick. He knew, even as Giovanni's dagger clattered to the floor, that he had no weapon.

Giovanni swung at Will, and in the same moment, one of the *Enigma* crewmen grabbed Giovanni's arm and twisted hard. The other Enigmas collared the Italian and wrenched him to the floor. Mr. Groves appeared from amid the Enigmas. "Take him away," he ordered.

The Enigma crewmen pulled Giovanni up and pushed him toward the door. Giovanni just had time to give Will a look of pure hatred. Will took a deep breath and rubbed his hands together, glad to have been spared a fist-fight. He picked up the broken walking stick. *Maybe,* he thought, *the silver handle can be salvaged.*

Mr. Groves turned to Will. He was not pleased. "You know you had that one strike. If you had missed, he'd have killed you."

"Aye, sir. I know, sir." Will had never been more thankful for the years of swordsmanship training his father had required or for the sudden appearance of a friend. He ran his hand down the walking stick and felt the broken end. *Mr. Groves is right. I had had only one chance to use this poor excuse for a weapon.*

"What in the devil's name are you doing here alone, anyway?"

Will sputtered, and Mr. Groves turned even angrier. "Does your father know you are here? Where's that strapping big brother of yours? Is he aware of this escapade of yours?"

"They were not home when Francesca—Signora Lenzini—came to visit Mother. I overheard what she said about Giovanni being a drunk and..." Will hesitated, "disgracing her, endangering Franci."

"And you thought you'd take on an angry drunk by yourself? A grown man at the peak of his strength? Without a decent weapon?"

Will stood straighter. "Immediate action was warranted. I know Giovanni, and I thought I could talk some sense into him. I didn't know he would be drunk." Will saw the flicker of a smile on Mr. Grove's face, a smile with no amusement to it at all.

Will steeled himself and asked, "Where will they take Giovanni?"

"I should think it obvious, Herr Kästner," said Mr. Groves. "The bloody stupid sod needs to be put to work. He won't stop drinking unless he's at sea. He ships out tonight. To Mexico City." He paused.

Will took a deep breath. "I thought he would —"

Mr. Groves waved off his excuses. "Let's go, Herr Kästner. This step was necessary, but Signora Lenzini still needs our help. We will bring her back to pick up her things. She and her daughter, that darling child, need a strong escort and a safe place to stay. They must not sleep another night in this hellhole."

Will followed the first mate out of the tavern and watched as the older man hailed a cab. Will was worried about what his father would say. He had disobeyed several of his father's strictest rules, not to go off alone, not to go unarmed, and always to outnumber the enemy. Moreover, he regretted having broken his new walking stick.

It was only later that Will realized that Mr. Groves never said how he knew what was going on. Or how he showed up at that perfect moment. Nor did he mention the name of the ship on which he had deposited Giovanni. Or seem to have a second thought about what Francesca would want. Mexico City was the destination of many coastwise ships leaving New Orleans, and in that crowd, Giovanni had vanished.

He was gone as completely as if the sea had swallowed him.

CHAPTER 4

ONE GLORIOUS WHITE FEATHER

"Why didn't you tell me?" Niklas's voice was a hiss.

The Kästner family had been in New Orleans three whole days when the world proved itself altogether too connected. It began innocently enough with a stroll through le Vieux Carre, whose streets had been hacked from Louisiana swampland little more than a hundred years earlier.

Niklas was still unhappy about his middle son's escapades and glad to have Will and Hans off on their own while he strolled along the boulevard with his wife and two daughters. Little Jakob, the five-year-old darling, was safely ensconced at Robichaux House.

Katrina's face was hidden by an enormous straw hat with an oversized white satin ribbon and a glorious white feather. The hat was new, an extravagance to celebrate being in the fabulous city known as the Paris of the New World.

"I must have it," Katrina had told him and then corrected herself. "The girls and I must have them. Our new dresses are incomplete without hats." This was indisputable.

Now, Katrina smoothed the fine linen cloth of her blue and white checked apron over the blue calico cotton of her dress. Wearing a decorative apron was the height of fashion in Paris, and she was determined to show New Orleans the fashions of the continent. This particular linen fabric, however, was not available to anyone in New Orleans. She had spun the threads and woven the cloth herself in their hometown of Berleburg, a charming village in the mountains east of Cologne. When she saw the blue cotton calico in Texas, she knew the two fabrics would be perfect together.

The three ensembles, one each for Katrina, Amalie, and Lisette, were sewn on their voyage from Texas to New Orleans. It took all of the blue and white checked linen. The girls now had matching straw hats, theirs tied with the same white satin ribbon but with no feathers, a step down, as befitted their status as children.

The trip from Texas was the last leg of their long voyage from Europe, a last delightful idyll on *Enigma*, nothing like the tribulation of the ocean crossing or the vicious hurricane that had pushed them away from New Orleans and tossed them onto Linnville, Texas.

As they walked along the streets of le Vieux Carre, Katrina kept sighing, relieved to be here at last, after an interminable braving of Atlantic storms and mal de mer, shocking deaths, pirates, and forced landings. With fresh joy, she sighed to see streets and houses in straight lines, the slanted morning sun glancing off them, lighting up the odd window as if glass panes were diamonds, and throwing alleys into deep purple shadow: the very picture of order imposed upon chaos, of man over nature.

And yet, the rush and clamor of it! Instead of the steady whoosh of ocean waves against the hull and the clink of halyards, the raucous calls of tradesmen and shillers sounded on all sides above a clatter of hooves and a rumble of wagons, carriages, carts, and wheelbarrows. Instead of fellow passengers and the familiar crew and officers of *Enigma*, there were a thousand new faces. It seemed that every New Orleanais was on the move, off in different directions at once. From above came a shrill, familiar note, a seagull's cry.

"The very air breathes of commerce, energy, and freedom." Katrina raised her face to whisper this in Niklas's ear.

Niklas smiled down at her and agreed. "Ancient despotisms dissolved and forgotten."

Deep in a jungle setting, New Orleans was darker and more verdant than Paris, but European-inspired architecture and newly installed streetlamps—gas-lit!—spoke of the city's reputation as the New World's own Ville des Lumières, its own Paris, the city of lights.

New Orleans may have seemed fully Parisian to those coming unschooled from one or another of America's frontiers, but to the Kästners, it was a pale imitation. Every little difference shouted, "New World, New World," none more loudly than the many faces of slaves around them. New Orleans was an imitation of Paris in a country that claimed to be the modern embodiment of democracy while embracing slavery. This was an irreconcilable conflict, and to Katrina and Niklas, a sin against its proclaimed love of liberty. Not even the joy of being on solid ground could save the Kästners from sensing the corrupt underpinnings of the city. By 1836, New Orleans, especially le Vieux Carre, was both thrilling and decrepit.

The sudden appearance of a beautiful woman like Katrina caused rampant gossip. Katrina's carriage was upright, her eyes bright, and her cheekbones smooth and high. She moved with confidence, though in truth, it was a quickness born of impatience. The impression she gave of being aristocratic was softened by her strawberry-blonde curls. Her immediate effect on men was attraction and on women intimidation.

Katrina was Niklas's second wife. He had been married for less than a year to Angelika, who died giving birth to their son, Hans. On that same day, far from the birthing room, a Russian sword had sliced open Niklas's face as he fought at the Battle of Borodino. Napoleon's Grande Armée won that day's battle, and thus Niklas was stitched up and carried on a stretcher into Moscow instead of being left for dead on a Russian hillside. Angelika was gone, and Moscow was burning, but Hans and Niklas survived that awful day, September 7, 1812.

Four years later, Katrina and Niklas married. Niklas had come home after the Battle of Waterloo, but he was not seen as a hero for long. Times changed, and the king of Prussia demanded a change in loyalties. Besides, Niklas would always carry the scars of battle, inside and out. Katrina married him despite her father's warnings, in part because of her sympathy for the child, Hans, and Hans's love for her.

On this, their third day on dry land, Katrina was not the only one catching the eyes of passersby. An equal number were drawn to Amalie. She was holding hands with her little sister, Lisette, whose happy smile, big blue eyes, and bouncing blonde curls were enchanting in their own way.

All of the Kästners were beginning to lose their sea legs, adjusting to an Earth that did not sway beneath them after their ocean voyage. It had been longer and more complicated than anyone could have imagined, but as the stultifying regimes of Old Europe dropped farther away by the moment, they felt the joy of having completed a fraught passage successfully.

"Mama, Mama, look!" Lisette had pressed her nose to the glass window of a dress shop, and Amalie was only a little less excited.

"Girls! Don't gawk." But to tell the truth, Katrina was also transfixed by the riches on the other side of the window. Lacy shawls, quilted capes, ruffled or tatted collars, embroidered slippers. Nestled among these were perfumes in glass bottles, lotions swirled into porcelain jars, and tiny, mysterious vials of various colors. In the middle, a dressmaker's mannequin showed off a confection in ivory silk. It had mutton sleeves tipped with lace and a skirt decorated with swirling lines of couched embroidery.

Niklas stood off to one side, forgotten, and could not help but tap one toe. At forty-five years old, he was a handsome man, broad shouldered, heavily muscled, and thick-necked with a square jaw and deep blue eyes. The wicked scar across his face had faded over the years, but it, along with his military bearing, hinted at battles fought, at danger and intrigue, at an extraordinary life.

Katrina stepped away from the window and went to Niklas. She clasped his arm. "It's a glory," she said, "to be on land and in the actual, real United States." The white feather in her hat quivered with excitement.

"In America!" agreed Niklas. "With all the family alive and well."

"Oh, yes!" said Katrina. "Though don't hex it by saying it out loud." She turned and called, "Girls! Come now."

They gathered the girls to them, turned a corner, and ran directly into a bent, peglegged man with a smallpox-scarred complexion.

"Ivan Ivanovich!" Niklas looked as astonished as ever Katrina had seen him.

"'Tis I," the peglegged man snarled, "and I never liked ye from the moment I clept eyes on ye."

Katrina gasped to see the stranger's hand fly to the hilt of his dagger. She recognized him at once as the vicious little man on the wharfs the day they arrived in New Orleans. As they debarked *Enigma,* an angry face had appeared in the sweltering confusion of dock workers and hurrying passengers, a face at first surprised and then furious at the sight of Niklas. Katrina had not known what to make of it. Now she pulled the girls to her. She and Amalie stood side by side, hiding Lisette behind their skirts.

"Nor I you, Ivan Ivanovich," said Niklas.

"You owe me for this," Ivanovich snarled, waving his dagger toward his missing leg.

Niklas's hand was on his sword, and his voice was low and steady, "Would you like to lose the other leg?"

The peglegged man hesitated. This was all the time Niklas needed to draw his sword. It came out of the scabbard silently. A long moment passed when no one moved.

The peglegged man let his dagger slide back down into its leather sheath. "Ye damned bugger of a Kraut." He turned his back and lurched away.

Niklas swore. "I should have dispatched him."

Katrina gasped. "But what then?"

"I am sure," he said, "New Orleans allows a man to respond to insult."

"But, but," she sputtered. A fine line of fear ran through her. "We are strangers in this city with no one to speak for us."

"I would not have you and the girls witness bloody violence. It is bad enough that you once saw murder on the streets."

He meant the event that pushed them to America in the first place, the murder by Prussian secret police of a fine young man, their nephew, a revolutionary like Niklas. Both he and his nephew had been members of the outlawed German Democracy Movement. By bad luck, Katrina had witnessed the bloody moment. The memory of it still shook her, but she focused on what had just happened.

"Who is he?" Katrina peered down the street, where Ivan Ivanovich had disappeared from sight. All she knew was that this horrid little man must be Russian. He and Niklas had spoken Russian.

"A pig. From Moscow."

"Here! In the New World!" Katrina desperately wanted Niklas to escape any reminder at all of his service in Napoleon's Grande Armée and in particular of the wound to his face and his recovery in Moscow.

For Niklas, the long march home from Moscow through a Russian winter was the source of nightmares. It was a retreat only one man in forty survived, and it was never far from Niklas's mind.

Yet even here, Katrina thought, *a Russian!*

Niklas lay a hand on Katrina's shoulder. "Let's away. No look of haste, mind you, but—" he scanned the crowds. "There is not a moment to be lost. Where Ivanovich goes, his brother Luka, a violent, bear-like man, will not be far behind."

"I saw him before—when we arrived," Katrina whispered. "At the docks."

"Who? Luka?"

"No, no, this one. Ivan."

"Why didn't you tell me?" Niklas's voice was a hiss, but he grasped the obvious immediately, and his voice softened. "But you couldn't have known. Ivanovich—here in New Orleans—it beggars belief."

CHAPTER 5

A MOST WELCOME SIGHT

"This could be the turning point."

"Herr Kästner!" They heard the voice first and then saw Captain Izak Peterssen step out of a tailor's shop.

Behind him, Erik Thorvald filled the doorway, his face red from the heat, his collar open, and the scars on his neck enflamed, fierce delight on his face at the prospect of a fight. Izak Peterssen's short sword was already unsheathed.

How out of place they look, Katrina thought, *these strong young men, with their weathered faces and pigtails announcing themselves as sailors.* Izak Peterssen was tall, blond, and Danish, captain of the barque *Enigma* that had brought the Kästner family across the Atlantic. His master gunner, Erik Thorvald, matched him in height, a muscular, redhaired Icelander. In this cosmopolitan, Francophone city, they were clearly foreigners.

Izak cast an inquiring eye over each member of the family, lingering perhaps a little longer on Amalie. Her face was drained of color, but even so, she surprised him. *How,* he thought, *has this butterfly emerged from the little caterpillar of a girl I took aboard in Rotterdam?*

"What of the boys? And little Jakob?"

"They are off by themselves," Niklas assured him. "You are a most welcome sight," he added with a slight bow.

"Are you all right, Frau Kästner?"

The feather in Katrina's hat bounced as she nodded. "All of us are untouched. Danke, Kapitän." *None of us,* she thought, *can ever repay you, who brought us safely to this shore. The strong arm of Thorvald is a comfort, too.*

"May I ask," said Izak, "who was this creature threatening you? We saw you look around—do you expect he has friends?"

"Ivan Ivanovich," said Niklas, "is a Muscovite rat who stayed on in 1813 when decent Russians—if there be such a thing—burned down the city around us as they fled. Ivanovich spoke a little French and saw the gold to be had by supplying us with goods plundered from deserted houses. He was with us while I recovered." He waved his hand at the scar running across one eyebrow and cheek. "He didn't hurt us today, and the danger has passed."

Katrina looked away as Niklas said all this, hiding her amazement. She knew his extreme dislike for speaking of his part in the Napoleonic Wars and thought it a good sign that he felt he could be so frank about it.

"When the orders for retreat arrived," Niklas continued, "I caught Ivanovich stealing from us. He ran, but not fast enough. We left him there bleeding—I did not expect he would survive—and certainly not that I would ever see him again." Niklas looked genuinely surprised, taken up with his memories.

"Russians." Izak's face hardened.

"Sailors who jumped ship, most like," said Erik Thorvald, motioning to his own plaited hair. Katrina recalled that the peglegged Ivanovich had a pigtail and caught Erik's meaning.

"And the others you are looking for?" Izak reminded Niklas.

"Ah, that would be Luka, his idiot brother, a huge, dangerous, profoundly stupid man."

Now everyone looked around, and with one mind, they turned down the largest, brightest street, moving swiftly. When Lisette skipped to keep up, Erik Thorvald swept her up with one arm. She had just had her eighth birthday but was still small enough for him to carry without a thought and still young enough to be thankful for his protection, so willingly given.

Before they parted ways, Niklas told the men about Robichaux House, and Katrina invited them to Sunday supper and begged them to extend the invitation to Thomas Segrave, who had sailed with them. Amalie said nothing, but Katrina saw her color rise at the sound of this invitation.

As Izak and Thorvald walked away, Katrina worried aloud, "We have just invited three men!"

"We can invite Madame Robichaux and Yvette," said Amalie. "It would help balance the table." Amalie was already enamored of Yvette Robichaux, the daughter of the house and a fascinating new friend. Yvette was Amalie's age, but far more sophisticated.

"And what about Francesca?" Katrina asked Niklas.

"And Franci!" said Lisette, her eyes lighting up at the thought. Aboard *Enigma*, Francesca's daughter had been Lisette's best friend.

"It would help," said Katrina, "and we must invite them anyway."

"I think that makes fifteen," said Amalie, who was counting on her fingertips. "Perhaps we ought to consult Madame Robichaux."

"I will," said Katrina. "But it's a grand house. I am sure she could seat twenty without thinking twice."

"Let Franci and me eat in the kitchen," begged Lisette. "We can take care of little Jakob."

"Oh, Jakob! I had not even counted him," said Amalie.

"We will need you two," said Katrina. "But Jakob does not belong at a dinner table."

It's settled, thought Amalie. She wanted to dance like Lisette.

"Achtung!" Niklas shooed them along. "Who stands in the street to talk of such things?"

It turned out that Niklas insisted they also invite Karl Schneider to Sunday evening's supper. He was the young New Orleans banker to whom they had been given a letter of introduction by Lennart Mueller, the only German in Linnville, Texas. Mueller tried to talk the Kästners into settling in a new German settlement being formed inland by Johann Ernst, writer of *The America Letters*. According to Mueller, Ernst wanted the new settlement to become a Prussian colony. He did not know how much Niklas wished to escape any allegiance at all to the king of Prussia.

Karl Schneider makes us an even seven and seven! Katrina knew the women's side was weak, including as it did two eight-year-old girls. *Good experience for them*, she thought, *but I pity their companions*. She was pleased to invite Marguerite and Yvette Robichaux, both mother and daughter as glamorous and charming as anyone could want. Marguerite was an authentic New Orleanais, an impeccable guide to the society of the city, and Yvette was decorative no matter what she wore.

"Which napkins?" said Amalie. She held out white linen in one hand and pale indigo in the other.

"White, of course. See the fringe on the indigo? It's too informal."

As she laid out napkins, Amalie lamented, "Will this evening never arrive?"

Katrina thought her daughter's impatience had to do with *Enigma*'s owner Thomas Segrave, and when Amalie blushed at the mention of his name, Katrina was sure of it.

The Kästners' new landlady, Marguerite Robichaux, was the kind of woman around whom others swirl, a very good-looking widow. She was German by heritage and had married a wealthy Cajun, and together, they had been the irresistible center of a wide social circle. Being suddenly widowed and impoverished, Marguerite Robichaux had opened her home to boarders. She ran her boarding house well, had an excellent cook, and came recommended by Elijah Bennett, innkeeper in Linnville, Texas, the tiny coastal village where *Enigma* put in after the hurricane.

The independence of Texas had come as a most welcome surprise to the newly arrived *Enigma*; it meant she had not run up against a dangerous coast in the midst of war. To many of those aboard, the larger surprise was that this mystery land existed at all, neither Mexico nor America, and birthed only days before by Sam Houston's defeat of Santa Anna. Despite their surprise, the large German family who had come over in steerage decided to stay in Texas, where land was free, since they hoped to start a summer crop. Of the family, only Francesca and Franci had come along to New Orleans, perhaps because of Francesca's shipboard romance with the rigger Giovanni. For him, only a port city like New Orleans was acceptable.

On being introduced to Madame Robichaux, Katrina was struck by how similar she was to Cousin Elizabet, who had stayed behind in Berleburg, a woman too beautiful, fascinating, and competent to be anything but the focus of society. Marguerite Robichaux was a little shorter than Elizabet, a little rounder, and had the added attraction of a gorgeous daughter, the two of them complementing each other in a kaleidoscope of silk and lace.

Katrina was immediately sure the Robichauxes were the perfect entrée to the best of New Orleans.

Robichaux House was near the center of town, ideally situated on a quiet side street, and big enough to accommodate the Kästner seven. Katrina saw to her satisfaction that its windows were kept spotless. This city, so like Paris, was even filthier and more pestilential. The cleanliness of Robichaux House was a welcome surprise.

She and Niklas were shown to a bedroom with dark red drapery, a large feather bed and just room for little Jakob's cot. The five-year-old could fall sleep anywhere but liked to be where he could crawl into his parents' bed before dawn. Amalie and Lisette shared a little, airless room next to their parents, which looked suspiciously as if it had once been a closet.

The older sons, Will and Hans, still called "the boys" even though Hans was twenty-four and Will sixteen, were bunked in the attic, under the eaves in a slant-roofed space unbearably hot and stuffy. The boys looked at each other with raised eyebrows, and Will knew immediately that they would find a sleeping niche on the porch. And that he would find Hans absent some mornings. His only hope was to be taken along for some wild nights out, as he had been in Havana.

By Sunday evening, Amalie was weak with nervous energy and impatient for the evening to cool down. The table had been laid immediately after the noontime dinner, and a young and otherwise useless slave girl had been stationed to fan the room and keep the flies off plates and silverware and savory dishes as they were brought from the kitchen.

All afternoon, Yvette Robichaux had blinked in delight to have this rich field of available men about to be brought before her: seven, counting the Kästner men, to be right at her own dining room table, and only one, the father, Niklas Kästner, unavailable. She tamed her curls and had herself laced into an hourglass of a dress. The smile came naturally, as did the dimples. Yvette was aquiver with excitement at the prospect of six eligible bachelors soon to appear, among them a ship's owner, a captain, and a wealthy banker. She was rehearsing their names and going over the details she had elicited from Amalie, who seemed to think the ship's owner was her own. This only made Yvette smile at the other girl's naïveté.

"Perhaps this dinner," Marguerite said privately to Yvette, "can make Robichaux House a center for important gatherings again. As it should be. As it was when your father was alive."

Marguerite was desperate to make a good match for Yvette, but she knew her daughter could be kept fresh and virginal for a few more years, while she herself needed a wealthy man right now, so she too was reviewing the names of her guests and wondering about their ages. Her hunger for a match grew every day as she watched her once-fine estate fall apart. It was already patched from shingles to slave quarters.

"This dinner could be the turning point for us," said Marguerite.

Yvette hardly heard her mother. But if Yvette was excited, her mother was even more so. Marguerite Robichaux had successfully converted the grand home her husband left her into a rooming house, but her cheeks burned at the thought. It was as highbrow as she could make it, but it was still a rooming house, and who opens a once-fine home to boarders unless poverty threatens?

CHAPTER 6

THE TAINT OF YANKEE SYMPATHIES

No one had made that point perfectly clear.

At exactly seven, the knocker on the front door was lifted and dropped, and Izak Peterssen, Thomas Segrave, Erik Thorvald, and Karl Schneider were admitted.

Izak was in his captain's uniform with its yellow waistcoat, a subtle tribute to Denmark, the land of his birth, though he had never sailed in its navy. He looked as impressive as a man in uniform can when tall, broad, and handsome.

Thomas was dressed as a ship's owner should be, in an exquisitely tailored suit with a lavender waistcoat and a silk cravat pinned with a pearl set in gold.

Erik Thorvald was wearing the cleanest, most decent clothing the family had ever seen on him and looked noticeably uncomfortable. His red hair had been slicked back into a pigtail, and his face was flushed with heat and incipient embarrassment.

The dapper and cheerful Karl Schneider was tall enough, but slight and slim, the very picture of urbanity in a double-black coat, the kind of man one saw in London or New York, a prosperous young businessman. He was immediately valued as the one among them who best spoke all three languages of the evening, having grown up in Germany, learned English in Boston, and been long enough in New Orleans to speak its particular Creole French. He was naturally outgoing, a friendly young man on whom these languages were not wasted.

Karl greeted Yvette and her mother as old friends. He was thinking warmly of his first few days in New Orleans, when he had been a guest at Robichaux House. Still, there was something of an awkwardness. The

Robichauxes could not ignore Karl; it would be poor business indeed to dismiss a wealthy, spirited young fellow, and besides, they were grateful that he had recommended them. But to be seen with an atheist! And one who was, besides that, a Yankee, over-educated, and a banker!

Remember his fine prospects, thought Marguerite as she smiled stiffly.

Hans and Will were happy to see the men of *Enigma*, with whom they had sailed and by whose side they had fought. Both boys had been to the barber, and both had had their travel clothes scrubbed into something presentable for social events. Hans, who was handsome no matter what, wore a full, dark beard in striking contrast to his white collar. Will, though at sixteen the only real boy of the group, had been transformed by a summer of working in the rigging. He moved in his body as if he were surprised by its new muscles and proud of them, which he was. Still, what one noticed first about him, as always, were his bright blond curls. They had made Ezmeralda, the Havanese girl who fell in love with him, think he was Apollo come to life.

While the men greeted each other like the old friends they were, slapping backs and grinning, Katrina watched her daughter closely. At the sight of Tom, Amalie blushed deeply. Tom himself may have turned a little paler than usual.

Katrina said quietly to Niklas, "Such a handsome gathering of young men."

"Yes, and muscle, a ready-made military unit. I long to seat them all on cavalry horses and take them through a proper exercise."

"But imagine the horse required for Thorvald!"

"He would need an Ardennes," he said, thinking of the enormous draft horse native to the Ardennes Forest.

"Like a knight in armor," she said. "And we would need a second Ardennes for Hans. Katrina chortled at the image of Hans and Thorvald as knights in armor, and Niklas did too.

Niklas had been told by drivers of the teams pulling Napoleon's cannon into Russia that Ardennes had been favored by medieval knights because they could carry a fully armored man into battle at a gallop. Napoleon's drivers had chosen wisely. Ardennes were the only horses able to survive the wintertime retreat of the Grande Armée. Niklas brushed this dark memory aside.

Now that the moment was upon her, it was Thomas Segrave who left Yvette most breathless. His fine clothing and aristocratic accent sent her instantly into visions of castles and crowns.

Tom could not help but see Yvette's admiration, and after introductions, he looked around approvingly at the Robichaux parlor and told her, "I have not seen such a gracious home since I left London." This was a lie, but a white lie.

Yvette took it as ample reason to link arms with Tom and take him around to the several framed items decorating the walls, stopping at her mother's favorite, a painting she said was of the French school after Jacques-Louis David.

"Ah," said Tom, "the painter of the Revolution."

"I am sure you are right," said Yvette, with a studious look. It was always her inclination to be agreeable though she did not know which revolution Tom meant or what David had to do with it. She tilted her head as if in thoughtful consideration of the painter's role, revealing the most delicate long neck.

Tom found this long neck and serious face even prettier than her smiles, so he answered by patting the soft white hand that lay on his arm. It had been a long time since he had had the pleasure of being thought a connoisseur by a young woman who was quite so decorative.

When Tom turned to greet Katrina, Yvette turned to Izak, wondering if the tall, handsome sea captain would be an even better match. *Is he both captain and owner?* She regretted that no one had made that point perfectly clear. She led Izak from the front door to the parlor, giving him alternating looks of adoration and coy shyness. In the parlor and then in the dining room, something about her laughter seemed too eager to suit Izak. It put him off to a degree that he did not, out of courtesy, dare reveal.

Watching Yvette, who looked angelic in shell-pink muslin, Amalie was amazed. She herself barely dared to speak to the captain, and here was Yvette doing so with ease. She fairly floated as she led first one man and then another into the dining room. Yvette moved with a supreme confidence, apparently so convinced of her ability to charm men that she had never imagined it could be otherwise.

Yvette was giddy as they gathered at the table, and she found herself seated between Thomas Segrave and Captain Izak Peterssen. Across from her was the banker, Karl Schneider.

"Captain," she said, "tell me about your voyage, about everything you saw and all the amazing things you did!"

Beside her, Izak stared at the tablecloth and took a deep, calming breath. He was not about to be drawn into a childish conversation by the frivolous daughter of the house. Many men in his position might have leapt at such a conversation, but he had his own unannounced preferences.

"It was long," he told her.

Seated some way down was Erik Thorvald. Yvette tried not to stare, but it was difficult. The man was so virile, redhaired, and large, a size as awkward at a dining table as it was advantageous on a battlefield. Thorvald seemed determined to say nothing and scowled whenever anyone addressed him. When he turned his head, Yvette caught a glimpse of the most barbaric scarring on his neck. Marguerite Robichaux saw it at the same moment and signaled Yvette with a cough and lowered eyelids, but Yvette did not need the warning. She recognized the mark of a slave collar and was horrified. She instantly erased Erik Thorvald from her list of possibilities.

Yvette studied Karl Schneider and was struck by how handsome he was. And yet her mother had said Karl dealt in filthy lucre. Yvette glanced furtively at his fingertips, wondering if "filthy" meant his hands were dirty. More shockingly, Marguerite said Karl Schneider was rumored to be an abolitionist, and one who advocated it in public. In any case, Yvette thought Karl ruined by his years in Boston, a town she knew to be rampantly immoral and filled with white wage slaves, many of them Irish and barely civilized.

Her dancing teacher, Mademoiselle LaCroix, had lived in Boston and told her it was cold, fishy smelling, and secretive.

"Bostonians," said Mlle. LaCroix, "are as remote and slippery as ice." She said they harbored dull scholars and duller-yet Quakers, "people who are traitors to their class, and who do not under any circumstances buy dancing lessons. The entire city is insupportable," Mlle. LaCroix had said in an aghast tone, raising her fan to hide her disgust.

In the end, it was the taint of Yankee sympathies that compelled Yvette to treat the handsome, personable Karl Schneider with a certain coolness. It was subtle, because her mother disapproved of Yvette's letting such opinions show in any way at all, and Karl himself found her behavior mystifying.

CHAPTER 7

TOO MANY GERMANS

"I see. You want an independent life."

By the time hot coffee had been brought in and stood steaming on the sideboard, Niklas had learned that repairs to the *Enigma* would be slow. He was surprised to hear that the work was not even on a boat builder's schedule yet. He was even more surprised that Thomas was not unhappy about it.

"The delay is an opportunity to explore the countryside. I am considering going north on the great river," Tom said.

Izak Peterssen's head jerked up, and he looked at Tom in surprise. Erik Thorvald turned a raised eyebrow to Izak.

Tom did not notice and continued to address Niklas. "Have you found passage north, my dear Herr Kästner?" He passed a slice of coconut and lime cake as he spoke, but the casual motion did not fool either Katrina or Amalie. Thomas Segrave appeared to be listening intently for the name of a steamboat on which the Kästner family might have found passage. Izak Peterssen was paying close attention, too.

"I have not secured passage," said Niklas, "but I will send a message when we do." He had not even decided whether to stay in New Orleans and make their home here, but only Katrina knew of these doubts.

Tom nodded. "We do not wish to come to America without seeing its great frontier." He seemed to be speaking for himself and Izak. Amalie lowered her eyes, but a hint of a smile was on her lips. The electricity she and Tom felt that moment aboard when their hands touched seemed to her a lasting connection, and for an instant, she felt that only the two of them existed in this room of many.

"Besides," said Karl, "it is a good idea to escape New Orleans' summer season of sickness."

Marguerite Robichaux's eyebrows shot up to hear a fellow Orleanais make such an admission, even if it were true and no one in New Orleans could reasonably deny it and half the city was already gone or packing up.

"My dear sir," she sniffed, "Yellow fever may indeed afflict Nouveau Orleans in the summer, but it is no worse than the consumption in the North each winter."

He nodded in agreement, but she was not mollified, his comment seeming to her so disloyal a thing, especially in mixed company and when a guest at her table. A few moments later, as she invited the men to cross the hall and use the parlor as a smoking room, she was still miffed.

The men trooped over to the parlor, more than one of them unbuttoning his waistcoat.

"Gentlemen," said Niklas, as he handed out cigars, "these are fresh from Cuba. Our delay in Texas did them no harm."

"Tell me about Texas," said Karl Schneider.

"You know about its winning the war of independence and declaring itself a republic?" asked Niklas.

"It's been the news all over town," said Karl. "Celebrated especially in the Irish émigré community, where so many—well, I mean, their fathers or grandfathers—tried to achieve independence in 1798."

"We didn't know any of that," said Izak. "As we approached the shore, the question was what scenes of violence awaited us."

Thomas said, "We were badly injured in the hurricane, you see, and in no shape to sail further."

"So we were prepared to fight," said Will. The other men looked surprised to see him jump into the conversation.

"Ja," Niklas said, "The boy is right. We thought we might be landing in the middle of a war. Then Major Forbes came out on a cutter and announced the war ended and welcomed us to the new Republic of Texas."

"They were glad to see a ship arrive and relieved that we did not pose a threat," said Izak. "Linnville is one of John Linn's towns and an up-and-coming center for the New Orleans trade."

"It's in a decent spot, with barrier islands and some depth to the creek," explained Niklas. "La Salle landed his colony there. The ruins of his fort are still visible."

"Not enough depth," Erik Thorvald said. "The creek will need dredging."

"Lennart Mueller wanted us to join the German colony in Texas. The Ernst colony."

"I am not surprised to hear it," said Karl. "He's a Texas enthusiast."

"He convinced the Ackermanns to go with him. We waved goodbye to their wagon train," said Niklas and then explained to Karl, "the family from Bonn who came across with us."

"Why didn't you go?"

Niklas looked thoughtful. "We value the opportunities of a river like the Mississippi. Besides, too many Germans."

"What?"

"My boys and me, we can farm, but it's not our preference. We are merchants. We need a river for trade."

"But, 'too many Germans'?" Karl looked mystified. And insulted.

"Ja. Why escape the Old World to immerse ourselves in it again?"

"I see," said Karl. "You want an independent life. So, tell me, how many went off with Lennart Mueller?"

Niklas looked at Izak, who answered.

"Eighteen. Three related families. They boarded as nineteen and lost one young woman mid-ocean. To disease, we believe. Which did not spread, thank God." The five men who had watched the corpse slide into the sea looked grim. None had forgotten that Hannah was a beautiful young woman whose death was mysterious or even suspicious.

"I'm sorry to hear you had a loss on the voyage," said Karl.

"We also lost two of the crew. A boy fell from the rigging, and a retired skipper who joined us in Gibraltar was swept overboard in a hurricane."

"We were lucky," said Niklas, "not to lose more to storms, especially the hurricane."

"Aye," said Izak. "It nearly sank us.

Tom asked, "Have you heard the news about Mr. Groves?"

The Kästner men looked up.

"There was a letter waiting for him here in New Orleans. All of his family, wife and children, dead of the cholera."

"Francesca Lenzini told us," said Niklas. "It's awful."

"The sort of thing," said Izak, "that makes one dread getting a letter."

"Did you know," said Will, "that Mr. Groves sent Giovanni packing?"

"What?" asked Izak.

Will told the story of Giovanni's being shipped out, making no hero of himself and avoiding his father's eyes. He studied the men from *Enigma*, still curious about how Mr. Groves came at the right moment to rescue him and grab Giovanni.

"I never liked the man," said Tom, but there was no further comment.

The group fell into a brief silence, after which Erik continued their earlier conversation. "We were also lucky not to lose more men to pirates."

"One of their bullets went right through my arm," said Hans, patting the wound that still ached now and then.

Karl's eyebrows shot up. "Pirates! I thought the Caribbean free of pirates."

"In Havana, they thought the same." Izak stroked his beard. "But pirates are famous for having hidey-holes."

"Perhaps we sank the last of them," said Niklas.

"Good riddance," said Hans, and the others nodded.

"We will never know," said Izak, "whether we battled the last of the pirates. Sunk ships take their secrets to the bottom."

They would learn, in a few years, that Linnville, Texas, John Linn's up-and-coming harbor town, was wiped out. Comanches sacked and burned the town, and the survivors moved on and left the ruins to molder.

In at least these two ways, the men of *Enigma* had, all unknowing, seen the last of several worlds even wilder and more vicious than their own.

The supper at Robichaux House was a huge success, and even on the streets, the Kästner family was given a rather extraordinary welcome in New Orleans. They soon considered their shocking meeting with Ivan Ivanovich a fluke.

The delftware they bought in the Netherlands and cigars from Cuba were easily traded, and Niklas replaced them with coffee, sugar, rice, and molasses to trade upriver. "They will also," he said, "provision our travels and the winter to come."

Katrina worried about this. Niklas had not decided how far north they would go or where they would spend the winter. The plantations lining the lower reaches of the river would be easy trade targets, but they would not bring the family much closer to cheap new land.

As she sat and sewed at Robichaux House, Katrina was also chagrined at how much more calico there was in New Orleans than in the newborn Republic of Texas. She had insisted on buying a bolt there when *Enigma* was blown off course and landed at Linnville's Matagorda Bay. The purchase had not been altogether foolish, for it had allowed her and the girls to use the days of sailing from Texas to sew matching dresses for themselves, a valuable result considering that heat was so oppressive in the city. In New Orleans, tissue cotton was the only fabric any of them could bear, man or woman.

"Let me see that line of stitches, Lisette." Katrina, Amalie, and Lisette were sewing lightweight shirts for all their men, starting with little Jakob, the five-year-old less able to bear the heat than his brothers or father.

Katrina inspected Lisette's seam. "I am proud of you, Daughter, except for these last five stitches. Rip them and try again. See how they begin to make the seam too wide?"

Lisette went back to her bench.

Amalie leaned over and told her sister, "I'm not sure I could have done as well at your age."

As she sewed, Katrina mused about New Orleans, a city like Paris: picturesque, crowded, and dark, except where evening gaslights were lit, and even more unhealthy. The beat of drums from Congo Square was different and unsettling, but at these, Marguerite Robichaux scoffed. Marguerite also seemed unaware of a powerful undercurrent of abolitionist sentiment, but Katrina felt it. The political unrest that simmered in Europe had made her aware of such things. To Madame Robichaux, the only worry was New Orleans' sick season.

Katrina was told, "There is nothing to do but escape." Hearing this, she thought, *Have we not already done enough escaping for one family?*

CHAPTER 8

JEAN FRANÇOIS GIROD

Ivan Ivanovich's revenge

The sight of Katrina, Amalie, and Lisette on the street caused many necks to swivel, but as it turned out, it was the Napoleonic cut of Niklas's coat that caused one man to stop and bow to them. There was a deep-seated appreciation for Napoleon in New Orleans, it turned out.

This gentleman, a certain Jean François Girod, unraveled an extraordinary tale of Napoleon's escape from Elba in 1815 and how the news reached New Orleans.

"Do you still remember the moment when you heard that glorious news?" asked Monsieur Girod. He twirled his cane and breathed a satisfied sigh, like a cat settling on a windowsill.

"Oui, that I do," said Niklas with a gracious little bow. In fact, he had been making his own escape from Elba alongside Napoleon, his regiment having been the one unit allowed to accompany Napoleon into his first exile. Niklas began his life in the military in 1809, when he turned sixteen, eight years before the regiment's brief stay on Elba. He served in Spain and Austria and barely survived the Moscow Campaign with its retreat through the Russian winter. Then, after Elba, he fought at Waterloo. *All of this*, thought Niklas, *is much more than an inquisitive little Creole needs to know.*

"Here," said Girod, who was too preoccupied with his story to notice Niklas's reticence, "in New Orleans, at the St. Philip Street Theatre, it was announced from the stage and met with the wildest cheers."

He told them the entire audience dashed from the theatre and gathered with many others at la Place d'Armes. Everyone thought Napoleon was likely to flee France and seek refuge in America, with New Orleans his best possible destination, indeed the only logical one.

"And in fact, this has recently been proven," Jean François Girod interrupted his story to add: "A few months ago, Napoleon's own nephew arrived in New Orleans! Colonel Achille Murat took up residence. He was once Prince of Naples and more recently the Prince of Tallahassee—that's in Florida—with his wife, Catharine Gray. She herself is a great-grandniece of George Washington's and as close to American nobility as anyone might desire. They are even now enriching the already glittering society of New Orleans." Girod lay a finger aside his nose and said to Katrina with a wink, "They are all the talk."

Achille Murat, frowned Niklas, *whose father was a traitor to Napoleon and whose mother was Metternich's whore, which allowed them to escape to America, where Murat can pretend to be a republican or a prince or a Bonaparte, whatever suits him on any particular day.* Niklas studied the ground to avoid having Jean François Girod notice the ire creeping up his neck in red streaks.

"In 1815, after Waterloo," Girod continued with a flourish of his cane, "when my uncle Nicolas was the mayor of New Orleans..." Jean François paused to let that impressive fact to sink in, "he renovated a home on the corner of Chartres and St. Louis to be ready for Napoleon, once the rescue was accomplished. When events turned," said Girod, "Orleanais did not give up hope, not for a moment."

Niklas was knocked breathless to hear the many shocks of 1815 and '16 dismissed with such brevity and New Orleanais described as loyal. *Is this city so remote,* he thought, *that there is no penalty for such dangerous loyalty?*

Girod went on to recount how a group of wealthy citizens—the pirates Jean and Pierre Lafitte, Dominique Youx, and others—planned a rescue mission to the remote island of St. Helena. The ship they prepared to sail was the *Seraphine,* a long, low schooner, painted black and with masts raked for speed, commanded by the esteemed Captain St. Ange Bossiere.

"The plans were laid," said Girod. "All was in readiness, but on the day the *Seraphine* set sail, word came of Napoleon's demise, and she was signaled downriver and brought back."

This had occurred fifteen years earlier, but even so, Niklas thought he saw the gleam of a tear in the French patriot's eye, and he forgave him a little.

"After this, my uncle Nicolas moved into Napoleon House and lives there still," Jean François Girod said. He added as an afterthought: "The spiral staircase goes all the way up into the cupola. You should see it."

The Girods were instrumental in bringing members of the Imperial Guard to America, Jean François said, where they settled in Alabama's Vine and Olive colony, in General Lallemand's failed—and suspect—colony in Texas, and in the end, in New Orleans.

Niklas felt his heart skip a beat at Lallemand's name, the man who commanded his own regiment at Waterloo. A more charismatic leader he had never seen, a faithful supporter of Napoleon to the very end, in spite of the cavalry's rout, the only one in its history.

"Lallemand is back in Paris, I believe, and returned to favor," said Niklas.

"So I understand," Jean François Girod said. "But France, God love her, has fallen back into tyranny with the July Monarchy. The light of glory may be dim just now, with the Americans taking over New Orleans—" he broke off to explain that he thought them barbarians—"but we Orleanais shall never forget Napoleon or fail to be inspired by him."

This was a conclusion so theatrical Niklas was not surprised when Girod added a deep bow before disappearing around the corner. Jean François Girod may have been an extreme, but the respect Niklas was generally accorded, and the interest various gentlemen had in his military career were most gratifying. Still, it worried Katrina to have it brought up so often.

Niklas had known Napoleon both as emperor and as man, and for Napoleon's sake, Niklas had nearly died in battle, suffered shame at Waterloo, and been driven out of his hometown, suspected of "old revolutionary" sentiment and of sympathizing with the underground resistance, the German Democracy Movement, the GDM. All the suspicions were right. Niklas had never entirely given up his admiration for the French revolutionaries and was a member of the GDM. Now, it was a comfort to be among these Francophile New Orleanais who admired a "revolutionary" heart. Still, a lifelong habit of reticence made him say little.

The city seemed to have dissolved the past into one glorious moment and credited Napoleon with a greater love of freedom than they themselves possessed in the here and now. Niklas often heard strange dislocations of fact: histories desired but twisted. This was especially so of tales of the Haitian revolution and the refugees who had escaped to New Orleans.

"The love of revolutionary France is something of a cult, wouldn't you say?" asked Katrina.

"Yes, that's the word. It's an adoration based on half-truths. Even so, it is pleasant to hear. And who are we to disabuse them?"

She nodded. "If we are to be honored in this new land without having to say so much as a false word, so much the better."

"We were dishonored in Prussia long enough, the monarchy determined to quash any hint of democracy."

Amalie had been listening and was recalling their frightening encounter with Ivan Ivanovich. "Perhaps being thought a traitor or a patriot is a matter of how one turns the coin?"

Her parents had forgotten the girls were there, so they were surprised to hear this, and Niklas thought it impertinent. Before he could correct her, Katrina put an arm around Amalie's shoulders. "You have given us food for thought, Daughter."

Niklas pulled his hat down and stalked off.

Later, at a particular café, Niklas and Katrina watched a group of French-speaking refugees from Hispaniola, known as Haiti these last thirty years. These old men drinking coffee had once owned fine homes in Saint-Dominque or on sugar plantations outside the island's capital.

"France will return," one insisted. He rapped a spoon on the table edge as if he could make it happen. "Any day now."

"Oui," said a second man. "If not for the malaria, the French would have recaptured the island long ago and given it back to us. 'Tis going to the devil without us!"

"Aye!" said a third, as he tugged at his wig. "Naught but chaos these days. I once had a mansion in Port au Prince, a plantation in the hills, everything a man could want—"

"Mistresses! Slaves!" another interjected, tears coursing down his cheeks.

Niklas and Katrina sat silent, glad to be a little distance from this maudlin group. They recognized the Haitian French accent, like that of Rafael and his family, whom they had met in Havana.

"It's been thirty years!" Katrina whispered to Niklas.

"More," he said.

"Remember what Missus Gaby told us."

"Ja, I know."

Missus Gaby, Rafael's mother, had spoken in hushed tones of unspeakable horrors inflicted upon the slaves in Haiti. That such horrors may have been cause enough for a revolution had not, apparently, occurred to the men in the café.

That night, when he woke in a sweat, Niklas thought, *'Tis Ivan Ivanovich's revenge on me.* His eyes were wide open in the dark, and his heart was beating hard in his chest. He had jerked awake from a nightmare in which Ivanovich burst through the bedroom door to attack him.

"I tried to raise my sword to strike, to stop Ivanovich from killing us both," he told Katrina. "But my arm was bound to my side, and I was helpless, powerless, able only to watch as we were about to be annihilated."

"You were asleep on that arm?"

He had rolled over and was waving his arm in the air, trying to revive it. "Yes, but the stupidity of it is no consolation."

CHAPTER 9

A WOMAN WHO KNOWS HER CHICKENS

Could this be an actor?

As strangers in New Orleans, it was hard for the Kästners to know what to buy and sell, although the Cuban cigars, Texas hides, and Dutch delftware were easy, having been bought specifically as trade goods. With cash in hand, Niklas and Katrina bought a clock for their new home, a copy of Webster's *Blue Back Speller* to help them learn English, and several bolts of calico for trade.

A bookseller urged Niklas to buy Alexis de Tocqueville's just-published *Democracy in America*, the result of his 1831 tour of the country, but Niklas had purchased it in Rotterdam and read it on the voyage. So did Hans, Will, and Katrina. Even Amalie read parts of it. Now, they were about to embark on their own tour of America with Tocqueville's words ringing in their ears: "Life is to be entered upon with courage."

Katrina sold their goats and the few remaining Westfalische Totleger chickens to a nostalgic German, one of Karl Schneider's friends, and soon found quite similar birds at St. Mary's Market on Diamond Street. These chickens were said to be local, but Katrina recognized them as the big, beautiful breed from East Frisia.

"I'm afraid these are too dear for me," she told the seller, who was a remarkably wrinkled old man with one clouded eye. He had four East Frisians for sale, a rooster and three fine fat hens in a wooden crate.

"J'aime une femme qui connaît ses poulets," "I admire nothing as much as a woman who knows her chickens," he said. "I'll tell you what I could do. I could keep back one of them hens."

His whole face smiled when he spoke, his voice musical with a dialect of Cajun French and the thoughtful pace of age and wisdom. He was nominally white below a deep farmer's tan, and the handsome man beside him was a Negro whose light skin glowed ruddy, a younger and stronger man. They were both dressed in rags, like many in a European village, and they talked and laughed together like family or friends. Katrina could not help but wonder: *Are they father and son?* It was a scandalous thought, but she knew such things were possible, as the many mulattos of New Orleans proved.

She and the old Cajun settled on one rooster and three hens after all, the old man going on about the fine points of the breed while the young man captured each bird by the legs and put one after another in a wicker cage for her to carry. She walked away happy with her purchase and in no way wiser about the complicated relationships of those involved.

Niklas again asked, "Is it quite necessary to carry chickens with us?" He had voiced a similar concern as they loaded chickens onto the *Holsatia,* the little steamboat that whisked them away from Cologne and down the Rhine to Rotterdam.

She looked at him with some degree of exasperation. *This from a man who does not do well without an egg for breakfast.* Katrina was a good cook, but no cook could do without basic ingredients. Not raising one's own chickens was as shortsighted as not growing one's own herbs.

Our very first purchase, she reminded herself, *when we are settled, will be a cow, a good, productive milk cow, perhaps a Vorderwälder, if it can be found. Preferably two. Or, even better, a Gelbvieh or Harzer Rotvieh to produce everything—milk, draft power, and beef. Then we'll shift to the higher quality dairy production of a Murnau-Werdenfels as time goes on.* For a moment, her mind filled with the image of a fine new cattle barn, with beef on the left, dairy on the right, and an impeccably clean milk parlor off the front.

Katrina cautioned herself: *I might have to take whatever strange cattle this strange country offers.*

"Remember those unlikely looking longhorns we saw in Texas?" she asked Niklas. "More horn and hide than beef or milk. All the more reason to seize upon these fine East Frisians when we can."

Niklas paid the old Cajun. She looked on and thought, *Perhaps I should mention the cattle. When some particularly soft moment arises.*

In 1836, New Orleans considered itself the most civilized city in America, and it might have been right. Like New York and Baltimore, it overflowed with immigrants, including those of obscure nationalities, the human oddities found in any world-worthy port who landed intentionally or by accident and never left. New Orleans was a not-always-happy mélange of rough frontiersmen, fortune-seeking Easterners, Cajun backwoodsmen, and grand old plantation families.

Half of the population was Black, but in no way homogenous. They were everything from well-connected, free, and cultured to the most wretched of enslaved new arrivals. Among these slipped the remnants of several Indigenous tribes, wise in the ways of the bayou, decimated by European disease, and disenfranchised by a long invasion by wicked strangers.

New Orleans was the gateway to the Northwest Territory, a label long used for land northwest of the Ohio River. Now, with three states carved out of it, the "Northwest Territory'" had shifted to the fabled and immense tract of land west of the Mississippi bought in one swipe by Thomas Jefferson. The only pieces still on the east side of the Mississippi were the Wisconsin Territory and an unprepossessing slice of northwest Illinois, recently cleared of Sauks, Meskwakis, and Kickapoos.

New Orleans was already an importer of more goods than New York City. The city throbbed with trade and hummed with street musicians. On any avenue, young scholars marched by with their slates in hand, artists promised a portrait for the ages, quacks hawked cure-alls, and frontiersmen lugged bales of furs. Merchants loitered, speaking the various languages of Spain, Italy, Greece, or the Ottoman Empire, even Egypt or Morocco, as well as the many Caribbean and African dialects. French was, of course, the lingua franca.

Into this city of shining prospects, the young moneyman, Karl Schneider, had come to manage the New Orleans Gas Light and Banking Company. It had been organized in 1834 by James Caldwell, an English actor and the visionary builder of New Orleans' latest venture, the St. Charles Theatre. The St. Charles was built to a degree of lavishness unsurpassed except perhaps, it was said, by the opera houses of Naples, Milan, and Vienna. People nodded wisely to hear this, though few in New Orleans could, in fact, make the comparison.

The new St. Charles was enormous and luxurious. Katrina and Niklas stood staring at the façade, a hundred and thirty feet wide and boasting statues of Apollo and the muses. It took up most of a city block.

Niklas said, "Shall we?" and guided Katrina inside.

The theatre was in its premiere season. It was the first building in New Orleans lit by gas, and even now, in the daylight, its huge central dome glittered with light from the mammoth chandelier: 176 gas jets amid 23,000 glass crystals. The lobby was almost empty, except for a trio of tittering girls along one wall and a husband and wife hunched together on the other wall, whispering to each other. They wore the drab clothing of religious conservatives, and they hurried toward the doors as if embarrassed to be caught in a theatre.

"We only came to see the lights." The man touched his hat as he spoke.

Niklas and Katrina, untethered to such scruples, crossed the lobby and peeked into the auditorium.

"She seats four thousand." In the dim light, the voice startled them, and then they saw the speaker.

Could this, wondered Katrina, *be an actor?* She was scandalized at the thought.

"And see those boxes—'tis genuine silk, if you were wondering." He saw Katrina's stare and said to reassure her, "The tickets are priced high enough to keep out the hoi-polloi."

She lowered her eyes, pink-faced to be caught staring.

Gilded columns flanked the largest stage Niklas and Katrina had ever seen. Loge boxes in crimson, blue, and yellow silk lined both sides.

A throne would not be out of place here, thought Katrina, *but it's only a stage.* Something about this seemed very modern and maybe sinful.

"Monsieur James Caldwell at your service," said the handsome man.

"It's quite something!" said Katrina.

"What she means is that it is an impressive structure." Niklas frowned at his wife's fawning enthusiasm.

Caldwell smiled. "The St. Charles is our winter home," he said. "I have theatres in river towns from here to Cincinnati on a circuit for my company of actors."

"Oh!" said Katrina. "A winter season in New Orleans and a summer season further north."

"Exactly, madame. My company in on the river already, and I will follow them this week." He bowed and excused himself.

"So that was Caldwell himself!" said Katrina. "At least we were not addressed by an actor. But why didn't you tell him we know Karl?"

"Sometimes it is wiser to know something the other does not," said Niklas.

Unlike his actors, who were adored but rarely considered respectable enough to marry, Caldwell had managed to achieve wealth and position. Perhaps it was because he had almost singlehandedly shoved New Orleans into the future as one of the first American cities to convert streetlights to gas. He had done it by providing three million dollars in capital, and subscriptions went so well that he soon doubled his investment.

Part gas company, mint, bank, and developer, the New Orleans Gas Light and Banking Company was one of six new banks to open in New Orleans in just two years. Watching over them was the great Louisiana State Bank, and behind it was the State of Louisiana itself, having put on its books a prodigious set of regulations that would carry some of these banks through the coming Depression of 1837, though that awful event was nothing more than a whisper in June of 1836, and indeed, a Cassandra's whisper.

CHAPTER 10

THE WORLD WITHOUT SLAVES

"Being cruel is the point."

Karl Schneider had been raised a Roman Catholic in Coblentz, not too far up the Rhine from Cologne, and he was one of the few immigrants to come to America with a degree from a university. Now he was a manager at Caldwell's and a proud American, thrilled with the growth of New Orleans, and able to quote the increase in the number of ships arriving and the quantities of cotton and sugar and hides going through his clients' hands.

"I love New Orleans and am proud to work for Mr. Caldwell," Karl said, "but for the city's entanglement in slavery."

He was walking along Canal Street with Niklas and Katrina, talking about their visit to the St. Charles Theatre. Soon, the afternoon rainstorm gathered, thunder rumbling its approach.

"Slave labor makes America's cotton and sugar cheaper," said Karl, "but how will it end? As surely it must someday."

Katrina looked at him with curiosity.

"It's already been almost thirty years since the Africa trade was made illegal. Individual manumission continues—like Mr. Henderson's. Universal emancipation cannot be far off."

"Mr. Henderson?" asked Katrina.

"Late of Destrehan Plantation. His will hasn't been read yet, but it is expected to free his slaves."

"Ah," she said, adding, "'Twas '07, the end of the Africa trade, just after Britain and her colonies." She was aware of Niklas's disapproving look. It had been their rule since the outset of this journey to say nothing about local practices, no matter how odd or abhorrent. In New Orleans, nothing was more unwelcome than espousing abolitionist views.

Before Karl could reply, the rain began in earnest, and the three of them rushed to a nearby café and stood under its tin roof, the tropical rain hammering above.

"I agree with Mr. Benjamin Rush," said Karl. "American principles do not allow for slavery of any kind."

When Katrina smiled her approval, Karl raised one hand. "Before you think too well of me, I have a certain self-interest at stake. Consider: how long can slavery last here?"

"In the 'Land of the Free' and when it is already despised in much of the civilized world," Katrina began....

"When," Niklas interrupted, "it collapses..."

"Exactly. When. The question is when, not if. When it collapses, what becomes of my clients? My scheme for a peaceful transition to paid labor, if it can take root, could save not only the slaves but the families that own them. And the bank."

"Preventing a convulsion such as happened in Haiti."

"Exactly!" said Karl. "And the best place to begin such a transition is right here, where more free Blacks live than anywhere else in America. Free Blacks who have been educated, some of them in France, so that New Orleans already has a cadre of Black doctors, teachers and other professionals."

"This is what Rafael said about New Orleans, that he could start his own medical practice here," Katrina said. An image arose in her mind of *Enigma* lowering a boat to the waves of the Caribbean with Rafael and his sister and brother in it. The three set sail for the Bahamas, which were free.

"Exactly! It should begin here," said Karl.

"What would that do to the price of cotton and sugar?" Niklas asked.

"I think it could be managed. It must be, ere buyers in England turn to India and Egypt. The rub is getting plantation owners to listen to me, a Yankee." He sighed and then laughed. "Some days I am despised as a foreigner and other days as a Yankee!"

Niklas smiled, but there was no humor in it. "Are there not some who will listen?"

"I think so," Karl said, "but few have ever seen life outside the plantation. They cannot imagine the world without slaves."

"Our landlady talks with fury about the poor wage slaves in the North," Niklas said. "She honestly thinks being enslaved is better."

"What are they thinking? How do they imagine this evil will end?" Katrina stamped her foot in annoyance, and Niklas laid a heavy hand on her shoulder.

"They don't think it will ever end and that saying anything at all about it will lead to an uprising." Karl's voice was sad. "So they tighten the rules every year. Most blame Yankees rather than see the beam in their own eye. But we can hope, and we can appeal to their Christian kindness." He glanced up to see the sky clearing, bowed to Niklas and Katrina, and departed.

He cannot yet be thirty, Katrina thought as she watched him go. Though he was whispered to be an atheist, she thought him a good man.

He had a ready smile and was handsome, wiry, and well-dressed. Niklas said many a man lost his faith—or found it—on a battlefield, but she had never known an admitted atheist. Between this and Karl's dangerously radical schemes, she had already decided to keep Amalie far away from him. Amalie was now fifteen and while still a child in her father's eyes, seemed a pretty young woman to everyone else.

"We are surrounded by the young," said Katrina. Niklas had been the oldest man aboard *Enigma* except for Methuselah, who was swept overboard in the hurricane. Niklas might also have been the oldest man in Linnville, Texas, she realized.

"If Karl were not so devoted to his scheme for hired labor," Niklas said, "he would see that his plantation-owning clients indulge him only for the sake of their annual loan and have not the slightest interest in freeing their slaves."

He glanced around to be sure that no one was listening. "His heart is in the right place, but he is deluding himself. Only the vast sums of money under his bank's control keep Karl from needing to sleep with a pistol under his pillow."

Niklas did not know that Karl already slept with a pistol below his pillow, and his elegant trousers were cut to conceal the dagger strapped to his ankle.

The horrors of slavery were widely acknowledged in Europe, where Niklas himself had belonged to Berleburg's Antislavery Society. Thomas Segrave had belonged to a similar group in England. This was not unusual. All across Europe, such groups met and talked.

Now, when Katrina began to speak again, Niklas raised a finger in warning. "Speak quietly," he said. "Here, as everywhere, tyranny is the rule. Those in power are dangerous."

Katrina nodded. "The old saw that 'a man's home is his castle' allows countless men to act the tyrant, and whether 'home' be a plantation or a hovel, men claim all the fruits of the labor of their wives and children."

"Well, children do owe their parents quite a bit," said Niklas, "but I agree that men should not beat their wives or children. You know this."

Katrina smiled at Niklas. She would always be grateful that he was against beatings. Then she frowned. "Remember what Rafael told us: 'Free men will not work alongside slaves, whatever the wages.'"

They had bought Rafael in Cuba, as well as his sister and brother, in order to free them. It was complicated by Rafael's having been trained as a physician.

"Rafael said those just brought across are the worst. He called them 'African monkeys' and said a free, civilized Black man like himself is infinitely superior." She had been surprised at his vehemence.

Rafael had told them he could not imagine being considered as having any similarity in thought or sentiment to the recently enslaved. "Of course, it is an unspeakable cruelty to be kidnapped in Africa and enslaved," he said. "I don't mean to be unsympathetic. But the distance between slave and free is so pronounced that assuming any fellow feeling at all is a grievous mistake."

With his medical training, Rafael dreamt of coming to New Orleans, gaining the support of other doctors and becoming part of a medical practice. "I can be on the staff of a hospital. I can buy a home," he told them.

This was before his former owner, Dr. Martinez, betrayed them and sent thugs to recapture Rafael and his siblings. The doctor meant to claim that Niklas had stolen the three, regain his slaves, keep the cash, and have the satisfaction of seeing Niklas and Hans swing from a gibbet. He was not the only Cuban who thought the Kästners interfering heretics. Once his attempt to recapture Rafael and his siblings failed, the old doctor might have thought to send a claim of legal ownership to officials in New Orleans, which made the Bahamas a safer choice. Katrina wondered whether the three of them had made it to the Bahamas and what those newly free islands could offer a family of such prodigious talents.

"Whatever Karl's opinion or Rafael's," said Katrina, "it's only rational to expect a transition to paid labor someday."

She and Niklas headed back along the street, dodging a dripping fig tree. As they talked, they agreed that Karl Schneider's scheme ignored the nearly universal impulse to feel oneself superior, an impulse so strong that many could not wait to clap chains on a man or breed another mulatto child.

"To such as those," said Katrina, "the cruelty of slavery is not an unfortunate side effect. Being cruel is the point."

He nodded his agreement, and they lapsed into silence. A little while later, Katrina spoke again. "Niklas," she said, "let's check the post office for general mail. Rafael promised to write from the Bahamas. It would be a relief to know those three young people made it to the islands safely."

She glanced at the people on the streets, wondering whether even a few could imagine a world without slaves. *Could it ever happen peacefully, intentionally, as Karl thinks it could?* A sudden premonition shook her of an awful convulsion, a blink of a battlefield image, like those Niklas described, horrible and bloody. She shook her head to clear it, and when Niklas put his hand on her waist as if to hurry her along, she was glad of it.

CHAPTER 11

SILK, LACE, AND CONFUSION

"This is why you are so important."

On Sunday next, they planned to dress well and be off to church, such as it might be. Today, however, they walked along Clio Street, taking comfort in tall white columns, carved stone fountains, and straight city streets that spoke of the French founding of the city.

"Oh, look," cried Amalie. "It's like Havana…or Gibraltar. With wrought iron balconies." On this lovely cool morning, with violet patches of Louisiana iris in bloom, everything spoke of advanced civilizations, and the distant strains of a pianoforte were a wonderful comfort.

Will noticed none of this, his thoughts filled instead with their land-lady's beautiful daughter, Yvette, whose perfect figure kept appearing in his dreams. He felt guilty about neglecting the memory of Ezmeralda, but he could not help it. He thought of Yvette all night, and just this morning they nearly ran smack into each other in one of the home's narrow hallways. Will was acutely aware of this precious opportunity and searched for a fine or witty phrase, an ounce of repartee. Instead, he blushed and came out with "Excusez-moi."

Oddly enough, Will could not seem to find his tongue with Yvette. It had been so easy in Havana with Ezmeralda. Just thinking of Ezmeralda made Will feel achy and confused.

To make matters worse, Amalie seemed to find everything about Yvette fascinating, including her conversation, precisely the point on which Will found Yvette least satisfactory. She made Cajun corrections to his French or advised him about how to button his new waistcoat a certain styl-ish way, but otherwise, their talk seemed to stall. He considered himself a creature of wide interests, so he was surprised that none of those interests seemed to overlap with hers. As he walked on Clio Street that lovely morning, he berated himself for their awkward encounter and wondered what he should have said and in which language.

Marguerite Robichaux had seen Yvette mooning over Hans and hissed in her ear, "That idiot wants to go to Indian Territory. People who go there are condemned to a crude life among savages who cannot wait to debauch a White girl such as you or scalp her outright."

For emphasis, Marguerite gave Yvette's beautiful long hair a yank, and the girl shivered at the thought of it dangling from a brave's belt. Yvette put Hans aside, despite the occasional surreptitious glance she allowed herself, such a fine figure of a man.

Of the six bachelors at dinner, Thomas Segrave attracted her most, but what about Amalie? Was he in fact Amalie's own? Yvette was certain she had felt some frisson with him. Izak Peterssen, the handsome sea captain, had been distinctly cold, and master gunner Erik Thorvald was nothing but frightening. Karl Schneider was triply damned as an atheist, Yankee, and abolitionist. And now her mother said Hans must be dismissed as well. The evening—begun so promising!—ended on such an unsatisfying note.

In the absence of the others, Yvette turned the full brunt of her attentions to Will. She sighed to think of it, such a plethora of possible suitors reduced so quickly to the youngest, shortest, and most unimpressive. At least Will was slender, muscular, and talkative. But those blond curls of his! They were perhaps too striking—what young woman wants to be the less noticed of a couple? Besides, the tan he earned from a summer on *Enigma* smacked of something déclassé. He told her with pride of scaling the ratlines, but she knew no gentleman would do something like that.

In fact, she wanted someone older, taller, and richer. And perhaps less German, though anything was better than an American. There was also, she was vaguely aware, her desire for a man whose suave, handsome exterior hid a strong, or even a dangerous, forbidden interior. This drove her to surreptitious glances at Hans. And to musings about the forbidden Thomas Segrave.

The Kästners, who were a naturally handsome family and clearly of some substance, had Karl Schneider to thank for an invitation to a Creole ball, the last of the season.

This excited a flurry of shopping and dressmaking, beginning with Katrina's purchase of cream-colored silk damask for the aprons of gowns to be made of the jade green silk brought from the Kästner shop in Berleburg. They would sew identical gowns for herself, Amalie, and Lisette, except for a lace ruff at her own neck, the better to set off the jade necklace Niklas bought for her in Havana.

The largest bedroom in the Robichaux House was declared off limits to men and was soon bursting with gauze, taffeta, damask, lace, and muslin. At Marguerite's recommendation, Katrina hired a Creole dressmaker, a poor but well-born widow breathlessly eager to learn what she could of the latest Parisian fashions. When the new dress was ready for Amalie, she tried it on and spun around in front of the looking glass. She looked confused.

In a quiet aside to her mother, Amalie said, "But...I've always been the plain one."

Katrina sat down on the bed and patted to a spot next to her. "My darling child, you are plain only in comparison to Lisette, whose looks are quite extraordinary. This is your moment."

Katrina reached out and lifted her daughter's chin. "Lisette's beauty is not an advantage! It will garner far too much attention. How will she know who among her admirers esteems her for herself? Most will want a decorative wife, not a life's companion. What are the chances that her head will be turned by all this?"

"I had not thought..."

"Of course you wouldn't! But this is why you are so important. You can show Lisette how to be a respectable young woman. How to navigate such difficulties."

"I'll try..."

"I know you will! You have always been quiet, respectable, and competent." Katrina shook her head sadly. "Think of this: What are the chances that some wealthy man takes Lisette away from us? Almost certain. We can depend on nothing with Lisette."

Amalie saw her mother's sad look. "Mama! None of that is happening now! Now we are here, among these silks and ribbons, and we are going to a ball! We'll show New Orleans what to look like!" Amalie spoke so bravely she surprised herself.

Katrina smiled. "That's my girl! You are right. How wonderful that we three are a grown woman, a brilliant girl, and a child, three stages of life all in the same impeccable jade and cream."

During these weeks of fancy dressmaking, Marguerite and Yvette watched closely. In their bedrooms, there soon was surreptitious stitching going on, a little tuck here, a new ruffle to be added. They were determined to be as beautiful as their guests.

CHAPTER 12

MORE THAN A WALTZ

How little I knew before I was beautiful.

On Saturday night next, the Kästners, except little Jakob and Hans—who flatly refused to go, and in whose place, they invited Francesca and Franci—filed into a large, gracious house in le Vieux Carré and through a receiving line of a splendidly dressed host and hostess. The foyer was crowded with incoming guests and overflowing with pots of ferns and the sweet scent of pink flowers Katrina did not recognize. They could hear from above them the welcoming strains of harp, flute, violin, and clarinet.

"Thomas!" said Niklas, "Izak, Mr. Groves!"

The friends greeted each other and then tromped up the staircase to the third-floor ballroom. It was beautifully paneled and lit with chandeliers, lanterns, and mirrors. Candles had been set into the mouth of an incongruously large fireplace at the far end. Niklas stared at the fireplace and could not imagine a fire ever being needed there.

At one side Marguerite Robichaux fanned herself, and Yvette looked cool and pretty in fresh, light peach silk. Katrina saw a man she did not know aiming for Marguerite. A moment later, he kissed her hand. To Katrina, Marguerite Robichaux seemed quite pleased with this admirer. A cluster of girls closed in around them, and the mothers of the fluttering girls surrounded the Robichauxes as well.

As Karl Schneider came to present himself to the Kästners, the harp and flute embarked on a lovely piece of music, and Katrina closed her eyes to treasure each note. Presently the clarinet joined in, and lastly, the violins.

Dancers swirled all around, enlivened by the cool evening air felt at each window, their slippers brushing the wooden floor and skirts swishing as silk will do, a tinkle of laughter or a bright remark adding a lively accent. It was as gay and unaffected a scene as ever Katrina had witnessed. All the girls seemed to have very fine dark hair, clean and shiny, and surprisingly, styled almost entirely in the same manner, without the side curls now de rigueur in Europe.

In this scene, Amalie was an exquisite exception in a glorious jade green gown with its cream damask apron, her auburn hair touched with golden highlights from a summer aboard ship and done up with dangling clusters of curls and an embroidered headband, a style sure to adorn many a girl at New Orleans's very next ball. Lisette's natural curls were gathered in imitation of her sister's, and Katrina's hair was more conservatively arranged with smooth waves on the sides and a slim green headband.

Francesca, who was in deep conversation with Mr. Groves, looked elegant in a purple gown. As Katrina surveyed the scene with satisfaction, she was frankly thrilled to see that she had succeeded in raising the fashion standards of the room. Niklas stared at Amalie in amazement, seeing his daughter transformed.

"Niklas," whispered Katrina, "don't stare."

"It's just that…I am used to seeing her in her shift."

"Her day dress?" Katrina was amazed at how blind men could be. For most of their voyage Amalie had worn a plain, undyed linen shift, perfectly suited to traveling. "Even that," said Katrina, "had a little embroidery that I did myself."

"Hmm," said Niklas. *My daughter,* he thought, *seems to be impersonating a grown woman, the way she looks tonight.*

Thomas Segrave had noticed Amalie long before Niklas and was escorting her through one dance after another. Amalie's hand rested as lightly as a feather on Tom's arm as they performed the first few steps of a quadrille.

Amalie wondered if Tom felt the same thrill she did until they turned to face each other, and she saw what she could only think was adoration in his eyes. Somewhere in the back of her mind, her girlish vow never to marry knocked at her, and she laughed at her younger self: *How little I knew before Tom,* daring to add, *before I was beautiful.*

Katrina and Niklas overheard one of the women nearby say, "Now them two, there's a pretty pair."

Then Tom handed Amalie to Izak Peterssen and went spinning off with Yvette.

All the conversation was in French, and the customs of France were observed throughout the evening. According to these, each gentleman was privileged to address and dance with any young lady in the company without going through the ceremonial ordeal of introduction. It was impossible to conceive of a regulation more suited to Will, with his naturally gregarious manner but no acquaintances besides Yvette.

Will excused himself from Yvette for an obligatory dance with Franci and then with his little sister, Lisette, a pretty child in her jade green and cream silk damask ensemble, a miniature of her sister and mother. While Tom took another turn with Yvette and Izak danced with Amalie, Will went through the entire line of Yvette's friends. He thought of it like picking flowers, one agreeable face and figure after the next, enjoying their bare pink shoulders, straight little noses, dark eyes fringed with long eyelashes, and eyebrows finely penciled into place.

The quadrille was performed as a contredanse, the dancers facing one another, a variation that Will seized upon in moments. The gallopade was kept to a leisurely pace, danced without devolving into a romp. It was the waltz, though, at which Will excelled, gliding across the dance floor with the grace and confidence to set tongues wagging.

Nodding to Will, Niklas murmured to Katrina, "That boy has more talents than I have credited." Will was not especially tall, but his natural slimness and athleticism, boosted by a summer of sailing, allowed him to cut an admirable figure.

From across the room, Niklas saw Mr. Groves kink his head to one side, a signal if ever Niklas had seen one. He excused himself and went to speak to *Enigma's* first mate.

Katrina saw him returning, staring at Will, a hard look on his face. She glanced at Mr. Groves, but he had now joined the dancers, Francesca in his arms. She ignored Niklas's mysterious turn of mood, and when he was close, she said, "Look at our daughter!" Tom and Amalie were sailing by in a Cajun waltz, her face radiating joy. *This is new*, thought Katrina, *and more than a waltz is involved.*

But when she looked up at Niklas, he was watching the violinists and bending to hear Marguerite Robichaux tell him the name of the tune: "Jeunes Gens Campagnard."

"We used to call this dance the Nizzarda," he said to Marguerite.

Katrina knew it had been a scandalous dance at the time. *He missed the moment*, she thought.

Very shortly, the musicians took a break, and Katrina wandered off with Niklas to the buffet tables set up at the end opposite the fireplace. These were stacked with crab étouffée, fried bayou shrimp with remoulade, grits, cakes, beignets, and ices, accompanied with quite presentable wines and champagne.

The glorious evening was too soon over, each of the Kästners departing much pleased with the mirth and agreeable manners of Creole society. Niklas and Katrina shared a meaningful look as they hesitated on the porch, the faint strains of music still audible, glad to be out in the cool evening air, but wondering when they would ever hear such sweet sounds again or watch dancers of such grace and sophistication.

As they waved goodbye to Karl Schneider and then to Francesca, Franci, and Mr. Groves, Katrina said very quietly to Niklas, "Perhaps we should make New Orleans our home."

He smiled.

They walked home with the young people, Amalie, Tom, Izak, Yvette, and Will trailing far behind, their laughter heard now and again. Will was quiet for once, filled with secret romantic imaginings, sweet memories of dancing with one girl after another. Tom said something funny and from Yvette there was a burst of hilarity. Niklas and Katrina smiled and shared a look. Ahead of them, Lisette went tripping away, dancing a dance of her own, lightheaded with exhaustion, a giddy smile lighting her bright young face.

"A most satisfactory evening," Katrina said.

CHAPTER 13

DEW DROP INN

"Best to keep the particulars of this event to yerself."

It would not surprise any close observer that on this same evening, Hans Kästner was eager to escape the clutches of his loving family. As soon as he had admired their new dance clothes adequately, looked concerned at the fretting over Amalie's hairdo, kissed Lisette goodnight, and seen them off for the ballroom, Hans hopped a horse-drawn omnibus down La Course Street, heading directly for the seedier part of town, breathing in his night of freedom.

The omnibus rattled through the gas-lit streets of wealthier neighborhoods, then past deserted wharfs where stacks of cotton bales cast long black shadows, and then into the darkness and earthy stench of poverty, not stopping until harsh laughter filled the air, accented by a badly played fiddle and voices raised in anger. Hans jumped off near a filthy, narrow alley, a few long steps away from a low, rudely built shack from which issued much of the noise.

So easy to escape, Hans thought. *As easy as falling off a log.* He laughed aloud at the new American expression. He had overheard it on the street, bandied about by two keelboaters, one with a red feather in his cap and both with admirable muscles and a boatman's swagger.

The shack Hans headed for was one of several similar establishments along the alley. Taverns, gaming dens, and brothels glowed through "walls" of draped calico or interlaced fringes of palmettos. These places were made to entice the dregs of the world, rough frontiersmen and rude sailors, and extract whatever coin they might have tucked away. Such deplorables loitered in the alley now, smoking clay or corncob pipes and passing a bottle around. The shack that was Hans's destination wore a crooked sign reading,

"Dew Drop Inn," and for the sake of unlettered patrons bore a drawing of a leaf dripping one fat dewdrop. Lantern light slid in long fingers through an open doorway and an oiled paper window.

As Hans neared the place, a woman screamed, and a man rolled out of the doorway. Behind him, another man was shoved, pushed, or tossed out. The men who had been thrown out scrambled away, grabbing each other in the stumbling way of drunks, both cursing.

Hans stepped deftly to one side and into the smoky den. He ducked as his hat brushed against rough-cut ceiling beams. Above the beams, smoke clung like a woolly blanket.

"Hans!" called the barkeep, "What's yer poison tonight?" The barkeep was a big man, as tall as Hans and forty pounds heavier, with a puffy face and close-set, porcine eyes that disappeared completely when he laughed. He was clad in his usual deeply soiled waistcoat of purple and pink striped silk. Hans stepped forward with a strut his parents would not have recognized, took a seat at the bar, and called for beer, a shot of whiskey, and a cigar.

A pretty girl slid onto his lap and kissed his cheek.

"Lainie," he said happily. Hans knew everyone else in New Orleans would be able to specify to the exact percentage Lainie's racial mix, but he neither knew nor cared. He admired her coral lips and stroked the smooth, cocoa-colored skin of her wrist. *How blind*, he wondered, *must one be not to consider such skin beautiful?*

Drinks in hand, they moved together to the table abandoned by the fighters, its ante of shillings, francs, and reales still glittering in the center. As Hans tossed in an American half-penny, a palmetto bug nearly the size of his fist crashed into one of the lanterns, dropped and skittered away. Behind him, a drunk patron, a thin man with a hooked nose, nodded off to sleep and fell against the bar, knocking it away from the barrels on which it sat. The thin man woke with a start as the barkeep swore at him, picked him up by collar and waistband and tossed him out the door. Hans laughed to see this, his big white teeth holding his cigar in place.

"Shall we play a hand or two first—with all this wealth to share?" Hans nodded to the pile of coins. The barkeep frowned as other men took the seats at the table. A moment more and he would have swept the abandoned riches into his own pockets.

"Oui, oui, chérie," said Lainie with a kittenish half-smile, a smile made crooked to hide a missing tooth, a souvenir of her time on Ramparts Street. She was once a debutante at a Quadroon Ball, in a silk gown and hair ribbons, pretty enough to "marry" a Creole fop. It did not last. Instead of living the fine life of a kept woman, she was kicked out, literally, losing a tooth and landing here, at the Dew Drop Inn. Now she hoped this big dumb German would be her second chance.

"Girl!" the barkeep barked, "Clean up!"

Hans saw a young serving girl jump. It was Lainie's little sister, Hans saw, who was called Tiny. The barkeep threw a rag at her.

About Lisette's age, Hans thought idly, and he turned back to Lainie, who smiled her crooked smile at him again, her eyelashes fluttering, giving him a look intended to be irresistible.

To Hans, it was. He had already swallowed most of a second stein, each with a whiskey chaser, and now he looked at her with adoration, sure that he knew many secrets and understood the multiple mysteries of life. His many doubts and insecurities floated away into the universe.

Hans left the Dew Drop Inn hours later, lurching out with a stupid smile on his face. The dark streets were moonlit, and the broken cobblestones were slick with wet grass sprouting up between them. He struggled to keep his footing. It would not do to slide into the wide gutters, flowing, as everywhere in New Orleans, with stinking brown effluent.

A man's step behind him startled him, and Hans spun around, lost his balance, and put one foot deep into the gutter. There was nothing for it but to climb out, disgusted at the filth now coating his boot and trouser leg. He flicked a cockroach off his knee, which put his face closer to the stench. It was enough to make him retch.

Now Hans was sure he heard the click-click of bootheels on the cobblestones. He pulled out his pistol and tried again to turn toward the sound, but the ground was not where he thought it was, and he slipped again, landing hard on the cobblestones. Someone stripped his pistol from his hand, and Hans heard a girl say, "Let me go!" He wondered if he had imagined it.

Then she was kneeling at his side, a little thing going quickly through his pockets. He heard the jingle of coins, his winnings of the night, before a kick landed in his gut, so hard it took his breath away.

"An easy mark." A disembodied voice floated somewhere above him, with a flash of pink and purple.

Hans lurched to his feet. Tiny was struggling against the barkeep. Hans grabbed her and pulled her free, but in the same moment, the night was split by the flash of a pistol firing, the bullet so close to Hans that he heard it hiss past him. He staggered backward, covering his ears.

The barkeep collapsed onto the cobblestones. Tiny mouthed "Merci" to Hans, and in one swift motion, picked up her skirts, turned, and ran.

Hans wobbled where he stood, staring after her. He shook his head, but he could not hear anything. By his feet, blood was pooling. He looked at it and stepped away, sorrow welling in him. He was aware of a strong impulse to leave, to go home.

A small man stepped up quietly to stand beside him. Hans could smell gunpowder.

"Best to keep the particulars of this event to yerself, Herr Kästner," the small man said in oddly accented French. "New Orleans loves le chaos." He nudged the corpse with one toe. "And if something nasty like this plays a part, so much the better."

The small man nodded to another, much bigger man, a few steps behind them. The big man lifted a cosh, a small, neat cudgel made of baleen with a lead ball wrapped in plaited line. He swatted Hans on the back of the neck. Hans crumpled to his knees, only vaguely seeing the big man going through the barkeep's pockets. There it was again, the jingle of coins.

A thief's thief, Hans thought.

He did not really hear the growl behind him, and he only faintly realized someone had him under the armpits and was lifting him, half dragging him. Hans struggled to find his feet. The growl became a language Hans did not know, a complaint, a question.

"Don't hurt him," said the voice in oddly accented French. "Par ici, this way."

To one side was a reasonably well-lit street, and the three men turned toward it, Hans stumbling, the second, a large bear of a man, supporting him. Trailing behind them was the small man who had shot the barkeep. He was older and slower, and his pegleg made him limp.

CHAPTER 14

C'EST FINI

People scrambled for the door.

At first light, there was a banging on the door of the Robichaux House, and Hans was found drunk and crumpled on the porch. Niklas and Will hauled him upstairs and dumped him into his bed.

"Get your mother," Niklas said to Will. "Not a word to anyone else."

Niklas looked sadly at his oldest son, watching the bruises flowering across his jaw and cheek, wondering if he had lost a tooth. Niklas thought of the important causes so many died for, and by comparison, how pointless Hans's brawling was.

Katrina came quickly down the hallway, a bucket in one hand and a wet cloth in the other. She looked worried. Hans roused himself at the sight of her, smiled sickly, grabbed the bucket, and was violently ill. He groaned as he lay back. She wiped his forehead and lips, and he drifted into sleep.

Niklas motioned to her, and she followed him into the hallway. "Did you smell the gunpowder, see the track it left on his cheek?"

Katrina gasped.

Niklas continued. "I might not have seen it either, had I not turned his head to look at the bruising. But there it is. He was almost shot."

Katrina shook her head sadly. "Maybe the Prussian army would have been a better place for him."

"No, no. We were right to bring him with us. But I should never have allowed him to go off by himself. Not here, nor in Havana neither. I blame myself for indulging him, and I blame him for being weak and for not knowing anything of honor, respect, or restraint."

"His foolishness almost got him killed!" She was shocked. Then she added, "And yet he must find his own way."

Niklas was angry. "Anywhere would be better than cities like this. Sinkholes of evil, depravation, and sin."

She took Niklas's arm, turned him away from the sight of his son and spoke soothingly. "But this morning, he cannot possibly be left alone. You go on now, go down to breakfast."

He turned to go, but then she said: "Just a moment, please." She took up the bucket and grimaced. "Take this away," she said, "and have another bucket sent up."

A few minutes later, in the breakfast room, Niklas talked quietly with the other children as he ate, telling them their older brother was ill and not to mention it or this morning's destination, a Lutheran church service in a private home. Then he looked appreciatively at Mme. Robichaux's eggs and grits and pain perdue and ate everything on his plate and encroached upon that which had been put aside for Katrina, slathering each slice of French toast with mayhaw jelly and dusting it with finely ground sugar.

The younger children were turned out as well as anyone could expect when they were in a strange home after a long voyage. Mme. Robichaux had used the intervening days since the Kästners' arrival to send their small clothing to the laundry down the street. They all had had baths before last night's Creole ball, and Will had been stuffed into his best coat by his father, who swept it clean with swats both effective and rather hard to bear.

"I was informed about your visit to sailor town where you apparently intended to save Francesca," Niklas had told Will. "What were you thinking of to go there alone? If Mr. Groves and his muscle had not turned up in time, we may have had you to bury, a dagger in your gullet. Never again, Wilhelm. We go with the strength of three men or not at all, do you hear me?"

Will said, "Yes, yes, yes." He felt it unfair of Mr. Groves not to mention that he had used his cane brilliantly to disarm Giovanni. All this time, his father swatted at the back of his coat, ostensibly against the dust. Will wanted to say, "Ow, ow, ow" but he was sixteen and as tall as his father, so he bit his tongue and bore it.

A few days later, in another café, the talk about Napoleon ran from grumblings about "that dreadful little man" to "atheist Sicilian monster," and other phrases too vile to repeat. These were despisers of Napoleon and of the new France, families whose grandfather or great-grandfather had lost his head or everything else, and who were even now watching for a chance to make things right or at least, to take revenge.

Overhearing this, Niklas and Katrina were about to move on. Niklas pushed back his chair and stood. He was stretching out his arm, reaching for the back of Katrina's chair when he felt the point of a knife in his back.

"You. You are Kästner, non?" The voice was low and fierce.

"Oui." Niklas stood stock still.

Katrina was oblivious. She was fiddling with her reticule, and now she said, "Niklas, did I have my best white kerchief with me?"

All of Niklas's attention was on the knife at his back. He swore at himself for choosing a new café, for not sitting against a wall.

The man behind Niklas grabbed his arm, hard. "Pour Grand-père. Pour Dieu. Pour la France."

The last word was garbled, mixed with a shriek of pain. The knife hit the floor. The tight grip on Niklas fell away. Niklas spun around to see a man in a tattered coat, once fine, dropping to his knees.

Behind the collapsed man stood Ivan Ivanovich, who wrenched his dagger free. He looked at Niklas and said, "C'est fini."

Blood burbled from the fallen man's mouth. He sank to the floor.

Niklas stared at Ivan Ivanovich. Luka loomed behind his brother, looking upset. "Ivanovich," said Niklas.

Katrina had at last looked up, and now she rose so quickly that her chair toppled over. People were looking their way. She took a step backward. She heard gasps. People scrambled for the door.

Ivan Ivanovich said, "How is your boy?" He wiped the blood off his dagger.

Niklas reached for his pistol, but Ivan Ivanovich grabbed his wrist and snorted. "Would I have killed this filthy French royalist for you if I wanted you dead? Besides, you owe us your son's life. Has he told you who saved him?"

"What do you want?"

"You could turn certain goods I have."

"Hah! Go sell whatever rotten thing you have yourself."

"No one trusts me. Qui sait pourquoi ? Who can say why? But it is my wish to die in Mother Russia. And this one," Ivan nodded at Luka, "he needs to be where they grasp his mumble."

"What do you want?" Niklas said again.

"Enough to pay for passage home. We want to go. You want us gone. Sell what I have. And there's more if you want to be in on it."

Niklas frowned, and Ivan backtracked.

"Or give us your own gold, whatever you please, so long as we have money for passage home."

Ivan Ivanovich kept still, studying Katrina, giving Niklas time. Then he dropped a cloth bag on the table. "Here. Find a buyer quickly. If you are not to be part of the operation, you don't want this in your hands."

They agreed to meet in three days' time. Ivan motioned to Luka, and they were gone as quickly as they had come.

Niklas reached for Katrina's arm. "Are you all right?"

"Yes, yes," she said. "Are you?"

Niklas nodded. He picked up the cloth bag, opened it, and peered inside at a cluster of white compressed disks. "Opium," he said. "Quite a lot." He glanced around. The room was deserted by now. No one had heard.

Niklas glanced at the dead man. "Let's away. There's not a moment to waste."

CHAPTER 15

ACH DU LIEBER GOTT

a cry for help, for mercy, for rescue

A clean and pressed Kästner family, without Katrina or Hans, made its way down Chartres Street that Sunday morning, heading toward Clio Street. The family passed La Pharmacie Francaise, at 514 Chartres Street, where the pharmacist Louis Dufilho had earlier the same day advised Niklas on dosing for Hans, selling him basil with spices for fever and elderberry leaf ointment for cuts and bruises.

Monsieur Dufilho, who had heard about Niklas's years in the French army, brushed off his own expertise in comparison with that of a Dr. Du-Bourg, once a surgeon of Napoleon's Imperial Guard. More recently, DuBourg became the first in modern times to save a child and mother with a successful Caesarian operation.

"Do you know the great doctor?" Monsieur Dufilho asked Niklas.

"I have heard of him," Niklas admitted, with his usual reticence about matters pertaining to the wars. He made a fist of his right hand, hiding the missing little finger, cut off by Dr. DuBourg when frostbite made saving it impossible. It was that or gangrene, and Niklas was rightly thankful for Dr. DuBourg's few precious minutes with him and for the neatness of his stitches.

Mme. Robichaux spoke of Monsieur Dufilho in hushed tones, telling of his bottles always lettered in Latin. "What a comfort," she said. "The new State of Louisiana actually licensed him as a pharmacist, what will the world think of next?" She paused, but not long enough for Niklas to say anything. "Oddly enough, Dr. Dufilho says he is just as properly addressed as 'Monsieur' as 'Doctor,' and ain't that gratifyingly humble?"

Niklas took the rare opportunity of being at a pharmacy to buy Peruvian bark, against the dreaded Walcheren fever and marsh ague, all too common in southern regions. Katrina had sent along a request for turpentine for rashes, to which Jakob was susceptible, and laudanum for any other problem that might arise.

The streets were, as always, filled with as many Africans as Whites. Free people of color were as numerous as those enslaved, but the family had not yet developed an eye as to the niceties of dress and bearing to distinguish. Everyone, Black or White, slave or free, spoke French. Many New Orleanais were tri-lingual in French, Spanish, and English. Some German was heard as well, and a sprinkling of almost everything else. Americans were the exception. Rough-dressed and monolingual, American frontiersmen and riverboat men spoke barely decipherable English, nearly as unintelligible as a Scotsman Niklas had heard in one of the shops.

"It's a kind of English," the shopkeeper assured him, "although..."

"Flatboat men! Americains!" Mme. Robichaux sniffed. "The worst sort of ruffians."

Niklas was surprised. He did not expect, here in America itself, to hear the word spoken with such venom.

On Wednesday, a handsome young man arrived at Mme. Robichaux's home in equipage so fine everyone on the street buzzed about it. He, whose name was Antoine Huber, delivered an invitation from his father.

The carriage was a cabriolet with a Negro groom up behind, dressed in a blue uniform with gold stripes on the trousers. The brass on the cabriolet was polished to a brilliance rarely seen and sported a blue and gold crest. It was drawn by a fine, smooth-trotting black Friesian, and the groom hopped down as the carriage slowed, before it had even rolled to a stop. He ran along to the horse's head, grabbed the bridle, and stood with it in hand, holding the horse perfectly still as Antoine climbed down.

The Kästners, it turned out, were to be the guests of Antoine's father, Jacques Huber, a German Coast plantation owner.

Yvette was left breathless. She found Amalie, grasped both of her hands, and said earnestly, "Did you see him? And that carriage? This is what I mean about New Orleans presenting fine opportunities for you to make an envious engagement."

She looked at Amalie with new respect, her mind racing on to imagine being Amalie's gorgeous friend, too beautiful for her poverty to be noticed, invited to grand balls at the Huber Plantation and exciting the devotion of some wealthy friend of Antoine's. Or even of Thomas Segrave, tossed over by a newly rich Amalie, and perfectly available. Yvette found the romance of it all irresistible, indeed, almost unbearable. *Nice!* she scolded herself, *Be nice to Amalie.*

On upper Chartres Street, a row of foreign embassies stood chockablock, including the Danish Embassy, where Izak had gone earlier in the week to hear his native tongue spoken. It might have brought tears to his eyes if he had not been with Katrina and Niklas.

"Over there is Sicily's embassy," Katrina said, wondering aloud where Giovanni might be.

Niklas shrugged. "Gone to one of the Italian countries, I presume."

"We must see Francesca again," Katrina said.

Niklas murmured an assent, but he was more interested in the embassies near Sicily's, which included several for newly minted South American countries, ones called "Colombia" and "Brazil." Then, at the same moment, Niklas and Katrina caught sight of the Prussian embassy. He took her arm, and as if of one mind, they turned the other way, back where they had come.

"Why are you bothering to write to Elizabet? Have you thought about what it will cost us to send these letters?"

"Why do I write? Because she's family, Niklas!"

"She's family beyond reach. As far away as if death took her."

"No, she's not! She may yet follow us here."

"She is a wealthy widow with plenty for a comfortable life in Berleburg. Besides, her sex makes her irrelevant. The king, the secret police, the monarchists, they'll never bother with her. Thus, she will never follow us."

"Family beyond reach," Katrina murmured. Niklas's words hurt. Then she stirred herself. "Not if we write to one another. Not if we understand one another. Not if our hearts are as one."

Niklas sighed. "You'd do better to concentrate on your daughters. Make your heart as one with Amalie. With Lisette. Leave Elizabet to her own devices, same as she has left you."

"She'll write back," Katrina said. "She will. And the girls, well, daughters are another thing. I love them, you know I do, but Elizabet..."

Tears welled up in her eyes, and seeing this, Niklas could not help but take her into his arms. She gave one big sob and was still.

"Write whatever you wish," he said. "We'll pay the postage, outrageous as it is. Your letters are a comfort to Elizabet, I am sure." *Your letters,* he thought, *are a comfort to you, whether Elizabet bothers to open them or not.*

On another day, Niklas was abroad with the younger children, and as they turned onto Clio Street, they saw a huddle of people on the other side of the street, coming toward them.

At the sight of feet moving in unison, linked by chains, Niklas recognized it as a "coffle." The word was new to him. He had heard in a discussion about Hewlett's Exchange, the nearby slave market, to which he supposed these slaves were being driven. A slave auction was posted for Monday, and Niklas had agreed to go, though not without trepidation.

The coffle went by with a clanking of chains, a tightly packed, anxious, gray cluster, shuffling and moaning, urged on by a man with a whip, his face half hidden by a sweat-stained leather hat, who was driving them into a holding pen. A flick of the whip, and a Black boy flinched and bent in submission, a stripe of blood reddening across his shoulders.

An exhausted young woman, no older than Amalie, had a newborn in her arms and a young child clinging to her bloody gray skirt. As the Kästners watched, a wail went up from one of the slaves and a string of words, incomprehensible but perfectly clear: a cry for help, for mercy, for rescue. People on the street turned at the sound and turned quickly away again. The whip cut through the air, followed by a shriek. The strange words stopped.

"Ach du lieber Gott," Will said, stepping between the whip and Amalie, who was hiding Lisette in her skirts. They were out of its range, but he couldn't help but shield them.

Niklas picked up Jakob and turned him away, but the five-year-old was having none of that. He twisted to see what everyone was looking at, and when he did so, his sharp, young ears picked up the first phrase of a sound as soft as a butterfly's wing. One slave, an old woman, whispered a song, and the others joined her. It was a sad, plaintive song, but it was theirs.

CHAPTER 16

IN THE GRIP OF A LIE

"The most dangerous thing is the lie."

Niklas always had goods to buy and sell, and now he was in the awkward possession of a rather large quantity of compacted opium disks. He hoped to find a buyer at Hewlett's Exchange, a trading and auction house where the Enigmas expected to sell the ship's cargo. Before that, though, he stopped at La Pharmacie Francaise.

Louis Dufilho's eyes went huge when he saw the quantity of opium Niklas had to sell. He guided Niklas to the back room, a laboratory with a marble-topped table and shelves all along the sides holding glass bottles, porcelain jars, cloth sacks, and wooden crates. "May I?" he said, looking up at Niklas.

"Certainly."

Dufilho reached into the sack, withdrew one disk and placed it on a marble cutting board. He drew a sharp knife across it, dropping a dusting of white powder onto the board. Dufilho picked up a pinch and put it on his tongue. "Ahh," he said. "This is good." He looked up at Niklas, tilted his head, and asked, "Where did you get this?"

"Monsieur, though it pains me to say it, I cannot tell you."

"Can you bring me more?"

"I cannot."

"This by itself is far more than I would ordinarily buy." Dufilho returned the sample disk to the sack.

Niklas backed up a step. "I do not mean to press you, Monsieur. I can sell it at Hewlett's Exchange."

"Please do not! Consider, kind sir, what damage this could do if used carelessly. And how it could help if properly cut and mixed to create laudanum for those in pain and for quieting babies, blessed relief for many. It should not be in irresponsible hands."

Niklas hesitated. "I cannot explain, Monsieur, but I must arrange a sale quickly. If you knew what danger this puts my family in, you would agree."

Louis Dufilho looked at Niklas with narrowed eyes. He did not know who in this German's family was addicted or whether he was looking into the face of the addict himself, but he said, "I will buy it. I cannot pay as much as some might, but I will weigh it fairly and give you a fair price. You will know it is going to good purposes, every ounce of it."

Niklas reached out a hand, Louis Dufilho shook it, and then set to the task of measuring opium.

On Monday, Niklas, Hans, and Will went to Hewlett's Exchange, there to meet Izak Peterssen, Thomas Segrave, and Mr. Groves. Besides the trades in which they were interested, a slave auction was posted for the day. Niklas had steeled himself against the sight, and he warned the boys. "You should witness this," he said, "the better to understand slavery."

The building was impressive, but it stank. Gigantic portraits of Napoleon and Washington lined the walls of the Exchange, and all around, men discussed the new Republic of Texas, inclined to believe it could be brought in as a slave state and thus improve the slave-to-free balance. They talked of Mexico and fair compensation. Above the chatter, four twelve-candle chandeliers hung from a nineteen-foot-high ceiling, a jarring stab at elegance amid the business of the day.

Hewlett's Exchange reminded the Kästners of the big exchanges in Cologne and Paris. They loved the excitement of such places, the sight of exotic goods from Egypt or India, and the feeling of being in the center of everything important in the city.

And then the first lot of human beings was brought in.

Will was surprised to see that some were naked. It seemed such an unnecessary extra cruelty.

Izak Peterssen saw this and nudged Thomas. "He shouldn't have been allowed to come."

Thomas looked grim. "He has age enough for it."

On the auction block, men and women were pinched and poked, their mouths opened for an inspection of their teeth, and their muscles squeezed.

Sometimes they were made to trot about to prove their fitness. Naked young women, some in neck collars, were made to walk at speed or trot, to show buyers the bouncing of their breasts, saying it indicated whether they were virgins or had borne children. Some were swollen with child, and this brought more money.

"Good breeders," a buyer seated next to Niklas said with satisfaction.

The first lot of slaves looked newly brought from Africa. They were moved about with the point of a whip, having apparently no grasp of French or English. One young girl crouched and ran when she was poked. Men laughed as the handler tripped her and then hauled her upright. Mothers and children cried piteously when they were separated.

Importing slaves from Africa had been outlawed nearly thirty years earlier, but as the man next to Niklas said with a conspiratorial wink, "We can always count on the Lafittes."

The men were sold like oxen or mules for hard labor on sugar, rice, or cotton plantations, though some were barely able to stand, having suffered horribly on the slave ships. Some had been oiled to hide the cuts and filth of their bodies, and some, both men and women, had decorative scarring on their faces, shoulders, or arms: circles, stripes, or dots in strange patterns. Will had seen such tattooing in Cuba and assumed it was Caribbean. Now he understood it as the mark of someone born in Africa.

In sharp contrast were those who had been "sold down the river," which meant being brought across from the Southeastern states. These slaves were better dressed, lighter colored, and could be given verbal commands. They behaved lightheartedly, laughing and smiling to prove how "willing" and "happy" and "easy" they were. Will could see that they were kept separate, not to be associated with those newly brought over. Many from the East were skilled cooks or seamstresses, wet nurses or midwives, shoemakers or blacksmiths, maids or butlers, and such talents were announced. A premium was paid for speaking French.

Izak had gone red in the face at the sight of this wretched trade. Thomas Segrave had been a boy aboard *Isolde* when Izak was reclaimed from the Barbary pirates and saved from both slavery and the sea. He knew something of what Izak had lived through. He pulled Izak out to the street at the first opportunity where Izak bent over the gutter and vomited.

"You can do nothing for them," Tom told Izak, "We have already helped save one man and his family. That's all we can do for now." Niklas, Hans, and Will followed the others to a coffeehouse where they ordered coffee with brandy, a good deal of brandy.

Will brought his coffee to his lips with hands that shook. "How do they sleep at night?"

"Oh, my son," said Niklas, "I have known men whose own experience of subjugation did nothing to temper their desire to subjugate others."

"And indeed," said Tom, "sharpened their appetite for it."

"Huh," said Will. "I will never hold anyone as a slave." A moment later he felt a stab of homesickness and anger. *How,* he wondered, *could Father have ever considered such a horrible country for us? I will go back to where people are civilized, I swear I will.*

Later, Niklas told Katrina how pathetic and horrible the slave market had been. "They treat slaves as property and the spectacle as ordinary commerce," he said, shaking his head. "There is no human kindness."

"They do not think slaves are human, and they do not want them treated as human beings," Katrina said. "Madame Robichaux reprimanded me when I thanked one of the serving girls. She told me, 'You'll give them airs.'"

"The entire institution rests on lies about the nature of humanity, a false sense of superiority, a whole range of falsehoods and idiocies."

"Idiocies that grown men and women accept as gospel." She looked thoughtful. "The more outrageous the lies, the better."

"They work to inculcate each generation."

"What worries me is the thick crust of cruelty that is not just accepted but encouraged."

"The most dangerous thing is the lie. Europe is based on a lie—that a few are made to rule and all others are inferior and must submit. I see now that America is in the grip of the same lie, though it is in direct conflict with her stated dedication to liberty. Democracy cannot survive a lie."

"Oh, my dear Niklas, let's not get ahead of ourselves. Slavery and the excuses for it are idiotic, but they infect only half the country. There's plenty of the other America left for us."

He told her then what they had seen on Sunday. "Being with the younger children made it even harder to come face to face with slaves being driven like cattle on the street. I picked up Jakob and turned him away, but you know how he is; he squirmed around to see what everyone was looking at."

"He won't remember it, Danke Gott."

"Some say children should know the harshness of life and become inured to it," said Niklas, "but I think a child will be soon enough hardened. It is better to shield children from awful sights such as worm into their minds and become the stuff of nightmares."

Nightmares, thought Katrina. *No one knows better than Niklas about nightmares.*

In the Old South of 1836, slavery infected everything. To its defenders, it was an inescapable way of the world, necessary for a wealthy and cultured life. Their preachers told them the Bible accepted and defended slavery, and that was enough.

To those who thought beyond the sermons, slavery was an inexplicable sin. The Kästners had been thrust into the midst of all this, and it was disorienting. The whispered tales they heard of further horrors only added to their dismay and discomfort.

CHAPTER 17

LA CÔTE DES ALLEMANDES

He is the kind of man I cannot possibly like.

"It wasn't all that bad, my dear," said Niklas to Katrina. He shifted his weight, glad to be in bed and safely away from the spot on the way home where the Hubers' carriage, elegant as it was, had broken a spring.

"Oh, yes, it was," she said. Lowering her voice, she added, "Jacques Huber may count himself a German, but he could never be a friend of ours, Niklas, a man so blind to the evil of owning slaves."

Niklas could not disagree. The only reason he was still awake was that he was contemplating men like Jacques Huber, who would never willingly dismantle slavery. Huber's anger about what was happening at Destrehan made that clear. Still, it saddened him to see Katrina's distaste for la Côte des Allemandes, the German Coast. He knew her opinion might extend to all New Orleans, but he worried that their other option, the American frontier, might be worse than any city. He wanted New Orleans to be an acceptable fallback.

Katrina was not finished. "I feel about Jacques Huber," she said, "like I felt about that despicable Ernst Zimmermann and the rest of the Prussian secret police. They are everything contemptible, unchristian, and immoral, the opposite of you and me, and when they are civil and invite us to dinner, we should find a way to refuse them." She took a deep breath. "I am in some way afraid of them."

"Katrina!" He whispered in the darkness. "Where is your courage? Your human kindness?" It was a dismal note on which to try to sleep.

The afternoon of that day had begun pleasantly enough with the family walking to the docks to meet a private steamboat the Hubers had hired to ferry them up the river. As they waited to ascend the gangplank, a parade of expensively dressed women disembarked, each living proof that no amount of money helped those unable to choose a dress well.

"Look carefully," Katrina murmured to Amalie. "It is one dreadful lesson after another."

A short, smooth riverboat trip later, the family debarked and saw a carriage arriving to meet them. It was larger than the carriage Antoine Huber had arrived in when he came with their invitation, but in the same Huber Plantation colors: blue paint, gold leaf detailing, and bright yellow spokes that seemed nearly royal. The driver was in a top hat and tails, and the team of handsome black Friesians was tacked up in an elegant harness with the blue-and-gold Huber crest.

Well done, thought Niklas, admiring the carriage, *most handsomely done.*

Monsieur Antoine Huber emerged and held the carriage door for them. It was a tight fit for seven, but not impossible, and there was much to admire. The blue velvet interior had gold-threaded silk pillows, a ticking clock, and a visiting list. Clearly, Antoine's father was interested in them, in the way anyone appreciates new money, especially with the added enticement of its coming from an officer of Napoleon's famed light horse cavalry. Jacques Huber was one of many Orleanais admirers of Napoleon.

The Huber family had been among the original 1721 German Coast settlers. Like the Kästners, they were Rhinelanders, whether nominally Swiss, German, French, or Dutch. They survived floods, hurricanes, mosquitoes, and other rigors of the frontier tropics to make their settlements a success, and in the process, grew the food that saved an infant New Orleans. In 1768, they helped oust the Spanish colonial governor, and they fought the British during the American Revolution and 1812's "Second Revolution." But their most important contributions to early New Orleans were the vegetables and rice that kept the struggling city fed.

On their way, the Kästners passed Destrehan Plantation with its distinctive West Indies hip roof and curved twin staircases. It reminded them of Havana. Katrina studied its wide porch and wooden window grilles. She turned to Antoine and asked, "Would I be correct to imagine that Destrehan has a central patio with a tile floor and a fountain?"

"Yes!" said Antoine. "How did you know?"

"It looks like homes in Cuba." The thought gave her a stab of regret about leaving the island. There were moments when the beaches of Havana alone seemed worth being surrounded by papists.

"Yet here we are," Katrina turned and murmured to Niklas, "still surrounded by papists."

"What?" he said.

"Nothing, nothing."

"The old part of Destrehan is bousillage," said Antoine. "It's brick made of clay and retted Spanish moss. There's no stone to be found hereabouts. Even now, stone must be brought in."

The hold of *Enigma*, recalled Will, carried limestone blocks as ballast.

His father had apparently had the same thought. He said to Will, "Remind me to mention this to Izak and Tom."

"There was a blight about 1790," Antoine said. "Indigo crops failed, and Jean-Noël Destrehan switched to sugarcane. Then, his brother-in-law, Étienne de Boré, invented a new processing method that made sugar more profitable. You could say de Boré spun sugar into gold!"

"Inventions like that," said Will, "make the world modern."

"Indeed. Destrehan was also the site of the slave uprising of 1811. Two or three hundred slaves rampaged across the countryside, killing two white men. They were captured, and ninety-five hanged or shot, the others beaten into submission. It was a good lesson, which they have not forgotten. We are more vigilant, too, even now."

Amalie peeked at Antoine from under her bonnet. *Ninety-five*. Out the carriage window were fields full of Black men, women, and children. She thought of the Germanies as the most civilized countries in the world, and now she wondered, *How can this be a German part of the world?*

Niklas asked, "What caused the uprising?"

Antoine shrugged. "So many new slaves from Haiti, Cuba, or straight out of Africa, I suppose. Sugar takes a lot of slaves."

Katrina tried to change the subject: "Who lives at Destrehan now?"

"It's awful unsettled just now, madame," Antoine said. "Last week Monsieur Henderson died—of a broken heart, they say. He married Zelia Destrehan years ago, when she was barely sixteen, but when she died, Mr. Henderson never recovered, and it's been an unhappy house ever since. Now with him gone and no children, no one knows what's next."

The Friesians cantered past huge cotton fields glowing white in the dim light and slowed to a walk as the carriage turned down a gracious allée of live oaks hung thick with Spanish moss. Pink crape myrtle and blue verbena edged the allée, and mint had been planted for the wheels to crush and add to the delights. It was an entrance out of a fairy tale.

"This is home!" exclaimed Antoine. Then he said, rather incongruously, "Laissez le bon temps rouler."

Antoine handed the ladies down, and the family stepped up onto a wide porch between immense columns, three on a side, and then into a foyer with a ceiling painted sky blue with white clouds. In its center stood a finely carved circular table and a huge bouquet. Antoine ushered them into a high-ceilinged parlor with yellow walls and tall windows. Blue velvet swags lined the windows, and a gold leaf mirror gleamed brightly over a gray marble fireplace. The Kästners looked about in admiration.

Wine was served and sumptuous hors d'oeuvre: Italian-style pâtés, shrimp and crayfish, artichokes with lemon and butter. As they nibbled and chatted with the charming Antoine, their host and the rest of the Huber family joined them, the candles flickering at their entrance.

Jacques Huber was a large, thick man, with an inflamed complexion and slightly bulging eyes. *Goiter,* thought Katrina as he kissed her hand. The circles under his eyes and the red tracery on his nose and cheeks reminded her of a drunkard she had known in Berleburg. She saw nothing of Antoine in this man. Monsieur Huber introduced his wife, Maria, a little woman of Katrina's size who had once been pretty, though her skin now had a pallor that suggested illness. Maria wore a black armband.

"Herr Kästner," Jacques Huber said, "Willkommen!" His German had a French accent.

After a sentence or two, Niklas switched to French, and the Hubers were happy to follow his lead. Monsieur Huber drew Niklas and Hans to one side and spoke earnestly to them. Katrina overheard a few phrases, "fresh blood," "the value of new capital," "Utopia." It was enough to know how the conversation turned.

One of the daughters, Juliette, was about Amalie's age. She smiled shyly from a face so pale and soft it must never have seen the sun without a parasol. She and her younger sister wore identical apricot silk dresses with very wide sleeves, the most up-to-date cuts Katrina and Amalie had seen in New Orleans. Like Antoine, his sisters took after their mother.

Jacques Huber led them to Great-Aunt Violet, who had been lifted into the room by two slaves and now sat leaning forward, her hands resting on a cane, her arms shrouded in black lace. As they were introduced, Antoine leaned over to Amalie and whispered, "She talks to the dead."

Amalie's eyebrows rose. *Did I hear correctly?*

"I mean," said Antoine, "she talks to her dead brother, her dead husband, and especially her dead sister, 'poor, dearest Dabney.' Right now, she is talking to your parents, but she hardly ever talks to people who are alive."

"Oh," said Amalie, "we had a great-uncle in Berleburg like that."

"Where…" he paused, "is that?"

Amalie did not think she could tell him exactly. "Our hometown, in Prussia, near Cologne."

He smiled politely, having only the slightest notion of Prussia and none at all of Cologne.

Someone looking at the two young people would have thought Amalie and Antoine oddly alike, both thin and he only a little taller. It seemed strange to Amalie, who was used to robust boys. She went on a bit about Berleburg, about its swift-running creeks and picturesque mountains, its fine half-timber houses, its ancient palace, until she heard what she sounded like and felt the blood rise to her face. "It's just a village," she said, "but a pretty place. It was Napoleon's when Mama and Papa were growing up and now belongs to the Prussian king." She sighed. "Berleburg was our home."

"Why did you leave?" Antoine asked.

Amalie hesitated. Then she brightened and said, "For America!"

"Oui! America."

Amalie felt herself blush again. She was not used to telling lies.

Antoine was distracted too, appreciating what a blush did to the cheeks of a pretty girl.

Mme. Huber smiled at Katrina. "Please call me Maria. May I call you Katie?"

Katrina hesitated. *I am, after all a guest in this house, but "Katie?" Not in this life.* "Trina, if you please," she said aloud. *If you must,* she thought.

Katrina inquired about the black armband, and Maria told her it was to honor their near neighbor, Mr. Henderson.

Over Maria's shoulder, Katrina saw Jacques Huber's large eyes assessing Niklas and Hans frankly and approvingly. Niklas was speaking now, and Monsieur Huber's eyes roved, dismissing Will at a glance and resting on Amalie in her new bloom of womanhood and on Lisette, an astonishingly pretty child, sweet and pink, with a mass of fine blonde curls.

Jacques Huber drew a lace-trimmed handkerchief from his sleeve, mopped his forehead and stared again at Amalie, looking her up and down. Marguerite Robichaux said Huber was thought to be rich. She also warned them that he was notorious for gambling and for his temper; he had fought numerous duels and won. Even here, in the family, Katrina saw, he was treated with extreme deference.

Moments later, a young slave in a footman's uniform slipped into the room and held out a silver salver with a folded note. He looked as if he dared neither to interrupt nor to delay the delivery of the message.

Huber took the note, read it, and swore under his breath. He excused himself and a jerk of his head told his slave to follow.

The rest of the party moved off to the music room, where the younger Huber daughter sat down at the piano to play. Beside her, Juliette sang,

"Horch! horch! die Lerch'im Aetherblau;
   Und Phöbus, neu erweckt,
Tränkt seine Rosse mit dem Thau,
   Der Blumenkelche deckt;
Der Ringelblume Knospe schleußt
   Die gold'nen Aeuglein auf;
Mit allem, was da reizend heißt,
   Du süße Maid, steh auf! Steh auf, steh auf!

"Hark, hark, the lark in the ether blue,
and Phoebus, fresh awake
Waters his steeds with the dew
which covers the flower's chalice.
The marigold's bud opens
its little golden eye;
with everything that is adorable;
Thou, sweet maid, arise! Arise, arise!"

The sisters finished, and their listeners clapped politely.

"It's Schubert, isn't it? The lyrics from Shakespeare?" Katrina asked.

"Oui," Marie said, "from *Cymbeline*."

As the girls shuffled through sheet music and whispered about what to play next, the elegance of the evening was split by an angry voice and a stifled scream. The young footman stumbled out of the library, one hand to a bloodied cheek, and ran, disappearing down the hall. Antoine swept the music room doors closed, but it was too late. Everyone had seen the outburst and must now pretend they had not.

Maria Huber suddenly became animated and filled the room with light-hearted chatter. Niklas sat stiffly listening, aware of a wish to have arrived better armed.

In a few moments, Jacques Huber opened the doors and strode into the music room, still red-faced. As he turned to close the doors again, he wiped the blood off the back of his hand.

"That blackguard Henderson has freed his slaves," he said. "The will was just read out. There will be no end of trouble. Even in death, that damned Scotsman makes my life difficult."

He waved his daughters to play on, and there was another song before Maria ushered the group into the dining room. It had red walls, a glittering chandelier, and a beautifully laid table. Behind each chair, a house slave stood, ready to seat and serve each person. Maria motioned her guests to their places, saying, "Mesdames. Messieurs."

Katrina was seated beside Jacques Huber, where she saw a smear of blood on his ring. *It matters not at all how rich he is,* she thought, *or how personable his son; he is the kind of man I cannot possibly like: rude, leering, easily angered, and dangerous.* She longed for the moment they would not be his guests on an estate where he reigned, its ugly realities draped in elegance.

CHAPTER 18

A SUDDEN VISION

"'Tis the way of all the world."

New Orleans in summertime was no fit place to live. But this year, 1836, the town had an excellent distraction: the shocking news about Destrehan.

Among many angry reactions, sages recalled George Washington's freeing of his slaves and discussed the founding fathers' intent. Lawyers said the matter was not settled. Though the Hendersons had been childless, heirs would surface, and the will would be challenged.

On Saturday, Katrina and Marguerite Robichaux were companionably drawn up in wicker chairs on the back parlor, with a pitcher of cold tea and their sewing. Marguerite wanted every detail about the German Coast and the Huber mansion, and Katrina obliged, telling her landlady about the magnificent hackney coach, the gracious allée of live oaks, the red walls of the dining room, the chandeliers, and the silver epergnes. She described the elderly grandaunt, the pale Madame Huber, and the two pretty daughters.

When the beat of drums from Congo Square filtered into the back parlor, Marguerite shuddered. "Such a primitive sound."

Katrina described the moment Jacques Huber received the message about the Henderson will and his burst of anger.

Marguerite was angry, too. "What was the Scotsman thinking? A mob will flood into town—newly freed, hungry, out of work, and with no way to feed themselves or their children. A few days of this—" she waved angrily at the sound of the drums— "and they will break into our houses, steal us blind, and murder us."

Katrina let a moment of silence cool Marguerite's ire, and then she asked, "The Destrehan slaves are Christians, are they not? They speak French and have been trained to a trade. Wouldn't they just join the free Black community?"

"Hah!" said Marguerite. "A few may be cooks or smiths or whatever, but most are fieldhands, crude, filthy, and unfit but for hard labor." She looked at Katrina with pity and spoke slowly, as if to a child. "If you want sugar," she said, gesturing to sugar bowl on the tea tray, "sugar takes slaves. You want rice? Rice takes slaves. You want cotton?" She held up the cloth she was sewing. "Cotton takes slaves."

Katrina could not resist asking the obvious. "Why not simply hire labor? Think of it: if you paid wages, you would be free of feeding, clothing, and housing slaves. You could charge rent for the houses out back and collect pennies for every meal."

At that moment, a houseslave appeared at the doorway and extended a hand toward the tea service, ready to take it away. Marguerite looked up and said, "Get out!" The slave disappeared.

They sewed in silence for a few minutes, and then Katrina said in her gentlest voice, "Marguerite, this is a democracy. How can slavery be here in the land of the free?"

"Democracy is an idea, an I-D-E-A. Are you and I free? Is anyone truly free? I'm afraid you are unrealistic, Frau Kästner." She lifted her nose and frowned.

Katrina stiffened. "Where I come from, the whole continent eschews slavery. The poorest of our peasants are free. Anyone can rise from poverty, and many do. Besides," she continued, remembering the miserable, unpainted slave quarters on the other side of the Robichaux garden, as bad as the worst hovel in Europe, "people who are free paint their own houses, teach their own children, pickle their own cabbage. Everyone has reason to do the best they can."

"Your continent still bows and scrapes to kings," said Marguerite Robichaux, "so don't think you can say anything about ours." There was a long pause while she sighed, thinking how tedious this conversation was and how inappropriate that this Kästner woman, barely dry from her ocean crossing, should have opinions.

A distant look came over her face as she recalled something unfortunate. Her cook's son, raised under this roof, fed, sheltered, and indulged, had run away just before she could sell him.

"None of this," she said, "is up to me. I can't change it, nor would I wish to."

She threaded another needle and picked up her work again. One who listened carefully might have heard her mutterings continue, something about the Jews in Egypt and the harems of China.

"'Tis the way of all the world," she said out loud, looking satisfied with her personal review of history. Then she remembered the Kästner gold, straightened her shoulders, and put on a proper landlady's smile. "Surely nothing for us to fall out about."

"He's twenty-four, Niklas, the same age you were when you came home after Waterloo." Katrina was dressing while Niklas lay on the bed, admiring her.

"Well, you're right."

"Consider," she said, "all you had experienced by his age—men dying around you on the retreat from Moscow, the sword that nearly blinded you, the first man you killed."

"In Spain. I was only nineteen."

"A few years older than Will is now."

"He would have killed me had I not struck him down. I have been able to protect these boys from such as that, Danke Gott."

"Danke Gott. But we should remember that by Hans's age you were a veteran, father to a four-year-old, and marrying for the second time."

"Yes," he smiled. "And a good thing it was for Hans that I married you. How could I have tried to raise him myself?"

"To tell the truth, I was thinking only of you, the handsomest man I had ever seen. The strongest, the smartest, the only one in the village who had seen the world and lived to tell about it." She was in his arms by now.

He snorted. "I see I pulled the wool over your eyes."

"Never take me for a fool, my good sir. You have never fooled me for an instant."

In one swift move he swung her around to lie below him. "A challenge then! Perhaps I can fool you today."

They laughed a sound full of love and joy, though barely above a whisper. They were so discreet that only one person in the house overheard them.

In the next room over, Marguerite Robichaux ground her teeth.

CHAPTER 19

LADY BANKS ROSES

"We will make it clear that you have powerful friends."

In the Robichaux garden, half-hidden below drifts of tiny white Lady Banks roses, Yvette and Amalie rocked themselves in a wooden swing hanging from a massive live oak tree. The roses had been trained twenty or thirty feet up into overhanging branches. Amalie felt unusually free, the little ones being looked after by a slave, a skinny girl Madame Robichaux had borrowed from a neighbor. Amalie thought she should, by rights, object, but she could not bring herself to do so. Not until she had had a little more of this lovely afternoon to herself.

The two girls were talking in whispers, breathing in the scent of roses and jasmine, their heads close together and their faces behind fluttering paper fans. Yvette took delight in shocking Amalie with the New Orleans practice of plaçage.

"Oh, you never did hear the like, I suppose," said Yvette. "There are Quadroon Balls at la Salle de Condé, where free women of color, quadroons at least and some of them octaroons…"

Seeing Amalie mystified, Yvette clarified: "A quadroon is one-quarter colored, octaroons one-eighth. And such are courted by the richest Orleanais men, who negotiate with the girls' mothers on the terms of a civil union.…" Amalie looked confused again. "It's sort of like a marriage but not really."

Jakob poked his head into the girls' bower. "Amy," he asked, holding up a green banana, "Can I eat this?"

"'May I,'" said Amalie, looking sideways at Yvette, who was shaking her head. "No, dear, it might upset your tummy."

"Not 'til it ripens up and turns yellow," said Yvette.

"Put it in the kitchen and keep checking every day!" Amalie said.

"Until it has brown speckles, lots of brown speckles," added Yvette.

"Oh!" said the little boy, who held the banana straight up and marched toward the kitchen.

"Give it to your slave girl," called Yvette, and as Jakob disappeared beyond the roses, she told Amalie, "They'll eat anything."

Amalie was confused. "Do you mean little boys or slaves?"

"Well," laughed Yvette, "both! But I meant little boys." With a smile she returned to her subject. "Mama says plaçage is concubines. The men acknowledge the unions, buy a house, and support the half-caste family. Some of them even send their natural boys to Paris for an education."

Amalie stared, and a satisfied Yvette added the coup de grâce: "They call themselves 'Creoles of Color.' They take French names, speak French, and carry on like real French people, and so do their children after them."

"These men, do they also marry white women?"

"Oh, yes! Of course."

"But that's polygamy!"

Yvette tossed her head. "Ain't the Bible got polygamy in it?"

"Do their White wives know about this?

"Of course," said Yvette. "But generally, they pretend not to. Some men give up their quadroons when they marry, but if they don't, their real wife might call out her husband, and make sure his nasty placée gets flogged."

"They are whipped?" Amalie was horrified. She had heard talk about flogging aboard *Enigma* last summer, and she knew some sailors died of it.

"Oh, yes. And in public, too. Sometimes," Yvette confided, "a man favors his quadroon. They can be beautiful. What's a real wife to do?"

A welcome breeze filled the yard, setting the palm fronds high above to clattering. Amalie thought it unkind of Yvette to spoil the afternoon with such nasty talk.

"It sounds awful," she said.

"You ol' softie," Yvette giggled. "It's just the way things are. Men can't help themselves."

Later that same day, Niklas spoke with exasperation to Katrina: "That Will! He falls for every pretty face, head over heels, hook, line and sinker, root and branch, as if there were no tomorrow and no chores that require his attention."

Katrina turned away, but not before Niklas could see a smile she could not prevent. Perhaps her shoulders even trembled with laughter. *I am not amused in the slightest*, he thought, *or believe that Will is an acorn fallen not far from the tree or a chip off the old block or whatever else she might be thinking.*

Several moments passed in silence, during which Katrina sighed and Niklas's pique turned to considering the stifling heat of the dim parlor. The room was closed up with heavy drapery, the color of claret, because Madame Robichaux believed in trapping the nighttime coolness, which worked until sometime in the late afternoon, which it was at this moment.

Niklas fanned himself with a sheaf of newspaper. "I sometimes think my prime has passed me by. But maybe it's just this damnable heat."

"The dampness is the worst of it," said Katrina, pulling her bodice away from the wet skin below and flapping the fabric. She looked around the shadowy parlor with irritation. It was a room that might have been considered well-appointed by someone born in an earlier era. She yearned to throw open the heavy drapery, toss the old furniture into the street, and buy the first new wallpaper she saw.

They lapsed again into heat-induced silence, and Niklas said, "Hans..." but did not finish his thought.

Both Katrina and Niklas had noticed how well Hans looked in his new brocade waistcoat and beaver hat, and how uncomfortable he seemed in them.

"As handsome as he is, he's not a dandy," said Katrina.

"Unfortunately, in decent clothing he's...he's... like a fly out of water," Niklas remarked.

Katrina hesitated before she spoke. Niklas was the one who knew several languages, and yet, this did not sound quite right. She thought for a moment and then asked, "Do you mean he's like 'a fish in the ointment'?"

Niklas looked rather annoyed.

"Or 'a flash in the pan'?" she asked, trying very hard to be helpful.

"Let's just say he's not himself and leave it at that." Niklas swatted at a horsefly whining by his ear. "Verdammt Fliege, damned fly!"

Katrina bent wordlessly to the patch she was sewing on Jakob's breeches. *'Tis best, sometimes*, she thought, *to let a stitch in time sew things up.*

Katrina had written to Cousin Elizabet several times while aboard *Enigma*, preserving the letters by wrapping them in oilcloth, and posting them after they arrived in New Orleans, safely within the boundaries of the United States. Now, she wrote again.

My Dearest Elizabet,

We have set foot at last in America, but I must tell you that we were almost drowned by a hurricane, saved only by the grace of God and the extreme bravery of our captain.

The storm blew us off course to a province of Mexico in the midst of war. But in fact, the province had won the war and just declared its independence, so we landed in a time of peace and celebration, Danke Gott. Have you heard of the new country, Republic of Texas? It is settled by a few Spaniards, Irishmen, Americans, and Indians. Great stretches of land are available for free or almost. A German agent wanted us to stay in the worst way and join a German colony.

A coastal tribe called Karankawa are handsome but wild and dangerous, actual cannibals! One wore a crucifix and styled itself a Christian, but as wonderful as that would be, I found it hard to credit.

At the seashore, Texas is marshland, but inland it turns to scrubby desert, as Niklas and I can testify, because we rode inland a ways. Niklas was tempted by the wild cattle with horns of a six-foot spread, which are there for the taking. But wisely, he decided to bring us on to New Orleans, so we set off once again.

This time the ocean was gentle, and we were soon coming up the Mississippi River, which is prodigious wide, twice the Rhine or three times, for a week before we saw an actual city, and what a city it is, my dear Elizabet, a miniature Paris in a jungle. Beautiful buildings and churches, almost all Catholic. Everyone speaks French, except the Americans. Most adore Napoleon, except those who hate him. The Napoleon loyalists have tried to entice us to stay, including inviting us to a wonderful ball, where, I must admit, we were paid quite the attention.

There's a German Coast here, of fabulously rich plantations with what they call "Big Houses," which are mansions done up as if for a duke. There, too, they want us to stay, because they think we are rich. These "Germans" came a hundred years ago, and they no longer seem much like anyone at home. They are enriched by the labor of enslaved Africans. They accept it, defend it, and say it cannot be changed. In short, they are thoroughly corrupted by it.

I wish I could send a magnolia tree home to you, my dear. It has huge white blossoms that light up the jungle like candles. There are roses in bloom and plane trees that make the city look like Paris, and many wonderfully exotic flowers, hydrangea, hibiscus, water lilies, and iris, and a beauty called crape myrtle.

Yesterday a fog rolled in, which the gardens seem to love. It bathes cheeks and drips off the nose and eyelashes. It was eerie to hear muffled sounds but see no one. When the fog lifted, the garden was more beautiful than ever, tree trunks black and every leaf as deep green as could be. You and I could spend happy lifetimes in a garden here, Elizabet!

Nevertheless, I wouldn't advise New Orleans to anyone without warning about its being plaguey. People say you won't get it if you don't think about it, but I don't know. The cholera was here recently, and the yellow jack sweeps through now and again. When it last came, they used mass graves and sank bodies in the river, horrible, horrible. We hope to leave soon and escape the worst of the sick season. Don't worry! We are all well.

Such a comfort it was to lay eyes on this civilized city when we had been at sea for so long, with French food and wonderful musicians. But the longer we are here, the more we feel the horrors of slavery casting a shadow everywhere. The other night we heard the African drumming, in what's called "Congo Square." It was frightening.

The whole problem is "politically intractable," Niklas says, but it is hard to conceive how a people who call themselves civilized can accept such a thing, and more than that, to embrace it as right and proper. All the while giving homage to "Liberty"!

They are blind, to its horrors, I think. You should hear the excuses!

Pray for us, Mein Lieber Vetter, that we find a new home more settled than Texas and more humane than New Orleans.

I remain your most affectionate cousin,

Katrina Beckmann Kästner

P.S. I have neglected to tell you about the children! Hans is uncomfortable here. He'll be better when we have farmwork to do. Will is in love again, but I expect that will fade when we leave New Orleans. Amalie is blossoming, I wish you could have seen her at the ball we attended, and the little ones are healthy and happy. Lisette's lisp is gone unless she is tired, and Jakob is sprouting up so fast I think he will be more Hans's size than Will's. Love to all the family.

With a snort, Niklas picked up the letter Katrina had written to Elizabet. He was dismayed to think of the postage needed to get it all the way to Berleburg. "Elizabet did not even know why we had to go."

"A lot of people," said Katrina, "want to believe the best of their king."

"Our nephew was murdered!"

"She thought he'd gotten in with a bad crowd."

Niklas snorted again. "The same bad crowd I had gotten in with. And Günter."

"Whose murder she still thinks was a highway robbery gone bad."

"Robbers who took nothing but the best horse? What does she need—a note pinned to the poor man's shirt explaining why he was murdered?"

"I know, I know," said Katrina. "He was murdered by mistake. Günter looked like you."

"Well, we were cousins."

"Yes, and he was driving our rig."

"I wish I had never asked him to help us."

"Yes. I agree."

They fell into silence, thinking of Günter's wife and children suddenly impoverished by their father's death. "I wonder," said Katrina, "if Addie has been able to keep the bakery."

"I suppose so. There's plenty of children to help. And Edzard is of an age to be a baker."

"He was meant to go to university."

"Well, now he will be a baker."

CHAPTER 20

THAT WE MIGHT SINK TO SAVAGERY

What would Mama think if ever I married a Catholic?

It was true that Niklas had armed himself and instructed the boys to be fully armed. He had trained his sons in the martial arts, and they had both been proven in the battle with pirates outside of Havana. On the street now, the three of them looked more militant than one generally saw in New Orleans. An older man took one look at them and ducked into the nearest shop.

The three Kästner men turned smartly into an inn, one very near the Owl and Crown, where Niklas was to meet Ivan Ivanovich and his brother, Luka.

"Herr Kästner!" said Mr. Groves, *Enigma*'s first mate, seizing Niklas's hand and shaking it. He smiled at the boys. "Hans. Will."

A few burly Enigmas stood in the background, and the Kästners shook hands all around.

Niklas began to explain, but the first mate waved him off. "You have told me enough—you need to be rid of dangerous men, Russians who threaten you and your family."

Niklas began again, but Mr. Groves interrupted again. "Do not think twice of it, my friend. Many is the time I have loaded a man, drunk or sober, willing or unwilling, onto a ship for his own good or that of others. You say these two want passage to France or points further east?"

"Their hope is to return to Russia," Niklas said.

"Ah. They will be pleased, then, with a passage to Constantinople, though they may or may not be enslaved there."

"What?"

"It's Constantinople, good sir. Nothing about traveling to that benighted city can be assured."

Niklas dug in his breast pocket for the opium money. "Will this be enough?"

"More than enough," said Mr. Groves, who quietly pocketed the gold.

"Give them some of the leftover," said Niklas.

Mr. Groves looked at him oddly, then brightened. "I see that you and your boys are well armed, but there's no need. It's wiser to take these blackguards by surprise. We will deliver them to the ship and make it clear that you have friends, powerful friends, here in New Orleans."

"You are too good, sir," said Niklas.

"The ship they sail leaves tomorrow, and we will post a guard. It will weigh anchor before we let it out of our sight."

Niklas thanked Mr. Groves again, and he and the boys shook hands all around. They had turned to go when Mr. Groves caught his sleeve.

"Tell your dear wife that after Giovanni set sail last week, I married Madame Lenzini. She will be safe now and well-cared for, I assure you, and Franci will be safe."

Niklas and the boys gave Mr. Groves their congratulations and started for home. Niklas was surprised by the news, glad not to have had to confront Ivan and Luka, and happier than he had felt in some time.

Will spoke in the dark to his brother. "Would you want to stay in New Orleans?"

"Ach nein! This is not the America I imagined. I will be bitterly disappointed if the old man decides to stay here. And look what he got us into with those Russians! Let's hope they are shipped out and on their way to Constantinople."

"Oh, Mr. Groves will make sure of it. Did I hear him correctly, that the Russians might be enslaved there?"

"Yes, but I don't know if it's true. Maybe it was Groves's way of assuring Father that they will get what's coming to them."

"Hmm."

"And what about the so-called Germans we met last week? They think Father is wonderful! And rich. Did you know Huber was trying to get him to buy Destrehan? Could Father afford it?"

"I really don't know," said Will. "Besides, this was before Henderson's will was read."

"It will go to the courts, they say, which will never uphold it."

"Whatever happens with Destrehan, if Father stays, I shall take the next ship I can engage back to Texas."

"Or up the Mississippi?" asked Will, who was not eager either to lose his brother or go with him to Texas. "I hear a new town there is booming. On the edge of Indian territory and a great lake."

"What is it called?"

"I'm not sure. 'Tsch'-something."

"Oh. You mean Tsch-ca-go."

"Yes, that's it."

Hans was still missing Lainie, but he had not known what to do with her either. Even the first step, introducing her to his family, was impossible. Now he could move on, as he had moved on from the girls in Havana. The American frontiersmen, despised by the landlady, were those whose strength and freedom he admired. *Still,* he thought, *everything considered, I was right to come along to America. Now to live here on my own terms.*

Earlier that day, Will, Hans, and Niklas had stepped into a dry goods store, a big, clean space where they bought blue linsey shirts: oversized, loosely woven, and belted. Linsey was cooler than the shirts they had bought from home. The store owner assured them that, up the river, such goods would be much dearer, if they could be found at all. When Will saw Hans in his new shirt, he realized how well it suited his brother.

Tonight, Will was surprised at Hans' vehemence, but not at his opinion, which reflected his own. He was deeply attracted to Yvette, but love was not everything, he told himself. He would be happy to leave her corrupt city far behind. Perhaps Texas was not such a bad idea, with its Christianized Indian princesses, like the Karankawa he had seen wearing the shortest skirt he had ever seen on a woman. Such a girl would not think he should wear fine white silk stockings and tight breeches and speak in proper Cajun French. Then he remembered the crucifix the Karankawa princess wore, and Yvette, and his poor, lost Ezmeralda and worried: *What would Mama think if ever I married a Catholic?*

"And you, little brother?" Hans asked. "Do you want to stay?"

"I agree with you," said Will, with a rush of conviction even if it might mean Texas. "Tomorrow, I expect we will learn Papa's intentions."

"Um-hmm," said Hans. He gave another fleeting thought to Lainie, then rolled over and was soon snoring.

Of all the things Niklas spoke about when the family met again, it was the strain in his father's voice that Will would remember: "We are tired of traveling, and these families have opened their homes to us most graciously and assured us of many fine opportunities. Their love for Napoleon after all this time is heart-warming. They are almost all Francophiles, the Creoles and the 'foreign French,' even the Germans!"

"And I suppose," Niklas continued, while mopping his forehead, "I could learn to live with this endless summer. But since we have escaped the Old World, I don't want to stop here. I want to get to an area with folk who are more like-minded than those here."

Heads nodded all around the family, Katrina noted with satisfaction. *Well done us,* she thought. *We have raised a family of adventurists. And a family of abolitionists.*

She nodded. "Of course, I agree with your father, and besides, there is a moral danger. Our souls might become compromised if we stay here among those who turn a blind eye to what they call their 'peculiar institution.' They think it is necessary and even *right*. If we stayed, I fear for us—that we might sink by some slow, unaware steps to their savagery."

"Never!" said Hans, and Amalie was shaking her head, too.

"But Papa," said Will slowly, "they think you are a war hero."

"That they do, and I will admit, it is a comfort to be esteemed. But I have lived both ways, as a hero and a villain, and I would not mind being neither."

"An invisible man?" Katrina smiled at him.

"Yes, I suppose so."

Niklas looked around at his wife and children. "Please consider that in New Orleans, life is recognizable. And soft. If we go north, we don't know what we will face, but it could be hard living."

At the moment, they sat comfortably at a magnificent breakfast, a feast good enough to weaken their resolve: quantities of fresh eggs, a lovely sausage pie made with hot boudin, fried cornmeal mush served with milk and cane syrup, and chicory-laced coffee with brown sugar and sweet cream.

Will pulled a straw basket closer and helped himself to a beignet. The last time he had had one, he was at the Creole Ball. He bit through the sugar glaze, thinking of the ball with its music and dancing and girls as pretty as flowers. *I will come back*, he thought. *I will get rich and come back and go to fancy balls and marry the prettiest girl I see.*

Hans spoke with conviction. "I would rather have stayed in Texas than be here! Except for French instead of Kölsch, it's like we never left Cologne! Except a hundred times worse with the enslavement of innocents. I can't wait to go up the river and find a better place."

His parents were relieved to find Hans in agreement. They were not sure what alliances he might have made during his late-night excursions or what vices might have ensnared him.

"It's actually smelly here, too," said Will. "I long for the sweet air of the forest."

In an aside, Hans said to their father, "He always has to stick his two cents in."

Thus did the Kästners agree to take passage at the first opportunity on the *Paddle Vessel (P.V.) Yellow Stone*, a Kentucky-built side-wheeler already famous for exploring the Missouri up to the Yellowstone River. Niklas told them the *Yellow Stone* had just returned from heroic service in Texas, and its owners were determined to make the most of the Mississippi's high-water season. Only the *Yellow Stone*, which had been built for long, difficult journeys, went all the way north to St. Louis.

"Maybe," he told them, "we will go even further, all the way to Tsch-ca-go. Though I am not sure what that will require."

Oh, but New Orleans had markets! The new Port Market in Faubourg Marigny, along the river, had a roof but was otherwise open air, tables on both sides loaded with fruits, garden vegetables, fresh and salted seafood, fresh-baked French bread, sweet and savory beignets, and achingly sweet pralines. Off to one side, hobbled dray horses stamped their hooves and quivered their haunches against the insects. Empty carts stood with their shafts tilted up, piercing the humid air, their mules unhitched and tied to one side.

A Cajun voice shouted, "I got crawfish and shrimp for you!"

Katrina filled hampers and bags, in preparation for their trip north. Unlike *Enigma*, *Yellow Stone* was said to have both a galley and a dining room, quite a grand dining room. This was not enough to assure Katrina about what the vessel would provide for the family. She had had to bring and prepare the family's food for the long ocean voyage, and she was not letting her guard down now. She herself, and Amalie, being small women, could get by on very little, but there were three men to feed, and the two young ones, who could not yet be trusted to eat whatever was put in front of them.

For Niklas, his astonishment had begun with his first sight of the *misi-ziibi*, the Anishinaabe's "Great River." The Mississippi dwarfed any European river, and it was said to go as far north as Canada, its source still undiscovered, and to connect with many tributaries, notably the Red, Arkansas, Ohio, and Missouri.

He salivated at the prospects for trade as soon as he saw the crowd of vessels on the river. At the main docks, dozens of steamers and steam barges called "smokers" added to the general cacophony with "whistle talk" signals. Downriver, flatboats of every design floated, including immense, ungraceful hay boats from Indiana, and further downriver were schooners, sloops, and all manner of ships built for ocean-going or coastwise voyages. Mixed in were paddlewheel tugs, lighters that could be rowed or sailed, and many smaller types of sailboats, ferries, bark canoes, rafts, and rough bateaux— hollowed-out tree trunks, their origins still visible.

Niklas was eager to judge the upriver cities for himself. Few Orleanais had been farther than Baton Rouge or Vicksburg, or at most, St. Louis, and no one knew much about Chicago. The few who had been there spoke of a stubby, whitewashed Fort Dearborn and a few log cabins set on swampy land. The Black Hawk War was recently concluded in spite of the cholera decimating the American troops sent west to fight it. It had been three years since the war or maybe four, but Niklas knew war had many repercussions, and it did not sound encouraging to him.

Even if one could find an Illinois River steamboat to Chicago, the river was not fully navigable. This was why everyone talked about the projected Illinois-Michigan Canal, which was to get underway soon. The Erie Canal on the eastern end of the Great Lakes had been a great success, and this new canal looked equally promising. It would replace a long, slow portage and create a grand inland waterway all the way from the people and cities and factories of the East to the sugar and cotton and rice of New Orleans. In anticipation of the canal, land prices were soaring in Chicago.

"You are so lucky," Karl told Niklas, "to be traveling there in time to make a killing."

This was a new expression to Niklas: "to make a killing." He looked quizzically at Karl, but the young banker went on without noticing.

"Indiana and Illinois are much troubled by expanses of empty wilderness, but it means cheap land, and if you stay near the river, a ready outlet to New Orleans."

Niklas had made arrangements with Karl's New Orleans Gas Light and Banking Company. He had also chosen the Louisiana State Bank at Royal and Conti Streets for a substantial deposit in anticipation of re-ordering fabric, coffee, spices, rum, tobacco, cotton, sugar, rice, red beans, and molasses once they settled up north. With credit established here in New Orleans, he could place an order with any respectable riverboat going south and have goods brought back without having to make the trip himself. Niklas had once had similar banking arrangements between Paris and Berleburg.

"We have a buying and selling system," Niklas gloated.

"Better than being in le Grande Armée?" asked Will.

Niklas laughed. "Much better!"

The army story Niklas had never quite managed to tell Will was of the vast stretches of boredom in the army, long blank days of inaction, exactly the thing that would drive Will wild, as it had him. There were sleepless nights trying to stay warm and dry because some simpering idiot in charge for the day had insisted that they camp by a riverside, assuring them that the water would not rise and the mosquitoes would not bite.

Long days had been spent ravished by hunger, scavenging for food, avoiding what every man knew, that behind the haystack or hidden in the attics or cellars or spying at them from the woods were people who had grown that food and harvested it and who would starve without it, if not today, most assuredly when winter came.

If Will is ever anywhere near an army, Niklas thought, sincerely hoping this son of his never would be, *he should know enough to get into supply at the very first opportunity, where he can read requisitions, and talk blacksmiths into good prices for swords and shoeing, and bring back enough bread and cheap whiskey to the troops that they will lay down their lives for him, the supply sergeant, and never let him come anywhere near a battlefield.*

Niklas never told Will any of this, but it hardly mattered. By his very nature, Will understood.

BOOK TWO

UP THE RIVER

"A [riverboat] pilot, in those days, was the only unfettered and entirely
independent human being that lived in the earth."
— Mark Twain, *Life on the Mississippi*, 1883

CHAPTER 21

SMALL, STURDY, AND FIERCE

New Orleans, June 1836

Being on a Mississippi steamboat was rather like entering another world, a
world suspended between the ordinary and what heaven—or hell—might
be. It began deep in the tropics and unrolled every day into something entirely new and unexpected. The Kästners would never forget the people they
met aboard—such people!

Katrina did not know any of this when their journey began, as she and
the other Kästners walked to the foot of Canal Street, trailed by a handcart
filled with their trunks and as much small baggage as they could pile on top.
There the steamboats lay. Canal Street was two miles upriver from sailing
ships going coastwise or crossing the ocean and one mile upriver from a
congestion of flatboats selling live animals, this year's spring vegetables, hay,
and the remnants of last year's harvest.

There, the Kästners were swept into eager throngs drawn to the sounds
of distant whistles and thrashing paddlewheels and to the thrilling sights of
steamboats coming 'round the bend with smoke billowing from the stacks
and showers of sparks swirling upward.

The *P.V. Yellow Stone* was not one of these new arrivals. It had reached
New Orleans four or five days ago and spent its time at the dock unloading
and doing repairs, cleaning, and painting. Today, she sat wide and low in the

water, freshly polished, sparkling in the sunshine, flags flying, and shiny black funnels burning pitch pine to create dark smoke. All boats scheduled to depart burned pitch to signal their imminent departure. Smaller vessels scattered, tacked sails, or bent to the oars; steamboats had the right of way. Strong men caught dock lines as thick as their arms, and roustabouts, stripped to the waist, hauled bales of cotton, sacks of rice, hogsheads of sugar, and barrels of whiskey or rum.

"Thieves, pickpockets, gamblers, ladies of questionable repute," warned Madame Robichaux, "and should you ever reach the frontier, awful privations on every hand!"

To tell the truth, Marguerite Robichaux preferred not to travel at all, despite the sweltering New Orleans summers when anyone who could escaped to the ocean breezes of Isle Dernieres or to the summer camps at Milneberg or Spanish Fort or Mandeville.

"Harmful and damnable characters, forgive my language, s'il vous plaît," she went on. "Keep your children away from them." She was pleased to have an excuse for strong language. She was thinking about Kaintuck boatmen when she spoke, but she despised all Americans, a feeling shared by many Orleanais, including free Blacks and those Marguerite thought of as the better class of the enslaved.

Her warnings seemed just a tiny bit out of place once Niklas and Katrina stepped aboard *P.V. Yellow Stone* and were taken to the dining salon with its mahogany paneling and long rows of curved windows. It was magnificent, as fine as a private dining room ashore with the added advantages of a view and a breeze.

"Only the finest food, wine, and music," Robin LeMoyne, the ship's purser, assured them. "The safest, most relaxing mode of travel ever invented. Did you note how easy she was to come aboard?"

Steamboats rode low on the water, and *Yellow Stone*'s long bow gangplank required only a modestly slanted walk, nothing at all like ascending the steep gangplanks of a sailing ship or the embarrassment, discomfort, and fright of being hauled aboard in a bosun's chair.

Niklas and Katrina murmured their assent, but they were drowned out by the final warning gong, and a howl from the hurricane deck: "All's that going ashore, git ashore! Now, please!" The boatswain repeated this warning in frantic French. A stampede of feet deafened them as the last visitors fled for shore and the most procrastinating of passengers leapt aboard.

A moment later the gangplank was raised, and the Kästner family stood with Izak Peterssen at the rail, waving goodbye. Francesca, Franci, and Mr. Groves were in the little knot of friends, along with Thomas Segrave, who had decided yesterday that the demands of boat ownership required him to stay. Katrina looked sideways at Amalie, who seemed brave at their separation and innocent of suspicion. She wondered what, if anything, had been said between them. Karl Schneider was there to see them off with Marguerite and Yvette Robichaux. Will was surprised to see an unusual radiance in Yvette's smile, and when he waved to her, he was also surprised to feel relief.

Robin LeMoyne said, "*Yellow Stone* is one of the first to have a separate dining room. On most riverboats, the men's room is cleared for dining." He did not mention that *P.V. Yellow Stone* was old by steamer standards, and many were now far more glamourous and featured separate family cabins. *Yellow Stone* had only two sleeping cabins, a sparse room with hammocks for the men and a smaller, more elegant one for the ladies, furnished with ruffled curtains and a red and black "Turkey" carpet.

LeMoyne also told them they could save a pretty penny if the boys paid only for deck passage, a mere $18, which meant sleeping wherever they could lay a blanket on deck, and they would pay even less if they agreed to help wood the boat at the woodyards along the way.

"Surely such fine boys with American grit need nothing more," LeMoyne said, "than a few inches of deck to sleep."

Niklas asked him to explain "American grit." In the end Niklas agreed, and the boys took deck passage. Niklas, Izak, and a half-dozen others filled the men's sleeping room.

Among these were Pastor John Ewing and his assistant, Josiah Bedford, a man who was thin and pockmarked. He was young but had already achieved a permanent look of sad piety, with eyes that sometimes fell shut even during conversation, in prayer perhaps or in sleep.

The Kästner men also met Mathias Cunningham, a handsome, if shabby, older gentleman who introduced them to Bert and Chester Harms, both strong, beefy young men with weathered faces showing brick red below their hatbands.

They had chatted for a moment when Niklas asked, "I assume you have an older brother?"

"Why, yes," said Bert with a tilt of his head.

"Whose name begins with an 'A'?" asked Niklas.

The Harms men laughed full belly laughs. Chester wiped his face and said to Niklas, "Now you're the clever one. Not one in a hundred guesses the scheme of our names. Not even when Alfred's with us."

"Or Dora," said Bert. "Now may we guess about you? Have you come just now from the Germanies?"

When Niklas assured them that their guess was correct and told them about Berleburg's being a village east of Cologne almost in Hesse.

"Our grandpa was a Hessian mercenary for George the Third," said Bert, "captured in the Revolution, sent to a Pennsylvania farm as captive labor and abandoned without pay after the war."

"Not a propitious start," said Chester, "but by the time the prisoners of war were paroled, he had decided to stay."

"The family's forgotten pretty much everything about the Germanies," his brother added, "except beer and sausages."

"And sauerkraut and 'gesundheit'" said Chester. "None of us but Fanny ever says, 'God bless you.'"

"And that's only because she married a Scots-Irishman," Bert explained. "We tell her she's putting on airs."

They both chuckled.

Hans asked: "How far did your parents get down the alphabet?"

"There are fourteen of us children."

"Including a 'Hans,'" smiled Bert, who had just met Hans Kästner. "And by now Alfred has five, I have two, and so does Chester."

"And our sister, Ella, is just starting out with one."

There was a short silence, and then Niklas asked in a respectful tone, "That's twenty-four. Surely not all have survived?"

"We lost only one, our little brother Misha, taken two years ago by the cholera."

There was another respectful silence, and then Niklas said, "Still, it's a sign of health and wealth and a tribute to your parents' care."

"Ja," said the Harms men in unison.

Off to one side, a tall, rail-thin man in a long, loose coat turned to stare out at the river. He was Jeremiah Brown, one of Kentucky's true believers, a man whose fierce eyes seemed yellow, they burned so with hatred of sin and sinners. He had preached his way across Kentucky, chopping out trails and heathens with blow after blow of his axe and his zeal, and was now going to save Missouri before everyone in it went straight to Hell. When Jeremiah Brown surveyed his fellow travelers, he judged none of them worth saving, especially these too-jolly Pennsylvania Dutchmen.

Pastor Ewing assumed authority as the men gathered, asked them to bow their heads, and proceeded to bless their journey. As he began, his voice rose in declamation against the onboard racket of shouted orders, crates being shoved into position, passengers coming and going, and the steady whap-whap of water against the paddle wheels. As Pastor Ewing waved one arm in the direction of Heaven, Jeremiah Brown turned, put on his hat, and left the cabin. Will's sunburn itched, and he longed to swat a mosquito, but he bore up with the thought that at least they had a proper, if long-winded, advocate of God with them.

P.V. Yellow Stone was a plain, strong, sidewheel steam packet built for the famous 1831-'32 exploration up the Missouri River. Compared to most, it was small, sturdy, and fierce, better able than most to face the current all the way to St. Louis, a task that might take twelve days or a few more. There were dozens of steamers leaving New Orleans, but few went beyond Natchez, Vicksburg, or New Madrid.

After her first Missouri River expedition, *Yellow Stone* went up the Missouri again with Prince Maximillian of Wied-Neuwied and his painter, Karl Bodmer. She followed that with a stint on the Brazos River in Texas, just a few miles from Linnville, where *Enigma* landed. Sam Houston pressed her into service as a ferry, and *Yellow Stone* made trip after trip carrying the Texan army across the river and out of Santa Anna's reach. In gratitude, a full league of Texas land—4,428 acres—had been promised to Captain Ross and to the engineer of *Yellow Stone*, each of the other crew members receiving a third of a league. A good number of the crew had suddenly become Texans, but others were still aboard, so *P.V. Yellow Stone* now had the richest, most independent, and orneriest steamboat crew on the Mississippi.

Despite the *Yellow Stone's* esteemed history, Mme. Robichaux was right about riverboat men. Their fearlessness, recklessness, and loose living were legendary. So was their strength and courage, which was required to take boats upriver and downriver past unfriendly tribes, vicious "banditti," as river pirates were called, and the challenges of the river itself. It threw everything at them, including unreliable currents, constantly shifting sandbars and islands, collapsing banks, and hull-piercing sawyers. Being a riverboat man demanded both fortitude and something of a lawless heart, since "running the river" had been illegal when Spain forbade American traffic.

"The life of the boatman," opined Pastor John Ewing, "is by turns indolent and strenuous."

As they stood at *Yellow Stone's* thin black rail, Will studied his elderly companion, admiring his girth, which suggested that he had never starved, and amazed at his wild eyebrows, which went up and down as he spoke. Wiry white hairs showed in his nose and ears, sprouting everywhere.

"For days," the pastor continued, "their work requires little or no labor and no special risk; then of a sudden turn, it requires all of man's capacity for toil and danger."

Here the pastor looked kindly at Will, who saw at a glance a lesson forthcoming and no easy means of escape.

"You may never face the difficulties of a riverboat man's life," said the pastor, "but a difficulty is an opportunity. Just look around, son; see the vast untilled fields of the New World. Many fine new arrivals are like yourself—educated, energetic, the best of the Old World. If you retain its riches and seize those of this one, you'll be doubly wealthy."

Pastor Ewing took a deep breath. "Every man thinks he is special, but most lack the persistence this frontier requires. Their weakness will be your advantage. They will fail. They will go back East and become wage slaves or stay here in poverty and degradation. Hang on when they give up and buy their failing farms."

The sixteen-year-old gave a brief bow to acknowledge the reverend's wisdom, but the older man was not finished.

"If you smile, chat nicely, and stay honest, you won't be short of friends. Courtesy, and kindness, that's what 'Love thy neighbor' means. Remember."

Will admired the articulate pastor, but he was a little amused. *Those eyebrows! And lessons only a child needs. I have plenty of determination, and I already see only opportunity and possibility and bright prospects.*

The old man and the young man stared at the greasy Mississippi water below the rail, watching a long black water snake glide by. When Pastor Ewing turned to speak again, he saw Will's crooked smile and decided he had said enough for one day.

At the same time, Pastor Ewing's assistant, young Josiah Bedford, handed Amalie a religious tract titled, "Everlasting Punishment," and cornered her in conversation. Bedford was as thin as the reverend was thick, with stringy black hair and a face announcing his having survived smallpox.

He told Amalie that he was a native of Virginia, a state known for its good tobacco and bad men. This was his only joke, all other talk revolving around the Bible. He gave her more tracts to read, and he ended every conversation with, "Thank God, our only shield against evil." In this way, he embarked on the kindly project of saving Amalie's soul.

Josiah Bedford had already decided that Amalie would be an ideal parsonage wife, despite her unfortunate beauty, and her foreign extraction, which would require significant correction. He expected she would be grateful for his instruction.

"Your piety does you credit, sir," Amalie told him.

CHAPTER 22

ANGEL ISLAND

all of these perils taken together

Once *Yellow Stone* backed out from New Orleans's steamboat landing, she wound through heavy traffic past noisy sawmills and stinking distilleries, sugar refineries, and soap factories on the city's edge. These faded into a region of villages with wooden cottages tightly packed at first and later with fields and gardens between, until the first of the great sugar plantations appeared. Amalie came to the rail as her parents were pointing out Destrehan's memorable West Indies hip roof and twin staircases.

A little further on, Amalie saw the Huber plantation, and remembered the neat, handsome Antoine and Yvette's rather obvious hope of ingratiating herself with the family. *Good riddance,* she thought. But Antoine made her think of Tom and his rather sudden decision not to travel with them. She did not understand, and she could not help but feel abandoned.

From Destrehan to Baton Rouge, a long parade of sugar plantations formed a nearly continuous settlement, mansions in front, double rows of slave quarters behind, and cane or cotton fields on both sides. Sheds, barns, and brick sugar houses lay amid orchards, gardens, and live oak trees hung with Spanish moss. North of Baton Rouge, Amalie was at the rail with Lisette when she saw something dangling from a far-off oak tree and recognized it as a man. She turned her little sister from the awful sight so gently that Lisette never knew what she had been saved from.

After Baton Rouge, civilization faded as if the jungle had won the day, the river drowning the land flat into immense stretches of cypress swamp and grassy marsh, a land of black bears, alligators, beavers, panthers, wolves, foxes, armadillos, bobcats, a thousand avian species, and immensities of insects. Eerily absent from the shores was the mark of anything human. The family heard the knock-knock-knock of the swamp's woodpeckers and the eerie call of loons, and everyone watched for ducks, pointing out new varieties. Soon Amalie begged a page of foolscap from her father and tried to keep a record by drawing ducks and penciling in descriptions: "iridescent backs," "spotted breasts," "bright red bills," or "ringed necks."

Several days of heat and humidity broke with a hard rain overnight and revealed a brilliant, cool morning. Katrina tossed the three youngest out of the cabin. "Get some air," she told them. "Give us some room to breathe."

The decks were still slick with water, but Amalie found a perch for them on a trunk and dried it with the hem of her skirt. They sat slumped down, three disconsolate monkeys in a stairstep row. Little Jakob yawned, and then his sisters did, too.

"Good morning, children." Mrs. Rogers stood in front of them, seeming to appear out of nowhere and looking intently at the two younger ones. "Are you at all related?"

"He's my little brother," said Lisette. Their matching heads of curly blonde hair made this rather obvious. Lisette took Jakob's hand, feeling a little protective, even though this woman with white hair escaping her bonnet was the picture of harmlessness: short, round, and smiling.

"Hmmm," said Mrs. Rogers. "You," she nodded at Lisette, "might be eight, and you," she said to Jakob, "could you be five?"

"How did you know?" Little Jakob was amazed.

"Just a lucky guess," she said, "and because I'm a grandma."

Amalie was sitting up straight now and smiling at the two younger ones. "Grandmas know these things," she said.

"Can you tell me," said Mrs. Rogers, pausing for drama, "three things you are lucky about today?"

Little Jakob shook his head, and Mrs. Rogers continued, ticking off each point. "You are lucky to have this sunshine; you are lucky to have your big sisters to look after you; and you are lucky to be aboard the *Yellow Stone*."

Lisette squeezed Jakob's hand. Then she cocked her head to one side and asked Mrs. Rogers, "What are you lucky about?" Amalie was surprised to hear Lisette be so bold.

"An excellent question!" Mrs. Rogers looked thoughtful for a moment. "I am lucky to share the sunshine; I am lucky to have had a kind and gentle husband, God rest his soul; and I am lucky to meet you!"

Still smiling, Amalie stood and offered Mrs. Rogers a seat. "Would you do us the favor of your company?"

Little Jakob scooted over so Mrs. Rogers could sit between them. Amalie dried off another spot for herself, looking down to hide a tear as she thought of her own grandma, whom Lisette did not remember, and Jakob had never known. *How very kind of Mrs. Rogers*, she thought, *to be our ersatz grandma, even for a few minutes.*

Later, Katrina joined the children, and Jakob went off with Niklas while the women of the family began to have what they would come to call their "angel morning." First, they spied the most enchanting flock of roseate spoonbills. Mrs. Rogers told them the odd name of these birds, a phrase that sped from mouth to ear across the deck as everyone watched these delicate pink creatures decorate a tree and then take flight. Soon after that, they passed a long, narrow, white sandspit entirely covered with white pelicans, an amazing sight made even more extraordinary when the flock took fright at *Yellow Stone*'s approach and rose as one.

"Like the robes of angels," murmured Lisette.

Katrina and Amalie glanced at each other with raised eyebrows to hear the little girl pronounce so lofty a notion. Amalie smiled and said, "Let's name it Angel Island, shall we?"

Beyond seemingly endless flat tracts, the Red River joined the Mississippi, and the current intensified. It had torn away points of land and undercut great sections of the banks, pitching trees headlong into the river.

Robin LeMoyne waved one hand to the west. "The Red River leads to the old Nakitosh tobacco region," he said. "'Tis rich land, but not a proper place to settle. All the good land is taken, and besides..."

Robin paused, and Niklas waited as he lowered his voice and glanced left and right, "It's hardly civilized, sir. The last outpost before the Spanish, Mexican, and Texan wildernesses, it attracts those who leave their homes and families for some reason, whether they ever admit it—the dregs of society, men fleeing arrest, bankruptcy, or a ruined reputation. No place for gentlefolk."

Niklas said nothing for a long moment. Then he pointed to a floating tree. "I believe you call those sawyers? Trees fallen in when the current undercuts the shore."

"Exactly right, sir," said Robin. "Big as a house and the whole thing ready to hole any boat so unwise as to come near."

Here, and in many places, the river was a shape-changer, piling heaps of driftwood onto mud bars or sandbars, making them unrecognizable overnight. Adding to the sudden changes were snags created by wrecks, tree roots, and "chutes," the narrow passages of fast-flowing water where sandbars and islands divided the river.

This said nothing of near misses between vessels. A hushed twilight or fog could be broken by the clanging of spoons pounding skillets and shouted imprecations from a flatboat or a raft suddenly visible through the mist. Many of these craft were large, but even when they were not, their log hulls were like battering rams to other vessels.

All these perils taken together created a passageway as tricky to a riverboat pilot as shoals and islands are to a captain at sea. Pilots going upriver stayed as close to the shore as they dared, to avoid burning wood uselessly against the fast-flowing middle channel. Where the current had scrubbed one shore cleaner than the other, a pilot might take a boat across the river and hug the other side. Every crossing cost time and wood, so each was judged carefully and timed precisely.

Hugging the shore meant risking shorelines messy with overhanging branches. Once, Robin LeMoyne told them, *Yellow Stone* hit a branch and knocked loose a water moccasin. "It fell onto the deck," he said, "as dangerous a viper as you're ever likely to see. You should have seen people scatter!"

"What happened to the snake?" Will's voice had a hint of panic.

"Oh, it's long gone," laughed Robin, who saw Will's eyes scanning the deck. "Big Mike picked it up by the tail and flung it into the river."

The shore also hid a surprising number of shipwrecks. Will stared at a bright red spot in one of these shipwrecks and tried to think what might be so colorful, until he recognized a riverboat man's red flannel shirt, saw a shock of dark hair, and looked away.

The spring floods were over or nearly so, but the river had not reached its late summer low. Boats going downriver tied up every night, because the strong current shoving the stern made a boat unpredictable. Going upriver was a different story, and *Yellow Stone*'s captain and pilots kept at it day and night, except for fog or intricate, dangerous passages.

CHAPTER 23

YELLOW STONE'S PREDICAMENT

to gild the lily

Every officer, hand, and passenger talked of nothing but Rattlesnake Island, which presented a complex passage, a narrow channel, and an unpredictable sandbar.

"If we make Rattlesnake before nightfall," they said, "we could keep going all night."

"But it would be crazy to run Rattlesnake Island in the dark."

Ordinarily, each pilot ran the stretches he was most familiar with, but this afternoon all three pilots remained in the pilothouse, pulling out their watches so often that at last they kept their watches out and open, braced on the wheelhouse windowsills. The sun fell lower in the sky as *P.V. Yellow Stone* bore steadily down on the treacherous passageway.

The pilot in charge of this passage was Doc Marshall, though no one seemed to know why he should have been given that honorific, his having been born on the Mississippi and surely never set foot in any medical college nor ever cured a single Christian soul.

Doc Marshall pulled the bell cord three times, and the watchman's voice called out from the hurricane deck to the leadsmen at the bow for depth readings.

"Starboard lead, there now, larboard lead!"

The cries of the leadsmen rang out: "Mark three!" from one side and from the other, "Quarter less three!" Then these were revised to shallower measurements: "Mark twain! Half twain! Quarter twain!"

Doc Marshall pulled the bell twice in quick succession. From deep in the engine room, a faint jangling was heard, and the boat slowed, steam whistling through its funnels. Passengers were caught up in the tension, Niklas and the boys among them, and had hurriedly been taught the finer notions of steamboat piloting, so that now the vessel was eerily quiet, with half-heard murmurings about *Yellow Stone*'s predicament and the disasters of other steamboats.

"When *Ben Franklin* blew at Mobile, it was on account of letting them there boilers go dry. Running into a sandbar ain't half thet dangerous."

"That one was in March of this year, weren't it?"

"Yes, sixteen daid and thirteen so badly burned as to wisht they were."

A pause: "God save us." This was the deep, sure voice of Jeremiah Brown.

"Now, now, if anyone cain do it, it's Doc Marshall!"

"We coulda made it, only now we're way too close in. He shoulda stayed further out."

One of the men said to Izak and the Kästner men, "If we hit the bar, it'll knock the boat's brains out. Better if your womenfolk were on deck should we need to swim."

"A steamboat is nearly as flat as yon broadbeam," another explained, waving toward a flatboat going downriver in the central current, "but top heavy. If she hits the sandbar hard, she'll tip, and we will be required to swim for our lives, those of us not fitted with wings right off."

"Least ways, we're on the *Yellow Stone*, a stronger boat never built." Someone laughed nervously, but most heads nodded in agreement.

Niklas went immediately to fetch the rest of the family. Amalie spoke quietly to Mrs. Rogers as they passed her, and now she joined the seven Kästners at the rail. Katrina was wrapped in a shawl, Lisette's arm around her waist and little Jakob asleep on her shoulder. She wondered if Mrs. Rogers's fat, of which the grandmotherly woman had quite a lot, would cause her to float, and she hoped it would.

Izak stood by Amalie and whispered in her ear: "I am a strong swimmer. Should we go over, don't panic. Just let me carry you." He studied the current to see what he would be up against and where might be the closest point of land. There was always the sandbar itself, but he knew that wrecked steamboats went up in flames, so nowhere nearby was safe.

Amalie looked at Izak in surprise.

Izak glanced at her, his eyes going down to her skirts. "Are you wearing a hoop? Is your mother or Lisette? Go take them off. Right now. The skirts are bad enough. Take off any extra layers. And metal hoops, for God's sake!"

It was shocking to be talked to this frank way, but Amalie was nothing if not sensible. She swallowed her feelings, spoke to her mother, and they disappeared into the ladies' cabin. In a very few minutes, they returned to the rail.

The water got thinner and thinner, until the leadsmen called out: "Eight feet! Now seven and a half feet!"

Suddenly, the boat shivered, and a deadly grating sound ran all along, passengers gasping and steadying one another. Hans reached over and took little Jakob from his stepmother. They knew without speaking that Hans had a better chance of survival. Her skirts would drag her down. Niklas took Lisette's hand. Amalie had a moment's panicked thought: *Where is Tom?* Then she remembered that he was not aboard at all.

Doc Marshall, calm and determined as ever, set the bells to ringing and called down through the speaking tube, "Now give it all she's got! Now! Now!"

The boat ground its hull along the sand and for one dreadful moment seemed to come to a halt. Then she lunged forward and was over the sand-bar and free of Rattlesnake Island! A cheer went up from the pilothouse, echoed by the crew and passengers. In the midst of the cheering, Izak let go of Amalie. She smiled up at him in gratitude and took a step to one side.

The story of Rattlesnake Island made Doc Marshall even more famous on the river and added another notch to the fame of *P.V. Yellow Stone*. Long before this, Izak had been watching their progress and the operations aboard with great interest, aware that steamers were the future, and although he knew ocean-going sailing ships would always be needed—no wooding-up stations mid-ocean—coastwise trade was another thing entirely. Now he could only shake his head.

"This is hard sailing, never to see blue water," he said aloud, as if to no one. Privately, he wondered if the hull was intact. When the cheering ended and the Kästners began to follow the others inside, he lay a hand on Niklas's arm and said quietly, "Not yet." With a look from Niklas, the Kästner family turned as one and retook their places along the rail.

Izak explained quietly about shock cracks and slow leaks, thankful no one in the Kästner family was the panicky type. They listened as they watched the sunset. As time passed quietly, there were no whispers among the crew, no shouted orders, no patter of sailors running. They began to breathe easier.

Presently, the men turned jocular and at a nod from Izak, began to make their way in. The women followed them. Katrina glanced at Izak, grateful for his knowledge of these things and for his caution. Amalie was the last, and just as she turned to go, Izak did what he had no right to do: he took her hand, held it for a moment and then pressed it to his lips. She touched his cheek in a motion so light and fleeting that later he would wonder if he had dreamt it.

When at last the terrain changed, the Kästners were carried through hilly and forested lands, where bottomland cotton plantations began to appear, as grand as those for sugar downstream. Soon, they were nearing Natchez, the most dramatic hill town, its new lighthouse two hundred feet above the river on a bluff crowned with church spires. Below was the infamous Natchez-under-the-Hill, a landing crowded with several hundred flatboats and steamboats. The largest of all the shoreline towns, Natchez-under-the-Hill was a shabby, run-down, rough-and-tumble place offering everything the riverboat man could want at prices determined to suck out his every penny.

As they approached Natchez, Katrina stood at the rail with Mathias Cunningham, a fine-looking older gentleman, if threadbare. He stood straighter than many his age, spoke with assurance, and was inclined to grand expressions, a wink, a nod, a gesture.

He pointed out a particularly gaudy boat on the shore. "'Tis a showboat, Missus," he said. "My company always tied up at Natchez-under-the-Hill. I was on *Noah's Ark* when we first brought her to New Orleans in '16, all the way from Pittsburgh, down the Ohio and into the Mississippi with never a stop longer than one or two nights, playing to whatever audience we found before the church element could set to with clubs and firebrands to teach us right from wrong."

He paused, and his large, brown eyes looked searchingly at Katrina to see whether she was offended, but her face was impassive, perhaps even interested. She was recalling the mysterious man in the shadows of the St. Charles theatre, whom she thought an actor until he introduced himself as James Caldwell.

"It weren't easy, ofttimes all hands called, even the women, to pole around a sandbar or frighten off banditti, such as were likely to frequent Plum Point, Rowdy Bend, and St. Francis River—we gathered at the rail with swords, though the swords were painted wood: stage props. A wicked band nearly wrecked us above Vicksburg."

The old thespian paused, lost in memory. "Aye, we played *The Honeymoon* or *The Lying Varlet* for laughs and *Maria and Petruchio* to confound the moralists. Once we said, 'Shakespeare,' it was so popular that it confused them about play people," he finished with a laugh that shook his jowls.

"I take it *Noah's Ark* was a showboat?" she asked.

Mr. Cunningham leant his better ear toward her, and then grasped her meaning: "So to speak. But 'showboat' is only what they come to calling them now that they are done up with a proper stage and all."

Here the old thespian dropped into a pretty verse:

"To gild refined gold, to paint the lily,

To throw a perfume on the violet,

To … add another hue unto the rainbow."

The lines sounded vaguely familiar to Katrina, but she was not on solid ground with poetry, so she just nodded and smiled as the old man continued to reminisce.

"But on *Noah's Ark,* pitiful as it was, we had some of the finest actors I ever saw, the Chapman family, one more talented than the next, from the London stage. England, you know, is ruinously expensive, so the lot of them came here. Not unlike yourselves?" He gave her a bow, and she smiled.

Mathias Cunningham did not mention the scandals that drove the talented Chapmans out of the east coast cities. "Nothing at all like the charlatans on stage now, born in Tennessee or the like."

Katrina stared at the water, confused about where Tennessee might be. She remembered how James Caldwell was transforming New Orleans. Then she shuddered. It was New Orleans that had left Hans drunk and beaten, a streak of gunpowder along his temple. She took a deep breath, happy to be free of New Orleans.

Mathias Cunningham straightened up, remembering himself: "Not that I disparage any fellow thespian, not when I consider how despised we all were."

The two of them were still in conversation as passengers began to debark at Natchez to put their feet on solid ground while the crew loaded the next batch of wood for the boilers. As they watched the passengers, Katrina saw Amalie and Izak on the gangplank, laughing as they went. She noticed a Mrs. Aloysius Green of St. Louis. Katrina had met her in the ladies' cabin. Even at a distance, Mrs. Green's immensity made her hard to overlook.

Katrina watched willow branches trail along the water's edge and the silver flash of fish at the surface. Very shortly, she went down the gangplank holding tightly to Jakob's hand, with Lisette following. It took some time before she stopped lurching around on sea legs, and they were almost ready to board again before she stopped feeling the big boat's vibrations or thought of anything but the old thespian and his stories.

CHAPTER 24

A FEARSOME PLACE

a fine force of volunteers

Amalie was still surprised and disappointed that Thomas Segrave had declined to travel with them. His decision had been sudden, and she hoped for an explanation.

"No doubt," Izak told her, "repairs to *Enigma* took longer than expected." He looked closely at Amalie and could see that tears were close.

There was a long pause.

Finally, she swallowed hard and spoke. "I suppose he had no choice."

Izak answered slowly. "I think he found himself in a difficult position."

"Do you think there will be a message in St. Louis?"

Izak looked away. "Perhaps."

Amalie considered when another boat would get to St. Louis. Nothing was faster or more capable on these waters than *Yellow Stone*. "But not for weeks or maybe months."

"Regretfully, that is so."

"I don't think Papa expects to stay in St. Louis. But it's another French city," she said hopefully. Then she frowned. "Which side of the river is it on?"

"The west side."

"Ah, that means Missouri, a slave state, doesn't it?"

Izak shrugged. "Yes. Summer is upon us. Maybe your father will decide to overwinter in St. Louis." He gave her a weak smile, bowed, and departed.

Amalie watched him go. *He knows more than he is saying.*

One evening, the Harms brothers chatted with Izak and Amalie as they watched a string of flatboats floating downstream, their stern lanterns twinkling magically in the dimming light and the faint strains of fiddling coming across the water. The brothers were in shirt sleeves against the heat of the day.

"Flatboats seem to have an easier time of it, being well out in the middle," suggested Izak.

"Oh, indeed," said Chester Harms. "They get the strong current behind them, whereas going upriver, we need the easy water along the banks, as ragged and changeable as the shore might be."

"That one's huge," said Izak, pointing.

"'Tis an ark," explained Bert. "An ark can be a hundred feet long."

"For hauling horses, cattle, hogs, hay, corn, or wheat," said Chester. "And see, they have little or no deck."

"It don't take much skill to go downriver," said Bert, "and besides flatboats and arks, there's barges. They is all cheap. You cobble one together, float it down to New Orleans, knock it to pieces, and sell the lumber. They will always be used for downriver, but with no keel, they cain't go upriver."

"It's how Abraham Lincoln himself did it," said Chester, "but in those days, they had to traipse back up north to Kaintuck, Indiana, or Illinois."

"Or ride if you could afford a horse," laughed Bert. "Or pole a keelboat upstream. Now there's work for you."

"Today," said Chester, "The price of a steamboat ticket is nothing compared to trying to sail, or pole, or warp a keelboat against the current. Twicet," he added. "Lincoln made the trip twicet."

Izak's curiosity showed on his face. "And who is this Lincoln?"

Bert told him to keep a sharp eye out for the man, "If you settle in Illinois. 'Honest Abe,' they call him, is a lawyer, a state senator, and a very tall man."

"I believe they say he's 6'4", said Chester.

"He saved the lives of three men," said Bert, "when they were building a flatboat together. Pulled them out of the river when they were sucked in and about to drown."

Chester Harms picked up the story. "Lincoln ran two flatboats down, broke 'em up and came back, even though on the first trip he was attacked when his flatboat was tied up at night. He and Allen Gentry beat the robbers off with oars, not true banditti but escaped slaves, most likely, seven of them trying to git the boat."

"Whoever they were," said Bert, "they were about to kill Lincoln and Gentry, but then, Gentry shouted, 'Lincoln, get them guns.' There were no guns on board, but it scared 'em off."

"We got this from the horse's mouth," Chester assured his listeners, "Dennis Hanks, Lincoln's own cousin."

"Anyways," Bert finished for his brother, "Honest Abe got himself a nasty cut to the ear and a scar he'll wear for life."

Chester Harms suddenly looked at Amalie, and seeing how young she was, he blushed. "Forgive me, Missy," he said, and turning to Izak, "Forgive me, sir, if I have spoken too freely of rough matters."

"Miss Kästner is, despite her youth, a world traveler."

"Your most humble, Missy," Bert Harms said, and with that odd American bow, he and his bother doffed their hats.

"Oh, sirs, I take no offense, I'm sure," said Amalie. "I only wish I had been there to fight off the robbers and save Messrs. Lincoln and …"

"Gentry," Izak murmured in her ear.

"Gentry."

"You would have been fearsome, missy, I am sure," said Bert Harms, smiling at this pretty young woman's pink cheeks and fine fighting spirit.

Amalie smiled to be called "missy," and the Harms brothers smiled at the thought of her slim figure swinging away at the robbers.

"Say," Chester Harms said, pointing upriver, "see that sandbar coming up? It don't look like nothing, but it reminds me of Crow's Nest, as was sunk in the earthquakes of '11 and '12."

"By divine retribution," said Bert.

"Crow's Nest sank and left nothing behind but an ordinary sandbar. Before that, it was a true nest of evil, home to the worst of the banditti. It took a posse of eighty or ninety to clean 'em out in '09." He turned to Amalie. "Most of them river bandits are gone, but not all, Missy, so mind your reticule when you disembark."

Izak and Amalie stared dutifully at the sandbar, which looked for all the world like any other, and tried to imagine its muddy shores and grass flats hiding a nest of evil.

"And," Bert Harms added with a smile and a wink, "stay close to that beau of yours."

Which made Amalie's cheeks pinker still. When the Harmses left, Amalie rebuked Izak: "Neither of us corrected him."

"There's no reason to tell strangers anything private," said Izak, who did not seem at all perturbed about it.

The boatmen's muscle and courage were admirable, and their love of a fiddle and a joke was endearing, but Niklas was not enamored with what he heard of their belligerence. Each boat had a champion pugilist known by the red feather in his peaked wool cap. He told Will and Hans about it and warned them: "Stay well clear of that man."

In truth, riverboat men seemed to have few vices except hot tempers, drunkenness, gambling, and a love of tall tales and what they called "frolics," which covered any other mischief. They were known to spend a year aboard and go ashore penniless, having lost it all in the flophouses along the river or to the luckiest man aboard. It was a bonus for Hans, who was suddenly possessed of lively friends to drink with at every under-the-hill town.

Such towns lined the shores of the Mississippi, one after the other, as *Yellow Stone* passed Vicksburg and entered the region of the upper delta, where the Yazoo River joins the Mississippi. Then the great river returned *Yellow Stone* to flat, jungle-like terrain on both sides with the only sign of settlement a few primitive huts of woodcutters and their families.

Katrina and Niklas were at the rail one dewy morning, drinking coffee and watching the swampy floodplains go by when Katrina cried out, "Oh, look, Klaus; are those Indians?" Along a small ridge standing just above the treetops, a column of people, horses, and dogs moved slowly away from the river, their long black hair and buckskin clothing distinctive even at this remove.

Behind the Kästners a woman's harsh American voice said, "Good riddance! Good Colonel Jackson, he's clearing out the country of them all."

It was Mrs. Aloysius Green, a woman of remarkable size and with hair piled high in a chignon. Mrs. Green extended her hand to Niklas, who touched it lightly. When she heard their destination, she gasped, clasped her bosom, and looked both ways to be sure no one could overhear.

"I'll tell you what, that frontier is a fearsome place. What with the slaughter at the Davis cabin, I would think long and hard before leaving civilization behind."

"The Davis cabin?"

"Oh, my word, yes, the Massacre at Indian Creek." Mrs. Green shook her head, growing more exercised as she thought about it. "My word," she said again, with an edge of outrage. "Fifteen settlers killed and scalped, men and children chopped to pieces, an innocent babe dashed against a tree, the dead women hung up by their feet."

She added in an aside to Katrina, "With their privates exposed! Two girls were captured and were gone ten or eleven days." Her voice dropped. "God knows what happened to them," she said, with a significant look, "before some tame Indians brought them back for ransom. All this right where you're aiming to go." She shook her head disapprovingly.

"Where is your home, Mrs. Green?" asked Niklas.

"Oh, we're in Sanct Louey. Some people call it the wild west," she chuckled, "but it ain't no such thing. It's been seventy years since the good King Louie gave us a land grant for the city."

"The Indian wars were recent?" Niklas hoped to drag her back to her story.

"The Black Hawk War, yes, 1832," she said with some severity. "It was the Sauk, Pottawamies, Illini, and some such other tribes." She paused. "We chased them across the Mississippi, into Iowa Territory." She nodded so vigorously at the western shoreline that Katrina imagined her chignon coming undone and flying overboard.

"This massacre you mentioned—it started the Black Hawk War?" Niklas had read about it; its gruesomeness had given it wings. Even in Germany, people gossiped about the Hall girls, Rachel and Sylvia, and tsk-tsked about the dangers of an uncivilized America. Niklas recalled how one girl fainted when she recognized her mother's scalp among those raised on a pike. The story was a little different each time it was told, and he wanted the local version.

"Oh, savages are wicked things. Our Illinois militia settled them, a fine force of volunteers, my brother among them, before General Scott's troops arrived from Buffalo, though two-thirds of those men had died of the cholera before they got to Fort Dearborn. It was the first time of cholera in Illinois."

"Madam, stand perfectly still," Niklas told Mrs. Green, who looked at him in surprise. A hairy black wolf spider had settled weightlessly on the woman's shoulder.

Niklas flicked the little creature into the Mississippi. Mrs. Green shrieked and skipped off to one side.

"They are fond of living on boats, madam," Niklas said apologetically.

"I am indebted to you, sir!" Mrs. Green backed away, as if it might rain spiders at any moment.

Katrina and Niklas waved goodbye and turned back to look at the long thin line of people disappearing over the ridge into the West, dogs and horses pulling sledges piled high, infants strapped to their mothers' backs, mounted men in army uniforms standing guard as the families filed past.

On the starboard side of *Yellow Stone* and at the northerly edge of an immense swamp lay Memphis, which was not much more than a dozen houses, and soon after that, the steamer neared the confluence of the Ohio, the first sign of which was a crystal-clear current splitting the brown waters of the Mississippi. The wide mouth of the Ohio appeared on the east as *Yellow Stone* hugged the muddy west shore, steaming hard against the doubled current until she could drop into the quieter waters above the Ohio.

This was the family's only glimpse of la belle riviere, as the French called the Ohio, the beautiful river. The *Yellow Stone* put in at Cairo to wood up and disembark passengers bound for Cincinnati and other points east. The Kästners were sorry to see the Harms brothers go. Then the *Yellow Stone* steamed north again, a clear and hopeful sign that they were making progress, getting closer and closer to the home they wanted and the dangerous frontier on which it lay.

CHAPTER 25

THE GREAT SHAKING

more than a tall tale

On long, lazy, hot days, the air was so full of water that the skin wore a layer of dew all day, the distance shimmered, the sunshine itself was blurred. This was late June, and along the river, full-grown magnolias were in bloom, magnificent trees that might be a hundred feet tall, filled with gigantic white blossoms like immense candles that lit up the riverside. The children were told to point them out to their mother, no matter when they saw one.

When Katrina saw her first one in New Orleans and exclaimed over it, Marguerite Robichaux said, "Oh, that ain't nothing but a magnolia."

Since they boarded, the boys were seen as likely crew, because they walked like and talked like the sailors they had spent three months among while crossing the Atlantic. When the weather kicked up and a storm threatened, they offered to lend a hand, and in that way, they met Big Mike. The thick-bodied, red-haired Irishman was new to *P.V. Yellow Stone* as captain of the aft crew. His father had been a rebel in the Irish Revolution of 1798 and escaped the hangman's noose by a nip and a tuck. The boys told Big Mike about the Irishmen they had met in Texas, many with links to the revolution of '98 and how the Irishmen expected to make a new country of Texas.

"Maybe I'll get off the river and go to Texas," Big Mike said, but neither Hans nor Will thought it likely. In spite of a barely discernible Irish lilt, Big Mike was a true "Kaintuck," a Kentucky-born boatman who wore canvas trousers and a red flannel shirt with a checked neckerchief. When a day was too warm, he and the others stripped to the waist, women and children notwithstanding, but no matter how hard they worked, they were always ready to go ashore for horse racing and what they called "wrastlin" and footraces and dancing and any other frolic they could find. "I am," he said, "half horse, half alligator, and half snapping turtle."

Hans and Will felt that something about riverboat life could get under your skin, but they had their doubts.

"Sure, everything is new this time," Hans said. "But why go up and down a river when there is such a great lot of country to see?"

"Or such a lot of ocean to sail," Will agreed. "Sailors don't strut about or love tall tales like riverboat men."

"There is that," Hans grinned. "But more frolicking."

"And less rigging," said Will, looking up, not sure whether this was a good thing.

Several passengers talked about heading for Chicago, and when they did, Hans and Will remembered Karl Schneider advising them to get to Chicago fast, buy land cheap, and sell at prices sure to go sky high when the canal came through. Those going to Chicago went on and on about deals already struck. Hans thought this was more American get-rich-quick foolishness, but since the sensible Karl Schneider had endorsed it, Will said they should reserve judgment. He did not admit to Hans that he could hardly wait to see Chicago. Will hoped their father would invest.

For some hours and days, a spike of doubt had been creeping into Will. He stared at the primeval shoreline, miles and miles of bluffs and bottom lands and piney woods or willows or cottonwoods with no sign of life more than a few rough cabins at far distance from each other or sometimes only a thin wisp of smoke curling up from a hidden homestead or a hunter's camp. *This country*, he worried, *is going to have to become more likely if we are going to turn our stake in cigars and sugar into ready cash.* He remembered the palace in Berleburg and the Huber plantation and wondered if a man had to have serfs or slaves to be rich.

He looked up to see Hans with a big grin on his face. "What makes you smile, Brother, when we are deep in a wilderness such as we never imagined?"

"A wilderness? Yes, but isn't it exciting when things are unexpected? We're on the edge of a whole new world, and that's the best place for the likes of us."

Hans punched Will in the shoulder, not hard enough to hurt. Will said, "Ow," but he also grinned.

Big Mike hooted when he heard that Hans' whole name was Hans-Jürgen. "Make it 'Hank,'" he said. "Strong man like yourself, you need an American name, a riverboat man's name."

Big Mike had heard talk about "goddamned foreigners coming over in droves," and he warned Hans about it. He did not mention his father's homesickness for Ireland or having heard whispers of "filthy Irish." Mostly, his liking for Hans was the same way a cattleman appreciates a likely young bull. Hans had the lines of a riverboat man.

Hans took Big Mike's advice to heart, especially about a new name. He began rolling "Hank" around in his mouth, considering it.

One placid evening under a full moon, the pilot decided to keep *Yellow Stone* running through the night even though it was a dangerous stretch, changeable and fraught with obstructions and impediments. Big Mike was on lookout duty, but not too occupied to talk. He liked having an audience and a tale to spin.

One of the crewmen asked him to tell of the Great Shaking of '11 and '12, and Big Mike was happy to oblige. He had a booming voice; Niklas said they could have heard him in Berleburg. Tonight, he began by swearing that what he was saying about the Great Shaking was the God's own truth.

"Yes, I was there as a boy on my father's flatboat crew," said Big Mike, "and like everyone, I felt the big quake in December of '11 and heard about the terrible happenings of the time, but no one expected the shaking to continue. It was the year of the comet, you know, Tecumseh's Comet, which caused everything."

Big Mike's father's crew laid up most of December and January in St. Louis waiting for the Earth to settle down. And on account of ice. When another big one happened on January 23, the ice cracked loose, chimneys fell all over St. Louis, and Big Mike's father figured that had to be the end of it, and "Besides," he said, "being on land is not safe neither."

They started downriver and ran through the night, afraid to tie up and get iced in, when the third and biggest quake hit. It was February 7, 1812, and the quake was big enough to ring church bells in Boston.

"It would have frightened the devil hisself," said Big Mike, "like all the thunder in the world, louder than any of us had ever heard, and flashes of lightning coming up from the ground, yes, lightning going upward."

Murmurs went through the listeners, and Hans heard someone say it could not be true.

"The river was all roiled," said Big Mike. "Our flatboat tipped almost over, and we all thought we were dead for sure, and a poor Tennessee boy slipped overboard and went under without so much as a peep."

The crowd murmured in sympathy. "This river," said one man, "makes cowards of us all."

Big Mike agreed.

"Suddenly," he said, pausing for effect, "we realized we were going backward, up the Mississippi. Even though the river had settled a bit, we were running backward."

The moonlight was bright enough for Big Mike to see Will's look of disbelief, and he swore: "It's the God's own truth! The river ran backward; upriver became downriver. My father, he said the world had turned upside down or inside out, and that we would likely land in China."

"Aye," said someone. "People said 'twas the end of the world."

"And you better git right with God."

"Now here we was going backward," Big Mike said. "The air smelled of sulfur. Da said it meant the gates of Hell had opened up."

Mike paused, and into the silence, he spoke. "The wind came up and then suddenly changed directions. The river slowed and then jerked and began moving rightly and picking up speed."

His hands swayed from side to side, trying to show them how powerful the reversing current had been. Just then *Yellow Stone* gave a lee lurch, bringing gasps and stumblings all around. Will slid off the coil of rope he had been sitting on, and leapt up with an embarrassed, "Hah!"

Big Mike paused, a satisfied smile just barely visible, pleased at this timely echo of long-ago events.

When everyone quieted down, Big Mike continued. "Now we came back past the same shoreline we had just traversed, "except everything was different. There were rapids and a waterfall in front of us, which had never been there before and which only by the hand of God did we get over them. Riverbanks had collapsed and were unrecognizable, huge trees were piled onto sandbars—new sandbars, old islands gone. When we came to where a big Indian village had been, it was gone with nothing to be seen of it. At New Madrid, there was nothing left. People on shore yelled for help, but we had no control and couldn't get to them. When they saw us passing by, they shook their fists and cursed us."

"Where did you finally make land?" asked Hans.

"Not until Natchez," said Big Mike. "We didn't see another boat the whole time, though we passed many wrecks and many corpses. One night we tied up to an island, and overnight the island sank! We threw off our lines just in time."

"I had family in the town of Big Prairie," said a man. "Gone. We heard about waterfalls that came and went, a big new lake on the Kentucky side where the Injuns had been, and sand that boiled and coughed up tar balls as big as a man's fist."

Here Big Mike, who had not seen the inside of a church in a decade, crossed himself.

Hans and Will sat still in the moonlight. It made them shiver to think they were passing along that same expanse of river right now. Later, they told the family about it and wondered whether to believe this, given a riverboat man's love of tall tales, but their parents had read of the Great Shaking, and their inquiries with others revealed no exaggeration but only more stories. Everyone in the West had a story about the earthquakes of 1811 and '12.

"We were all sure," said one man, "that it was End Days, with every new tremor. Which happened all the time for a year or so, but not like the three big ones."

Niklas kept his worries to himself, but the evening brought home his big worry, that this adventure into America could be the death of them.

CHAPTER 26

A NEW WORLD UNTAMED

a bitter acrimonious hatred

Aboard *Yellow Stone*, Izak relaxed his captain's demeanor and became a friend to all the Kästners. Hans was almost an age-mate, and they shared a love of travel and adventure. Izak listened with attention to Will and his talk of inventions, new business ventures, and grand schemes for becoming a wealthy landowner. He even played with little Jakob. Most often though, Izak was seen in conversation with Amalie; they became daily companions.

Niklas was surprised. *What*, he thought, *could she possibly say of interest to a man who is a sea captain?*

He thought it good of Izak to indulge her, especially when it saved her from the attentions of other men aboard. Niklas shared Amalie's low opinion of the weaselly assistant pastor, but his distaste for Bedford was nothing compared to his genuine worry about the wild-eyed Kentucky fanatic, Jeremiah Brown, who was also studying Amalie. Young women were scarce on the frontier, and Niklas supposed that accounted for the attentions of these men.

Will noticed Amalie's situation, too. He was alarmed about protecting her and envious of the attention she attracted. He was also annoyed not to find a single female of interest to him on *Yellow Stone*. It was, he feared, only the beginning of a frontier scarcity. He thought ever more fondly of the coquettish Yvette, but in his dreams, she stood next to Tom Segrave and with a brilliant smile, waved goodbye.

Yellow Stone passed the confluence of the Ohio and entered the American Bottom, a vast region of fertile floodplains. Magnificent cliffs appeared off one or both sides of the river, and on quiet evenings, the Kästner family marveled at the sunsets stretching over a wider expanse of sky than Berle-burg's ancient forests had ever allowed them to see.

One evening a colossal flock of birds appeared, slate-blue with copper bellies and gleams of purple, passing north to their summer quarters. Lisette heard them first, like faint distant thunder, and pointed; then the others gaped at the enormity of the flock. It darkened the sky, chattered too noisily to talk over, and sent the passengers running for cover. The flock took most of the dusk to pass by.

The galley cook and his crew went immediately to the bow of the boat, shooting upward and collecting birds as they fell. Several men joined in for the fun of it, an unexpected chance for hunting practice. These were passenger pigeons, they said, and one fellow from Columbus, Ohio, claimed to have waited from morning to night for the sky to clear.

"Squab is delicious," said the cook. "You can rely on its being on the menu tomorrow."

To the Kästners, the passenger pigeons were like manna from heaven and another instance of America's seemingly endless bounty.

Most evenings they watched the sky until the light faded. The wonder and amazement of these quiet evenings invoked what some philosophers called a "feeling of sublimity." For them, it was the gift of a New World untamed, so different from the tired, abused, and blood-stained lands of Europe.

When at last Saint Louis hove into view on July 1 of 1836, the excitement aboard was palpable. For days, riverboat traffic had been increasing, and now the Mississippi was crowded. St. Louis was a promising-looking town with the Missouri River just in sight beyond. On the east shore lay a barely-there settlement called Illinoistown, where *Yellow Stone* prepared to dock.

Besides steamers from points south, flatboats and trading scows came down the Missouri loaded with bales of furs. Others were poled up from Indiana. Rapids above the confluence of the Missouri made St. Louis the northernmost navigable port for most vessels, but as *Yellow Stone* bore off for its Illinoistown landing, a keelboat went on directly up the river.

"Its draft is so shallow it can go where a proper steamer cannot," said Big Mike.

As Will watched it pass by, five or six deckhands walked in a row on a narrow running board from the front to the back of the boat, each with his shoulder fixed firmly against the knob of a long pole, whose iron point was set in the bottom, and with all his strength "walking" the boat against the current. When a man had walked the length of the boat, he raised his pole, went back to the bow and renewed his set.

"I saw," said Will, "men passing the young willow trees on shore hand over hand to bring a keelboat upriver."

"That's called warping," Big Mike said, "done by hand or with ropes slung around tree trunks."

"Whichever way they manage it, going upstream looks like hard labor for slow progress."

"Yes," said Big Mike, "and at any moment, the current can catch them and sling them back down river."

More than a hundred and fifty steamboats were at the St. Louis levee, landing or departing, loading or unloading, but far fewer were on the east side. Big Mike told them that last year the east shore landing was made directly on mud. The limestone landing they saw now was new.

Izak squinted at this scratch of civilization. "At least it makes debarking drier."

"The streets beyond will put us in mud soon enough," said Hans.

"Humph," said Niklas, who was looking off the west at a set of new cathedral spires. "I would like to see what there is of St. Louis."

Yellow Stone maneuvered herself into position, threw out docking lines, and lowered a gangplank. A man hopped onto the foot of the gangplank, threw open his arms and cried, "Welcome to Illinoistown, in the great free state of Illinois!"

Big Mike said this was Gordon McArthur, a hotelier, who now extended his hand to the ladies, as well as to children and the infirm of either sex, handing them down to the safety of solid ground and talking in a steady stream about the McArthur Hotel and its dining room.

As Hans and Will watched the parade of departing passengers, Pastor Ewing scowled at Mr. McArthur and waved him away. He did not consider himself old enough to need help, and he certainly did not want the touch of a man who was a free stater.

Robin LeMoyne, the *P.V. Yellow Stone* purser, shook his head. "McArthur is unwise to mention Illinois's being a free state. That's all it takes to awaken a bitter acrimonious hatred in the heart of Southerners."

"But Illinois is in fact free?" Will asked. "And Missouri a slave state?"

Robin explained: "Yes. Illinois entered as a free state in 1818, and the 1820 Missouri Compromise allowed Maine as a free state and Missouri as a slave state. But it really didn't settle anything, and today nothing is as divisive as slavery. McArthur will get no trade from Southerners by taking sides."

"Even," said Will in a lowered voice, "a man of the cloth?" In German, he said to Hans, "How can the Golden Rule square with slaveholding?"

"Principles have nothing to do with it," said Hans. He wondered if anyone had understood their German. It was never wise to embrace abolition in public. Lainie had warned him about Southern preachers and their condemnation of foreigners, along with Freemasons and Jews, all evil, they said, and in league with Satan. Most congregations, Lainie said, had never met a Jew or a Freemason or a foreigner.

"Why the bitter hatred, then?" Hans had asked.

She laughed and said it was to tighten the screws on the devil they knew, the Black man. They thought, Lainie said, that bringing a slave to Christianity was a fair trade for enslavement. "Nay, more than that," she had said, "since thus is his soul saved."

Niklas decided Gordon McArthur's hotel was just the place for the family. He said as much to McArthur, who helped load their baggage onto the mule cart at the end of the gangway.

What the family heard the very next day showed how deeply Illinois and Missouri were divided.

A mob had attacked the offices of the *St. Louis Observer*, a weekly religious paper, furious that its editor, a Presbyterian minister named Elijah Lovejoy, denounced the horrific murder of a Negro. The man had been broken out of jail, trounced up in ropes, and burned to death. Lovejoy had had the temerity to condemn this. The Kästners were glad to be on the Illinois side, though here too, the fear was palpable. All the talk was of the Lovejoy incident and what might happen next, especially because the Lovejoy family was said to have escaped across the river to a town just north, a boomtown named Alton that was growing as fast as St. Louis.

CHAPTER 27

ARE WE AGREED?

"The first wagon train headed... all the way to Oregon."

The arrival of *Zebulon Pike* on August 2, 1817, marked the beginning of the steamboat era in St. Louis. Over the next decade, steamers replaced many of the working boats in the river, although flatboats remained the cheapest way to transport anything downriver, especially hay and meat on the hoof. Among the steam tugs, lighters, and ferries docked at St. Louis or Illinois-town lay an unprepossessing little sternwheeler named *Ottawa*, newly built for trade on the Illinois River. It had a sailing schedule posted to its rail and was, Niklas learned, in its first year of scheduled runs up the Illinois, the only steamer doing so. The family could book passage in just a few days.

Izak, it turned out, was once more to accompany them. *He's a man full of surprises*, thought Niklas. Izak's decision might have aroused Niklas's suspicions except that he was glad to have the ship's captain along, his strong hand having proven its value more than once and his steadiness welcome.

The era of steam had transformed St. Louis into a bustling boom town and inland port, or at least so it seemed. On the frontier, none knew which village would prosper and which would not until the last settler pulled up stakes and left the buildings empty of all but ghosts. By 1836, St. Louis was as sure thing as a frontier town could be, seventy-two years old, founded as a fur trading outpost by Pierre Laclède. His thirteen-year-old scout, Auguste Chouteau, chose this spot on the Mississippi for its sloping bluff, a barrier to Mississippi River flooding. In April 1764, Laclède named the site for the patron saint of his king, Louis IX.

Gordon McArthur told anyone who would listen, "The great General Marquise de Lafayette disembarked here in '24 to rejoicings and gratitude. We saluted him, the hero of the Revolution, with thirteen cannon." He paused to allow his listeners to grasp the significance of the number. Katrina was mystified, and the children studied their shoes.

"Such a glorious sight was he," said McArthur, "with his long, sad face, though he was stooped with age and lame with injuries received in the Revolution." St. Louis had been thrilled with Lafayette, a city where French was heard as often as any other language, but everywhere, Americans cheered General Lafayette. His 1824 tour swept political parties away with nostalgia.

However, when Katrina tried to make conversation with a new acquaintance by mentioning Lafayette, she was rebuffed.

"Humph," said the well-dressed lady. "The best families, the old families of Sanct Louey, have deep connections to the aristocrats of the old regime, who detested the man as 'le traitre Lafayette.' My grandfather was among them, and to this day I share his opinion."

No one exploring St. Louis in 1836 could miss Big Mound, the largest of many ancient Indian mounds. St. Louis was called "Mound City," and Big Mound was a favorite picnic spot. The Kästner family decided to ferry across with Izak to see it and take in the view it afforded.

As they boarded the ferry, Katrina noticed Jeremiah Brown at the rail. He was staring intently at them, and Katrina realized with a start that it was not she herself but Amalie who had his attention. In the sunshine, Amalie's auburn curls were touched with blonde, her cheeks were rosy with health, and her bonnet swung happily on one arm.

There she is again, thought Katrina with a frown, *without a proper bonnet. That bounder Thomas Segrave deserted her without a word, and now on this barely civilized frontier, she has far fewer prospects and is the object of much unwanted attention.*

"Amalie," Katrina barked, "come here! Put that bonnet on."

Katrina did not quite grasp that Amalie was smart, observant, and able to manage her older brothers, a skill that would transfer nicely to other men.

Sister Rose Duchesne founded the first free school for girls west of the Mississippi in 1823 and soon lamented, "Temptations are great in St. Louis...we have to fear for the girls who are still in our school. I consider St. Louis as bad as Malacca in the days of St. Francis Xavier."

She was right to impugn St. Louis, which was then emerging from an era of manic fur trafficking and riotous riverboat men. Things were uncertain enough that another of St. Louis' nicknames was "Pain Court," "short of bread." The settlement was dominated by Frenchmen who considered Americans Johnny-come-latelies disturbing their rightful monopoly of the fur trade—New York's John Jacob Astor the worst of them.

By the time the Kästner family arrived a decade later, St. Louisans starved less often and the town had many new buildings, the most impressive, a cathedral named Basilica of Saint Louis, King of France.

"It was completed two years ago," Father Pierre Jean de Smet told Niklas and Katrina, and in '32, we, by which I mean St. Louis College, became a university, the first west of the Mississippi." Father de Smet was a Belgian-born Jesuit priest often away on missions among the Salish, Iroquois, and Nez Perce, but happy to show the family around on this golden summer's day.

"Young gentlemen from as far away as New Orleans come here for an education," Father de Smet told them, nodding significantly at Will, who yawned behind his hand as the priest continued about the town's having its own Catholic diocese, a courthouse, a United States Arsenal, the Jefferson Barracks military base, and Mullanphy Hospital, built on land donated by John Mullanphy, an Irish immigrant whose name was Ó Maolainbhthe in Gaelic, which the priest respectfully spelled out for them in the dirt.

"Monsieur Mullanphy," Father de Smet told them, "paid $150 in 1828 for four Daughters of Charity to travel to St. Louis and $350 toward the building of the first hospital west of the Mississippi." He explained that the hospital, now a fine brick building at Fourth and Spruce Streets with room for both patients and nuns, had been housed in a log cabin before Mullanphy's generosity.

Father de Smet and the Kästners turned at the deep rumble of a line of covered wagons going through town. One of these wagons was a heavy, low-slung Conestoga, having come across the river from much farther east, and having once worn a coat of blue-green paint on its sideboards and brick red on its wheels. It was now battered and with a much-patched canvas top. The others were newer, having been built on this side of the river and painted shiny black on the sideboards and bright yellow on the wheels, topped with new canvas bonnets stretched taut over metal hoops. The Kästners had seen many covered wagons in Europe, including the multi-colored ones of wandering Gypsies, but these were larger and bore a distinctive high arch.

"Many more wagons are camped outside town," Father de Smet said. "This is the first wagon train headed all the way to Oregon."

"Unimaginably distant," murmured Niklas.

"Most go to Kansas or Nebraska or the Dakota Territory," said Father de Smet. "God save them." He crossed himself, horrified that these people, women and children among them, were ready to travel so far through raw, unsettled Indian lands. An intrepid traveler himself, he knew more about the dangers than he cared to tell anyone.

In 1836, one would not have been wrong to bet on this fine young city. It was about to become the departure point for a century of travel into the Far West. For Niklas, however, the lure of Chicago thrummed in his ears, and now that they were just a few weeks away, he was impatient to be going. Not even he, however, was impatient enough to ignore a warning Mr. McArthur confided over breakfast.

"Prices in Chicago," said Gordon McArthur, "are sky-high, and on the Illinois River, I'm sorry to say, the only settlements of any size are Havana, Peoria, and Hennepin. I beg you to expect nothing whatsoever of the clusters of log cabins springing up here and there. Nothing can be procured there beyond a broken-down mule or a glass of whiskey."

"We will need livestock for the winter," Niklas said, "—horses, a milk cow or two, and a hog to butcher—it makes no sense to buy here and carry these aboard *Ottawa* unless there is no alternative. What do you suggest?"

"Hmmm," said Gordon McArthur. "Ah! Two possibilities! Buy direct from a Hoosier wagon train. They run north up Hubbard's Trace into Chicago and camp there before their return trip. Or buy in Peoria before you get to Chicago. Prices may have risen there, but not likely as much."

Niklas thanked him but as he turned to go, McArthur touched his sleeve and added, "However, if you will need anything else for homesteading, you would be well advised to purchase here." Mr. McArthur said this within the hearing of Katrina, which left little for it but to go on a buying expedition. "If you need anything at all…" the man had said, as if they had not left a thousand imminently useful things behind in Berleburg.

When Niklas looked over his family this early morning, it was with pleasure and pride: Hans in his prime, Will as bright in intellect as in aspect, Amalie on the cusp of womanhood, and two little ones as pretty as any man could wish. And yet, below this happiness was a twinge of apprehension, and perhaps more than a twinge. He was admittedly a prosperous man, but nearly all that he possessed and that stood between his family and dire poverty lay in the hold of *P.V. Yellow Stone*, to be transferred today to *P.V. Ottawa*, and worthless without a buyer. In a single, small, iron-bound casket was the last of the gold carried from Berleburg, the leavings of a small inheritance, the sale of everything they had once owned, and his own scrimping from fifteen years as a shopkeeper, now sadly, sadly diminished after four months of travel, gold having been required for every inch forward and at every mealtime.

After breakfast and at Mr. McArthur's recommendation, the Kästners ignored three fine-looking shops and stepped into the fourth, Grafton's Big Store. The family spread out through the store, not one of them noticing that Will had stayed behind on the porch talking to a pretty girl, Lottie Grafton. They were soon deep in conversation, their having instantly discovered a mutual attraction.

When the two young people entered the store, Lottie moved demurely behind the sales counter, a slab of wood sanded smooth and marked smartly with brass tacks for measuring yardage. Now the counter was filling up as Katrina and Amalie chose two cast iron skillets, a Dutch oven, a soup kettle, a flat baking stone, a pair of sharp butcher knives, a crock of sauerkraut, and a dozen jars of jelly or jam: apple, apricot, rhubarb, and raspberry.

Will found his father and brother inspecting buffalo robes, Niklas wondering how cold winters in Illinois could possibly be. Mr. Grafton recommended three robes for the family and an extra for winter travel in a sleigh.

Niklas swore to himself that this was his last extravagance.

Mr. Grafton gently suggested deerskin moccasins; his were especially well-crafted, decorated with red beads and blue-dyed porcupine quills. Niklas turned these last items over in his hands, marveling at the simplicity of the design. Here in the West almost everyone was barefoot, men and boys, women and girls. He had once been trained as a shoemaker, and it was something he noticed.

"Everyone," said the shopkeeper, "wears moccasins in the winter."

"How comfortable looking!" said Katrina as she came up to her husband's side.

No doubt an Indian maiden made these, thought Hans, who was now introducing himself as "Hank" and even beginning to think of himself as "Hank."

"Winter will come soon enough," murmured Mr. Grafton. "Many people buy two pair to last the cold season." He did not say what had already occurred to him, that there would be a long summer between now and then or that it would be most rewarding to have fourteen pairs of these particular moccasins gone from his shelves before another hot day dawned.

Lottie Grafton had her father's ear now, and she whispered to him with a jerk of her head toward Will.

Will turned to Niklas and said in a confidential voice, "It's a good deal, Papa: rice, molasses, coffee, and Cuban cigars for Mr. Grafton's goods, not a penny from our coffers, a clean and clear barter."

Niklas looked at his younger son with amazement and a certain annoyance as he felt himself slip from wealthy buyer to fellow merchant. He was not inclined, however, to let such a propitious trade slip by.

"I believe my son has arranged a barter," he said.

"Indeed he has," said Mr. Grafton. He smiled and extended his hand. "Are we agreed?"

CHAPTER 28

ON THE ILLINOIS RIVER

He had used this very sword while charging on horseback.

Above St. Louis, the Kästner family and all aboard *Ottawa* had a wild ride as the little steamboat forced its way past the mouth of the Missouri, an altogether faster and larger river. Where the currents joined, they intensified, digging a wide, deep cut through islands and rapids. Off starboard, the Illinois River welcomed them with spectacular limestone cliffs, and once past the turbulence, *Ottawa* steamed happily into calmer waters.

It was a delight. The wooded bluffs rising on one side or both made the Kästners feel at home.

"How like the Rhine!" Katrina smiled.

"Yes. It needs only a castle at the top," said Niklas.

Will noticed, too, and felt a sharp pang of homesickness. He made a vow to go home again. *But not now*, he thought, *not yet.*

Gone were the tight bends of the Mississippi, replaced with a gentle sway from side to side and a mild current. The days were perfectly warm, and the progress upstream encouragingly quick. They passed the Sangamon River and steamed on until the shores pulled back to reveal Spoon River coming in from the west and a long beach on the east shore, the sandy edge of Havana, Illinois, where they were to moor for the night.

Havana was a hub of activity, with fishing boats and small sailboats busy on the river and a string of canoes along the shore next to a "Fer Hire" sign. Most impressive was a rectangular building several stories high with the first floor built of stone. It was a surprise to see it in this wilderness, dwarfing the log cabins of the rest of the village.

"Ossian Ross, at your service," a tall passenger volunteered. "Me and me boys built 'er, and you won't see another of its size in Illinois." He added a little sheepishly, "I own the canoe ferry, too."

Before Niklas could ask, the tall passenger added, "'Tis eighty feet long and with the porches on both sides, fifty-six feet deep. Zenos Herrington, he burnt the lime for the mortar and drug it down from Thompson Lake. Built the carrying cart himself with nary a nail nor a lick of iron. That's how we had to make do back then. The way the cart squeaked, you could hear him coming a half mile away, but it was a strong thing, and with two yoke of oxen he could carry a full load of lime."

"Did he carry the stone, too?"

"Oh, no, sir! That was floated down the river. There was a dozen or so who brought different things. Took us two years, on account of having to do everything by hand. No sawmills closer than Cincinnati at the time. Now there's two mills at Peoria."

Niklas and Katrina came down the gangplank at Havana as people ashore went about their business, a few stopping to see what strangers *Ottawa* had brought into their midst this time.

"A fine place to stretch our legs," said Niklas.

"And to buy a hot supper," Katrina said.

"From Havana, Cuba, to Havana, Illinois!" exclaimed Will. He considered himself a world traveler, but the big hotel surprised him. He was also hungry. It would be pork and beans and gravy and biscuits, he supposed, along with sassafras tea and whiskey.

Smoke rose from summer kitchens, going straight up in air so quiet that Izak shook his head: *Doldrum weather and yet no impediment to a steamer.*

There was nothing grand in sight except the hotel, no mansions, no cathedral built of coral like the one in the real Havana, none of New Orleans' cobblestone streets or gas lanterns or Spanish ironwork, no fiddlers or harpsichords.

"In spite of the hotel, I think we may be in the American frontier," said Niklas.

"I wonder," said Katrina, "how many people here have ever seen the Havana their little town is named after."

"I wonder how many have even seen New Orleans," said Will.

"I imagine," Amalie said, "some have not even seen St. Louis."

Will wandered off, and Niklas and Katrina explored, too, taking advantage of the long midsummer evening. They saw no slaves, and the air had the lovely, healthy coolness of summer nights in Berleburg.

"If we closed our eyes," said Katrina, "we might think we were in the Hoch Sauerland."

"Yes," said Niklas, "This is more like it."

Then Katrina looked around for Lisette and little Jakob. She called out, and when the children did not answer, Niklas called, and the urgency of his voice brought Hans up from the riverbank, where he had been watching otters play, and Amalie back from a woodland path into the clearing. The two little ones were missing. As was Will.

"Will must be with them," said Amalie. "They'll be all right."

Now all five were calling, Izak using his big captain's voice first one direction and then the other. Niklas waved for silence, and they strained to listen. No response. Nothing.

A shiver ran through Katrina as she remembered Mrs. Aloysius Green and the massacre at Indian Creek. She stopped a woman passing by. "Are there Indians here?" She asked. "Savages hiding in woods?"

"No," said the woman, looking mystified. "Not to speak of."

Katrina explained about the children, and the woman went to get help. The other passengers joined the Kästners in the clearing, and people from the village appeared. Hans ran back to *Ottawa*, where he opened trunks, grabbed pistols and blades and pocketed ammunition. In the clearing, the briefest of introductions: Lewis Peel and his family from the village, *Ottawa* passengers Messrs. Samson, Black, O'Neil, and Mrs. O'Neil.

Niklas listened to Lewis Peel's description of the lay of the land—river, woods, prairie. Women from the village brought lanterns—sunset was not far off—and the Peel boys came with saddled beasts, two horses and a mule.

Lewis Peel looked askance at the silver-handled sword Niklas was strapping on. "That will get in your way," he said with a nod to the sword. "Take this instead. Don't lose it." He handed Niklas a Bowie knife.

Niklas was already in the saddle. He frowned down at the villager, with a quick flash of memory. He had used this very sword while charging on horseback to cut off the heads of villagers not unlike Lewis Peel. He kept his sword and accepted the knife.

The Peel men would go on foot into the deepest woods.

"You would only get lost there," Lewis Peel said.

Niklas, Hans, and Izak would go southeast into the prairie on horseback, and the *Ottawa* group would go along the river and beat through a thick stand of willows there.

"Keep the river in your sights," Lewis warned them. "No man is to fire unless he is sure not to be aiming at another man."

"Be thorough, not fast," Niklas said. "These are young children. They cannot have gone far. Three shots in quick succession means they are found."

There were wolves, bears, panthers, and maybe a stray Indian, but being lost was far more likely. Two Peel youngsters were gathering wood for a bonfire when Katrina frightened everyone by brandishing her pearl-handled pistols and saying she would not sit by the fire and wait. Mrs. Peel suggested searching the beach, so the two women and Amalie became a fourth team, with the younger Peels to mind the bonfire.

Niklas, Hans, and Izak took the trail Lewis Peel pointed out. It passed two small log cabins in the woods, barely more than huts, and opened out into the last of the bright sunlight, shocking them with the immensity of the prairie before them.

"It's like the Russian steppes," said Niklas. "Easy to traverse, easy to get lost."

Izak blazed a tree where they came out so they could find the trail again. Niklas took the center position, and Hans and Izak spread out to his left and right. A grouse startled and flew up in front of Hans; his horse reared and backed a few steps, but Hans held his seat. The three men began to move forward, calling out in rhythm, each calling in turn with time to listen between shouts. They understood why the horses had been brought: not for speed but because only a man on horseback could see over the six-foot-high prairie grass. Here and there, perhaps along some hidden creek, a strip of tall orange lilies bloomed. Before long, the golden-green prairie began to turn pink in the setting sun.

In the dark woods where Lewis Peel and his two older sons searched, there was never any light to speak of, but their eyes adjusted quickly, and besides, they had tramped these woods day and night for years. They knew every deer and elk path, every foxhole, every panther's lair, every wolf's den, and every bear's cave; now they traipsed through dense undergrowth and over logs and roots with ease. At a giant sycamore, where the trail split, they agreed to meet again in no more than an hour. Lewis looked up—a clear sky and a full moon would help.

"What's his name again?" asked Eddie Peel, who at age fifteen was an exceptionally capable woodsman.

"William. They called him Will."

"What kind of idiot goes off into woods he doesn't know and with children in tow?"

"Enough!" said their father.

A half hour earlier, Lisette had come running out of the woods, wild-eyed and in tears. She grabbed Will and pulled him back into the trees. "Jakie's hiding from me—we were playing hide and seek, and now he won't come out. I can't find him!"

She turned from Will and ran ahead, crying, "Jakie! Jakie! Come out, come out, wherever you are!"

Will ran pell-mell after her, down a broad trail. "Jakob! Not a game anymore! Show yourself!" He caught Lisette by the shoulder and held his finger to his lips. Away off to the left they heard the little boy giggle. Will and Lisette followed the sound down a smaller trail, if it was a trail at all.

"Jakob!" called Will in his most authoritative tone, "Halt! Stop this very moment! Hold up!" But little Jakob did not stop, and they ran on after the laughter and the rustle of leaves.

Then they heard him scream. Will ran even harder, glancing back for Lisette. He did not want two children lost in the woods. That was his undoing. He fell hard over a snaggle of roots, tumbled forward, and grabbed at branches, grass, whatever his hands touched. When he stopped, he found himself at the very edge of a ravine. He scrambled to his feet and caught Lisette as she leapt over the roots and ran full force into him.

He set her down firmly and said, "Stay here. Don't move." She gasped as she saw the ravine's edge.

He turned and peered over the edge. Jakob lay in a crumpled heap at the foot of the ravine. Will groaned. He looked back at Lisette's terrified face and said, "I'm going after him. See that tree? Climb it. Keep watch for anyone who can help." He had seen Lisette climb gnarly apple trees in Berleburg just like this one, and he hoped this perch would keep her both occupied and safe.

"Don't leave me here," Lisette called out. She hitched up her skirts and began to climb the apple tree. "Be sure to come back for me."

"I'm going down, not away," Will said as he scanned the ravine, looking for a way down. Then he saw it—a knot of exposed roots and something below them that might be a footpath. He was as lithe, strong, and monkeylike as young men come, and thus he ran down where most would not even have found a foothold.

The little boy was breathing and seemed unbroken, but Will could not rouse him. He looked up at the height of the cliff: sixteen feet and maybe more, but Jakob had landed on a deep pile of last year's oak leaves. A foot further out, where the ravine ran wet with a creek, Jakob would have hit rocks. Will was trying to get the little boy to respond and thinking about how best to carry him when he heard a low, dangerous growl and looked up to see a mangy old wolf, head lowered, teeth bared and the ruff on the back of its neck standing up. In one swift movement, he picked up a stone the size of his fist and launched it squarely at the wolf. It jerked back and ran away yelping.

Now, before the wolf could recover, Will needed a way out. It would be easier, carrying Jakob, to follow the ravine in hopes that it led to the river but faster to go up the way he had come down. He draped the unconscious child over his shoulder and started to climb, surprised at how much harder it was to pick his way up. Tree roots lay exposed on the surface, and Will used them like rungs of a ladder.

Oh, he thought as he began to puff, *what I would give for* Enigma*'s proper rope ladders.* Will had just reached the knot of roots at the cliff's edge and was trying to find a safe way to get past its thick fringe when he heard voices, Lisette's and another, a man's voice.

Eddie Peel was staring up at Lisette, trying to make sense of what she was saying—in garbled English, French, and German—and why she was up a tree, pointing into the ravine, when he heard a voice at his feet.

"Good day, sir. May I have your assistance?" Will knew this was not a frontier way to put it, but it was the first English phrasing that came to mind.

Eddie Peel dropped and lay out at full length, grasping at Will's shirt and trying to lift Jakob off him.

"No, no, leave him be. Just help me get past the overhang."

Eddie had a length of rope at his waist, and now he undid it, wrapped one end under Will's arms, put a square knot in it and wrapped the other end around a stout oak tree. "On three, come up!"

One strong pull, and Will landed, sprawled on the ground, twisting to keep his weight off Jakob. Lisette was down from the tree and hopping with impatience to get to the little boy. Will rolled to one side, and Eddie Peel pulled the little boy away from the edge. Lisette knelt at his side.

"Little Jakob, Jakie, wake up, you little dummkopf." She found quite a lump on the little boy's head.

Will stood, put out his hand, and told Eddie, "I am indebted to you for my life, my dear sir, and for my brother's."

"Of course," said Eddie, who was impressed with the bravery, strength, and elegant language of the young man opposite him. He glanced over the edge of the ravine. "That's quite a climb you had."

Eddie had no gun to sound the signal, but he led the way back to the sycamore tree. Once there, he set to work chopping down a tree. That was his family's usual signal.

Lisette and Will made a little bed for Jakob, propping him against the sycamore tree, and continuing to call to him. They looked at each other with deep concern.

"What would Mother do?"

"Splash his face with cool water, perhaps?" But they had no water.

"Shall I spit on him?" asked Lisette.

"I don't think so. Give him time. He only seems sound asleep; surely he will wake up."

And true enough, when they looked back at little Jakob, his eyes were open, and he was staring at them in confusion. In moments, he dissolved into tears and sobs and climbed into Lisette's lap. She and Will shared a smile of relief.

Between the sound of the hatchet and the child's wailing, it did not take long for Lewis Peel and his older son to find their way back to the sycamore tree. Lewis sounded the three-shot signal, and the little group set off for the clearing. Jakob was back in Will's arms, his tired little head resting on his big brother's shoulder, and Lisette held onto the back of Will's jacket. Will thanked God for sending true woodsmen to the rescue, now that the sun had set and darkness filled the woods with shadows as double-black as he had ever seen.

"You have some explaining to do, Will." Niklas was dismounting, the firelight showing his face dark with anger and worry, his having counted up all the many ways three of his children could be dead or dying since the alarm was first raised.

"No, no, Papa, he saved us!" Lisette could not keep herself from breaking in, afraid as she was of her father's black look. Will raised his eyes to his father and saw what he had seen from childhood, a man in his prime, a hero still. He had no hope of comparing to his father.

But the little girl's outburst was not everything in evidence; the best of it was little Jakob half-asleep on Will's shoulder.

"Is the babe hurt?"

"He has a sizable goose-egg," said Will. "He was knocked out of his senses by a fall, but he came to whilst we were in the woods, cried, and then fell asleep. The Peels deserve our gratitude, Father. I'm not sure I could have made it out of the ravine without Eddie here and the rope he so wisely had with him."

"He had come up the cliff like an Injun," said Eddie, "where I could not even see a footpath, carrying the child on his shoulder."

"Actually," said Will with a smile, "I came up like a sailor."

"And he caught me and saved me from going over the edge, and he fought off the wolves at the bottom of the ravine," said Lisette, who had seen the whole thing from her perch in the apple tree.

"One wolf," Will corrected her, "and a decrepit old one at that."

"And one lucky toss of a rock, I expect," said Lewis Peel, who had already heard the story.

"Aye, a lucky toss," Will said, with an inner shiver to think what might have been had his aim been poor. *Even one old wolf has sharp teeth, and I did not even have a knife with me,* he thought. *That's twice I have not been well enough armed.* "The Peels led us out of the woods through pitch blackness," he added. "Thank you again."

Katrina took little Jakob into her lap and felt him all over, searching for broken bones and regretting that she did not have plaster of paris in their baggage. He was bruised, but no bones appeared to be broken. Once she had kissed each tender spot, she turned to Lisette and Will and gave each of them a kiss as well, even though they were all right out there in public.

In the days to come, the family honored Will for the hero he had become and wondered at the strange coincidence, little Jakob having fallen twice and Will saving him twice.

Later, Hans told Will, "Now you have saved little Jakob, just as I once saved you. Maybe someday Jakob will save you and me!" They clapped each other on the back and chuckled at the miracle of brotherhood.

In the morning, as a few new passengers boarded, the Peels stood on the shore, waving and calling out thanks to the Kästners for their kind invitation to come visit.

"Such good-hearted people, and God's own blessing that they came to help us," Katrina said to Niklas. "I do hope we see them again." As she said this, she remembered that she had no home in which to receive them.

Katrina looked at the new people coming aboard, pondering the shocking difference in their journeys: her family's all the way from Prussia and these new passengers' lazy day trip up the river to Peoria or Hennepin or Ottawa. Niklas and Izak gazed out through the last wisps of morning fog in wondering approval at the forests stretching off into the distance and thinking of the endless, untouched prairie they had seen the night before. When Niklas asked Lewis Peel about its being so empty, Lewis told him the tall grasses have such dense roots the sod cannot be broken.

"What you saw," Lewis Peel told him, "is the Great American Desert."

One of the new passengers was a land agent who explained that the wooded, rolling hills off to the west were bounty land, awarded to veterans of the 1812 war in 160-acre tracts. Those who decided against taking up their claims—which was most of them—sold their tracts to speculators, who were even to this day re-selling them. The land agent unrolled a copy of a newspaper, the *Illinois Bounty Land Register*, smoothing it out to show the list of claims and looking inquiringly at Niklas and Izak. Neither so much as raised an eyebrow, so the land agent sighed and folded up the paper again.

This is some fine land for very little, Niklas thought, *such a change from home, where every tree and stone and rivulet was claimed ages ago and is now soaked with the blood of generations disputing those claims.*

Soon they entered the Peoria Lakes, where the river spread out on both sides, the flowering prairie came into view now and then, ducks and geese abounded, and small settlements added a friendly aspect to the shores.

Izak told them they were lucky to have come this far unobstructed. The crew had told him of buffalo once so abundant they delayed passing boats for hours, huge herds crossing from side to side, the animals too big and dangerous to be herded or to venture in amongst. Hans was disappointed.

"What," Hans asked Will, "in a journey of such length as we have had, would a delay of a few hours count against the chance to see such rare beasts?"

Will nodded, and each knew the other was thinking of a magical afternoon in Berleburg when they had seen a wisent, the vanishingly rare European bison, and had sworn to each other: in America, they would see vast herds of bison.

But not today, Will thought, *not today.*

CHAPTER 29

FORT CRÈVE-COEUR

another dreamlike hour

One of the Havana-to-Peoria passengers, Dr. Rudolphus Rouse, was a physician of some repute, the first "president" of Peoria, and the son of immigrants from Hanover. Rouse was middle-aged and impressively built, but still trim when he turned certain ways. He wore a white silk cravat and a dark green velvet waistcoat with two rows of silver buttons. His mustache turned up at the ends, and he smelt of tobacco, boot leather, and pomade.

Dr. Rouse introduced another well-dressed Peoria man, John Detweiller, a native of Lorraine who switched to German as soon as he and Niklas began talking. Their dialects were similar, and they were happy to use the old language.

"How long did it take you to get across?" Detweiller asked. His journey from Le Havre to New York City, he explained, had taken forty-eight days.

Niklas laughed. "It was complicated. The captain had arranged to pick up a passenger in Gibraltar, then we were forced to put in at Havana. We were seventy-one days from Rotterdam to Havana. Then it took us another three weeks to get to New Orleans, thanks to a hurricane that pushed us into Texas."

"Mein Himmel!" said Detweiller. "It took me thirty-five days, to reach Peoria from New York, for a total of eighty-three days."

"How did you come across?"

"Up the Hudson to Albany, west on the Erie Canal to Buffalo, across Lake Erie to Cleveland, down the Ohio and Erie Canal to Cincinnati—that leg alone was four days but saved weeks of time—across on the Ohio River to the Mississippi, up to St Louis, and this last stretch on the Illinois River."

"Ach du Lieber Gott! So far in so little time! We've been on the rivers for..."

"Two weeks, counting our two nights in St. Louis," supplied Will. "And we stayed two weeks in New Orleans. That's twenty-six days plus seventy-one plus twenty-one. A hundred and thirty days compared to your eighty-three."

"We are not home yet," said Niklas. "We are aiming for Hennepin tonight, and later I expect to have a look at Chicago."

"Oh, you don't want Chicago," Detweiller said. "It's a muddy mess. And rough. Uncivilized. Peoria, now, was the first European settlement in the territory of Illinois, founded by the great La Salle himself. It was called Fort Crèvecoeur, which means 'broken-hearted.'"

"What!" said Will, "La Salle again! Is his ghost haunting us?"

"Perhaps," said Niklas with a smile.

Detweiller looked mystified.

"The de Crèvecoeur were an old, noble family of France," said Dr. Rouse quietly. "The name has nothing to do with being broken-hearted."

"But wait 'til you hear this," said John Detweiller. "Fort Crèvecoeur was abandoned after four months, and this message was found burned into the side of an unfinished boat: 'Nous sommes tous sauvages,' 'We are all savages.'" He shrugged and grinned.

"Fort Crèvecoeur was not well-sited," Dr. Rouse said. "After the War of 1812, Fort Clark was built, but Indians burned it down in 1818. When the first Americans arrived the next year, all they found were remnants. The area was known as Peoria, and that's the name they began to use."

As they stared at a promising-looking town, Dr. Rouse added, "Early on, a prosperous French village grew up."

John Detweiller jumped in. "With a blacksmith shop, a chapel with gilt lettering, a winepress, and a windmill. Jean Maillet led it and then sold it in the 1770s to Jean Baptiste Pointe du Sable, an African-French-Canadian..." Here Detweiller paused to see if his listeners would object to hearing about a Negro, and seeing no startled looks, he went on. "Du Sable left Peoria and went on up to Lake Michigan with his Potawatomi wife, a woman named Kittihawa or in English, Catherine."

Dr. Rouse said, "Du Sable and his wife had a trading post in Chicago. The name is Potawatomi for garlic or onion, that's how woebegone its swamps are."

"Things are changing," said Detweiller, "what with the canal and all. They say the Ohio and Erie Canal has bumped land prices by 360 percent."

Niklas asked what they thought of investment opportunities in Chicago.

"We hear tales of a lot of money being made," Dr. Rouse said. "But if the canal goes through, it will transform things all along the route. Hennepin and Peoria are already thriving and better situated to make the most of it."

John Detweiller added, "Chicago is a new, uncertain thing. Here in Peoria, your family would have a settled town and a county seat as can give you a clear, official title to land. That's something to watch for."

Dr. Rouse looked appraisingly at Niklas and his family, thinking about the advantages of having this handsome, well-educated Prussian family settle in Peoria. He wondered how much money they had.

Niklas could see where this conversation was heading and demurred: "I think, having come this far, I want to see what's going on in Chicago."

"Well. The lake is amazing. They call them 'great lakes,' but that hardly does them justice. They are as big as oceans, but the water is sweet."

"That reminds me," said Niklas, "why do I hear people here called 'suckers'?"

Dr. Rouse snorted. "It's a nickname for people settling on the Illinois grasslands, which not many do. Have you ever seen a prairie, a good look, I mean, not the bits and pieces we spy through the trees?"

Niklas told him of seeing the prairie outside Havana.

"Then you understand how vast they are. Once you leave the river, it can be hard to spot a creek in the tall grass, but no one ever dies of thirst on an Illinois prairie. The grass stems are hollow and so stiff they can be thrust into the prairie soil. A few feet down, water is always to be found and can be sucked right up. It takes a few muddy mouthfuls, but you'll soon have water to drink, no matter how huge the prairie you traverse. That's how we came to be called 'suckers.' In Peoria, of course, we have the river, endless sweet, fresh water."

Izak Peterssen stared at the pretty town, his mind going back to the utterly different way the ships of the British Navy, those he had served as boy and man, had approached a landing: proudly outfitted in shore-going white trousers, ribbons marking the outside seams, blue jackets with brass buttons, and straw hats with ribbon around the crown, often embroidered with the ship's name.

"How different the approach of this casual steamboat," said Izak to Niklas, "from our nerve-wracking approach to Cuba."

"Yes," said Niklas. "And to Linnville."

"This is safe, civilized, and unremarkable," said Izak. *Here I am*, he thought, *aboard as an ordinary civilian, commanding no one, indistinguishable from all the rest.*

The whistle blew to announce a stop at Peoria.

"We became an official, incorporated village last year. The captain will stop here for an hour," Dr. Rouse said with a smile, pulling out a pocket watch. "Everyone will have heard *Ottawa*'s whistle, and some will contrive a reason to gawk," he added, with a nod to Katrina and Amalie, "once they see that there are the fashions of New Orleans to be admired. New Orleans is our Paris, you know."

Oh my, thought Katrina as she acknowledged his smile. *At least in New Orleans they know this is authentic Parisian fashion we wear, not Orleanais copies!*

Turning to Niklas, Dr. Rouse asked, "Am I so fortunate as to have the acquaintance of the merchant with such a prodigious quantity of goods aboard?"

"You are, sir," replied Niklas, and this led to a longer conversation, the upshot of which was the sale of sugar, molasses, rice, coffee, a sack of pecans, and a few cigars. As it happened, Rouse and Detweiller were forward-thinking gentlemen, happy to try something besides their usual preference, the pipe.

"A bird in the hand," Niklas told Katrina later, "a bird in the hand!" He was relieved to have found ready buyers and of such high quality as well.

When they boarded again and the afternoon wore on, one pleasant view revealing itself after another, the Kästner family was lulled into an odd state in which this lovely and placid river promised an Illinois Eden, peace and possibilities greater than they had dreamt of.

At the same time, everything they had known at home was slipping away—they knew they were not who they had once been. They were acutely aware that their journey, their very long, hard, and treacherous journey, was about to end, and yet another vast unknown lay before them, a new world indeed. That very evening, they hoped to disembark for good, and then the further trip by stagecoach to Chicago would happen or not, depending on what they found in Hennepin and whether they could bear to go further.

The Peoria Lakes ran on and on until at last the Kästners perceived a change in direction, as the sun, now lying low in the sky, came around to their backs. Izak noticed it first and said this was the big bend of the Illinois, which now headed east to Chicago, and that they had almost reached the limit of the navigable portion. *Ottawa* would moor at Hennepin that night, and on the morrow, it would go on without the Kästners about twenty miles further to the village of Ottawa, at the mouth of the Vermillion River, the absolute last navigable waters. Once there, *Ottawa* would drop off its last few passengers, turn and begin the downstream trip to St. Louis.

For another dreamlike hour, the excitement built. The Kästners gathered by the rail, little Jakob held by his father, Will on one side, and Katrina on the other with her arm around Lisette. *Will*, thought Katrina, *might be taller than his father if you put them back-to-back and measured.* She hoped he had passed the growing boy phase, when he was almost always in motion and either vastly hungry or chasing a girl.

She glanced at Hans, who had gone through this phase, too, but more fiercely, leaping from skinny, sad child to big-muscled, morose giant of a man. She could not for a moment discourage his plans for traveling west, much as the family would be diminished without him, not when she saw how his eyes lit up at the thought.

Hans stood a little behind, tall enough to see over the others, and Izak and Amalie stood with him, where their clasped hands would not be visible to the others. If they spent as much time looking into each other's eyes as at the passing scenery, no one was the wiser. They knew that these precious days aboard, providing such extraordinary opportunities for unchaperoned moments, were about to end, a courtship of conversations masked by the noise of the paddlewheels and the rush of water alongside, noise that was music to them, an excuse for heads being tilted toward each other, even lips put to the ear.

The light was fading as *Ottawa* rounded the last bend in the river and gave them their first glimpse of Hennepin, now bathed in a golden glow. They were to moor at the town's downstream edge, as a narrow, shallow bypass to upstream rapids was best approached in the full light of day. They could now see a marked change in the river from the wide, lazy stream to a faster current divided by a large island and rushing through narrowed chutes. In the fading light passengers were asked to stay aboard for supper and sleep.

Morning would be time enough for unloading baggage and trade goods and for securing lodgings, and for discovering Hennepin, Illinois, the United States of America, a fabulous new world where everything would be different. It would be time enough to discover whether, by chance, in this little village, by some act of magic and courage and long travail, they had found a new home.

CHAPTER 30

HENNEPIN

She looked like an angel.

Will leapt out of bed or as nearly as was possible from a hammock in a cramped cabin on a boat. For an instant, he stood stock-still, wondering where and when he was. *Ah,* he thought, *1836, the Illinois River, on the* P.V. Ottawa. He remembered that he was newly a hero: thanks to him, his little brother Jakob was safe and asleep in their mother's arms this morning.

He had had the help of Eddie Peel who was his own age, but a woodsman born and bred to Illinois, who later told everyone: "He came up the cliff like an Injun and carrying that young'un like a feather." Will hoped he would see Eddie again. Lisette had called him a hero, too, saying he had scared off a pack of wolves. That exaggeration was quickly corrected, but like the whole incident, it was sweet to recall, amazingly sweet.

Will snuck out of the cabin and stood at *Ottawa*'s rail, looking down at the dock where she had tied up the night before. It was new, the wood still bright, but scarcely big enough to hold the steamer in place. *That's because* Ottawa *is in its first year of regular service,* he remembered. *They weren't really thinking of her and didn't build it big enough. How lucky we are to be here when everything is new but not so new that we had to tramp all the way from St. Louis. It's a lucky start!*

The pale blue sky was laced with white streaks and dotted with peach-tinted clouds. *Like embroidery in the sky,* thought Will, laughing out loud at this high-flown notion.

In the dark last night, a few ramshackle log cabins were just barely visible on the riverside, lit comfortingly from within by lanterns or firelight. This morning, things looked less romantic but far more promising. On the rise above the river stood a building or two, and just upriver, straddling the south shore and the island, was a mill of some sort. It was an imposing structure, built to make use of the waterpower of the rapids.

Something about the mill reminded Will of Berleburg, the ageless, pro-vincial town of their birth, built in circles within circles. The ancient palace on the hill was surrounded by a cluster of houses and these were surrounded by long, thin, medieval farm fields which were in turn surrounded by the dark green forests of the Red-Haired mountains. Berleburg lived in history; every cobblestone had a story; every turn hid ghosts. Will had been born in the same slate-roofed, half-timbered house as his father and grandfather.

Here in America, the Kästners were surrounded by forests and prairies and wolves and Indians, and they would not even have a place to lay their heads until they built it themselves. There were no massive stone blocks hewn by the Romans and ready to be hauled over and put to new use, no fields dug to a fine tilth with all the rocks stacked into fences by skilled hands long forgotten. There were no ancient grudges to dodge or ancient privileges that handed undeserved wealth to one family. Only one.

Suddenly, Will was ravenously hungry, so he stepped back inside the men's cabin and knocked his half-brother in the ribs.

Hans preferred "Hank" now that the family was on the rough new edge of America rather than in stuffy old Berleburg.

Hank rolled over, grunted, and reached out to swat his little brother. Will ducked and bumped into his sleeping father.

"I'm sorry, Papa," he said, patting the second growling form.

In a few steps, Will was out again and curious about this little town. *If,* he thought, *this becomes our new home, that will make us "Suckers"!*

After such a long time traveling, the entire family was ready in every sense to disembark. Hennepin, he recalled, was named for a French priest who had sailed by and maybe landed here long ago, with La Salle, great ex-plorer of the Mississippi River. *Surely,* Will thought, *we will not wind up in a place forever reminiscent of La Salle.*

Will stared at the big new mill, and in the coolness of dawn, his eye caught a movement, the blue of the sky brought down to Earth, a girl's dress! She was carrying something, swinging a bucket as she walked toward the mill. Her blonde braids caught the dawn light even from here, creating a sort of halo effect. As he watched, she transferred the bucket to her other hand, becoming nothing but that glorious hair and a gently swaying column of blue. He blinked and shook his head. *She looks like an angel.* He watched until she disappeared into the mill. It took all his restraint not to go right after her. Instead, he ran his hand through his own blond curls.

Little Jakob caught him around the knees, giving him a fierce morning hug, and his sister Amalie swept the little boy into her arms, kissed him, and took him back to the ladies' cabin to dress, tossing a greeting over her shoulder to Will: "Guten Morgan! Isn't it beautiful today?"

This was not a moment any Kästner wanted to waste. They threw on clothing and marched with something like abandon down *Ottawa*'s gangplank, Will glancing every other moment at the mill. Everyone in the family knew they might go on to Chicago, depending on what Niklas decided, but for the moment all seven of them were filled with delight to be on land again.

They walked past the few habitations on the waterfront, old log cabins with walls awry and clay chimneys aslant. As they climbed the embankment, they could hear axes and hammers and saws. On the rise, they saw a few genuine houses with fresh clapboard siding and shake roofs, homes enough for perhaps twelve families, and a main street of several buildings.

On the southeastern side of the great bend in the Illinois River lay a beautiful expanse of flatlands, bounded on the north and west by the river, and stretching out to the south as Hennepin Prairie. The first official deeds for land in Hennepin had been issued two years earlier, and a considerable number of lots had sold at prices varying from $11.68 to $87.86, but now, with canal enthusiasm spreading, many blocks had been laid out, surveyors' stakes dotting the village outskirts. No one guessed that most would be abandoned within a few years, the development of the town long delayed.

On this morning, though, several houses were in various stages of completion, being built balloon-style of timber framing and clapboard. The axes and saws and hammers they had heard were off to one side and not far away. They could just catch a welcoming scent of sawn pine, reminiscent of the forests around Berleburg.

This summer, land prices in Hennepin were rising in reaction to Chicago's real estate boom and the Internal Improvement Bill passed by the State of Illinois. It supported the Illinois-Michigan Canal, which would connect the Chicago River and Illinois River to create a cheap new way to float all the way from the eastern cities to New Orleans. It also provided money to dig the Hennepin Canal west to Rock Island as a direct path to the

Mississippi. When both canals went through, Hennepin was guaranteed to become one of the most important cities in Illinois, being a terminus of both and their connecting point.

Two squares in the town had been reserved as commons. One, Hanover Square, was to be used for a school, as yet unbuilt, and on the other, was a modest building that Oskar Miller would later tell them was a Methodist Episcopal Church, three years old, with a preacher who divided his time between Hennepin and Peoria.

Not far from the church was a jail, which, they would learn, was the second jail on that spot. The first had been a log structure 12'x12'x7' high, in which only one prisoner had ever been held, a man named Will Tallmadge, though it was hardly right to say "held," since Tallmadge had knocked out a log and escaped. The new jail cost $334 and promised to be much more secure.

The money for the new jail had come from the Internal Improvements Bill; it was the only improvement made with almost $10,000 Hennepin had received from the state. The rest had disappeared into the coffers of one Jeremiah Cotton, county treasurer, a man blissfully unaware of anything like fiduciary responsibility. He had been generous to his friends and himself.

The largest building in Hennepin in 1836 was the blockhouse. As the family walked by, a sentry dozing outside scrambled to his feet and came to something like attention, any military effect ruined by an early morning yawn. He might have seen Niklas's look of disapproval and heard Amalie giggle. Katrina saw her husband's frown and, eager to make friends rather than enemies, asked politely about the building.

"'Tis the blockhouse, ma'am," the sleepy young man told her, and seeing that he was expected to go on, he added, "Headquarters for the Putnam County Rangers during the Black Hawk War, you know, ma'am."

"This served as barracks, then?" asked Hank.

"Yessir, for the volunteer militia until General Scott came through with regulars. In those days, there was not a safe square foot of land north of the Illinois River. Just there across the river," he pointed, "the Arent cabin was attacked, and Elijah Phillips killed and scalped, whose own brother lives here in town still and has the tavern."

The Black Hawk War lasted less than a year and by the end of it, the Fox and Sac Indian tribes had been driven across the Mississippi. Now the land north of the Illinois River was safe and being settled, the sleepy soldier assured them, and he added, "When Black Hawk was paraded through New York and Boston and people heard his side of the story and how he came to bury the hatchet and was attacked instead, he became a hero, and his eldest son was made much of. He's a handsome sod, you have to admit." The young sentry, now thoroughly awake, cleared his throat and glanced around to be sure no one in Hennepin had heard him say that last part.

The family's first impression was of a new, orderly, little settlement. Clean. Fresh. New Orleans was many good things, but few would describe it as clean. The deep gutters along Orleanais streets were filled with fetid water, and its above-ground boneyards were better not even mentioned. The Kästners' hometown in Prussia, Berleburg, with its vast forests and mild climate, was meticulously clean, streets swept and windows hung with freshly washed curtains. It was a pleasure to see this new little frontier town being given similar attention.

CHAPTER 31

OSKAR MILLER

"Why did you come west?"

The Kästners stepped into the only inn in Hennepin to the very welcome scent of breakfast. Bacon and biscuits and potatoes frying with onions and parsley made them feel more at home than they had in a long time. Clean, whitewashed walls and a scrubbed pine floor greeted them.

"Mama, look," said Amalie. She had a pepper shaker in her hand, turned upside down. "Its mark says 'Prussia.'" A hand-painted salt cellar and a mustard pot matched the pepper shaker.

"Oh, lovely!" said Katrina.

The friendly proprietor of the boarding house where the Kästners breakfasted was Oskar Miller, who laughed as he told them he had come to Hennepin to trade in furs "before there was a Hennepin." In a blue linsey shirt with a belt and knife, Miller looked more like an American frontiersman than an innkeeper. Hans looked admiringly at the knife, a Bowie or Arkansas Toothpick, he could not tell which. Oskar Miller described the early days, working with Hubbard and Hartzell and Bourbouvis and Jean-Baptiste Beaubien of the American Fur Company, the first to build a trading post on the river.

"It's a rude log building, but warm and comfortable," Oskar said, "and still standing, near twenty years on."

"Such pioneers you were," said Katrina.

"I think you yourself would be considered a pioneer, ma'am."

Women, especially handsome women with daughters, were a rarity in Hennepin. Katrina had seen more men as they traveled north, and she was glad that Oskar Miller was married, so there was a woman in the inn.

The village had been laid out in twelve blocks in 1834, and sixteen blocks had since been added. Oskar Miller told them that he had been born in Bucks County, Pennsylvania, as had his wife, Ula, a tall woman who was slim, pretty, and friendly, with big blue eyes and an exceptionally expressive face. Katrina felt immediately that they would become friends. Ula was second-generation, her family displaced Swedes who emigrated through Hamburg in 1810, just in time for Ula to be born an American. Oskar's family had been here longer, coming from Switzerland when it was dangerous to have certain religious beliefs.

When he heard the Kästner hometown was Berleburg, he was amazed. Oskar said his family had sheltered in Berleburg on their way from Switzerland to the coast, taken in by the Pietists there. Their first purchase in America had been a Sauer Bible, also sometimes called the Berleburg Bible.

"In Pennsylvania," Oskar said, "my father knew the younger Christoph Sauer. Do you know the family?"

"Wasn't Christoph Sauer a cousin?" Katrina asked Niklas. "Distant, but still a cousin on your mother's side?"

Niklas's eyes narrowed ever so slightly, just enough that she regretted having mentioned it.

"Well," Niklas said, "they don't call it the Sauerland for nothing. In Berleburg you could hardly toss a stone in any direction without hitting a Sauer or at least the cousin of a Sauer."

"And knock him out, too," said Will, nonsensically.

Smiles lit the table, and then the discussion turned to other places and people. Katrina wanted to know more about Hennepin's early days.

"Gurdon Hubbard," said Oskar, "when he was a boy of sixteen, worked for Beaubein as a clerk. Beaubein was illiterate, you see. Tom Hartzell, who now has a fine store down the street, and Antonie Bourbouvis ran competing trading posts, but then they switched sides and signed on to the Astor's American Fur Company, and Beaubein's trading post folded. By then, Hubbard had his own trading post on the Illinois—at Crooked Creek, I believe, and now he's on the Iroquois River."

Niklas asked, "Are we correct that this town is named after the explorer who was a French priest?"

"Yes, indeed," said Oskar, "Father Louis Hennepin, of the Récollet order, who explored the Illinois and Mississippi Rivers with La Salle and then wrote memoirs."

"I believe he is thought to become more and more fanciful as he wrote," said Niklas tentatively.

"Oh, yes," said Oskar. "He even went so far as to claim that he, Hennepin, discovered the mouth of the Mississippi two years before La Salle! How did he expect people to believe that?"

"He got a little carried away with himself?" asked Will.

"Whatever the case," Oskar continued, "his name will no doubt survive everywhere. This is the happy fate of scribblers, to become better known than those who are more important. This particular place, our Hennepin, was named honestly, but whether the man actually set foot here or just pointed as he floated by, we don't know."

Hans asked, "Why did you come west?"

"For elbow room," Miller said with a grin, "And for the 'easy' life of a fur trader. The Illini had been pushed out by then, but you can still see what's left of their Big Village—the ruins of their longhouses—up the river across from where the Vermillion joins it. The Fox, Sac, Ho-Chunk, Potawatomie, and Dakota trapped a bunch of Illini up on a cliff there and put an end to the Illini. It's still called Starved Rock."

"Is the fur trade good here?" asked Hans.

"No, it's trapped out—all gone west," Oskar said. "Antonie Bourbouvis will leave soon. He says a man can still make a living in fur along the Missouri River."

"Are there buffalo here?" Will asked.

"We used to see gigantic herds, and maybe they roam north of the Illinois; there's a lot of empty land up there. But here there's a patch of prairie littered with the bones of buffalo, elk, and deer, the leavings of the Winter of the Deep Snow, 1830, sixty straight days of snow. The herds were trapped, and the Indians say their children will not go south of the river."

At this, Oskar coughed discreetly and made his move. Much as he liked these new arrivals, an innkeeper had work to do. Ula had long ago drifted away and was now wondering what was wrong with him, this being about as much talk as he had ever done at one time.

The long morning's conversation did not keep Oskar from pulling Niklas aside, inviting the older man to smoke a cheroot with him. "When I heard of your likely relation to Christoph Sauer, sir, I felt obliged to tell you of his sad end, or I should say the sad end of his press and his son."

Niklas looked at him inquiringly.

"Christoph Sauer, I mean the son, was a Tory in the Revolution," Oskar said. "He was a pacifist and besides, grateful to King George for the refuge he had given their sect. This made him a target of Revolutionary patriots, in particular Ben Franklin. The Continental Army arrested him, seized his press, threw him out of his home, and confiscated his property. He was stripped, coated in paint, and run out of town as a warning to other Tories. He was reduced to living in poverty and died at a nephew's house."

Niklas had heard all of this, of course. Christoph Sauer, his son, and grandsons were well known in Berleburg. The family had come from Schwarzenau, the village next to Berleburg. Many Germans had emigrated because of Sauer's early reports about Pennsylvania. His letters about the civil and religious liberty in Germantown had been printed and reprinted in Germany and, as he himself once wrote, had "provoked many a thousand people" to immigrate to the Pennsylvania colony. Sauer said America was where "One could live as a good Christian in solitude, as one pleased," and "earn his livelihood with abundance." But that was before the war.

Niklas had read many of those letters but had avoided Pennsylvania as the home of "Dunkers," radical German Baptists, Mennonites, and Amish, even though he agreed wholeheartedly with their antislavery sentiments. Christoph Sauer was the first man in America to publish antislavery tracts.

Privately, Niklas made two mental notes: even here in the land of liberty, it mattered whose side you were on. And Oskar and Ula Miller had moved away from Pennsylvania, a sure sign that they had wished to separate from the very conservative religious communities there. This was nothing more or less than he expected, and it was still a far cry from his own situation with the Prussian secret police having his name on their list, waiting for an excuse to murder or imprison him and its thugs waiting to seize Hans and Will for the King's army.

The most immediate happy result of their acquaintance with Oskar Miller was that he had a warehouse available for the Kästner trade goods. He also had three rooms for the family to let, and he said a store and a house could be built for the Kästners before the winter snows.

The Kästner family unloaded everything, attracting quite a crowd and selling many items right from the wharf; rice and sugar and molasses very welcome with winter not far away; ginger, cardamom, nutmeg, and cloves wanted for baking; and the newly fashionable Cuban cigars irresistible to many. Much of this was bartered, coins of any kind not common on the frontier, and it went for wheat flour, potatoes, apples, turnips, onions, carrots, hominy, pease meal, dried beans, a dry-cured ham, a small, precious sack of dried cherries, and a larger one of raisins to fill a Kästner root cellar not yet dug. Young men with no goods to trade offered to hire on as labor, starting with cutting down trees for a house.

In Ula's kitchen, the women exchanged the fruits of the fields and woods, corn and beans and cornmeal, oats and chestnuts, for Cuban sugar and tea and coffee, Texan pecans and New Orleans' rice, tobacco, and the last of the pralines. Ula threw in some sourdough starter and was glad to have some of Katrina's European saleratus in return.

"This is what I need for biscuits," said Ula. "Men can hardly ever get enough buttermilk biscuits."

"Where do you get the buttermilk?" asked Katrina. Ula had her own cows, and she promised to supply the Kästners until they could buy their own. The two women worked in silence for a good while until the quietness of the kitchen made Katrina ask, "You have no children yet?"

"Nor do I expect to," Ula answered with unusual forthrightness. "Oskar and I have been married for seven years, long enough. I suppose it might still happen, stranger things have, but by now, it would be quite a surprise."

"Or maybe a child will come about another way," said Katrina, and told Ula about having married Niklas when Hans was already a seven-year-old. "There are often stray children in need of a mother."

Niklas made a list of the foodstuffs they had traded for and observed that they would need meat, at least a hog butchered before winter. Still, they had made a propitious start to shopkeeping in the New World and to setting up housekeeping. In fact, they had already sold as much in a month's time at the various stops up the river as they would have in a year in Berleburg.

"This is the true 'streets paved with gold,'" he told Will. "We can make twice or ten times as much as in the Old Country."

Will nodded with enthusiasm. None of this was lost on him. Becoming a rich American by finding such opportunities occupied his mind almost as much as meeting the girl in blue. He had come to think of her as the Angel of the Mill.

New people were arriving in Hennepin all the time. Some dreamt of making a fortune in fur or corn or hogs, but most just wanted ten or twenty or forty acres to farm. Some were already busy filling the chinks in new log cabins and applying whitewash or transforming a cabin into a comfortable lap-sided house.

Oskar said, "Coming west is just about the best way to escape any sort of trouble. Which means you should keep one hand on your purse when you meet someone newly arrived. Most are fine, but there can be liars, sneaks, and horse thieves among 'em."

Niklas's eyebrows rose, and Oskar's tone softened. "Some states, like Kentucky, make a mess of land records, so folks get cheated out of land they homesteaded. And then, consider that if you sell ten or twenty acres in Pennsylvania, you can buy eighty acres here."

One newly arrived family was made up of twelve Yankees from Connecticut, parents and ten healthy children, each a half a head taller than the next. They had come across on the Great Lakes steamers. Another family had come on foot from Kentucky, losing a mother and child on the way. Another had emigrated from France, landed in Baltimore, sailed coastwise to New Orleans, and come north. On the outskirts, past the pincushion of surveyors' stakes, were men camped in ragged wagons, Mormons scouts who had traipsed west from Kirkland, Ohio, to investigate the cheap land between the Illinois River and the Mississippi. Others had come up from New Orleans on their way to Chicago, hoping to profit from the promise of the Illinois-Michigan Canal, named for the river and lake, not the states.

Niklas now had substantial goods safely stored in Oskar Miller's warehouse, and he was sure that if he took *Ottawa* south this fall, he could bring more sugar and rice and calico north and sell it all before Christmas. That evening, when he did a reckoning of his books, he was amazed at how very well it had gone already. *At this rate, I will soon be ten times as wealthy,* he thought to himself, although just then some dusty saying about chickens and eggs and counting and hatching floated through his mind, not quite clearly enough to shape itself into words.

CHAPTER 31

THE TWISTER

"Schauen Sie nicht," he said to Katrina, "Don't look."

The Kästners settled comfortably into Hennepin, exploring the clean, new-built riverside town, the vast prairies to the southeast, the limestone bluffs along the river's edge, and the picturesque hills and dark forests on the far side of the Illinois. The view to the north so recalled stretches of the Rhine that Niklas and Katrina sometimes spent the last hour of light watching the last golden rays of sunlight slant across the pine and spruce trees on the north shore.

"There," Niklas said, "are gentle, south-facing hills just asking to be cleared for a vineyard."

On one long, long summer's evening, they had gone southeast to see the infant village of Florid, where a promising schoolhouse was being built of brick. It was surrounded by open prairies dotted with grazing cows and horses. Niklas pointed to a black blur moving south across the prairie.

"Hogs," he told Katrina. "Razorbacks. Everything's free range here, hogs, cattle, and horses. The prairie grass is free."

"We'll need to fence in our garden and our fields of corn and wheat."

"Yes," he said, pointing to a farm. "With wood scarce, they dig ditches or plant hedges—Osage orange—to keep the animals out."

"Which take a while to grow," she answered.

As Niklas and Katrina rode back toward town, a sudden shower engulfed them and passed quickly to the east. The sun came back out again, and in the east a rainbow formed, the entire arc visible from end to end on this flat prairie.

"See there—we could easily find the pot of gold," Katrina said.

Niklas laughed. "Look! A second rainbow is forming." In the soft evening light, the battle scars on his face faded, and he looked as young as ever Katrina had seen him.

They reined in and turned to watch this glory develop in the sky, side by side, so close that Niklas reached out and took Katrina's hand.

"Tomorrow to fresh woods and pastures new," he said happily as they stayed to watch the double rainbow glow and fade until fireflies twinkled all across the prairie, and it was really darker than two sensible people should have been out.

A few days later they were again out on the open prairie, searching for Niklas's carefully imagined Eden. He was sure that with all this untamed land, he could find a place to settle so naturally advantageous that it would give his family and his heirs important and long-lasting benefits.

The natural advantages he was looking for began with very gently rolling hillsides, neither steep enough to wash off in heavy rain nor flat enough to puddle and drown a crop. Grape-growing hillsides, south-facing, what an advantage to be there first and claim such a sweet spot! He would test the soil and choose what was rich and deep and friable. He had lashed an iron spade to his saddle and was using it this afternoon, determined to find topsoil that had lain fallow for years, not rocky or overused or worn thin. Now he found that lying fallow was not the half of it. These were virgin soils that had never been cut or farmed, black with richness. He had never seen anything like it. Out on the prairie, grasses stood six to eight feet tall, and he guessed correctly that their roots were equally long and dense. When he tried to put a spade to it, he found it was very hard work to displace these intertwined roots, and in spite of the potential reward of the prairie, he and Katrina thought it wiser to stay close to the woods, where the soil, though it was thinner, was plenty deep enough, easier to turn, and just as virgin.

Besides, timber was essential for building and heating a house. These basics of choosing a site were overlooked by many immigrants, who often settled wherever they became too exhausted to walk another mile. Niklas heard about a family who had made a disastrous choice when he talked with a Yankee who had crossed Ohio's Great Black Swamp.

The Yankee said the swamp was an oozing mass of water and mud almost the size of Connecticut and filled with snakes, wolves, wildcats, biting flies, and clouds of gnats and mosquitoes. Water and muck, often up to the belly of a horse, filled the surface until it froze in winter or evaporated in the hot summer months. Much of the swamp was a thick forest of giant oak, sycamore, hickory, walnut, ash, elm, maple and cottonwood, except where water rotted the trees or limestone bedrock rose up and would not support timber. There, scrawny fields of grasses had taken root.

Not even Indians went into the swamp except to hunt, and unless you could follow a blazed trail, it was easy to become hopelessly lost. In these awful conditions, the Yankee felt blessed to find a house for refuge one night. It was owned by a family who got partway through and refused to take a single step more. They settled in this morass, housing travelers and when that trade got thin, putting up a chain across the only dry path and charging travelers a fee to cross. Worst of all, the place was cursed with malaria, its fevers and chills so severe that victims shook violently, rattling the beds and floorboards. This was so common that these people kept quinine powder on the table to sprinkle along with salt and pepper. The story of the swamp people only steeled Niklas's determination to take his time and choose their new American home wisely.

So intently were Niklas and Katrina talking that they were surprised when they heard thunder and shocked to see a nasty storm brewing in the west, thick clouds with ragged edges roiling fiercely. It came on quickly, and they took refuge by a creek that zigzagged across the prairie. It was a slightly lower area with big trees for shelter. They dismounted and tied their horses tightly to the leeward side of the trees, the two animals snorting and rearing. Katrina stood at the head of her horse, trying to soothe the animal. The sky took on sickening shades of violet and green with huge, fast-moving clouds illuminated with lightning and fringed with curlicues dipping down and being sucked back up into the clouds.

"Ach mein Gott!" said Niklas, as a funnel cloud formed in the sky. The air had suddenly turned cold, and moments later they were lashed with hail as they crouched together behind the horses. A roaring rain began, and then the roaring became louder than rain, louder than anything either had ever heard. The funnel cloud now touched the ground, kicking up a wide cuff of debris. It crossed a distant creek and tossed trees about like toothpicks.

The roaring became impossibly loud, leaving them unable to do anything but cling to each other, cover their heads, and pray. And then, as quickly as it had come, they heard the roaring move off beyond them, and in a few minutes, they dared to look about. Their faces and arms had been lashed by flying debris and their hair was littered with straw and twigs. The temperature had dropped precipitously, and both were soaked to the skin.

One of the horses had been slashed open by the fall of a splintered tree branch and lay dying in desperate agony, breathing hard, the blood pouring from it, it having sunk to its knees, its head pulled up by the reins still tied to the tree. Niklas circled it, studied the wound and pulled out his pistol.

"Schauen Sie nicht," he said to Katrina, "Don't look," as he shot the poor animal in the head. The other horse jerked back at the sound, its eyes white with terror. Niklas mounted and pulled a shivering Katrina up behind him. They were not sure whether to expect another blast of the storm, but it was time to get out of the creek bed. It was rapidly filling with water.

"See this," Katrina said, pointing out the windward side of the tree they had sheltered beneath. It was a pincushion of projectiles. Katrina touched one. "It is just a straw; see how it bends. Yet it went into the tree like a nail."

They rode a short way to the center of the pathway that the storm had plowed across the prairie. The trees there had been blasted, stumps three feet high, whittled down as if by the hand of some vengeful god. On either side, mature trees perhaps ninety feet in height had been twisted and stripped bare of leaves, and next to them were other trees that looked almost untouched.

Niklas turned the horse's head toward Hennepin, and the couple rode in silence. They knew they might have come so far only to die on this godforsaken prairie, leaving their children to find their own way alone in this wide open, new country, and not even to be buried in the churchyard in Berleburg with the two children they had lost. Katrina felt the familiar, painful sparks of grief run across her chest as she thought of her two lost boys, two beautiful boys who would never see America, and when tears ran down her cheeks, they were not for herself or Niklas.

Later, when they talked with Oskar Miller, he called it a twister and said he thought it appeared more often and with greater ferocity than in Europe. It was one of the terrors of this part of the world.

If they were ever again to see the black clouds of a storm turn greenish and curling wisps form at the bottom edges and a howl arise of unspeakable noise, they were to lie flat on the ground. And their home should have a root cellar large enough for all to squeeze into if need be.

"A twister is violent," Oskar said, "but it lasts only a few minutes and can pick up your house and leave your neighbor's untouched."

"Like a hurricane," said Niklas.

"Not really," said Oscar. "A twister is horrible, but smaller. Most people live their entire lives without being hurt by one."

Later, Will, Izak, and Hans rode out to find the dead horse. They retrieved the saddle and made ready to haul the horse back for butchering. The three young men looked around at the flat, peaceful landscape and the crooked little creek bed that had been Katrina and Niklas's refuge. They could not help but scan the sky, now as blue and beautiful as if the storm had never been.

CHAPTER 33

ONE LITTLE GARNET

gone for good

"Your mother and I," began Niklas, and already he saw Hans' distracted look and Will's polite boredom. "Your mother and I," he began again, "have decided to go on to Chicago alone. Hans-Jürgen...I mean Hank...and Will will build a house for the family in our absence, and Amalie will cook. Lisette will help her and look after Jakob."

Now the boys were wide awake and listening.

"We may decide to settle the family in Chicago, but even if we do, I expect that we will return here for the winter. A house here will be easily sold. Boys, we have purchased a lot, and I have drawn a plan for the house."

Katrina had been with Niklas when he bought the lot, and she noted the care with which he was "sounding American." She had seen him sign his name, "Nicholas Costner." It was not subterfuge, but what so many immigrants did to adapt and what Niklas was especially glad to do. Niklas had been called "Claus" as a child, had been reborn in the army as Niklas, and now he would be reborn in his new country, a man free of his past and happily settled into a new life and a new name. He would not put his German name on any document in this new country, and when he became, five years later, the first naturalized citizen of Bureau County, it was as Nicholas Costner. Their melting into America would be complete.

Now Niklas explained how the boys were to throw up a log cabin first and escape the rates Oskar Miller was charging. Thankful as the family was for Oskar and Ula, it was still a hotel: six cents per night per person. The boys would build a proper timber frame house next, turn the log cabin into a barn. Building a henhouse and digging a root cellar were the first orders of business, more urgent even than the log cabin and to be started tomorrow on their new lot.

Niklas and Katrina had tested the ground when they bought, digging deeply. Both were amazed at the rich, friable loam, as black as either of them had ever seen, no clay, no stones larger than pebbles. The soil in Berleburg required generations of labor to clear and make friable.

The seller told them it went three feet deep here and as much as six feet on the prairie south of town. "This is such soil as has never been seen before," he told them. Gottfried Duden had written about the high quality of America's soil, but this amazed them. It went beyond all their expectations.

In an aside to Katrina, Niklas said, "'Tis 'too fabulous to be believed.'" He was quoting Gottfried Duden, whose book they had read aloud, taking turns by the firelight in their Berleburg home, a house that had been occupied by generations of Kästners and was now lost to them for this chance at safety and wealth in America. They shared a conspiratorial smile.

Katrina had returned later the same day with what remained of her roots and tubers and starts. Some had rotted on the way despite her precautions, but now she sorted through the rest, digging them into the turned-over patch where they had tested the soil: asparagus, onions, chives, leeks, grapes, tarragon, sage, lovage, tansy, horseradish, and rhubarb. Each plant would be separated and moved into position later, but at last these precious remnants of Germany had a new home and could begin to grow what they, like all of the family, really needed: new roots.

Niklas paused expectantly, and the many questions his children suddenly had for him began tumbling out. The sun had moved a goodly distance along its track before the family finished its discussion, and at that point, Niklas and the boys left for the sawmill at the river's edge, a substantial modern affair hovering over the Hennepin Rapids. The Kästners had logs they had bartered for, and they would harvest more—Hank already had some cut and waiting at Herr Guttmann's mill. Now that they had a plan, they could order beams and lapboards and shingles and have floorboards cut and planed.

Before their last night at Hennepin, Izak made arrangements to wait upon Niklas and Katrina, prepared, Niklas thought, to make his goodbyes at last. Niklas had come to like and admire the big young Dane, and he would be forever thankful for Izak's bringing them across safely and especially for his intervention on the stone quays of Gibraltar, where he helped to save Hans. Izak was not a landsman; even Niklas could see that he needed to make his way on the sea, but all of the family would be sad to see him go.

Ula served up a sumptuous supper of roast pork, heaps of roughly mashed potatoes, green beans in thyme-scented cream, sliced tomatoes of a sweet red and yellow kind she called "Rainbow," and burnt sugar cake. It was the best American country fare, and its excellence did not go unremarked.

"Aw," said Ula, when they sang her praises, "It ain't as good as you'd make for yourselves, but I guess it's worth eating."

Talk and hilarity spun around the table, picked up from one of them to the other and tossed like a bouncing ball. Even Hans wore a broad grin. Here they were, with solid ground beneath their feet, health glowing in every face, freedom and prosperity in the wings, and plenty of food on the table.

Thus, just when all seemed perfectly settled and full of promise, it was a shock or at least a considerable surprise for Niklas to receive Izak's request for Amalie's hand. A murmur of excitement went around the table at Izak's words, and all eyes turned to Niklas to see how he would react. He, in turn, looked searchingly at Katrina, whose secret smile told him all he needed to know. And when he had given his assent and Amalie rushed to embrace him, he knew the lovers (the word stuck in his throat) had had it all planned and needed only his agreement.

Very gently, Izak pressed a small, beautifully made wooden box into Amalie's hands; it was obvious that she knew what was inside, as she turned to her parents, opened it and showed them a lovely gold chain with a pendant centered on one small garnet. "This is Izak's pledge to me," she said.

Then Niklas heard the details: Izak was committed to return to New Orleans and carry the ship's owner, Thomas Segrave, to Liverpool aboard *Enigma* before winter closed in. He would go thence to Copenhagen to pick up his son and to settle certain financial affairs.

"Naught but happy affairs," Izak assured a frowning Niklas, the man who would become his father-in-law. "I have prize money and not just from the pirate ship we defeated together. Every successful action in which I have engaged has made me a richer man than ever I had expected to become."

He went on to explain about his first marriage, his son Lars, and the house he owned in Copenhagen. He would be back in the spring or summer for Amalie, he said, sailing *Enigma* or his own ship, God willing, and bringing along Lars, now five or so, about the same age as little Jakob.

Hans bowed his head to hide a look of envy. Here was a man nearly his own age who had experienced and accomplished so much, a sea captain, a father, a rich man, now choosing a second wife. He knew Izak had not had an easy life, having seen his father killed and having survived a short but horrific enslavement by Barbary pirates. Hans grew even more determined to test his mettle against the challenges of the wild Northwest Territories. He steeled himself for the announcement he would soon make.

"So much will be different by the time I return," Izak said. "Hennepin will be a thriving city. Chicago will have drained its swamps and its new canal will link New Orleans to the cities of the East."

Izak planned his return trip via New York, the Erie Canal and steamers across the Great Lakes. "It will be much quicker," he said, and here his eyes flickered to Amalie, her head modestly bowed, but a smile showing. "Maybe the Illinois-Michigan canal will be dug by then," he said, "and I will arrive at your doorstep by water!"

Will looked down, hiding his disbelief. Izak did not miss this polite movement.

"The ocean is impartial," he said with a smile. "It will carry anyone anywhere, and so will the rivers and the 'sweet oceans' on whose shores we are at rest now. But of course, no journey can be guaranteed."

Katrina had prepared letters to her beloved cousin Elizabet, remembering to add dates at the last moment, and wrapped in oilskin for Izak to carry with him. He would post them in Copenhagen, where no Kästner lived or could be traced to.

Niklas looked wonderingly at the bloom on Amalie's cheek, at the willowy figure that had taken shape so recently, and at her shy, happy smile. *These things happen, but so soon! And to my most sensible of children.* Surveying the table, he was annoyed to think that everyone else seemed to have known or guessed the couple's intentions.

As his eyes rested on Hans, the young man rose to toast the now-engaged couple, and when the cheers died down, Hans followed his toast with an announcement of his own:

"In the spring or perhaps yet this fall, Antonie Bourbouvis, the fur trader, will leave for the upper Missouri and a new trading post there. He has asked me to go with him, and I have agreed."

Katrina gasped to hear this. They were already so far west! Hans glanced over and gave her a guilty smile; it faded as he saw his father next to her, his jaw clenched.

"I can serve as a clerk," Hans said, struggling to regain himself. "Most trappers are illiterate, as Bourbouvis himself is, and in return for clerking, he will teach me to trap beaver and hunt buffalo. He might want to make the trip yet this fall, or at least the stretch down to St. Louie. *Yellow Stone* will go up the Missouri as soon as the ice breaks in February or March."

"Fur trading here is done for," Hans told them, "but it is still lucrative further west." All this would be so if his parents had no objection, Hans said, bowing in their direction.

Niklas looked grim, but he returned a gracious nod. He was fully aware that by law, sons owed their wages to their father only until they were twenty-one. Hans, at twenty-five, had been generous in his support for his birth family, and now he would continue being dutiful by making sure they were snug in a new house before he left. Niklas had no cause for complaint, but he was not at all happy.

For Niklas and Katrina, it was a stunning evening. She added a note to Elizabet about Hans's decision, obscuring his real destination and avoiding the American name he had chosen, for he would surely go west as Hank Costner.

Later, in private, Katrina told Niklas that Izak did not take fifteen-year-old Amalie with him because he did not think it would be fair. He thought she deserved time for a bit of life on her own before she married, which was a nice way of saying she deserved to live a while without risking an early death in childbirth. This, more than anything else, made Katrina sure that Izak would make a fine husband. Sailors as a class did: often gone and handy about the house when at home. "Did you, Niklas, truly not suspect a thing?"

He said that he had not.

Katrina changed the subject to Hans and worried aloud about him. "We must support his decision," she said, "but what do you think?"

"He needs to break free," Niklas said. "Young men must try themselves against the world, and if they are lucky, they survive the error of their ways, recover from their many follies, and live to become old men."

"Will you talk to him?"

"Of course I will," he said, "but I might as well give advice to a stone." As he drifted off to sleep, the thought that rang through Niklas's head was, *How can he do this to me?*

In the middle of the night, Niklas woke with that thought still ringing in his ears, but he also remembered with what joy and carelessness he himself had ridden off with the French cavalry all those years ago. Now, here in far-off Hennepin, Illinois, he clasped his hands and asked his mother and father in heaven to forgive the callousness of his youth.

The next morning the entire family gathered to wave Izak Peterssen bon voyage. At dockside, the rest of the family turned their attention discretely away for a few moments to give the young couple a chance for a few last words to each other—all turned away except Lisette and Jakob, who were busy making kissy faces and kissy sounds until Will cuffed them.

A thunderstorm had passed by in the pre-dawn, and its clouds now darkened the eastern sky and left the air misty and the gangplank slippery, but this was nothing to Izak or to *Ottawa*, soon steaming southwest to St. Louis. Amalie waved a white lace handkerchief until he and the sturdy little steamer disappeared into the mist. She touched the little garnet on a gold chain around her neck and prayed for his journey to be safe, fast, and successful in every way.

As they turned to walk up the hill, Amalie took her mother's arm, glad to have someone to hold onto as she blinked away her tears. *Without him,* she thought, *I am a child again*—and suddenly her mind was flooded with the memory of the hurricane and that awful moment when *Enigma* broached and they all thought they were dead and gone for good. *This is not a disaster,* she scolded herself. She straightened up and repeated it to herself: *This is not a disaster.*

BOOK THREE

HOMESTEADING

*"The greatest fine art of the future will be the making of a
comfortable living from a small piece of land."*
—Abraham Lincoln

CHAPTER 34

THE GARDEN OF A GIANT

"We were once young, too."

"What exactly did he say to you?" Niklas looked out across the pretty waters and passing shoreline of the Illinois River as he and Katrina floated upriver. He was still annoyed that everyone in the family seemed to know about Amalie and Izak except he himself.

The river was pleasantly cool this hot September day, and equally pleasant was the prospect of buying and selling properties in the boomtown of Chicago. Besides, Niklas did not object to leaving the hard work of building to his children. He and Katrina were to go seventeen miles upriver to the mouth of the Vermillion, where that river's influx of water made the Illinois deep enough to float a steamboat. Beyond that, it would be a matter of taking stagecoaches to Chicago.

Unencumbered as they were, with nothing more than a carpetbag, nor trunks, nor trade goods, nor children in tow, they had hitched a ride on a keelboat, little more than a raft with a wigwam attached, to take them to the limits of the river's navigability, another precious day of floating serenely before the rough trip overland began at the village of Peru. Niklas smiled in spite of himself, happy to be aboard again, even for such a brief time.

"Izak is a young widower," Katrina said, "as you once were, having lost his wife and one of the twins she bore. The surviving twin is a boy a few months older than Jakob. He lives with Izak's sister and her family in Copenhagen."

"She will be a very young mother to that child, before she has any of her own."

"As was I," Katrina reminded him. "Hans was about that age when we married. I know he thinks of me as his mama."

"And the language difference!"

Katrina looked sideways at her husband. *Of all the people to think language a barrier to love!* "Izak," she said, "did not like leaving Amalie, but he thought it wiser—and kinder—than taking her along. I think they are very much in love."

"But she is so young!"

"We were once young, too," Katrina said gently. "Amalie's youth is exactly his concern. He thinks to settle her in one of America's port cities, but that will take her away from us. Besides, it requires selling his house and settling other business in Copenhagen and bringing the child back with him. At least he did not whisk her away to live in Copenhagen!"

This much Niklas knew, as Izak had assured him that Amalie would not be poor or swept back to Europe.

"Oh, my," said Katrina, "This child, if he becomes Amalie's, will be our grandchild! We could become grandparents next year, and to a child as old as our little Jakob." She could not quite imagine their being called "Oma" and "Opa," but she shook her head and continued, "Taking this year's trip by himself will give Amalie a year, more or less, to mature and prepare."

"Not many engaged men would be so scrupulous."

Katrina nodded. "He does it out of love, I believe." She did not try to explain to Niklas what she saw in Izak's face: guilt that his impatience to wed had brought his first wife to childbed and death at so young an age. He wanted to assure Amalie a longer life, as much as he could, even though it meant being without her for a time.

"But what about his livelihood as a sea captain?"

"He does not expect to change his living. Thomas Segrave waits for him in New Orleans with *Enigma*. Amalie says Izak has talked about living in New Orleans, planning to be at sea during the plaguey summers or to send Amalie north to us then." *How,* she thought, *will I do without her? Especially....*

"New Orleans! I don't like the sound of that."

"It's closer than Boston or New York, and with his trade at sea they won't have to engage in the slave trade."

"Perhaps." Niklas was coming around, she could tell.

"Or maybe they will settle in New York. I don't understand the route, but the new Erie Canal has made it much shorter. He will come back to us that way, so he will know more then."

"They might feel more at home in French New Orleans than English New York," said Niklas, and Katrina was quick to agree.

That night in Peru's White Horse Inn, they enjoyed a degree of privacy that might have made them lonely had they not been so occupied with learning one another's deepest thoughts on the several momentous changes before them: Amalie's future happiness, Hans's adventures (they were determined to begin thinking of him as "Hank"), Will's new position as apprentice to Augustus Guttmann, owner of the sawmill, and his instantaneous love for Herr Guttmann's lovely daughter, Dora.

"At least," said Niklas, "this one…"

"Dora," said Katrina.

"This Dora is German."

Will seemed to adore the opposite sex, and they found him irresistible, too. He had been sorry to leave his little Sophie behind in Berleburg, had fallen deeply in love with Ezmeralda in Cuba, and toyed with the idea of their landlady's daughter in New Orleans. In Illinoistown, an immediate, mutual attraction with Lottie, the daughter of the shopkeeper, resulted in a most advantageous trade deal.

Niklas and Katrina turned from talk of the children to discuss the best town for their future home, whether (and how much) to invest in Chicago property, the house being built for them in Hennepin by their boys, and many other interesting topics. They talked later into the night than long-married people usually do, accompanied by the song of cicada with bullfrogs on the river adding a bass note.

Much later, in the pink glow of dawn, warm under a stranger's comfortable quilt, Katrina allowed herself to loll happily between sleep and wakefulness, aware of a near-miraculous dearth of immediate obligation: no children to tend, no breakfast to cook, no animals to feed, no garden to weed, no house to clean. And to top off her happiness, a day for something new.

It was later still when the two of them lounged together on the rustic porch, admiring the long prairie view, warming their hands around steaming cups of coffee, and feeling their youth restored.

Presently a freckle-faced girl appeared at the doorway, announcing, "Victuals, they is on!" with a jerk of her head toward the tables within.

There they found eggs scrambled with onions and poke salat, fried pork rinds, and pancakes topped with fresh butter and rhubarb sauce. They were speaking of their hopes for Chicago and of their joy in the voyage already accomplished when Niklas's face clouded.

"Trina," he said, "I do worry about Addie's family."

"Oh, so do I!" she exclaimed.

"With all our good fortune, what say you to sending back fare for their boy, Edzard? Günter always thought the boy a likely one."

"It's an excellent idea," she agreed, "although we might ask Addie to name which boy. Edzard is something of a scholar; he may not be adventurous." She paused and thought. "It's a lot to ask of a young boy to travel alone. Maybe Elizabet would come at the same time. Oh, joy if we should have her here!"

A few moments later Katrina laid her hand on Niklas's arm and looked at him seriously: "Do you think the Erlingers might blame you for poor Günter's death?"

He looked down, studying the wide pine planks of the floor, noticing a gap that should be caulked. It had long ago occurred to him: Günter might not have been the murderers' target but a case of mistaken identity. Even if the Erlingers had not thought of this, would they blame him for involving Günter? He was not even sure whether the letter he sent from Gibraltar surreptitiously had ever reached Addie, and if it had, whether the judge had believed it or torn it up. If she never received it, she could rightly think he had deserted the Erlinger family.

"I think it's impossible to know."

"If they did," Katrina said slowly, "we might be bringing a viper into the nest—it's a horrible thought."

"It is indeed. Let's think on this."

Breakfast finished, they set off at a quick pace for the stagecoach now running three times a week from Ottawa to Chicago, a big improvement from last year's once-a-week coach. Run by Frink and Walker, it was a Concord, also a big improvement, they were told—and no doubt it was true: Concords had springs! But it still meant long hours of jolting along, with eight passengers cheek-by-jowl inside and another six on top. This would carry them seventy miserable miles to Chicago along what was variously called "The Ottawa Road" or "The Canal Road," though the canal itself was little more than an investor's dream.

Niklas decided to err on the side of optimism and call the route they bounced along "The Canal Road." Their Concord coach was able to make a steady eight miles an hour on the flats, but as soon as they encountered any grade at all, the team dropped to a walk, making only a miserable four or five miles an hour, at which point most of the passengers hopped off and walked for a while. The exercise felt good, and it helped the horses out. Much of the afternoon, the coach took a ridge across the Sauganash Slough until Mount Juliet appeared. They overnighted there, where the tiny village was distinguished by a huge Indian mound, the "mountain" in its name, and a few log cabins, one of which was a sometimes-inn that fed travelers the customary bacon and beans, black coffee, and hot whiskey. What the area lacked in amenities it made up for in frontier humor, since the next village up the river had been named Romeo.

An unusually hard overnight rain had cleared the air to a degree of freshness that cheered all but the most recalcitrant passengers, but it also produced a quagmire of clayey mud and required both determination and strategy to pick one's way from inn to stagecoach. Once out of the stable's muddy yard, the stagecoach descended an almost imperceptible slope onto a ridge through what was called a "wet prairie" by one of their fellow passengers. Mr. Lemuel Drake, a Peoria merchant with thinning hair and a rather unfortunately large nose, said he came this way often. The wet prairie was a long, flooded area through which the horses' hooves splashed and splashed. Neither Katrina nor Niklas was at all happy to be on such a strange and invisible "road." Off to one side, or sometimes both, they saw ominous signs posted: "No Bottom."

Lemuel Drake said, "This wet prairie would have been eight or nine miles in April or May; we are lucky now 'tis half of that, even with last night's rain."

Presently, the team pulled the stagecoach onto a ridge of drier land where the horses' hooves kicked up thick clods of mud, and soon it was drier yet. The stagecoach could run along with greater speed, the trace chains jingling. Away to the south, unbroken prairie stretched to the horizon, its waving grasses mingled with a rich profusion of wildflowers. Niklas and Katrina marveled at the broad swaths of brilliant purple ironweed, orange coneflowers, and yellow sunflowers. All were tall enough to match the grass in height or nod above it.

"It looks like the garden of a giant," Katrina murmured.

"Yes, or ocean waves with plumes of multicolored foam," said Niklas. "Look how the grasses sway."

For some time, they proceeded as fast as six horses could draw them until a cacophony of warnings arose from the men on top, and the stagecoach came to a sudden halt, horses whinnying, and passengers thrown into each other. A cottonwood tree had fallen across the road. The passengers on top were called down to assist, and those inside disembarked to stretch their legs, lighten the load, and watch the brave attempt.

Niklas, who was pleased to appear too old or too wealthy to enlist, stood by Katrina on the grassy verge of the road as the men heaved and heaved and at last succeeded in shifting the huge tree trunk to one side, its drying leaves rustling like water as it rolled down a small embankment. The stagecoach was drawn gingerly over the deep rut left by the fallen tree, and the passengers walked forward to where the stagecoach stood waiting for them. Niklas leapt the gap and reached back for Katrina's hand, pulling hard to bring her flying across.

Presently they reached the Vincennes Trail and turned north toward town. One of the passengers knocked on the carriage roof and called out to the driver. "Ain't this called Hubbard's Trace?"

Lemuel Drake nodded solemnly. "It goes by both names. Hubbard's Trace was originally a buffalo path—that's what 'trace' means. Ain't it something to imagine—enormous herds trampling it twenty feet across—maybe more—moving en masse to winter or summer pastures and unstoppable. Naturally, the Indians used the trace, too, why wouldn't they, a cleared and packed pathway through the grasses and timber, and even now it's the easiest way to the shores of Lake Michigan."

Gurdon Hubbard had used it for years, Drake said, taking wagons all the way south to Louisville and coming back through Wabash Country carrying corn, hay, and hogs in distinctive wagons called Hoosiers, which after some time became the name for the drivers, too—"Hoosiers acomin'!" Sure enough, their stagecoach soon passed a train of five heavy wagons lumbering along, eight oxen pulling each wagon and at the lead ox, a man. Some men walked, and some were on horses with reins lined with tinkling bells, men in old-fashioned, broad-brimmed wool hats and gray coats, looking to Katrina very much like European peasantry.

The Hoosiers originally came to supply the soldiers at Fort Dearborn, who needed more food than the gardens and hunting parties of that rather small log stockade provided.

"The fort was built on one of the ancient sand ridges," Lemuel Drake said, "built twice—did you know it was burnt to the ground in 1812 by the Potawatomis—everyone killed?"

Niklas and Katrina shook their heads in unison.

"Well, anyway," he said, "you can't miss it. Sits up high, is whitewashed. The garrison lives there, and City Hall used to meet there, but last month it moved to the new Saloon Building at Clarke and Lake Streets."

After a long time on the Vincennes Trail, the stagecoach turned onto an old Indian trail known as the Road to Widow Brown's, which would much later become Archer Avenue. Houses were still scattered, built upon stilts or little rises that afforded dry feet. Now they began to see gatherings of covered wagons with horses hobbled or tied alongside and campfires with women cooking. These migrants from Europe or Ohio or Indiana or the former colonies lived in their wagons as they re-provisioned.

"They are headed to Iowa Territory or north to Wisconsin Territory or southwest into Missouri," said Lemuel Drake. He told of coming into Chicago in March unable to find any place to lay his head: "One innkeeper told me he already had people sleeping three deep, and another said he did not even have a hook to hang me on! People are flooding in. The last two years, the Sauganash's been selling meals and blankets in shifts, and it ain't the only place."

Drake began ticking them off: "There's Caldwell's Tavern (built by James Kinzie), the Miller House, and Mark Beaubien's, which he calls the Sauganash Hotel, since he put a frame addition on the original logs." The Tremont House had gone up in 1831 and just this year, the Lake House.

"Oh, it's elegant," Drake told them, "a brick building three floors high." Here he lowered his voice, as if there were people leaning in to listen: "heerd it cost 'em ninety thousand dollar."

The building boom, with no end in sight, ended three decades of Chicago's being little more than Fort Dearborn and a dozen cabins, that being an improvement from the earliest years when Jean Baptiste Pointe du Sable's cabin, barn, and outbuildings were the only structures. They served as trading post, inn, and family home all at once.

CHAPTER 35

OH, TO BE SO YOUNG AND SO RICH

"as motley a collection as you'd ever seen"

Adam Schwartz was a truly rich man at age twenty-six. He was back in Chicago having supper at the Wentworth Hotel when he heard the musical sound of German at the next table, and after craning his neck to hear it, shamelessly eavesdropped. Surmising that the speakers were in Chicago to invest, he introduced himself to Niklas and Katrina Kästner.

They listened to the history of this handsome, black-haired youth with interest and concern, having bought several lots earlier that very morning. Their worries were soon submerged by the pleasure of reminiscing about the old country, especially with Adam's uncle having been a lieutenant with Napoleon's Grande Armée and having filled his head with tales of it from the time he was little.

Adam Schwartz had arrived in Chicago from Baden as a twenty-year-old in 1830, before anyone dreamt of a boom. He made a modest living as a tinsmith and said he had been both invigorated and dismayed at the crudeness of the little frontier village.

"I was amazed to find myself so far west, and often considered moving even further west, just to set a record, but Chicago in those days was irresistible to a young man, if you don't mind my saying so, ma'am." He nodded to Katrina. "Mark Beaubien called it 'a village of boys,' and said he did his inn-keeping 'like hell,' begging your pardon, ma'am, them was his words."

Katrina smiled to acknowledge his gentlemanly sensitivity but did not object. She did not want to interrupt him, and besides, she had certainly heard rougher language than "hell," what with three months of keeping company with sailors.

"Mark Beaubien held dances most nights at his place, the Sauganash," Adam said, "and played the fiddle like a madman—it was something to see!

We worked hard and played harder, gambling, wolf-hunting, and horse-racing whenever we weren't dancing or ice-skating by moonlight! There were no schools in those days, no women besides squaws, and no religiosos, just 'the boys,' as motley a collection of French Creoles, Potawatomi, Yankees, and Virginians as you'd ever seen! And there I was in this wild place!"

"But, my dear sir," asked Katrina, "were there no…signs of higher civilization…at all?"

Adam Schwartz looked shamefaced at first, but then he brightened. "Hospitality was the rule, it being like breathing to Potawatomi and French Creole alike. There was no shortage of wit, with all the Yankee lawyers coming in, and children were sent off to Detroit, Grosse Point, or Princeton for an education, even most of Mark Beaubien's twenty-three."

Katrina's eyebrows shot up and so did Niklas's, but Adam went right on. "Or to Isaac McCoy's Indian Mission School, the half-breed ones from J.B. Beaubien's Ottawa wife. The Methodies and Presbyterias came in about '32, which helped some. The same Methodies moved their church across the river this year into the 'free zone.'"

He paused, considering whether to mention the circus pitching a tent on Lake Street earlier in the year and thought better of it. Before Niklas could take all this in and comment, Adam began to wrap up: "In those days, everything went to extreme in Chicago, from boys who worked all day and drank all night to the endless prairies and the gigantic lake—we pulled a ten-foot sturgeon from it one April—a welcome addition to Easter's feast, I'll tell you. I can't even begin to count the blizzards and tornadoes and wolves and mosquitoes as big as your hand, oh, and mud up to your knees.

"It began to change a couple years ago," Adam told them, "what with General Scott arriving with troops—they didn't all go home again—and the war being over so quick, and the canal being bruited about, and investors coming in from the East." He hesitated and then said, "I must admit to making a fortune myself."

Niklas and Katrina were still giving him their entire attention, so he explained. "It started because back in '31 I built a little tinsmith's shop for myself. It wasn't hard, the land being cheap and my being able to build it myself. I was pretty proud to have it, a property owner and only twenty-one, something my own father had never achieved. Things went along quietly for a while. I am naturally frugal, so I saved my pennies and sent money back to my parents in Baden. Then, a year ago, a year and a half, now, right after the first thaw, a well-dressed gentleman walked into my shop—a Yankee from Boston. He looked around and offered to buy the shop and the land under it for almost ten times what it had cost me! The night before, John Kinzie had been crowing about a thing like this happening to him, so I did not hesitate, but said yes immediately, whereupon this Yankee, he produced the gold and slapped it right down on my counter! When I walked away that day, I felt like the richest man alive."

"Quite a story," said Niklas, who had listened carefully and noted when this took place. *We have missed the market,* he thought.

But Adam Schwartz laughed, "Oh, that's not the half of it, sir! With all that gold, I bought a larger lot, rebuilt my shop and one on either side to rent out. On April tenth, this year, I sold all three, at a price that made me dizzy! That's when I put all my tinsmith equipment in storage and went into the real estate business. I, it turns out, have both a good eye for property and the connections of an 'old-timer.'" He laughed again.

From April to August of '36, Adam Schwartz bought and sold as quickly as he could, amassing a fortune unlike anything he had ever imagined. Then one day in mid-August he heard that his first little shop had been sold for the fifth or sixth time, bringing a thousand times the price he had paid. A thousand times!

"That night," Adam told them, "I woke up in a cold sweat, and in the next few days I started selling in earnest. I sold everything but one piece, a hundred and sixty acres up on Green Bay Road—that's to the far north— and I must say, sometimes those buyers' eyes shone with greed, sure that they were sending me to the poorhouse, they paid so little. But I was done, I was out of it, now I can sleep at night. When I finished selling, I went out to my hundred and sixty acres on Green Bay Road and built a house and a barn. That's how I earned my fortune, I, whose grandfathers never owned more than an acre and a half, which my father lost to Baden taxes."

Niklas shook the young man's hand, clapped him on the back, and gave Adam Schwartz his heartiest congratulations. He exchanged a significant look with Katrina, both thinking of their own twenty-six-year-old son and his determination to set off for the wild new territories across the Mississippi. They were worried about him, but now they wondered if magnificent new opportunities might await him there.

"If I were not hearing this from your very lips, sir," Katrina said, "it would be too fabulous to be believed."

Adam smiled, bowed to her, and said, "I feel much the same, Frau Kästner."

Then he began to tell them about the burgeoning German-speaking community in Chicago. Nicholas Berdell just arrived from Bavaria and was already organizing a German band; a tall man named Schnaebele—Adam could not think of his first name just now—from Pennsylvania in '32, a German Evangelical Association; the Sauter brothers, Charles and Jacob, who had come with their families in 1834, boot and shoemakers, and Jacob was now in Nicholas Berdell's band; Adam had heard them play at the dances at John Berg's Inn on LaSalle Street and the Ten-Mile House at Eighty-Third and Vincennes Roads. Wilhelm Haas and Konrad Sulzer were new arrivals with a hundred and fifty barrels of ale and had already founded a brewery.

"I'm sure the beer will be better soon," confided Adam, before continuing his list: John Schermerhorn and Johann Schmidt and Charles Stein, who brought his wife, Christine, and their baby son.

"You won't want for a friendly German community here," Adam assured them. Then Adam Schwartz cleared his throat, sat back and told them about the land far north, on Green Bay Road, quite remote but mighty pretty, he said, much better than being crowded here in town, if you don't mind the wolves.

Niklas asked him about that. "Why is everyone buying and building on top of one another with empty land a thousand miles in any direction?"

"Ah," said Adam, "you can see there's hardly anything to call a real sidewalk, and here and there single planks are laid up to doorways. It's because the mud is so fierce in the wet season, which is about half the year," he confided. "If you get off your plank, you sink immediately. Why, a young woman and her beau did just that last winter. Their plank tilted beneath them, and they sank and sank, were up to their waists before their cries for help were heard and they was rescued with ropes and a pile of men pulling.

"Or a friend of mine, Granville Sproat, who moved to Mackinac Island last year to teach the Chippewa up there. He was our first schoolteacher and a fine one, too, who used to carry the smaller scholars to school and take them home on his back, not daring to trust them on the slippery planks. One day he made a misstep and went down into the thick mire, with a little one in his arms. He struggled to regain his foothold and climbed back out and saved the child, too, but both of his boots had been sucked off by the mud. He never found them."

"Lost his boots!," said Niklas. "If all you have is a single plank to get from building to building, you won't want those buildings to be far apart."

"That's it exactly," said Adam, while Katrina smiled as she remembered their little cousin Berta, who honestly believed America's streets were paved with gold.

As the new friends prepared to part ways, Niklas asked another question. "Tell me, now, what you do with your newfound wealth? Will you go back home?"

Adam looked away, and his face might have colored a bit. "I've already sent more money back than anyone ever expected, and I hope my younger brothers will join me here, but no, I won't be going back anytime soon."

"Ah," said Niklas. He should have known better than to ask.

They shook hands and smiled. Adam kissed Katrina's fingertips, and as he walked away, he was whistling.

"Oh," said Niklas when Adam was out of hearing, "to be so young and so rich!"

CHAPTER 36

ON A BEACH AGAIN

I would believe almost anything that voice told me.

On Tuesday, Niklas and Katrina stood with a big crowd cheering the launch of *Clarissa,* the first sailing ship built in Chicago. The lake wore the same white ruffle as an ocean that day, with no opposite shore in sight. Never had Niklas or Katrina seen or dreamt of a lake of this enormity, one that required ships as big as those on the oceans, at least to their landlubber eyes. They imagined Izak would know better.

Amid the coos of an admiring crowd, Niklas picked out an authoritative voice and nudged Katrina; they both directed their attention to the voice. The speaker was short and thin but impressively dressed. *He might be a ship's captain,* Niklas thought, *or a naval officer. The casualness of American attire makes it hard to tell.*

"Aye, *Clarissa* should do well," the man said in a deep voice, something of a surprise for a man so small. "Designs adapted to the lakes, especially for schooners, are pretty nigh perfect by now, and they are fast."

"Yes indeed, Mr. Watt, sir," said the man next to him, "In July the brig *Indiana* broke the record—I'm sure you heard—from New York City to Chicago in only seventeen and a half days. *Agnes Barton,* a schooner out of Buffalo, done it last year in twenty-one, although no one ought to count on fewer than thirty days, wouldn't you say, what with the wind failing or storms?"

"To be sure," said the small man with the deep voice.

I would, thought Katrina, *believe almost anything that voice told me.*

In 1836, an Atlantic crossing averaged forty-five days, and travelers would be aboard another month if they took a steamer up the Hudson and then a Great Lakes schooner. This was the fastest route to the interior, and much better since the 1825 opening of the Erie Canal, which moved goods and people west or east at one-tenth the previous cost and in less than half the time. It was no wonder the prospect of the Illinois-Michigan Canal excited so many people.

"Last year," said Mr. Watt, "two hundred and fifty sailing ships arrived at Chicago, almost all schooners, and this year, we expect about fifty more. Fifty! Thirty-nine steamboats have already landed, and perhaps another ten might be expected before shipping closes for the winter, though days like today slow down our progress."

"You mean the westerly, Mr. Watt?"

"I do; wind like this can blow the lake all the way over to Michigan. Today, all it's doing is making us smell the slaughterhouses. Paugh!" Mr. Watt laughed, and said, "but with three thousand souls crowded into Chicago, what can we expect? Men have got to eat!"

Niklas made a mental note: the wide mud flats they saw were not there every day. As the launch party dispersed, Niklas and Katrina stole down to the nearest beach, took off their shoes and stockings and stood on the shore, balancing against one another, soaking in the sun, admiring the hypnotic blue waves of Lake Michigan, and reminiscing about the glorious beaches in Havana.

The excitement of the city was palpable, and the pace of building frenetic, but what Niklas and Katrina saw all around them was also disturbing. They were accustomed to houses built to stand for generations, roads solidly paved, and steeples soaring above cities like symbols of stability. Instead, on every hand they saw houses going up in the new "balloon" method of framing, never a thick, sturdy beam in sight.

"Look at that," said Niklas, gesturing discreetly.

Even Katrina, no carpenter at all, could see clapboards twisted before they could even be nailed tight.

"That's green wood being used," Niklas explained, "not properly dried. It's everywhere."

Contracts for construction, they were told, sometimes required completion in a week. Roads were a mess. It was impossible to lay cobblestones or bricks where these would sink into the mud overnight. Whole areas were nothing but surveyors' stakes, with no pavement or houses or public buildings to define a street plan.

Some thrilling camp meetings had been held, and some religious congregations had been organized, but the paint was barely dry on the few churches actually built. Adam Schwartz told them the Chicago Bible Society had been organized last year, and other benevolent societies were talked of, groups dedicated to good works and the conversion of lost souls.

"The city is filling up with missionaries and preachers of all kinds who worry about Chicago's many ungodly pleasures," Adam told them. He was trying to reassure them, but he looked a little hangdog about it.

It's a start, the Kästners thought.

As they stood gazing at a little, bright white church, its only enhancement a Gothic-style window above the door, Niklas said, "Close your eyes a moment, Meine Liebste." With a smile, Katrina closed her eyes, and he whispered to her, "Now picture Kölner Dom, the Cologne Cathedral, with its twin towers capping the largest church in Christendom."

She giggled and opened her eyes. "I believe what we see before us," she said, "is a fine example of church architecture. Though it is small, it is rendered in admirable simplicity."

"It might be insufficient," he said with a smile, "in a place like this, with its love of gambling, dancing, and whiskey." He became serious and turned to her. "Perhaps, one of these new-built Lutheran churches would welcome me if I should propose to teach Sunday School."

"You? With a roomful of children?"

"Yes, and why not? We are fresh come from the Fatherland, kept safe von Gott across the ocean, which should give me authority enough. Such a thing was not my practice in Berleburg, I will admit, but now I think I could attempt a homily for children, something to inspire their little hearts—say what? What do you find so amusing about my teaching a simple Sunday School class?"

Katrina had bowed her head to hide her face in her bonnet, but her grip on his hand had tightened almost to pain, her shoulders were shaking uncontrollably, and little gasps of titters escaped.

"Well, my word," he said, and at this, a louder gasp was heard, and Katrina dug into her sleeve for a handkerchief.

Niklas looked around with exaggerated calm in case any passerby should wonder at his wife.

At length she wiped her eyes, blew her nose, and dared to glance upward at him. "Forgive me, my dear, it was nothing but the oddest confluence of thoughts, nothing to do with whatever you were saying."

Niklas looked at her with raised eyebrows.

"Nothing to do with you, but the way you said, 'my word,'" and here she succumbed to another little fit. "When you said, 'my word,' I could not help myself." She wiped her eyes again. "God bless you, dear. If I could laugh like that once a day, I think I should live forever."

CHAPTER 37

A MORAL SNAKE PIT

"It was lucky you had gold."

"A moral snake pit," Ula Miller had once called Chicago. Katrina and Niklas thought this might be considered a somewhat hysterical opinion, combined with her remark about "Yankee Puritans who would keep you from having a decent German beer just because it's Sunday."

Oskar said in an aside to Niklas, "Ja, Ula has her humors and talks wild sometimes. But most families have someone like that."

Still, the scarcity of religious feeling in Chicago concerned them, as well as the lack of any other signs of civilization: music for troubled souls, schools, parks, and handsome civic buildings. Fort Dearborn, they privately agreed, could not be called handsome, and they were not sure that anything built with this new cobwebby framing would last the winter, let alone long enough to merit the name of architecture. Even with all the energy in the city, it might be quite a while before it pulled itself up by its bootstraps.

Niklas bought a thin newspaper, the *Chicago Weekly Democrat*, from a barefoot newsboy even though it was in English. He would study it this evening and make out most of it. He looked around for Katrina and saw her figure, as small as a girl's, among the larger, corseted women greeting one another and chatting or inspecting shop windows. From wooden plank sidewalks, five-or-six-step staircases ascended to buildings whose owners had paid to be lifted out of the mud and "built high." Other walkways were flat to the ground into buildings whose owners had not.

Turning the corner was a lone woman, Polish or Bohemian, Niklas guessed, dressed all in black except for a colorful babushka, looking very like the peasant women he had seen when crossing Poland with Napoleon's army in 1811 and '12, no adaptation at all to a new era or a New World. She pushed a cart along the street, hawking sausages and sauerkraut and apples.

A hackney cab swerved, its driver yelling at her to make way, its curtains down to protect the passengers from the dust and the inquiring eyes of the street.

Just past him, the cab rolled to a sudden stop, the driver hauling on the reins and its iron wheels clattering. A passenger leapt out. To Niklas's surprise it was Adam Schwartz, who was striding toward him. "Herr Kästner," he called, his black hair flying and one hand raised.

Niklas stepped forward to greet him as Adam told Niklas how glad he was to find him. "Come with me," Adam urged. "The lots you bought—I may have a buyer for you. Are you still in possession of them?"

"Yes," Niklas said, "but Katrina..." He looked around for her, but she was nowhere in sight.

"Niklas, flour is twenty dollars a barrel! It was six dollars in Hennepin. Oh, Adam, what a pleasure to see you again." Niklas spun around to see that Katrina had come up behind him.

The men delivered Katrina to the Wentworth Hotel and proceeded to the North Side where they paid a visit to the home of William Ogden, a recently arrived, rich Yankee who had supported the building of the Erie Canal in upstate New York and was now enthusiastically buying land in Chicago and promoting the Illinois-Michigan Canal.

Later that night, Niklas and Adam sat comfortably on rocking chairs on the porch of the tavern run by Wilhelm Haas and Konrad Sulzer next door to the new Haas-Sulzer brewery. As they rocked, the chairs creaked, emitting the faintest scent of freshly cut hickory. The woodsy scent mixed with the scent of German beer, better German beer than Niklas had had in some time.

"Are you pleased?" Adam asked.

"Immensely pleased and more thankful than I can say."

"It was lucky you had gold," Adam said, mouthing the word "gold" to keep it from nearby ears. "The *Specie Circular* says western lands can be purchased only with gold or silver, and who knows what the next law might say."

"Yes indeed," said Niklas.

"I am glad" said Adam, "to do something for a fellow countryman. It was just luck, you know, just luck that I had a connection."

"You are too modest, my dear sir," said Niklas, who knew that it was his great good fortune to have met this young man whose own parents were so far away.

"What will you do now? Will you stay? Will you reinvest?" Adam waited for Niklas to answer, and after a moment he added with alarm, "Some go back to Prussia...?"

Niklas paused. He had risked his whole family for freedom and safety. Günter had died helping them escape. Niklas's mouthful of beer was suddenly bitter, and he leaned over the porch railing and spat it out.

"Not this family," he said. "We are here to stay."

On the Saturday after next, September 24, 1836, Katrina was in their Chicago hotel room, having just taken possession of a delicious-smelling breakfast, delivered covered with hot towels.

"Niklas," called Katrina, "come have your breakfast or the tea will be no more than tepid."

In short order, they devoured eggs scrambled with cheese, a Swiss cheese so good that it was, by itself, a recommendation for Chicago, and flaky, salty biscuits with honey. Soon they were sipping tea together in comfortable conversation, glancing at one another now and then with deep affection. When Niklas sold their Chicago lots, to their amazement, he had quadrupled their money, no small thanks to Adam Schwartz. Niklas had bought a brass-studded strongbox to carry their new little fortune home, to bury and thus safely preserve against the vagaries of the future.

After some time, Niklas reached across for Katrina's hand and said, "My dear, what I am going to say may sound overly cautious, but I should like you to know my plans. On the one hand, Chicago may become a great city, and a man more inclined to speculation might want to stay and reinvest. On the other hand, Chicago right now is unsettled in the extreme. Its immense lake and the steamers to the East promise a great trade advantage, but its swamps are filled with poisonous miasmas and unhealthy water; these could steal every advantage from our family.

"Berleburg suited us more than the hurly-burly of Cologne, and in the same way, I think we may find Hennepin's advantages, situated as it will soon be at the crux of a fine, clean river and two canals, more to our liking.

I suggest we put Chicago behind us and choose Hennepin as our new home."

She was about to reply when Niklas held up his hand and continued. "I will admit it is something of a leap; it might not work out, but it's the best choice I can make right now, and the thing any man must do is to choose. What say you? Does this plan please you?"

Katrina rose, stepped around the small table and embraced her husband. "Thank you, my dear Niklas. I am in utter agreement. Thank you for carrying us safely to America, for making this decision with care, and for salvaging our fortune after all the costs of travel. For all of this I owe a debt of gratitude to you, my dear husband."

"Nonsense," he said, "There will never be such a debt between us, my love."

"When will your family be on its way again, dear Frau Kästner?" the heavy-set, well-dressed man opposite her asked. He had a thick German accent, so thick that Katrina thought he might be exaggerating it.

His eyes flickered downward, and she suddenly knew he was a wolf in sheep's clothing.

The word, "Wednesday" was already on her lips, and she said it, following as smoothly as ever with, "two weeks."

"Wednesday two weeks"—by which time they would be long gone. She too lowered her eyes, but only to make an inspection of her teacup and not before he had returned to studying her face. Which revealed nothing.

There was, after all, the ninth commandment to consider, she mused silently, running her fingertip along the rim of her teacup. It, however, had clear limitations, since she would not for the world endanger her family by revealing the actual date to this grasping and probably newly impoverished American, his malicious intentions barely concealed.

The talk at the table went on around her as she considered the commandments and one in particular. "Thou shalt not bear false witness" was a fine rule for children or for the courtroom. It was a rule every authority, from parent to priest, from owner to judge, wanted their children, parishioners, and those in the docket to obey. It was also a precondition of that special trust that cemented the love of true friends and of true husbands and wives.

Clear as all of this was, so too were its limitations. There was ein kleine Notluge, a little white lie, one of a packet of morally preferable lies. The lie told by a captured soldier to save his regiment. The lie told by a doctor to bring peace to his patient's last hour. The lie she had just told to deceive a thief.

Katrina sighed at the strain of such close thinking. It made her feel old to ponder such things and older still to work out resolutions, even though they were sound resolutions. They would have been out of her reach as a young woman.

On their way back to Hennepin, the Kästners were happy to leave behind the swampy, mosquito-infested Chicago, noisy with too many horses and lively saloons. It was a town, they agreed, of fabulous possibilities, but curiously overheated. Niklas had freed them from it with his decision, to the satisfaction of them both.

For Niklas, being in the saddle again, and on such a luminous morning, was a long-sought joy, especially astride a fine new Morgan stallion and with saddlebags full of gold. The horse had been purchased from a Vermont man reluctant to sell until he saw Niklas in the saddle. Niklas rode easily, with military precision, and it was clear that he liked and valued a good horse. Katrina rode their new Morgan mare. Morgans were a breed newly developed in America and quickly becoming famous for power, agility, and stamina.

Together, horses and riders took delight in this crisp, sunny September day, passing between swaths of goldenrod animating the prairie and cardinal flowers glowing flame-like in every marshy spot. They made quite a procession, with a pair of Hoosier oxen pulling a farm wagon driven by a Hoosier boy, Benji Wolfe. They had contracted with him for six months' wages and bed and board. Benji Wolfe was happy for the wages and perfectly willing to walk back to the Vincennes Trace when the weather cleared next spring.

Behind the wagon and tied to it were a third Morgan, a gift for Hans's trip west, and two milk cows with calves, not the Vorderwalder or Harzer Rotvieh Katrina wanted, but big rangy Holsteins, whose milk, she had been assured, was just as plentiful and rich. They would have their own milk, cream, butter, and cheese for the winter! Soon Katrina was deep in thought about the evening's supper; with their hampers full, it would not be difficult.

The day was stunningly beautiful, a morning of dewy light and soft breezes, the prairie stretching away like an invitation, red-winged blackbirds flitting among gold-tipped grasses and Canada geese on the wing, heading south. In the middle of the sandy dirt road, a pair of mourning doves sat, foolish and sweet, barely lifting off before Niklas's horse put its hoof down.

Katrina said "Shoo, now!" in a voice that sounded distinctly girlish, laughed, and called out, "I thought they would never move!"

Niklas looked at her with some surprise. He had come to think of her as old, and indeed there were days when she was stooped with labor and care, but now the early morning sunlight brought a golden glow to her face that reminded him of the girl he had married, and he realized with a knock that it had not been just Lisette or Amalie the sailors stole glances at. Just then, Katrina lifted her chin in delight with the changing colors of the dawn, and Niklas had a fleeting thought as of something half remembered—this look, this glow from within, presaged something but confounded him; he could not put a name to it.

Presently, Niklas slowed down to ride abreast of Katrina and asked, "How do you like this new saddle of yours with its high pommel, there?" The saddles they had bought were western-style, little else being available, their Spanish heritage showing in its design and tooling.

"Pommes?" she asked, "apples?" Privately, she thought Niklas took inordinate pleasure in switching about in languages, a skill she admired more than she could say, but for all the usefulness of his polyglot genius, it sometimes confused her.

He looked at her blankly.

"Or pommes de terre?" Wondered Katrina aloud. "How do you say Kartoffeln in English...potatoes? Or do you want Himmel und Erde, Heaven and Earth?"

"No, no, no, pommel—that object whereupon your left hand rests."

"Oh!" she said, snatching her hand up as if the pommel were suddenly ablaze. "And here I was wondering if you wanted fried apples or fried potatoes! Or Himmel und Erde, mashed together. Or shall we slice these new leather pommels and fry them for supper?"

Katrina set into giggles exactly as Will would have.

Niklas laughed with pleasure to hear such a sound. He had brought them safely across and now the two of them were headed home—home!—

to a pretty little village as fresh and clean as anyone could want and with bright prospects. They were at last to be settled in a home built by their sons. It was a result greatly to be desired, and together they had managed it.

The day's coolness predicted the coming winter, a season full of promise, Hans having become steadier and more cheerful with his decision made, Amalie filled with quiet joy, and Will, for once not in love (that they knew of), intent on becoming Hennepin's favorite tradesman, making friends quickly. Niklas would build a loom for Katrina and make a good pair of boots for Hans and shoes for the rest of the family. Together they would have long, lovely days with the swoosh of the shuttle and the tap-tap-tap of a cobbler's hammer.

Niklas sat comfortably on his splendid new stallion. He was one of the free and the wealthy now, he realized. It had all come about as he wished and by luck as much as wisdom. He had lived when those around him died in Russia; he had helped the cause of German democracy but had wisely chosen to escape the coming chaos. He had become prosperous in both old country and new, prosperous enough to bring his family across the ocean and settle them safely in as fresh a new town as he could imagine.

Suddenly, he realized that he had been blessedly free of night terrors. He had not even thought of the horrors of war for some time. Niklas looked again at Katrina, at her youth and health, and remembered when he had seen her glow in this way before: was she with child? A child to be born an American? It might be true—she would tell him in her own good time, but it might be, it just might be.

Niklas rubbed his chin and glanced sideways at Katrina. It did not occur to him that he himself and Katrina too, could now be called Americans, but neither did he need that thought yet. Instead, he settled back into the saddle, patted his handsome new stallion, and smiled into the golden sunshine, happiness springing all about him like new grass.

CHAPTER 38

THE HERO OF ST. LOUIS

October, 1836: and then he himself was out the window

Izak Peterssen, at twenty-six already the captain of *Enigma*, a handsome three-masted barque, now repaired, re-laded, and waiting for him in New Orleans' harbor, was at the moment far inland, at Illinoistown, across the river from St. Louis, sharing a hotel room with a certain Albert Hesselberth, a Bavarian-born wanderer even younger than Izak, although his prematurely white hair made him look much older.

Neither man smelled the smoke filling their room at once, but when Izak's eyes opened, he recognized the red light flickering on his bedroom wall in an instant and leapt out of bed, pulling on his boots and yelling at Albert: "Wake up, you lazy bugger, you poxed son of a lubber! Albert, get up or I'll break your neck!"

The other man moaned and rolled about, too groggy to make out more than the disturbing volume of Izak's voice. Izak put his face to the other man's ear: "You'll burn alive if you don't move your fat arse," which did serve to wake Albert Hesselberth at last.

Izak was out the door by then, and Hesselberth was considering going back to sleep when the words, "burn alive," echoed in his head and he thought better of it. The acrid smoke and the flickering light of fire were evident enough by now to alarm even Albert Hesselberth. He rolled to one side and felt for his trousers and boots.

In 1836, anyone traveling alone would find that requests for private accommodations would be met with a stare of astonishment, and single men were thought foolish indeed to expect a room of their own. Thus it came about that two utter strangers, young Captain Izak Peterssen and Albert Hesselberth, shared a room, but even so it was luxurious, its having only two cots and those separate, and only two men assigned to it. This generally clean and bright room was assaulted with noise and the smell of manure every morning, as it looked out over the back of the inn where ducks and geese and chickens kicked up a noisy fuss at dawn. Izak and Albert may have been strangers to each other a week ago, but they had easily become friends, despite an almost comical difference in their appearance and manner, as well as Izak's clumsy German and Albert's smatterings of Danish. Both were somehow of a similar cast of mind, and both were detained as they waited to book passage on a steamer to New Orleans.

Izak pounded on the other second-floor bedroom doors and shouted.

His landlord, Gordon McArthur, was running down the attic stairs, when he grabbed Izak in desperation and shouted, "My twins, help me find my twin babies!"

Lizzie McArthur was huge with child and lumbering down the stairs to the first floor, shooing their three oldest in front of her. Izak dashed into the smoke-filled attic after Gordon, blasted by the hot air and blinded by smoke. Instinctively, he dropped to his knees and felt his way forward. He ran into something soft on the floor, a baby's body, grabbed it and scuttled backward to the attic door, flames now licking their way up the walls and Gordon visible against them for an instant, frantically searching.

"I have 'im!" Izak roared, breathing in far too much smoke in the effort to speak. Gordon fell to the floor and came crab-like toward the attic door, cradling the other child in one arm. They fell down the attic steps and raced for the stairway to the first floor, but it was too late: with an immense crash, the stairs gave way, and the floor beneath them shook and threatened to buckle. Izak grabbed Gordon's arm and shoved him to the far side of the rooming house, through a deserted room, dark and smoke-filled, but not quite yet an inferno. Izak smashed out the small window with one elbow and searched wildly below, where Albert Hesselberth, God bless the lumbering big fool, was waiting with outstretched arms. Izak dropped the child and reached behind him for the second child, plucked it from its father's arms and dropped this child too into Albert's waiting arms.

He swung Gordon, dazed and barely breathing, out the window, hanging him down for an instant and dropping him. For an instant, he saw people below rush to drag Gordon away from the burning building, and then he himself was out the window. He flung himself away from the flames, falling in an arc, a horrific sight with his shirt and his long blond hair on fire. Izak could feel the shirt on his back flying up or off, but he did not know it was on fire; the pain had not yet come through to him. There was no other way out, nor a single moment to be lost. Behind him, the building reached its flashpoint and exploded into the sky. Below, everyone watching gasped, covered their eyes, and ran.

Izak hit the ground, rolled, and then lay still, stunned. A burning timber crashed down beside him, and then Albert was there, grabbing his legs and dragging him away.

Amy Costner, once Amalie Kästner of the beautiful little town of Berleburg in Westphalia, the westernmost province of Prussia, and now Americanized in name at least, stood brushing her hair, counting one hundred strokes. It was a lustrous auburn with highlights gleaming gold in the morning sunshine, the result of a spring and summer aboard one boat after another. She had come down the Rhine on *Holsatia*, then sailed across the ocean on the barque *Enigma*, a long journey seeming strange and dream-like by now, fraught with dangers and death as it had been, nearly lost to mysterious plague, to drownings, to vicious pirates, to hurricane, then up the Mississippi on the famously rugged steamship, *P.V. Yellow Stone*, and up the Illinois River on a wonderfully cozy little steamer, *Ottawa*.

When she considered her family's long journey, with its detours in British Gibraltar, Spanish Cuba, and the newly independent Republic of Texas, it felt strange to find herself standing before a looking glass in a neat little bedroom of a newly-built frame house in Hennepin, Illinois, a bedroom she shared with her little sister, Lisette, and their brother Jakob, who was still thought of as a baby although he had already turned five.

"I suppose it was a kind of death," Amalie said aloud, even though she was alone in the room, "to cross an ocean and leave everything behind." Homesickness overcame her, though it was the German word she thought of, "Heimweh." She often thought in German, even if she tried not to. Sometimes it kept her from feeling cut off from everything she knew and liked and that made sense.

As the world changed, so did she. She left Prussia a plain, sensible fourteen-year-old child and arrived in Illinois a fifteen-year-old woman, beautiful and beloved as she never dreamed she would be, longing to be married and frighteningly soon to be mother to a stepson, a little boy in Denmark almost the same age as Jakob and entirely unknown to her except for his name, which was Lars.

Amy felt in the top drawer for a small wooden box, pulled it out and lifted the lid, turning it to the morning light to see the red gleam of the small garnet on a gold chain that was Izak's pledge to her. It was like a drop of blood, he told her, heart's blood, a symbol of his love and loyalty.

It was a good thing, she thought, *that I have this necklace, or I might have wondered if I had imagined him. I still don't know what he sees in me.*

Izak was tall, blond, and strong, with the oversized shoulders and fore-arms that come from a lifetime of hauling lines and climbing ratlines. He was also kind and observant, making her feel beautiful for the first time in her life, sandwiched as she always had been between her beautiful mother and the beautiful Lisette, whose platinum curls and blueberry-blue eyes al-ways drew admiration. Now she had a long winter to endure and endless waiting through spring and summer before Izak would be back from Co-penhagen with his son, but this long stretch of time was hardly enough for everything she must make and learn to become a proper sea captain's wife.

"Amalie!" Katrina called, and the happy girl skipped down the stairs, ran to the kitchen, picked up little Jakob, gave him a twirl, and kissed Lisette.

"The oatmeal is ready," said her mother, handing it to her along with a bowl of sliced apples. A blue and white pitcher, delftware bought in Hol-land on the family's escape from Prussia, was on the kitchen table, filled with good, sweet milk from the Holsteins found in Chicago. These animals had nothing to do with that wild boomtown, being bought on its fringes from an itinerant Hoosier family, whose son, Benji, had been contracted out to Niklas and Katrina as a hired man. In the center of the table hot biscuits gave off puffs of steam from a napkin-lined basket.

Amy set Jakob to kneeling on a bench, tied a cloth around his neck as a bib and handed him a spoon. Her mother smiled at the little assembly of her younger children, all pink-cheeked and healthy, Amy now almost a grown woman. The men had gone out early, Niklas preferring at least an hour of work before breakfast, and their sons expected to share his opinion.

"You're up late," scolded Katrina, but there was no bite to her voice. Amalie was her right hand, as helpful with the children and household work as a fifteen-year-old could be expected to be, and a skilled needlewoman to boot. "The men will be in soon."

Katrina counted the sausages she was frying and tossed another three into the skillet. As a small woman, she found it hard to conceive how very much the men would want, particularly Hans, who always seemed to eat for six. She smiled at the thought of her robust oldest son, her stepson really, though no one in the family thought of him that way. She had raised him from a skinny, sad little boy, who kept surprising both parents as he transformed into a giant of a man, tall and strong beyond what anyone could have expected.

Amy breathed in the scent of sausages grilling on the big wood stove. It was she who was most often at the cookstove, an improved version of the Franklin installed a month ago when the house was finished. She had stood by making helpful suggestions when Will and Hans wrangled it into position with the help of two men from the wagon train that had brought the stove from the infant city of Chicago. It had been built in Erie, Pennsylvania, floated on a lake schooner from Erie to Chicago and purchased in Chicago by Katrina and Niklas—imagine the surprise and delight when the wagon with it appeared at their doorstep.

Now it stood in the corner of the kitchen, back-to-back with and sharing a chimney with the kakelugn, a tile stove in the parlor, hauled to Hennepin from Norway, Illinois, where a new, small settlement of Norwegian Lutherans built these stoves. Kakelugns heated a room evenly while having to be fed with firewood only twice a day.

Two more kakelugns, also back-to-back, shared the chimney on the other side of the house, one in the dining room and one in the front room, which served as the family's little general store. The kakelugns were Will's discovery, a result of his mushrooming trade connections, as pretty as the blue and white delftware tiles the Kästners carried across the ocean and that now lined the walls behind the stoves. Together, the tile on the stoves and on the walls radiated warmth and cheerfulness into the rooms.

Amalie could hear hammering outside, close enough to be the Kästner men at work. All of Hennepin was building as fast as it could, pushed by the coming winter and by the high hopes many cherished that this clean new village was soon to be the western terminus of the Illinois-Michigan Canal, which promised to transform it into something bustling and prosperous. In

Chicago, the eastern end of the canal was already being dug. Her parents had seen the work in progress. It was a filthy, thankless job. In Chicago's swampland, the ditch kept collapsing and killing hapless diggers. Leave it overnight and often it was flooded by dawn.

Will straightened up, hammer in hand, and surveyed their work. In little more than a month he and Hans, now with Benji hired and their father back from Chicago, had built a fine house with clapboard sides, plank flooring, and a shake-shingle roof, such an improvement over the thatched-roof log cabin they might have had for the winter. The boys had built a dirt-floor log cabin first and lived in it with the younger children while they worked on a proper frame house. Now the log cabin served as the barn, with two horse stalls and a lean-to for the cattle. The loft where the boys had slept was now the haymow. From scraps of lumber, the boys built a pigsty and a hen-house—tightly caulked against winter winds—for the East Frisian Gull chickens their mother purchased in New Orleans last summer.

Will and Hans had dug a root cellar for the family to squeeze into if there was another tornado like the one their parents survived in August, and now in the bright, cool last days of October, all three Kästner men and their hired man, Benji, were at work on a stockade fence to surround and connect the garden and farm buildings. The barn itself formed one end of the enclosure and opened on the far side into a feedlot and pasture for the animals. The pigsty and henhouse formed a wall along most of one side, and the back of the house formed the other end.

"Hand me a nail," said Niklas, and Benji was ready for him, three nails held conveniently separate in his skinny outstretched hand. Hans returned with the next log, sliding it neatly into place between the crossbars held by the other two men. Niklas and Will hammered the new log in place, one on each side of the fence.

It would take so much more work, thought Will, *to do this without the four of us, especially one like Hans, who can manhandle a log single-handedly.* Hans strode back to their stack of logs as the other two men hammered the last one in place, securing the top crossbar first and then the lower one. *Come spring,* Will thought, *Hans will be gone, up the Missouri. If anyone can make his fortune as a fur trader, it's my big brother.*

The men had been working since before dawn, beginning with chores—feeding and watering animals, mucking out stalls, spreading new straw, and doing the milking. Niklas had bought three Morgans in Chicago, a stallion, a gelding to go west with Hans, and a gentle mare; two big Holstein milk cows with yearling calves; and two sturdy oxen, used immediately to plow three acres behind the barn and haul the logs as they were chopped down. One ox was kept for the winter sleigh, and one was sold to a farmer in Florid, a man with forty acres to turn and who promised to lend them the use of the ox for next spring's plowing.

Their new Hoosier wagon would also be sold; it had done its job of carrying their Chicago treasures home. There were quite a few treasures, since Niklas had done well in land speculation during the boom and much was needed for their new home: a dining table, chairs, and sideboard; a desk and upholstered chairs for the parlor; and for the bedrooms, armoires, bedframes, and mattresses. In the evenings, Will and Hans built kitchen counters and shelves, a table, and benches. They also built a counter and shelves for the little general store occupying a quarter of the first floor. It had its own entry off the front porch.

The house was a simple, four-square design of two stories with porches on the front and back, the framing put up with amazing speed in just two days of house-raising with every able-bodied man in Hennepin participating and the women bringing food and Amalie baking for a week before the grand event.

Their ability to build a new-style balloon frame house rather than a log cabin was a matter of wonderful luck in having a sawmill right in Hennepin, where it hung out over the Illinois River rapids, with a waterwheel to power the saw. Will was already hired out for the winter to the miller, Herr August Guttmann, a recent arrival who had built his sawmill as a fine, sturdy structure just a year earlier, and who was the father of the beautiful Theodora, or "Dora" as the Guttmann family called her.

Will called her Dora, too, now that he had a name for his "Angel of the Mill." The family was from Alsace and while they spoke both French and German, they preferred French, which made Will glad to have spent time immersed in New Orleans. Dora filled his daydreams, and he fell asleep each night planning a glorious future together. Every now and then, he remembered Ezmeralda.

Hans-Jürgen Kästner, who became Hank Costner in America, had never minded using his muscles. Horsepower and manpower ruled, and he was perfectly aware that his stature, his grip, and his muscles gave him a tremendous advantage. He was like his father but on a larger scale, both having the same thick neck, heavily muscled shoulders, and inborn athleticism.

One look at Hans, and other men made way for him or accepted him on their crew, as had Richard Billings, the master carpenter of the barque *Enigma* and Big Mike on *Yellow Stone*. In Gibraltar, he had looked a likely enough prize that a press gang had tried to seize him, and only Will's fleetness of foot, and his father's deadeye aim, and Izak Peterssen's fierceness had kept him from becoming unwilling crew on some sleazy Mediterranean ship. These physical advantages, so important to everyday life, were not lost on women either, though they seemed to expect some facility in conversation, a difficulty he had not overcome.

Today, none of that mattered, except his ability to manhandle eight-or-nine-foot tree trunks and set them upright in the trench they had dug. The stockade fence was the last big project their new home needed before winter, although Hans could always count on his father to find some new dangerous or difficult task.

A long summer of hard work aboard ships and his father's insistence on military training had prepared him well to go west, his destiny, he was sure. He wanted to go west of the Mississippi, past the cliffs and the swamplands they marveled at as they came north up the river, and into truly wild lands, Indian Territory, inhabited only by wolves and bears and bison and savages. In the West, Hank Costner would make his own decisions for the first time in his life with neither his father nor Will by his side.

It had been agreed upon: Hank would go with Antonie Bourbouvis, long a fur trader here on the Illinois River and now finding it trapped out, what with the Indian Wars of '32 and the last of the tribes pushed across the Mississippi and the land north of the Illinois opening for settlement. Bourbouvis would go up the Missouri to a new trading post in the spring or maybe even this fall. He was even now making that decision, checking the thickness of corn husks and the abundance of acorns and the girth of woolly bear caterpillars and watching for woodpeckers sharing a tree or crickets on the hearth or, God forbid, snowy owls arriving early. Bourbouvis knew better than to set out into a winter promising to be severe.

Hank knew how to handle knives and guns and was an excellent marksman, but he sometimes felt like a babe in these woods where he knew neither plant nor animal habits, and faced entirely new creatures like raccoons and possums, and large, dangerous animals like bears, wolves, and bison—once denizens of Europe, but which Hans had never seen outside a book, except for one extraordinary moment. Two summers ago, he and Will had the briefest sighting of the almost mythical European bison, the wisent.

A fur trapper's main target was beaver, virtually extinct in Europe, with a pelt worth a fortune in St. Louis or New Orleans or New York. Most were shipped to London hatters to be felted and shaped into top hats, fedoras, and the new bowler styles.

Hank needed Antonie Bourbouvis, and Bourbouvis, who was not a young man anymore nor a literate one, needed Hank. Bourbouvis was glad of Hank's intimidating appearance, strong arm, and ability with firearms. His ability to clerk in Bourbouvis's native French was valuable, too.

What Bourbouvis had not mentioned to Hank was that everything would be different on the upper Missouri, where the trade was in buffalo robes and bearskins, and maybe not so much in beaver anymore. Bourbouvis himself no longer needed to hunt; he could make a living running the trading post, and Hank could act as his clerk, since his being literate was a rare advantage in the deep wilderness, but as to becoming a hunter and trapper the way Hank wanted, that might be another thing entirely, the era for it fading fast and maybe soon to disappear.

A few days later, Katrina was in the kitchen finishing a particularly spectacular apple pie, fruit piled high until it pushed up the upper crust, and popping it into a hot oven when Niklas walked in. Her exertion had turned her a fine rosy pink, and she was happily musing about the child resting inside her, so that when she smiled at her husband, all of her years faded away, and he saw the pretty girl he had married. Not for the first time in recent weeks, Katrina seemed to be thriving on the very air of their new home in a young, energetic country that breathed freedom. He knew, of course, that there was more than a new country or a new home or a fresh apple pie that made her smile, and that behind it was a secret satisfaction at being in a condition neither of them had expected to occur again.

He motioned to her to sit—her smile faded at the look on his face—and he handed her the letter from Izak.

She saw that the return address was a hospital, St. Louis' Mullanphy Hospital, and she understood the gist of it with the opening words, which had been written not by Izak himself but by a different hand:

> I am terribly scarred, my hair is burnt off, and I may not regain full use of one arm. I tell you this so the sight of me shall frighten you less. I have lost everything in the fire, and my ability to continue as a ship's captain is in some doubt, as is, indeed, the question of whether I have long to live.
>
> Should you or Amalie wish to retract our engagement, I will not object. I think it most sensible, though my heart breaks at the thought.
>
> Should she wish to proceed and you to allow it, I beg your permission to marry forthwith; the events I have witnessed since we parted have proven again the awful brevity of life. I do not wish to spend another day apart from your daughter, but only if she would wish the same, despite my diminished self and diminished prospects.

Katrina rose and paced the kitchen until she stood looking out the back door at the new stockade fence, smoothing the surface of the letter. The light had faded from her face, leaving it pale and drawn. She reached for the edge of the table to steady herself.

"He's alone, injured, and destitute, Niklas. We must go. Amalie must see him. Whether she wishes to marry him is a separate question, but she must not abandon him. I cannot in good conscience tell her what to do about the marriage."

"How can she even consider a marriage under these circumstances?"

Katrina sighed. "Perhaps they love each other."

A flash of anger crossed Niklas's face, not something anyone but Katrina would have caught. *He is,* she thought, *angry with me for putting my daughter's foolish heart above her well-being.*

She made her voice low and kind: "Despite this letter, we do not truly know what manner or extent of injury Izak has suffered or how long his life may be. True, people mostly go to hospitals to die, and I am not suggesting she must marry him, but I will urge her to do what is best."

Niklas was troubled. "She is so young. I was willing to agree to this engagement in part because it gave her a year to grow up."

"I know. What will this mean to her? We must tell her."

Niklas's thoughts turned to New York's Second Great Fire less than a year ago, said to be the worst since London's Great Fire of 1666. It had been disaster upon disaster, breaking out on a vicious winter's night during a blizzard with temperatures down to minus seventeen and gale force winds. Firemen chopped holes in the ice on the Hudson River to get to water. It froze solid in their hoses. Fifty acres were destroyed, seven hundred buildings, including all of the financial district, several ships in the harbor, and the last of the buildings of Old Dutch New York. When the firemen tried to blow up buildings to create a firebreak, they ran short of gunpowder.

Many of New York's buildings had had newly installed gas lines. When they burned, people said it was like immense furnaces in full blast. In some places, the heat melted iron doors and copper roofing, the metal running off into the streets. Flames were seen in Philadelphia, ninety-seven miles away. Now, months later, the city was being rebuilt in stone and brick with a new aqueduct, and the pitifully small fire department was hiring, hiring, hiring.

The fire in Illinoistown was like the Great New York Fire only in that the river acted as a firebreak. It involved only a few dozen houses and shops before a bucket brigade put out the flames. Niklas had heard about the fire but had not imagined Izak was still in St. Louis or caught up in the fire. He shivered to be standing in their new little house of wood. *It's foolishness to build in wood. The next house will be stone or brick.*

Katrina, whose thoughts had never left Izak and Amalie, said, "I would never have wished such difficulties on our daughter. Their wedding, if it is to be, will depend on his recovery, which will probably delay it."

"We must encourage her to refuse him. Her life and her happiness depend on a husband able to provide for her."

"It may also be that..." Katrina shuddered, "she becomes a widow before she becomes a wife."

CHAPTER 39

MULLANPHY HOSPITAL

No one yet imagined the many years of famine.

In the early morning of the following Thursday, when *Ottawa* was scheduled to depart from Hennepin for St. Louis, Amalie sat despondent on the stairs, waiting for her parents to finish packing. Her own carpetbag had been packed since Tuesday and was now on her lap, where she hugged it to herself. She had learned about Izak on Monday, the horrific news destroying the beautiful life she had imagined and everything she had hoped for.

Lisette came to sit beside her and put an arm around her, the big sister who had cared for her like a second mother. When Lisette was a baby, she could not quite pronounce "Amalie" and had turned it into "Amma." Will had laughed and said it was like "Mama" turned inside out. Katrina was less than pleased, but she considered it a small price for the daily care Amalie gave the little girl, and something she could not do much about in any case.

"It's all right, Amy," said Lisette. "We'll take care of him, you and I will, and he will be as good as new in no time."

Amalie reached for Lisette's hand and then gave in to her larger impulse and took the little girl in her arms. Amalie had already had three days of tears, so she was dry-eyed, even when Lisette began to sob.

"Whatever lies ahead," said Amalie, stroking her sister's curly hair, "we must do our best. We must trust that God will see us through."

Lisette shook herself. Amalie had taught her to be brave, clear-eyed, and sensible. If there was one strain that ran through the entire Kästner family, it was an insistence on rational thought. Being flighty, impractical, superstitious, or foolish was considered inappropriate for a Kästner. It was as bad as lying around in bed of a morning. "Self-deception," her father said often, "is like choosing to wear a blindfold." And again, he would tell the children, "Give strict attention to the facts, especially those you don't like."

Lisette did not exactly understand these sayings, but she knew better than to sit around in tears, so she took her sister's hand, pulling her up and saying, "Let me make you a cup of tea."

Amalie gave a surprised, pained laugh. At eight years old, Lisette could indeed make a cup of tea, but she did not usually take care of Amalie.

"That's a good idea," Amalie said, getting up, setting the carpetbag by the front door, and smoothing her skirts. "Let's have a cup of tea, you and me."

In St. Louis, Missouri, Sister Ignatius, director of nursing at Mullanphy Hospital, had, by the same date, received a letter from her brother Patrick in Ireland telling of the widespread failure of the potato crop and begging her to come home, she who was a mainstay of the family. He allowed that she would be another mouth to feed, but she would also be the caring touch for their elderly mother and besides, their mam was not the only one as might need the hand of a nurse.

Even earlier and from other sources had come news of an Irish summer colder than the oldest man or woman could recall, no warmth at all to it, and now hunger spreading through the poorest parishes. This season of cold and potato blight reminded everyone of Irish famines before, and people shook their heads again at the poverty and backwardness of Irish peasants and their overdependence on the potato—many owned but one kettle for boiling potatoes or oatmeal and not even an oven for baking bread.

No one had forgotten the Great Frost of 1740-'41, Bliain an Áir, the Year of Slaughter. It had decimated Ireland, and it was far from the first time, famine being so common in Ireland as to be considered an ordinary risk of life in the poorer parishes and on the more distant farms.

In spite of these memories, in 1836, no one yet imagined the many years of Irish crop failure and famine to come, of mothers dying, giving their children a last scrap of soda bread and that stretched thin with straw and children reduced to eating grass, their green mouths announcing their poverty and making them look less than human. This year, everyone would think they had only to make it through one admittedly sparse hard winter; such things were not unknown, and most had laid by some resources against a bad, even a very bad, harvest.

Patrick wrote on a thin, cheap piece of paper, apologizing for not having better:

My Beloved Sister Maggie,

Received your long-wished-for letter on the 22nd, and felt very much delighted at hearing that you are enjoying good health, as are I and our mother, brothers, and sisters at present, thanks be to God. Our brother Denis and wife are in good health, and they got another son called Patt, after me. I am in pretty good health myself at present, thank God for it; I am happy to state to you that Mam's health is good at present, and she is desirous to lay it as an obligation on you to avoid going to work among the savages or any dangerous work, if you have any say in the matter, although we acknowledge you must do whatever Mother Superior says, may God's many blessings be upon her.

We have enough to eat here, have no concern about us, but potato failure has spread dreadfully in the west, especially amongst those at Connaught, remote poor farms where we hear they are in a starving state, able only to procure "yellow meal"—that of maize—and the poorhouses there crowded with people, and some are dying. There is some kind of a strange fever in it, and it is the opinion of the Doctors it will spread over town and country when the weather grows warm.

I hope that as you went to America you will make the most of your work in the Church that you possibly can consider in yourself that it was not to remain during all of life you emigrated but that after spending four or five years in that Country you may come home. You would find consolation and comfort amongst your friends and neighbours, your brothers and sisters, who feel very sorry for your absence, but we hope that it is not a departure for life and that you will have some nights as yet in your own native village.

If you can at all, I hope you will still write, as it is all the comfort we have here. I hope you will let me know all the particulars how all things are getting on with you. I do not understand what is the reason Hannah has not wrote all this time. I was afraid something was wrong or she would have wrote.

I remain your loving brother,
P Lynch

Sister Ignatius laid her brother Patrick's letter aside and looked around at the stark whiteness of the hospital, sorry for her family's troubles but taking comfort in the color of cleanliness, the better to focus on miseries right here in Missouri, with the mighty river to the east and the immense and mysterious prairies to the west, miseries of the sort any hospital collects as its right and its due.

One of those miseries was Room 105, a burn patient, one Izak Peterssen, age twenty-six, though most days, the pain etching his face made him look decades older. The burning of the McArthur Hotel had occurred more than a month earlier, part of a fire that took seven city blocks and injured many, including one of the twin babies Peterssen had saved in an act of selfless heroism the newspapers had made too much of, no ordinary boarder expected to risk his life for his innkeeper's children. Both infants had lived, and he had saved the father as well, leaping last to safety after dropping the others from a second-floor window, a leap that was still talked about, his shirt and his hair on fire as he flew out of the building as it exploded, a sight no one present at the scene would ever forget. Sister Ignatius had frankly thought Izak Peterssen would not survive, but the crisis was now past, and he was improving daily.

Today, waiting in the sunroom again was a man odious to her, one Albert Hesselberth, a large, bulbous-faced gentleman from somewhere in the Germanies, almost bald and sporting a bushy white beard that gave him a kindly grandfatherly look, absurd at his young age, who was now sitting as usual with closed eyes waiting for her to allow his friend into the sunroom. Sister Ignatius had had to knock Albert Hesselberth into wakefulness more than once.

Hesselberth had come north to St. Louis on the advice of Adolph Wislizenus and Theodor Engelmann after a group of them fought in the war of independence in Texas. They were part of der Burschenschaft, the outlawed Student Union, who fled to America when their 1833 revolt against the monarchy failed. Then came ferocious days of battle in Texas, where one of their friends, Gustav Bunsen, died for Texan liberty. Later, Wislizenus would go west with the Rocky Mountain Fur Company and Engelmann up into Wisconsin territory.

Hesselberth, disenchanted with St. Louis, had thought to resume his studies in New Orleans, but after the fire he could not abandon this tall Dane, Izak Peterssen, his own savior on that awful night and the Hero of St. Louis. Now Albert Hesselberth seemed a very long way from the gracious townhouse in Frankfurt am Main where he had been born and where he and the others had conspired to bring down the Bavarian king. He realized they had been too young, idealistic, and disorganized, but they had been right, his stubborn intellect insisted, they had been right. The days of kings were drawing to a close.

In Room 105, Izak Peterssen was waiting grimly to endure the morning cleansing and changing of bandages and to be dismissed to the sunroom. He had, Sister Ignatius noted, the very slightest hint of health coming back into his cheeks, not that anyone but she could have told the difference. What she could not know was that Izak was coming back to himself, and today he expected to begin making plans for moving on. What she did know was that he would ask if a letter had arrived for him, and she would have to tell him "No, nothing" once again.

CHAPTER 40

AN ADDED TORTURE

"Do you not live in terror?"

On November 1, 1836, Niklas, Katrina, and Amalie boarded *Ottawa* again. Within the hour, *Ottawa*'s pilot, James O'Keefe, was looking hard at the changing hues of the river; there off the port bow a certain ripple worried him. *Was the water twisting around something submerged, out of sight but close enough to the surface to cause a dark wrinkle?* O'Keefe decided to cross the river in spite of the cost in wood and time. Every sailor knows extra tacks delay a ship, and every steamboat captain knows each crossing of the strong central current is a delay. But O'Keefe also knew the much higher cost a snag or a sandbar could extract in time, in repairs, and perhaps even in lives lost.

The Illinois River was almost always a dream of a river to navigate, and O'Keefe was delighted, when he thought about it, with the success of his first year of *Ottawa*'s running the river. It had been a year of immense change along the thin, diagonal line etched by the Illinois River across the state's flat, fertile bottoms from St. Louis to Chicago.

O'Keefe owed the immediacy of his success to the land boom in Chicago, prices rising a thousand percent in less than a year, bringing investors from the eastern states and making speculators out of otherwise sane, sensible and frugal Yankees, Kaintucks, immigrants, and outlanders from Canada, Mexico, Europe, and even South America. Not long ago, O'Keefe himself had carried two brothers from the little republic of Colombia to Chicago, rich men from the look of them, and a long way from home.

"Do you not live in terror at what you may find in St. Louis?" Louisa Grady spoke kindly, having already heard the horrific tale of the Hero of St. Louis, and newly aware that this serious, pretty child across from her was the Hero's intended.

"Ah, Missus Grady, I am not." Amalie looked down at her shoes and gathered her courage. They were alone in *Ottawa*'s ladies' sitting room, steaming downriver to St. Louis, and Amalie felt she could speak openly. "I have steeled myself for an initial shock, but there is no horror in me, only sympathy and love. I know that Captain Peterssen may be disfigured, disabled, or on the point of death. I have spent sleepless nights testing myself with what such possibilities mean, and my answer is constant: I would rather spend a lifetime caring for my dear Captain than thirty seconds married to another man."

What Amalie did not say was that she was even more dedicated to the task ahead that she dared say aloud. She had already realized that she would rather be forever childless than carry another man's child, she would rather be impoverished with Izak than rich with any other man, and she would rather be Izak Peterssen's widow than any other man's wife. She looked back at her crush on Thomas Segrave with disdain. Never again would she love another man.

The older woman was astounded at the romantic devotion so evident in this speech and could not reply—she could only take the girl into her arms. Amalie was dry-eyed and a bit surprised to be embraced, but Louisa Grady's eyes ran with pity and admiration. *This,* she thought, *from a mere child, a nothing special girl with an unfortunate German accent. Though I admit, her dress is well made. It suggests that she comes from substance.*

On the other side of the thin pinewood door between the cabin and the ladies' sitting room of *Ottawa*, Katrina had heard Amalie's speech and was driven to tears as well. They were tears of love and of sorrow for what faced her dear brave child. She had long known that Amalie had a good heart, but she was surprised and proud to hear such a demonstration of courage, devotion, and self-sacrifice. Katrina rehearsed her daughter's words in her mind so she could repeat them to Niklas. Both had worried about whether their daughter was ready for the challenges ahead and unsure about where the girl's heart lay and what advice was best.

Niklas shook his head in wonder as Katrina recounted Amalie's words.

"Is young love alone enough to inspire such courage?" he mused.

"Perhaps," she said, "although one thing rarely causes another altogether without ghost causes, flittings of causal dust, going unnoticed."

"Sometimes, Trina, I have no idea what you're talking about."

"Umm," she nodded, "I know."

However it had happened, they now knew the direction of their daughter's future and her courage in facing it, whether Izak Peterssen lived or died.

Gordon McArthur was there at the dock, ready to greet newcomers and searching among them, as he had every day, for the Kästner family, who had stayed with him earlier in the summer, long before the fire, and who had sent Izak Peterssen back to his hotel in the fall, a blessing the importance of which never left him.

"Mr. McArthur!" cried Niklas.

Gordon looked up at the rail to see Niklas, Katrina, and Amalie waving to him. He smiled. In spite of his genuine gratitude, it was a tired smile, his having become father to newborn twin girls since the Kästners were last here and his having spent weeks helping his toddler twin boys recover from their injuries and at the same time recovering from the scorching of his own skin. It was a smile of relief as well. Gordon McArthur knew of Izak's letters; he himself had delivered the injured man's letters to a steam packet bound for Hennepin.

As much as he was indebted to Izak Peterssen, once his boarder and now the man who had saved his life and his twin sons, Gordon McArthur did not know exactly what to do with him. It seemed clear that Izak would live, but how much he would recover and what the young man's future held was quite uncertain. Nor did Gordon McArthur know anything of the relationship between Izak and the Kästners, only that Izak had written to them.

He collected the Kästners and their baggage and deposited them at his brother Neil's inn, the Purple Thistle, both brothers being innkeepers. The Gordon McArthur family now took up half of the rooms in the Purple Thistle, not that it mattered much, the season drawing rapidly to a close. All of them, the Kästners, the Gordon McArthurs, and the Neil McArthurs were soon seated around one table, having supper and talking about Izak Peterssen and that awful night, the night of the fire.

The Kästners had arrived too late to visit Izak, the Mullanphy Hospital having highly limited visiting hours and strict enforcement, but Amalie already wore a smile, the very worst of her fears having been allayed. Izak still lived! He was in fact recovering, though the turnaround had barely begun. His head was still bandaged, but his face had recovered. It had a new layer of tender skin, 'tis true, and would need a winter indoors before he gave the slightest thought of going out in the sun or boarding a ship. Gordon McArthur did not know how bad the burns on Izak's back were and whether the muscle there would ever recover. There was the broken arm as well, but again the news was good: a surgeon had set the arm rather than take it off. Izak's arm was bound to his chest, and Gordon had no idea how badly it might be damaged, but Izak had not lost it, and he could wiggle his fingers.

This was the advantage of being in St. Louis and having the Mullanphy Hospital at hand with enlightened doctors and advanced methods. Izak had been taken across the Mississippi the same night as the fire. Neil McArthur had made sure everyone injured in the fire was transported immediately to Mullanphy.

When the Kästners arrived, they went immediately to the hospital to see if an exception could be made for their late arrival (no, it could not), but they left a note for Izak, so he would know they would see him tomorrow. He would know Amalie had come with her parents and that "We most eagerly await our reunion."

The occupant of Room 105 did not sleep well that night. He rarely did, braced as he had to be on his one good side and unable to move at all, but this night he had the added torture of anticipating the morning's interview, an event to set the course of the rest of his life as surely as the fire itself. He had imagined such a visit might be made by Niklas alone or even Will, appointed to deliver the bad news, but the letter dispelled that fear.

Still, he was determined to let Amalie go if he could detect the slightest reluctance on her part. She was only fifteen, which had given him pause from the first stirrings of his love for her, and now it was insupportable to ask a girl so young to take on the task of caring for him with no guarantee he would ever fully recover. And yet the thought of doing without her hurt his heart with such a physical stabbing he almost called the nurse, thinking that it must be some delayed, unidentified fatal injury.

In the blackness of the night, he thought he would die from it, and when morning came, he was gray and stiff. Sister Ignatius could see he had

had a setback. She was determined to keep his visitors to the absolute minimum time. If it had not been for Albert Hesselberth, the persistent German who had wormed his way into occupying the sunroom for hours on end, thus demonstrating that Izak was permitted visitors, she would have denied them entry entirely.

Sister Ignatius had written Izak's letters for him, so she had some idea how much this morning's meeting would mean to him. Frankly she expected him to be "let go." How many young girls could or would willingly do what she herself did, caring for a man so badly injured? This girl's being promised rather than married posed yet another problem, it being considered inappropriate for an unmarried woman to see or touch a man's body. She herself was a member of the only class excepted, a virgin nursing nun given access to the body of anyone. It was no good, this business of administering an emotional shock to a patient, and yet families did it, being demanding or thoughtless and often adding to the emotional pain by hauling the patient out of the hospital much too soon in hopes of saving a penny.

Sure, and this is the way to disaster, she thought. *I will read about him in the obituary column unless I put my foot down and stop any nonsense, any nonsense at all.*

At the same time, Sister Ignatius looked carefully to be sure the bandages this morning were spotless, and she took extra care to wind the one around his head so he was as presentable as possible. She helped him into a shirt Albert had provided, one arm in and the other hidden, strapped to his chest. She helped him get seated in a wheelchair, wrapping a robe around his legs, tucking it in firmly.

They will not think this man poorly cared for, oh no, not at Mullanphy and not under my supervision.

CHAPTER 41

NOTHING IS SETTLED

October, 1836: time for one question

The sunroom blinded Izak for a moment. He held his head sideways and blinked at the light. Albert was there as usual, and beside him a cluster of people, who now leapt up and came rushing toward him, the nearest being his own dear Amalie, whose smile was irresistible, lit by happiness too genuine to be denied.

He smiled as she knelt by his side and gingerly reached for his hand, afraid to touch him. When her hand at last touched his, he felt the amazing, healing power of her presence, a shock such as he had first experienced aboard *Enigma*.

He could find few reasons to speak to Amalie in Texas, and New Orleans offered little more opportunity, but when the family left to travel up the Mississippi River, he had no choice but to follow her. What a glorious two weeks it had been aboard *Yellow Stone*, time aplenty to fall in love.

Then his well-grounded, sensible, sunshiny Amalie broke into tears: "I have been so very worried about you."

"There is no reason to worry; I am almost well, as you can see."

Sister Ignatius was astounded to hear this, there being not an iota of truth to it, and these being the only hopeful words Izak had said since he came into her care. But even in this first moment she began to be reassured, Amalie being so clearly fresh and honest and caring, despite her obvious extreme youth. Niklas and Katrina were there, too, and Albert was out of his chair and hanging around in the background.

"Let's not crowd about," Sister Ignatius said. "Please take a seat. Just there behind yourselves, please, and let me bring him a little closer."

She got them all seated and Izak drawn up close, not with them facing him like inquisitors but so that Izak and Amalie could hold hands, since they seemed so inclined to do so.

"I had almost given up hope that you would come," Izak murmured to Amalie.

"We came as soon as ever we could," she replied. "It has only been…" and here she looked at her mother for help … "a week…"

"Ten days," Katrina amended.

"…since we received your letter."

"But *Ottawa* did not sail for another week."

Sister Ignatius listened as the talk ran on past inquiries about his health to questions about the rest of the family and their exploration of Chicago and their new house in Hennepin. As Albert Hesselberth launched into a retelling of the fire, she quietly left them, looking at her watch with a warning that visiting hours would be over in half an hour, no more, and "That means you too, Mr. Hesselberth."

In fact, Albert Hesselberth circled around the hospital halls while the family was ushered out amid promises to be back on the morrow. He reappeared in the sunroom before Sister Ignatius could wheel Izak out the door.

"Please," he pleaded, "let me have just a few minutes with him, time for one question, that's all I ask."

She threw up her hands and gave them three minutes more.

"What do you think?" asked Albert as soon as the nun was out of hearing, "Are you satisfied that her devotion is genuine?"

Izak looked exhausted but happier than Albert had ever seen him.

"Nothing is settled. We did not talk about the future. But her happiness is contagious, and I am much encouraged by her parents. They should know which way the wind blows, and they do not look as if they will stand in the way. Soon I shall try for a specific answer, but tonight I will sleep soundly. I think my girl is still my girl."

"I do too, Izak, and a luckier man I have not ever seen," Albert said and then gulped with dismay. "I mean 'luckier in love,'" he stammered.

Izak grinned at him: "I know what you mean, Albert, and I agree. It's a new day when anyone at all can call this crippled old man lucky, a happy new day."

In the weeks that followed, in St. Louis, in the Mullanphy Hospital sunroom, with Albert Hesselberth acting as their chaperone even though they could hear a very faint snoring where he sat dozing on his favorite chair, Izak and Amalie talked.

Izak's head was free of bandages, but he was nearly bald, only a fuzz of new growth showing, and one arm was still wrapped tightly against his chest. He had trousers on today and had walked to the sunroom on his own. Amalie seemed average in every way—in height, in hair color, and in looks—until she spoke, until she smiled, until one looked closely. And then one might, like Izak, see her beauty and so much more: kindness, capability, and intelligence. She had her mother's clear, pink skin and her father's white teeth and wide smile, but her voice was all her own, a musical ripple with a calming effect like water over stones.

Understanding the sorrows of others came easily to Amalie. Izak saw this in her face as he told her of his first wife, of that beautiful young woman's death in childbirth and of the death of one of the twins a day later. The two Astrids, mother and daughter, shared a grave in Copenhagen.

"One child was too small to survive," he told her. "It was a girl I named Astrid after her mother. Even the boy, Lars, was so small I was afraid to carry him except on a pillow. Without Ingrid, my sister, who is a mother herself and knows about these things, I could not have kept the poor little thing alive."

"How is the child now?"

"Oh," said Izak with a smile, "he knows nothing about the tragedy of his birth, and to look at him now, you would never see the slightest sign of it. I left him surrounded by cousins, my sister's children, five of them at the time, and she has probably added another one or two by now, as happy and healthy a family as anyone could want."

Amalie returned his smile, and he could read in her big gray eyes her thought: as happy and healthy a family as we shall have.

Lars had been three when Izak last saw him and almost in breeches— "Don't hurry him," his sister Ingrid told Izak. "It won't do any good." It was clear already that Lars was fated to be a big man; he was long and heavy for a baby, but this did not protect him from ear troubles that woke him screaming.

"He'll grow out of it," Ingrid said, as the boy clung to her, her own eyes shadowed from having been up half the night with him. It was as if this pain drummed all other crankiness out of him. When free of it, he was as sweet-tempered as a child could be. Like his cousins, Lars was a towhead, but unlike them, his eyebrows were so blond as to disappear against his skin.

In this way, Izak always saw his beloved Astrid in his son's face, Astrid who had been tall and blonde, the very picture of a strong, healthy Nordic woman. Together, Izak and Astrid had drawn eyes wherever they went, tall, fair, and handsome. It was an unspeakable tragedy to have such a fine woman die in childbirth and that before she had yet reached her twentieth birthday.

Later in life, when Amalie thought back on these days she and Izak spent together in the hospital and then at that first house in Hennepin when the wood still smelled new, she would think it a deep and necessary sharing of sorrows and hopes, a perfect interlude before they married, with time to talk almost endlessly, to share their most intimate thoughts, to become one in mind and spirit.

CHAPTER 42

GOOD FER BEER AND SAUERKRAUT

slipping unseen into America

The women of Hennepin were no brighter than those of any other frontier town, but even they soon knew the cause of Frau Kästner's discomfort, her having run out of church on a Sunday morning with a certain green look around the gills. More than one was a little smug about the delicate condition of this beautiful foreign woman. Katrina's elegant manners, jade necklace, and quite fashionable silk dress could do that to the most generous of women. But all these women were or had been or soon would be pregnant, and they could not find it in their hearts to be anything other than kind, especially with winter setting in.

Women on the frontier were scarce. They needed to stick together, and besides, this poor woman was, just a few months after the family's arrival, about to lose the only daughter she had of a useful age. The girl was to be married off, come springtime, to the Hero of St. Louis, whose story had been told in a little broadsheet that sold for two and half cents and was read by far more Christian souls than had paid the publisher for it. At that point this poor woman would have no one but her men, great strapping gentlemen though they were, especially the one of them, and a wispy girl-child, barely eight, and a little boy not long in breeches. This poor woman would need their help.

Katrina did not feel like a poor woman. She and Niklas were pleased and secretly a little proud of themselves to have another child on the way. She suspected, quite rightly, that this wave of exuberance would not last. It would wither in the face of the hard work of raising an infant to the age of reason.

Amalie was embarrassed, of course, and even the older boys looked at Niklas with some surprise. Katrina was glad that Amalie would be with her for the first year, in spite of her grief at the reason for it. The girl would certainly be useful at a time like this, and it would be good practice for her to care for a baby and even to witness the childbirth, which was enough of a shock for any woman without ignorance making it worse. Besides, a late child, should it thrive, was insurance against a lonely old age. At such a time, anyone would understand their desire for a girl, one whose purpose in life would be to care for her elderly parents.

The Kästner family had arrived wealthy, at least compared to many of those trekking across Illinois from Ohio or Kentucky or Virginia, but their stock-pile of goods for trade—rice, sugar, molasses, tobacco, calico, and a few odds and ends—was already shrinking as winter arrived, when few ventured outside their house or cabin.

As the season turned, Niklas grew ever more reluctant to spend the gold coins he had buried in a pottery crock beside the barn. It made no sense to bury this cache, considering the success he had had in Chicago's real estate trading, but the rate of change made his head spin. When he thought of what he had risked and might have lost! Already there were whispers of bank failures in Vermont and although that state was a long way from Illinois, it gave one pause. Besides, too much had already been spent to bring the family across, and he had bought more supplies on their recent visit to Izak, perhaps more than could be sold before winter set in, and there must be enough cash left to buy in the spring. He and the boys, Hank and Will, sought every opportunity to hire themselves out. They needed to replenish their savings and make connections with those they hoped would be customers when next summer gave people something to trade.

This week the work had been easy, Niklas thought, bitter cold, but easy. As a veteran of the Napoleonic Wars, Niklas had come to America well-armed. He and his two older sons were skilled in the sword, knife, pistol, and musket. Such expertise with weapons was not lost on the residents of Hennepin, and now he had been asked to be the rifleman, killing several steers for butchering.

One of the farmers with animals to be killed was a Yankee from upstate New York, Michael Taylor, whose farm was a mile outside town. On his way there, Niklas rode through burned-out areas left by the autumn prairie fires and strips burned intentionally around settlers' homes and outbuildings to keep them from being engulfed by wildfires. He rode past homesteads with smokehouses at work, puffing away in the friendliest way with the promise of ham and bacon and smoked sausage for their owners. A frosty month like December was the proper time for butchering, salting, and smoking. Here in America, no one built smoke closets into chimneys as had been done in the old house in Berleburg, such a good idea and a pity to lose it.

The Taylor farm was tucked up to a stand of woods and looked fairly well established. Michael and his sons had built a sturdy chute with a gate and a hinged side panel. It is never easy to drive cattle into a narrow space, but wiser to tie an animal tightly to what looks like an innocent corner of fencing and swing a side panel and back gate into place. Niklas looked it over and was pleased with the structure. On the front length of fencing, a platform and gun brace had been built, and it was here that Niklas took his place, stepping onto the platform and standing quietly so as not to add to the animal's fear of finding itself in an enclosure.

Quickly and quietly, he aimed the rifle at the creature's forehead and fired. The dead animal was dragged away immediately, in hopes of leaving little smell of blood on the chute. It was loaded onto a waiting oxcart. Another steer was brought out from the barn, and in this way, he dispatched five animals in one afternoon, including three from nearby farms, but even though the chute was kept out of sight of the steers, enough escaped in the way of shots, screams, and the smell of blood to make each animal wilder than the next, and he was lucky to get the last one down, a big brute of a steer, before it could break the chute and escape. *That one,* he thought, *should have gone first.*

Work done for the day, Niklas was invited in for supper at the Taylor house. It was a clever design he had not seen before, two log cabins with about a twelve-foot open breezeway between them. Michael Taylor saw Niklas studying it as the two men walked toward the house.

"It's called a dogtrot or possum trot," he explained. "I spent some time in Alabama as a young man, and I reckon it works better down south where the breezeway can be used all year. Next week I'll bring the wood pile over to the back side to block the winter wind."

The room into which Niklas was ushered had a board floor and log walls, skillfully planed, caulked with mud, and whitewashed. A fire kept the room bright, and a lantern was lit to chase the shadows out of the other side of the room. On the mantle were candles, a Connecticut clock, a Bible, a neat stack of newspapers, and four fancy cups and saucers.

Michael Taylor motioned Niklas to a chair with a deftly caned seat, saying, "I learned caning as a boy. A most useful art." He lit his pipe and looked inquiringly at Niklas, who had not thought to bring a pipe.

Niklas asked, "You said you lived for a while in the South, sir. May I ask how that came about?"

"You may, sir. I went south to visit my sister, who had married an Alabama man. I never liked the cold myself and wished to see if settling there, near her, might be preferable to our farm in New York."

"And yet I observe you here, so you must have concluded that the North has advantages over the South?"

"Not as regards winter, sir!" Michael Taylor laughed. "But as a matter of making a living, so I did. There it takes slaves and not just as labor but breeding 'em and trading 'em. Which pays better than cotton or sugar. Even if I had wanted to, which I did not, it would have been out of reach. The best I could hope for was to be a tenant farmer. And go into debt every year! Small farmers there live a miserable, no-account life, not even able to afford shoes, let alone a book or newspaper." He waved with pride to the stack on his mantle. "I decided I was happier to work where my own labor and that of my sons and daughters would be enough to live in comfort."

Michael Taylor was a man of curiosity, so he asked one question after another about the Germanies and about the family's journey here.

Presently Mrs. Taylor and two pretty daughters served the men supper, a tasty beef hash with potatoes, carrots, and turnips mixed in, followed by an apple brown betty. The daughters faded into the kitchen, but Mrs. Taylor brought in a third chair and joined them for supper. Her gentle conversation showed her to be as kind and intelligent a woman as Niklas had met in a long while.

Katrina will like her, thought Nikas.

The only blot on the day had been neighbors of the Taylors, two tall, rude, emaciated Kentuckians, making fun of his accent and his marksmanship.

"Whew, that was fast," said the taller of the two, after a particularly quick, sure shot of Niklas's.

"Yaah," said the other, trying to mock the German "ja." "They's good fer dat and little else."

"Wahl now, give 'em credit," said the tall one. "I bet 'Dutch' here is also good fer beer and sauerkraut." They both laughed. The two men spoke freely, having heard Niklas's German accent and imagining, unaccountably, that he could not understand English.

Dummkopfs, thought Niklas. *Who is so dimwitted as to insult the man with the gun?*

Niklas himself had no great love for Prussia, quite the opposite, having been exceedingly happy to escape it. But his hometown of Berleburg was as clean and pretty a little town as existed anywhere on Earth, and his German-speaking compatriots, conscripted by Napoleon as he had been, were the finest men he had ever known. It was infuriating to hear small-minded men think only their kind belonged in America. They had forgotten their own immigrant ancestors and imagined that the door should now be slammed shut. If he had to hear insults about Germans, Niklas decided, it had better be he himself doing the insulting, not some ignoramuses whose knowledge of the world stretched all of two states.

Niklas came home with a hind quarter of beef and a thick chunk of beef liver in payment and now, he and everyone else in the family were hard at work making the most of this glorious meat, putting flank, round, and shank cuts to cook in a kettle with plenty of melted snow and onions. Potatoes, carrots, and turnips would be added tomorrow and perhaps the odd beet or parsnip could be found. Mrs. Taylor had kindly dug into the snow to send along a few sprigs of sage and parsley.

Niklas sliced off steaks and roasts, three steaks to share tonight, more to sell and some to be hung outside in cloth bags, to freeze solid overnight and then be packed in a barrel with salt. Hank was at the meat grinder, readying the toughest parts and trimmings for sausage, also to be frozen. Will was outside, tramping through the snow to visit nearby houses and tell about cuts available from the saddlebag slung over his shoulder and tomorrow in the little general store in their house.

The Kästner family slept downstairs in this coldest part of the year, clustered around two of the Norwegian stoves, the boys in the dining room and the parents and little ones in the parlor, all of them under the buffalo robes Mr. Grafton had so wisely recommended. Germany was cold in the winter, and Niklas had known deadly cold on the retreat from Moscow—minus forty or fifty degrees, when a man's luck or skill in finding shelter was the difference between life and death—and he was not eager to suffer cold again.

In the coming summer, Niklas swore, every chink and crevice in their hastily built frame house would be stuffed with wool roving or linen tow, coated with clay and lime stucco outside; whitewash, paper or cloth would be hung on the walls inside and wool rugs laid in as many rooms as he could afford. This light frame house would never be the thick, sturdy, half-timber home they had left in Berleburg, but it could be made far more livable, and Niklas was determined to do it.

On this cold night with raw beef hanging half-frozen in a small cupboard on the back porch, Niklas was the first to hear boards being smashed and a deep growl. He had known a thief might come in the night, before the meat had frozen solid, and he was ready for it. He was up in a flash, Hank having heard it too and right behind him, their rifle, muskets, and pistols at the ready in the kitchen. Niklas threw open the shutters on the kitchen window, stared face to face with an angry panther, dodged the animal's swipe with claws the like of which he had never seen, and slammed the shutters closed. But the Kästner men were not defeated, not by any stretch of the imagination. A small window on the stair landing was directly above the kitchen window, and Hank was already leaping up the stairs.

"Fire on my signal," shouted Niklas, as he opened the shutters just enough for the barrel of his rifle.

"Ready!" Hank was at the upper window and pointing his pistol directly at the panther's head, which was not at all far from him. The creature had smelled the meat, and its head was already twisted to one side, jaws open and tearing at the beef.

"Fire!" shouted Niklas. Both shots went home.

"Got it!" Hank yelled. *What an excellent omen,* he thought, *for my journey west.*

On the porch, the animal looked dead, but both men waited to see if it moved again. In the morning, they would skin it.

"We stand watch," said Niklas, "until first light. It could have a mate. It could draw wolves." He turned to Will, who was standing at the entrance to the kitchen. "Bring a buffalo robe."

Niklas and his oldest son might have their differences, Hank being naturally pessimistic and chafing in his father's orderly household, but no one could take his place when he went west in the Spring.

"Congratulations!" said Will. "A trophy and a panther-skin rug, exactly what the parlor needs...or what we can sell, Father."

"I'll take the first watch," said Niklas, who knew he would not sleep anyway. Katrina was up by now and snuggled under a buffalo robe with him, wanting to know exactly what had happened, and inspecting his face to see that those claws had not reached him, not that adding to the many scars already there would amount to much.

When the butchering and preserving was done, Niklas, Hank, and Will delivered the last of the steaks to the inn and stayed to share a beer with Oskar Miller. Niklas told Oskar about the anti-German feeling he had heard expressed.

"Should we expect this in all Southerners—is it 'Whites' they are called or 'Kaintucks'?" He wanted the boys to hear Oskar's answer.

"It's often enough you will hear it from 'em, not so much from the Yankees, though you never can tell. It won't last long, though. In a few years accents fade, and my Mueller became Miller. Herr Guttmann will become Mr. Goodman..." He grinned at telling them how his own name had been anglicized, and it was true that the Oskar sitting before them looked as American as anyone. He was thought of as Pennsylvanian, not Pennsylvania Dutch.

"Maybe half the Whites," Oskar continued, "are inclined to be..." He searched for a word, "prejudiced...whose only consolation is thinking they're better than Blacks. Their womenfolk are just as bad or worse. The irony is, maybe half of them came north to get away from the plantation system, where a poor White man has no chances at all. He's as despised by the plantation owner as slaves are, and to rub it in, he must stand silent witness to the sins of slavery, never saying a word. They say Abe Lincoln's family got out of Kentucky like that—well, that and what everyone comes here for, cheap land. But not so many come so far, like you and yours did!"

"There's few things better for a family than land," Niklas agreed, smiling to think that no one in this new country, including Oskar Miller, knew of how very unwelcome Niklas had been in Prussia or how the Prussian army lay in wait to seize Hank and Will. Some facts, he thought, are better buried at sea.

Hank was not happy to have escaped the Prussian army, and he certainly did not want to be tied down to land. Dirt-grubbing, he thought, was not for him, or at least not until he had traipsed through the Great West, seen its buffalo, and discovered what riches it held.

Oskar is right, Will thought, *about slipping unseen into America.* He was determined to lose his accent as quickly as possible. Will shared some of his father's glibness with language, and he would use it to become an American before anyone even realized where he had come from. Even at this moment he was silently working his tongue around the most difficult English sounds, practicing them. Somewhere in the back of his mind a thought took root, an idea not yet completely formed, about how land might become more to him than fields and homestead.

CHAPTER 43

THE SUDDEN CHANGE

December 20, 1836: an icy hell

In Hennepin, the Kästners had a crowded house for the winter—the seven of them; Benji, the Hoosier hired man, really no more than a boy; a ninth, Eddie Peel, having come up from Havana to work at the lumber mill with Will; and a tenth, Amalie's intended, Izak Peterssen.

The eleventh soul in the house that winter was Katrina's unborn child. Although her pregnancy was now showing, Katrina continued running a household with six hungry men, two women, and two children. The unborn child added another to the imagination if not the reality of the house, an happy but difficult time ahead that made everyone, especially Katrina, pleased to have Amalie still at home and able to cook and clean. It had been to everyone's satisfaction that Izak had come to live with them, an odd arrangement with the marriage delayed, but one that gave Izak a few more months to heal and Amalie a few more months to grow up.

If Niklas occasionally felt inclined to grumble at the crowding, he knew that most houses in Hennepin held ten or twelve or even more—think of Mark Beaubien with his wife and twenty-three children! And most of those families were in log houses with dirt floors and half the comfort of the Kästners' own. As in most houses, youth dominated, six between fourteen and twenty-seven. Niklas found this invigorating, especially as it led to lively conversations at table, but he sometimes felt he should declare the house a university. And charge tuition.

Except for her nights, Amalie spent much of her time in the boys' room, where she and Izak waited and hoped for him to regain the use of his arm and continue recovering from burns on his back and scalp. He no longer wore the turban of bandages he did the first time she saw him in the hospital. The skin on the back of his head had healed, and hair was beginning to grow.

After years of wearing his hair long and braided in the old-fashioned sailor's way, it seemed impossibly strange to Izak to feel nothing but stubble behind his ears.

Sister Ignatius of the Mullanphy Hospital had shown Amalie how to cleanse and wrap Izak's wounds, pleased to see the girl so intent on learning and so sensible about seeing her fiancé's bare and wounded back. Amalie had brothers of her own, of course, and had seen the naked backs of each of them often enough, but most girls would have turned giggly or been too embarrassed to touch a man's skin.

Sister Ignatius could see that Amalie had both of the most important characteristics of a good nurse: the ability to understand another's pain and the ability to stay calm and take action, to do what needed to be done. *It's a pity*, thought Sister Ignatius, *to see such nursing talent go to waste, though I suppose she has plenty of private nursing ahead: her injured fiancé, the many children she will probably bear, and her aging parents.*

On December 20, 1836, a deep layer of snow covered the ground, but it dawned unseasonably warm. It was a sunshiny delight, an unexpected midwinter pleasure, and the sunshine and southerly wind quickly turned the snow into thick, dirty slush.

"Another day of this," said Niklas, "and we will be free of snow."

Katrina glanced out the kitchen window. "I think you are right. But as much as we like a thaw, it's hard on plants." She was thinking of the roots and starts carried from Berleburg and now dug into the Illinois soil.

"Should I cover them?"

She thought a moment. "Yes, if you would please. Shovel a thicker blanket of snow on them. It might be just the protection they need."

The back porch had already been swept free of snow, and Jakob begged to go outside. A boy almost the same age, Gus Shepard, had stayed overnight. His parents, Smiley and Catherine, were the first to settle in Hennepin besides fur trappers, and Gus was the first White child born here. Both boys were hopping with excitement to get outside. Katrina told Lisette, "Keep the children on the porch—no puddle splashing, no sopping wet moccasins!"

By midafternoon Niklas went out with Hans and Benji to begin evening chores, knowing dark would come soon enough. It was too warm in the barn, and they soon stripped off their barn coats. They worked without discussion, listening to horses and cattle chomping steadily, their teeth moving like mortars and pestles against one another, the animals stomping or snorting as hay was tossed into mangers, the dust flying into their nostrils, the pleasant smell of ground-up hay and oats filling the barn. Will and Eddie were away at Herr Guttmann's sawmill, bringing in good hard cash for the family. They had been gone since dawn. Evening chores done, Niklas set the other two to work on building a wider, sturdier haymow ladder. *Good to get it done*, he thought, *when it is warm enough to work in the barn.*

Not long after Niklas returned to the house, Katrina, her hands covered with bread dough, asked him to light a lantern.

"Of course," he said, but it seemed early, and as he reached for the lantern, Niklas glanced out the window at the northwest sky. A huge black cloud was moving fast toward them, something of a size and color he had never seen. He grabbed his barn coat and turned to the door.

"Weather coming on," he said. "Gather the children and stoke the fireplace. I'm going to bring those boys inside."

When he opened the back door, the wind whipped the door out of his hands and slammed it against the side of the house. Katrina gasped at the smack of the door, the sudden cold, and the deep bellow of the gale. It reminded her of the tornado she and Niklas had survived in August and the hurricane they had just barely survived in the Gulf of Mexico.

She dropped the dough she had been kneading, wiped her hands on her apron, and ran, yelling as she went. Lisette and Jakob were by her side in moments—Gus had gone home after lunch—and she could hear Izak lurching down the stairs. She knew Amalie would be coming down in front of him, to steady him and catch him if needed. The house was already almost as dark as night, a very cold wind howling through every crack and crevice. They heard loud cracks, thinking first of distant guns, and then realizing it was the clapboards of their house warping and cracking as they froze.

Katrina pushed logs into the keeping room fireplace, fanning the embers. "Lisette, draw chairs up to the fire. Enough chairs for all of us. Amalie, bring the buffalo robes." Izak took Jakob on his lap. With his injured back and one arm still in a sling, he could do little except keep the child warm and out of the way.

Outside, Niklas slogged to the barn through thick slush, one arm folded over his face. Hank had already seen the cloud, had brought the cows in and was struggling with the last of the Morgans, trying to get the skittish horse into the barn. Niklas reached out to push the animal and realized the fingers of his hand were frozen together. Together they got the horse inside, tied the animals up next to each other, and threw every saddle blanket in the barn across their backs.

Niklas saw that Hank and Benji were already cold, their boots soaked through, and their gloves wet.

"We have to get to the house," he told them. "Each man is to hang on to the man in front for dear life. Hans, you go first, Benjamin, you go in the middle, and do not lose your grip on Hans. As fast as we can, boys, as fast as we can."

They stepped out onto a thick layer of ice, the slush frozen into eddies, waves and clumps that made walking on it awkward and slippery. For their first few steps, they were sheltered from the full force of the wind by the barn, but then the wind hit their backs in full force, fairly skating them across the ice. They stumbled up the porch stairs, the door blew open as soon as they cracked it, and it took both Niklas and Hans to force it closed again. Their eyebrows and beards were full of ice.

"They'll be in the keeping room," Niklas told the boys. Benji had already plopped down on the kitchen floor and pulled off his frozen boots. The tops of his socks were frozen to his skin. He jumped up at Niklas's words and ran to the parlor after Niklas and Hans. There the fire was burning brightly, and chairs were drawn tightly up to it, buffalo robes stacked to one side, and Amalie coming back downstairs with an armful of sweaters and blankets.

As soon as Benjamin's socks had melted enough to be pulled away from his skin, and Niklas and Hans got out of wet or frozen clothing, they wrapped up as warmly as could be and looked about in apprehension. The house seemed to be holding for the moment, but it creaked and cracked all around them. The walls and floors were more like sieves than solid barriers, cold coming in everywhere and snow forming streaks at every crevice.

I will build again in the spring, Niklas swore to himself, *and this time we will have none of this newfangled balloon framing ready to fall down about our ears, but solid logs at the core of the walls, every chink filled with clay and lined inside and out against the ferociousness of blizzards and tornados, clapboards on the outside, thick wallpaper on the inside and Turkey rugs to keep the floors warm.*

He had anticipated rough weather in America. Many "America letters" sent by early immigrants made a point of it. Besides, his family was soft in this way, with their hometown, Berleburg, famed for its gentle and agreeable climate, but still, this was more than anyone could have expected, last summer's tornado and the hurricane in the Caribbean—it was really more than any one family deserved to be hit with. They could thank their lucky stars for Mr. Grafton, of Grafton's Big Store in St. Louis, who had recommended four buffalo robes, a number that seemed absurd to Niklas at the time, but now was barely enough to share on this very cold day.

Katrina quietly asked Niklas the obvious question, "What about Will and Eddie?" The two boys were at work at the mill when the blizzard hit.

"We shall find out soon enough," he said. "Augustus Guttmann is a sensible man. He will have known to get everyone to shelter." They knew the mill was the strongest building in Hennepin and that Augustus Guttmann would not send anyone home in the face of such a storm. The mill was built out over the Illinois River rapids, source of the water that powered its wheel and turned its millstones. It was indeed the strongest building in town, built to hold up to spring floods. It was also the most exposed. If the wind was strong enough to destroy the mill, everyone inside would fall into the river, and if that were so, it had probably already happened. Besides, no ordinary sawmill was equipped with buffalo robes or any other way to stay warm, a dismal set of facts they felt no need to rehearse aloud, especially in front of Lisette and Jakob. Amalie and Izak had already exchanged grim looks. They knew.

"I will get them," said Hank, throwing a robe aside and starting to rise.

"No, you will not." Niklas was the only one in the room who understood such extreme cold as this, having suffered it in the Russian winter of 1813, on the Grande Armée's disastrous retreat from Moscow. "In cold like this, shelter is the difference between life and death." To make his point, he held up one hand, showing the fingertip lost to frostbite all those years ago. It was a motion he had never made, and it surprised him even now.

Izak looked up in surprise. Niklas rarely spoke to Hank like this, as if he were a child. The two of them, Hank and Izak, were almost the same age, but Izak was a full-fledged sea captain and now, most regrettably, the Hero of St. Louis. He could hardly remember his own father.

Hank sat again, glum, unhappy, but knowing that his father was right and that his father would not let him go.

Little Jakob had fallen asleep in Izak's arms, and Lisette was drowsing off and on, but everyone else felt a new bleakness settle over the family. Katrina rocked as she prayed, thinking of their repeated decisions to move on, to leave Cuba, Texas, and New Orleans. Surely none of those places ever suffered a blizzard like this, of a ferocity such as she had never seen. Niklas looked as discouraged as she had ever seen him. She could imagine that he was wondering why he had brought them to a place like frozen Russia, the source of his nightmares. She wondered if Niklas would want to go south again. For warmth, might he accept life amid the scourge of slavery?

Hank's thoughts echoed Katrina's with an added worry about his plans for the wilderness. Fur trapping was winter business, something of little concern until this demonstration of the ferocity of an American winter.

"Are we guilty of pride?" Izak and Amalie heard her mother ask this, even though she had spoken in a murmur meant for Niklas alone. They were together under one of the buffalo robes, and now Niklas shook off his mood and reached for her hand.

"Never, my love. This is but an interruption, an odd and unexpected delay. Today looks like an icy hell, but Will and Benji are young and strong. They'll survive, and then we'll see what tomorrow looks like."

"It can hardly be worse."

He nodded in agreement.

Many hours later, Will and Eddie Peel finally burst through the front door of the Kästner house and found everyone still clustered about the keeping room fireplace. They were welcomed into such a vortex of cheers and hugs and congratulations that it made them giddy, even though they were more man than boy and had that very day proven themselves strong and courageous in several important ways.

When the welcome quieted down, they told of how the wind had sliced through the big gap in the mill around the waterwheel and the way the mill itself shuddered and shook and cracked. In spite of the thickness of its timbers, they thought it would give out. Then the river froze solid with a suddenness no one thought possible and gave the mill a stability and strength it would never have otherwise had.

"Dora was with us at the mill, Mother, and we took in several travelers," Will said, "saving them from certain death. No one had ever seen anything like this. Antonie Bourbouvis was one of the men who sheltered with us, and he swore no such a thing has ever happened before."

Bourbouvis ought to know, thought Niklas, who had some time ago realized that the vineyards they dreamt of while watching last autumn's sunsets would never last through such extremes of weather. *And what loss of stock might we find,* he wondered, *when it is safe to venture out to the barn?*

Dora had sat by Will as they all got as close as they could to the wood stove. He had not dared to reach for her hand, but he was convinced she had crowded in a little closer to him than was really necessary, and he felt sure the shared threat of death had brought them closer in an afternoon than an ordinary year might have.

"It came on so fast," Eddie added, "we had no chance to leave the mill, but Augustus, I mean Herr Guttmann, he has a snug little office in the mill with a Franklin stove. It was crowded, and the wood was running low before we left, but it kept us alive."

"Yes," agreed Will. "And, Gott sei dank, our boots and pant legs had dried by then. The men we took in from the street had a rougher time of it with their wet feet and legs. By the time Monsieur Bourbouvis got to us, his pant legs were frozen solid."

"It's still very cold out now, said Eddie. "Everything froze so quickly, the road is rough, full of clods and bumps. Little waves frozen in place."

"Ja," Will agreed, "but the wind has died almost entirely. We may even see a clear sky and stars tonight, but who can say? I would not be sure of anything on such a day as we have had."

Later still, Oskar Miller pounded on their door and was quickly admitted. "Just checking on you," he said, looking with satisfaction at the group surrounding him, counting heads even as he spoke.

"Will and Eddie were at the mill—," Niklas began.

"—which almost collapsed until the river froze solid and held it up," Will added. His chest tightened as he recalled that instant when he thought their long journey had been pointless, at least for him. That he would die, he and the Angel of the Mill together, a horrible icy drowning.

"—and we saved Antonie Bourbouvis," Eddie said.

They told the rest of the story then, falling over themselves to add this detail and that.

Hank scrunched down in his chair to hear again about Antonie Bourbouvis, frontiersman extraordinaire, who was to guide him into the deep western wilderness, having to be saved.

"They are already calling it 'The Sudden Change,'" said Oskar.

"Better they should call it 'Ein Sudden Einfrieren.'" Niklas said: "A Sudden Freeze."

"Whatever you call it," said Eddie, "It was no ordinary blizzard."

Eddie might be only sixteen, but he had lived all of his life in Illinois or Indiana. "For the love of God, I hope we never see anything the like of it again."

Word had already come in, Oskar told them, of a man and his daughter killed by the storm. They had gone out to a far pasture to call in the cows, lightly dressed; it had been so mild just before the storm. The pair of them were frozen in their tracks trying to get back to barn or house, frozen as they stood, embracing each other. The rest of the family found them and sent word to a neighboring farm, but even with help the corpses could not be freed from the ice and brought inside.

"That will be the sad work of tomorrow, and you will be called upon to help," said Oskar.

"Is there someone to make the coffins?" asked Hank. He had never made a coffin, but after a summer of work with Richard Billings, master carpenter of *Enigma*, he knew he could.

"Oh, yes, with all the building going on, the town is full of carpenters, and Herr Guttmann will have boards cut already." Oskar heard himself say, "Herr Guttmann," with some surprise. He had grown up among German-speaking Pennsylvania Dutch but had long ago put aside that language for English. It was the effect of the German accents all around him at this moment. "I expect their near neighbors will have already set to coffin-making."

"This poor man and his daughter, are they, were they, English?" Niklas was thinking of Michael Taylor and the daughters he had glimpsed when he had supper with that kind, intelligent family.

"English, last name Smith. Yankees from Vermont or New Hampshire. A mother and five surviving children with no father now. The girl who died was the oldest—fourteen or fifteen, I think."

My age, thought Amalie.

Not Michael Taylor, thought Niklas.

"How can we help?" asked Katrina.

"Well, now," Oskar rubbed his chin. "The men are going out tomorrow to cut the bodies free and move them; these men will need to be fed. And any further kindness will be appreciated, I am sure, as the wife..." He corrected himself, "widow ... gets on her feet again and has to make guests welcome for the wake and funerals. Good to be known for kindness, as a newcomer and as a German, I think."

"Hank and I will go with you tomorrow," said Niklas.

"With enough bread and cheese," Katrina said, "to feed you and others and to leave for the family." She had been making bread when the storm hit, a big batch of four loaves. Now she rose, shook off the buffalo robe, wrapped a thick shawl around her shoulders and went to see about the bread, little enough sacrifice on such a day and one she was glad to make.

"Westward, ever westward."
— Henry Wells

CHAPTER 44

STRANGE BUT SATISFYING

January 1837: "I only wish to be there for you."

The Kästners were doubly lucky to have the boys back safe, but they lost the chickens. It was the least of their concerns.

No matter how cold it was or how deep the snow, chores had to be done every morning and evening, and when the weather was mild, there was firewood to split and a dozen other outdoor tasks to be seen to. Even on days when the cold drove everyone inside, there was not a moment wasted, nor a hand idle. Niklas was in the store, seeing to customers or at the desk doing bookwork. Will and Eddie Peel left every morning but Sundays for work at Herr Guttmann's sawmill. Hank had built a cradle for his new little stepsister or stepbrother to come, and eight-year-old Lisette was knitting caps and mittens and baby blankets, having become quite accomplished with her needles.

Benji, the Hoosier boy, mostly quiet and good with animals, did both the morning and evening chores with Niklas, except for the chickens, which had been Amalie's responsibility. One cow had gone dry, but Benji milked the other. About the only time Katrina saw him smile was when he handed her the milk can each morning, still warm, the cream still rising. She poured it off and set Lisette to churning. They had milk to drink and a nice lump of butter for suppertime and every few days there was enough milk to make a pudding or a cream soup.

Only little Jakob, now six years old, was oblivious to coming events and the constant labor it took to keep the family warm and fed, concentrating only on the wheeled wooden boat Hank had carved for him, the spinning top his father had made for him or whatever stick, rock, or string he pretended led a charmed life.

Katrina was often at her new loom, weaving baby clothes. Another of her rightly famous baby blankets was already cut off the loom, and she worked madly at it in the evenings, quilting the cotton side to the handwoven wool side and embroidering when she was too tired to sit at the loom or quilting frame.

Amalie cooked and cleaned and in every spare moment cut and sewed and wove, making baby clothes for the new one to come and a matching set to go with her in the spring. She had been a little shocked when her mother insisted on this.

"It's inevitable, you know," Katrina had told Amalie, looking at her kindly. "Well, not inevitable," she admitted, "but highly likely."

Amalie was rarely abashed, but now she was. "I'm sure you are right, Mama." she said.

"I only wish I could be there for you, my dear."

"Maybe you will be, Mama, as I may be here, home with you." Amalie thought how strange it was to be expecting both a stepson the same age as her little brother and that she and her mother might be bouncing infants on their knees at the same time. It was a strange feeling.

Katrina sighed to think of Amalie among strangers when a baby came, and if she were to be so unlucky, surrounded by sailors, who, kind as they might be, would be entirely ignorant and incompetent. The least she could do was to send Amalie off with a supply of cloths and clothing for a baby, including a beautifully woven and quilted baby blanket, though if Amalie wanted it embroidered, she would have to do that herself.

When both of them were tired and their fingers stiff from sewing, Katrina regretted the baby clothes left in Berleburg and now being worn by the youngest of Günter and Addie's children, but this thought was quickly quashed as she reflected that there would be no more of those children, Günter having been slain a year ago as he helped them escape the Prussian secret police, enforcers of the king's repression, capable of every barbarity, from spying and torture to outright murder.

She and Niklas would never know whether it was Günter's friendship that made him a target or his own too vocal enthusiasm for the underground German Democracy movement. Perhaps everyone else who shared that particularly rousing evening of solidarity in Cologne had been killed, Niklas escaping only because he was already on a path of escape, or maybe it was just the unluckiest of chances, Günter becoming a victim because he was mistaken for Niklas or simply because he was alone on a deserted road deep in the forests of the otherwise quite civilized country of Prussia.

CHAPTER 45

THE GREAT WEST

July, 1837: rendezvous at Green River Valley

Hank left in February. He and Antonie Bourbouvis waved goodbye as they disappeared on their trek into the Great West. They had pack mules and horses and a buffalo robe and rifles and well-sharpened knives and beaver traps and hampers of food. Hank had named the Morgan gelding for Lainey—how often he thought of her fondly— and at the last minute his father had pressed a surprising number of gold coins on him, as a stake for buying supplies and trinkets for trading with Indians.

There was still a month of ice, or maybe two, before *Ottawa* or any other steamer would try to navigate the Illinois, but Bourbouvis thought the ice might be broken up below Peoria, and if they found it so, they might stop and build a flatboat.

"If not," said Antonie Bourbouvis, "we have feet. And plenty of time to reach the Missouri before the spring season."

Today, with winter, spring, and half the summer gone, it was July 15, and Hank was at Horse Creek in the Green River Valley of Nebraska Territory— an area that would become Wyoming—at the great rendezvous. He lay on a thin straw mattress calling himself a dummkopf and cradling his aching head in his hands, eyes shut against the sunlight and wishing he could stop up his ears.

These people, he thought, *their whooping and howling and dashing on horseback through the camp, yelling like fiends, and the barking and baying of their savage wolf-dogs, and the incessant cracking of rifles and carbines! It makes a perfect bedlam of the camp.* He needed quiet and a real bed. Preferably a perfectly soft feather bed.

For days on the trail, trapping as they went, Hank had looked forward to the rendezvous, listening to stories about it by Bourbouvis and their traveling companions, three of Captain Walker's men and Jean Baptiste Charbonneau. Charbonneau had been born on the Lewis and Clark expedition to Sacagawea, the Shoshone guide, and her French-Canadian husband. He and Hank quickly became friends. Charbonneau spoke French and had learned some German from his years with Duke Niklas Paul Wilhelm of Württemberg, a man known for his love of wilderness. He and Hank could be heard talking in a wild mix of English, French and German, with a little Shoshone thrown in to give Hank a head start with the language, should he ever need it.

Hank had not expected the journey to be easy, and although he was proven right, the winter months were bearable, and it had been a long, beautiful springtime as they went north and into the Rocky Mountains, hunting buffalo, deer, elk, and bear for sustenance and trapping the beaver streams. They avoided attack several times, fought once, rescued two starving trappers who had spent the winter in the mountains, and for a time, when game was scarce, they themselves almost starved. By the time the rendezvous was scheduled, they felt like rich men coming down from the mountains, their mules loaded with furs.

The American Fur Company's mule trains had come the other way, packing whiskey and supplies from St. Louis to Horse Creek and setting up a trading fair—a rendezvous. This year, as always, the valley was alive with singing, dancing, gambling, games, shooting contests, fighting, and races.

A rendezvous had "all [the] extravagances that white men or Indians could invent," as Jim Beckwourth put it. After nearly a year of wilderness-enforced temperance, whiskey flowed always and everywhere.

Jim Bridger, Osborne Russell, Joe Meek, Robert Newell, and Joe Walker were the first to arrive on June 10th. A contingent of Hudson's Bay Company traders came under the direction of John McLeod and Thomas McKay, and a brigade came up from Bent's Fort on the Santa Fe trail, bringing tales of smallpox devastating the Great Plains.

Joseph Thing, second in command of the Columbia River Fishing and Trading Company, came over from Idaho's Fort Hall, and William Gray appeared for the second year in a row. He was one of the missionaries who traveled west with Marcus and Elizabeth Whitman in 1836 and was now returning east from Oregon to find a wife.

Hundreds of Pawnee, Sioux, Shoshone, and Nez-Perce were there, as was a painter all the way from Baltimore, Alfred Jacob Miller. It happened that Miller had studied in Paris and had been most recently in New Orleans, such a surprise for Hank to meet someone in such a remote place who knew those cities. Miller had come with his patron, the Scottish nobleman and adventurer, William Drummund Stewart, who could always be picked out by his flat-crowned hat with its single jaunty feather, and his black cravat. His was one of a thousand remarkable get-ups, the mountain men in buffalo or beaver hats and full sets of fringed leathers, and the men and women of each tribe in their own costumes.

The most eccentric of all may have been what the famous mountain man, Jim Bridger, donned for ceremonial moments at the rendezvous. It was the uniform of the British Life Guard cavalry regiments of the Household Brigade, a full suit of medieval armor, topped with a steel helmet with a red horsehair plume. William Drummund Stewart had met Bridger at earlier rendezvous and brought him the brass and steel armor from England. It clanked most rewardingly when Bridger was in the saddle.

Rendezvous were not to be missed. They were known to be lively, joyous events, where all were welcome—a disparate assemblage of company men, free trappers, Indians, mountain men, trappers' native wives and children, the cheats and buyers of the American Fur Company, and everyone else west of the Mississippi. There were perhaps 2,500 men, women, and children in attendance, half of them native, and twice that number of horses.

It began slowly over a week or more as people arrived and then was kicked off as a proper event by the Indian Cavalcade, a procession of Indigenous men and women in finery on horseback, who circled the entire camp. It would have been intimidating except that all had arrived with one peaceful goal: to trade.

Days later, gallons of whiskey later, the rendezvous drew to a close. Hank and Antonie Bourbouvis hired on with Thomas Fitzpatrick to pack the furs out. The plan was to load the furs into bull boats and float down various streams, named and unnamed, to the Missouri River, their ultimate destination St. Louis. This was known to be dangerous work, the men carrying furs worth a thousand dollars per bundle and facing weeks of managing unwieldy boats through heavy currents, white water, and stretches too shallow to float.

In late August, not far from Joseph Robidoux's trading post at Blacksnake Hills, outside St. Joseph, Missouri, not far from civilization and safety, the Sioux attacked.

By the time the battered little band of White men had crossed Missouri and arrived in St. Louis, Hank was limping badly. Lainey, the Morgan gelding his father had given him, had been lost to a Sioux arrow, and Hank had been shot, too, the second time in his life that a ball had gone right through him. He needed a horse. He needed a bath.

Most of the money Hank had earned in a winter and spring of trapping had gone to whiskey at the rendezvous, and half of the furs had been stolen or ruined, but he could be glad of one thing. He was glad not to have been buried outside St. Joseph, as Antonie Bourbouvis was.

Now at last the bedraggled band of survivors entered St. Louis. Their hearts and hopes were high. They were elated to be among the civilized and ready to be rich men at last, with enough furs left to make it happen.

They found things changed. The States were in the grip of a financial panic, and the price of furs was plummeting.

CHAPTER 46

A MAN WITHOUT A SHIP

late summer, 1837: Tiskilwa

Will stared hard at the top of his father's bent head, the hair now gone gray and thin. *This,* he thought, *is a man who risked all our lives to save us, a man for whom risk was once second nature. Now that same man craves certainty, and keeps his gold buried and going to waste. It is I who suffers this loss, me, the faithful son, the obedient one, the loyal one, of whom everything is expected and to whom nothing is given.*

Had Will but seen the secret smile on his father's face, hidden as Niklas bent low over a plank to which he applied an adze, he might have been more like his usual cheerful self. Niklas was looking forward with pleasure to the tasks of the day, the continuing work of building a stout house, its walls thick with logs and clad in and out.

Niklas was having a lively chat in his mind with Captain Aldo, the friendly riverboat captain who kept the family safe on their run down the Rhine, floating away from Germany and into the Netherlands on the spring flood, bypassing certain inquisitive towns with a wave. He wished he could tell the good captain how much more easily attainable the comforts of life were here in America.

Niklas and Will were in Tiskilwa, a new village on the beautifully hilly and wooded north side of the Illinois River, where they and a crew of strong young men had hewn the timber for their house, split shingles for the roof, and hauled stones for the foundation, all of it either bartered for or found for free on the eighty acres Niklas had purchased as soon as he scouted this land, ten times what he might ever have been able to afford in the Rhineland, if it were available (which it was not), and rich with resources the like of which he had never seen. It was, he sometimes thought, like stumbling upon Eden.

Tomorrow, thought Niklas, *if the weather holds, we will let the house go and harvest the first cutting of hay.* Niklas looked up from his labors to tell his son this, wiped his brow, and saw Will stepping away.

Where is he going now? Niklas wondered.

Izak Peterssen, once a sea captain and now a man without a ship or a ship's owner throwing money at him, raised an axe to slice off another shingle. With his still-weak left arm, he pushed a pile of new shingles out of the way and raised the axe again. A roof takes a lot of shingles, especially on a house like this.

Niklas insisted on a larger, sturdier house to the degree that surprised Izak. It began with thick foundation blocks rough-cut from the bluffs along the river, and then it rose on large logs, which would be well-caulked and clad with lap siding on the outside. Most simply whitewashed log interiors, but Niklas wanted a snug interior, wind- and waterproof. He had given up finding tapestries and decided on wood paneling for the two front parlors, and for everywhere else, he would settle for thick wallpaper.

The house had a central hallway straight through, doors at both ends leading onto front and back porches, and a grand staircase, a wide curve of cherry, its rails and spindles being carved even now by a finish carpenter in Hennepin. The two front parlors would have high ceilings touched with whatever elegant designs the plasterers dreamt of. Tall windows would be set into the front walls at a depth and height for window seats. The central hallways on both floors would be wide enough for furniture. Downstairs, there would be a china cabinet, extra chairs, and two settles. Upstairs, the hall had room for clothes cupboards, chests of drawers and blanket chests, not that the Kästners owned all the furniture yet.

In a design repeated from the frame house in which the family spent its first winter, four flues fed two chimneys. Three flues were linked to their Norwegian-style stoves made in Norway, Illinois, and backed with delftware tiles the Kästners themselves brought from Holland. The fourth flue, in the kitchen, led to a Franklin-style wood stove standing to one side of an open fireplace, the only place needing to be watched for flying sparks. It would be a safe house, a strong house, a big house like the one the family had left in Berleburg, worthy of generations of Kästners.

Izak bounced the axe in his hand, found its balancing point, and thought, *I would rather be doing hard labor than what my sweet Amy faces every day with her mother.*

Katrina still lived and worked, but she moved in a fog of grief. She had lost the child, the one she and Niklas had been so glad about. It was born dead, a beautiful little girl who was to be their first American child, the umbilical cord wrapped around her soft baby neck. They named her Caroline, and she became the first to be buried up on the hill in a beautiful spot chosen as the family graveyard.

Katrina's long, difficult labor had sobered the men in the house and frightened everyone, perhaps Amy and Lisette most, or perhaps little Jakob, who now clung to his mother. She dealt with the birthing stoically, but there was so much blood afterward, and her face was so gray that everyone in the family feared for her life.

Niklas was afraid to touch her. The midwife had looked at him sternly before she left, raised one index finger and said, "No more." In recent weeks, Niklas had tried to interest Katrina in the choice of wallpaper, but she was having none of it. If she could not find interest in color and pattern, he took this to mean she found joy in nothing.

Amy was as good a nurse as any family could hope for and a godsend to her mother, but her own plans to be married to Izak and off to Copenhagen melted like snowflakes with the death of her little sister. That Katrina would grieve, Amy expected. That she would cry so unexpectedly or snap at little Jakob, or suddenly be unable to manage something simple, this was unexpected.

Katrina could not warp the loom, though she had done it for decades. She quit reading to little Jakob, telling Lisette to do it. Worse yet, her nighttime rambles were unnerving. When she could not sleep, she would appear like a specter at Amy and Lisette's bedside, listening to hear their breathing, studying them to see that their chests did in fact rise and fall.

It was hard to help Katrina. She did not want to be touched, she would not eat, and she was often so far away in her thoughts she did not reply to a question or comment. Just yesterday, when Amy tried to get her mother to eat something, Katrina said, "Why? Better to save it for the others."

Now Amy and Izak would wait to marry, perhaps as long as another year. At first, this fact took her breath away, but when it became clear that Izak would stay, she tried to tell herself that perhaps the delay was for the best. With Hank gone west, her father needed the help, and Izak needed yet more time to regain his full strength. In a year, Amy hoped, her mother would be recovered and so would Izak. She prayed for patience.

BOOK FIVE

1848: THE WORLD TURNS

"What is history but a fable agreed upon?"
— Napoleon Bonaparte

CHAPTER 47

MEIN GOTT IM HIMMEL

December 1, 1848: Tiskilwa

From the beginning, when he and Will and Izak built the first Tiskilwa house in the spring of 1837, Niklas would have preferred it to be clad in stone, and now with the Stephens Brickyard open in Tiskilwa, and John Stephens's grand new house in town showing off what handsome things could be done with brick, he was considering replacing the original lap siding. It had only been eleven years since the house was built, but the Sudden Change of '36 was never gone from his memory. This house should be made strong, ready to stand like the one he had been born into, a home built for generations of Kästners, even if they were now called Costners.

The original farmhouse had served them well, and a spectacular first year's crop had made all their efforts seem worthwhile. For a time, it seemed farmers in the North would escape the pain of the Panic of '37. It had hit the South hard, with that region's dependence on annual loans. The Panic slowly came north, and by 1839 and 1840, it spread its gloom everywhere. By now, it had depressed growth for a decade, nearly bankrupted the State of Illinois and imposed a snail's pace on digging the Illinois-Michigan canal. The canal had been finished at last in 1845, and now it carried passengers and goods as long intended.

Such troubles as these had cooled the ardor of many for America, but not for Niklas. He had made it a point to become the first naturalized citizen of Bureau County. Little Jakob had grown up strong and willing, an indispensable help on the farm, and Lisette was being courted by a nice boy from down the road who almost swooned whenever he saw her. Apparently, the very sight of her made his knees weak.

Amalie and Izak had married, and a better match Niklas had never seen. Although they were childless, they had Izak's first son to help them on their farm, the next one over. Will had been married early to Dora, his Angel of the Mill. They lived with Niklas and Katrina and had filled the house with three grandchildren already.

Hank had survived his wilderness year, and come back with tales of grizzlies, Bourbouvis's savage murder, and near-starvation. He had not stayed long in Illinois but had gone off again to farm in Iowa when it was still Indian Territory. He married a girl who had grown up there with no childhood friends but Indians. Perhaps this made them safe and content living where other White settlers feared to build or plow.

Now, as 1848 drew to a close, the entire country boiled with ambition, its eyes glittering with dreams of easy wealth. Gold had been discovered in California, although it might as well have been in China, as far as Niklas was concerned. All sorts were hitting the road any way they could, trying to get there. A few days ago, on December 5, President James K. Polk confirmed the gold strike in an address to Congress, and not a day went by without more foolishness about heading west. Just last month, nearly thirty thousand men left Independence, Missouri, in wagon trains bound for California. Thirty thousand!

The place had already been fought over and maybe made a state already, as if gold were all it took. It disgusted Niklas. *Was not family more important than gold? Was not owning land more important? The Bible was clear: "Ye cannot serve God and mammon."*

Will looked for all intents and purposes like any comfortable, well-off farmer, a certain thickness around the waist, the long curve of a pipe, and the crinkle of a newspaper in his hands. He and his father sat side by side in rocking chairs in front of the parlor fireplace, stoked this winter evening to a pleasant blaze.

The chairs squeaked as the men rocked, Niklas reading the family Bible, as he did every night. Hank had made the chair during the fall and winter he spent at home after his long ramble west and before he took himself off to Iowa. Hank's horse, the fine, sturdy little Morgan Niklas bought for him, had been shot out from under him, and Hank would always have a wound from a fusée ball in his right calf, not a lethal injury, but one making him use a crutch that winter and happy to sit and whittle. The chairs' squeaking reminded Will of this, and he looked up from his paper to muse on adventure and why he had so little of it in his life.

Will's early dreams included none of his brother's desire to dodge arrows and sleep rough, but he had had ambitions. He had dreamt of traveling, trading, and becoming wealthy. No, he had dreamt of traveling afar, trading largely, and becoming a man with wealth to spare. The advantages of this new era, the things he had seen when others missed them, things he had wanted to seize upon, like canals and railroads, seemed stuck in a quagmire, yielding only talk, talk, talk. Some of them, notably Hennepin's becoming an important center of trade, had been proven false, and the delays in others had dimmed his hopes.

Now it was the black gold of Illinois land that tempted Will. Sod was being broken where it was once impossible, and it was rich black soil, able to be tilled at last, thanks to a self-scouring plow young John Deere up in Grand Detour had invented, another opportunity Will saw while his father scoffed at the idea that a different plow would matter much.

Besides, Will could almost taste the gold in California. No mining for him, no, he would be the one who was handed the miner's gold the easy way, in trade for flour and coffee pots and pickaxes and saddlebags, all at a huge mark-up. His father would have given up their fine little store in Hennepin, but they kept it, and it was manned day to day by Benji Wolfe, who had come to Hennepin as their hired man and had never gone home. Will watched over this store, and dismal as Hennepin had become, he managed to bring it to a tidy profit each year. It was also his excuse to travel to Chicago, where Adam Schwartz had become a dear friend, and to take *Ottawa II* down to Peoria or St. Louis or New Orleans once or twice a year.

All of this would have been much easier if his father had not kept stubbornly to his cache of gold. All Niklas's brave talk of wanting a home for the next generations and yet Will could see that he had no desire to invest.

Instead, the gold was buried, and his father would not even tell him where. Slowly, painfully, Will had scraped together enough to buy the farmland next to his father's. In spite of another child arriving every two years, he had saved enough. Not that he had spoken to his father of this.

Now he felt the heat rising up his neck. *Where was my Morgan, my stake for a year of rambling, my investment in Iowa land?* He had done all that Hank had done, given his father more than the expected duty of serving him until he was twenty-one. He had even, at his father's insistence, undertaken a long and dangerous trip into Iowa Territory to talk Hank into returning to the safety of Illinois. Hank, his arm slung around a pretty young wife with their baby on her hip, had laughed at him. Then he had had the long trip home and the difficulty of explaining. Here he was still, at twenty-seven years old, a father of three, giving his labor to his father for mere room and board, handing over his cash winter wages, though perhaps not every penny.

No wonder, thought Will, *that Hank rode away when he was twenty-six.* That evening, rocking beside his father, looking straight at the fireplace, Will swore to himself, *It's now or never.* And then he spoke.

"Here's the thing, Father. I bought the acreage next door. It's a fine little farm, and this spring I can build before the planting season."

His father said nothing for a long while, and then Will thought he heard him say, "What next, Mein Gott im Himmel? What next?"

Will felt a trickle of sweat trace its way down his spine. "Little Jakob is old enough now to do the farming here." Will paused. *By rights,* he thought, *I should be complimented on my initiative. Father should be congratulating me on saving enough to strike out on my own.* "We're done harvesting," Will said, "and I'll help with spring planting. I'll have the sod broken by then, and we'll do my spring planting, too."

"Mein Gott im Himmel! You will abandon the family?"

Will jumped. He had not expected such fury. "But I'm not!" He stood up, not sure what was going to happen next.

"Mein Gott im Himmel! Do you expect me to bless this idiotic new venture?" Niklas seized the Bible off his lap, stood, and threw it into the fire.

Behind them, Katrina gasped and started forward.

How long, thought Will, *has she been there?*

Katrina grabbed a poker and pulled at the Bible, but it was already ablaze.

"Leave it, woman! Let it burn." Niklas turned and stomped from the room.

Katrina looked up at Will, accusation in her eyes, and went back to batting at the burning Bible, the family Bible where she had carefully entered every birth, marriage, and death, as his parents had done before her.

"It's not like I'm going to California!" Will headed for the door. "I'll be in the barn if he comes to his senses. Enough is enough."

CHAPTER 48

GOLDDIGGERS

December 5, 1848: Tiskilwa

"Enough!" cried Amalie Peterssen, as her stepson, Lars, climbed the ladder with a fresh-cut pine log on his shoulder. Izak held the other end in place and waited for Lars to drop his end into position. He did, grinned, and raised one arm to the sky in triumph. It was the last of the logs needed for a new outbuilding.

Amalie stood back to judge whether it was level. The boy, now seventeen, liked nothing much more than using his muscles, and now he slid down the ladder, flexed those muscles and did a few wild steps that could not for the love of God be called dancing, but were instead sheer explosive enthusiasm.

"Shameless showoff, you." Amalie launched the insult at her stepson, but since she had to duck to hide her smile, it wouldn't stick. Nothing much stuck to Lars when his strength proved itself to him a dozen times a day.

When Izak and Amalie sailed to Copenhagen and brought Lars back with them, the boy was a bold eight-year-old and ready for adventure, even if it meant leaving the nest of cousins he had grown up among and accepting a new stepmother and a father he had been taught to admire but hardly knew.

The return voyage was Lars's chance to become a sailor like his seacaptain father, and he took to it with the energy and enthusiasm that marked everything he did, beginning as a cabin boy and rated as ordinary seaman—at age nine!—by the time New York harbor hove into view. In the long hours aboard, the three Peterssens discovered a wonderful truth: they liked each other immensely. As the years wore on without the appearance of more children, they became a tight-knit unit of energy, intelligence, and mutual support, tackling one problem after the other.

Izak had intended them to stay in Illinois only a year or two, breaking sod he thought would be farmed by his father-in-law and building a snug little house he thought would become Will and Dora's. He owed the Kästners a great deal for taking him in, and it seemed only right to repay them.

Now the years had passed in a blur, and he missed the sea. He and Amalie had given up a decade to be sure her parents would be well-settled, her mother able to smile again. Niklas and Katrina were still strong, surprisingly so for their advanced ages, and now life was easy for them with the first backbreaking labor of homesteading accomplished, a comfortable house well-furnished, and Will and Jakob doing most of the farming for them.

Izak could not help but look west; there was gold to consider. These nights, he fell asleep debating about whether it would be better to go overland from St. Louis or sail from New York and go around the Horn or through the Panama shortcut. Any landlubber in Illinois would elect the overland route, but Izak was a sailor, and to tell the truth, Amalie was, too, having crossed the Atlantic three times and never a touch of mal de mer.

He wondered whether to sail as passengers or to try for a berth as a captain or first mate. While it had been years, the salt air was in his blood. He was sure it would all come back to him.

Thinking this way reminded him of Thomas Segrave, who had long ago sailed away to England, leaving Yvette with child. She called herself Mrs. Segrave now and purported to be a widow. The two of them, she and her mother, were widows running Robichaux House. There was no one to know better but he himself and Amalie, who were not about to say a word to anyone. Another memory came flooding back of the night at the Creole ball, when all had seemed innocent and full of possibility.

Izak shook himself and returned to debating the best and fastest way to get to California. By sea was more expensive, but they could afford it. And if California was dripping with gold the way they said it was, they would soon be repaid for their journey.

Besides, he missed the sea. All three of the Peterssens did.

CHAPTER 49

THE PRODIGAL SON

December 30, 1848: Tiskilwa

When he got home from his midwinter trip to Chicago, Will, out of concern for his father's age and increasingly temperamental behavior, hid the November issue of the *Chicago Democrat*.

The next morning, after he had slept deeply and washed off the dust of his trip, he thought this tactic childish. No matter how disturbing the news, it must come from him and no other. He took the precaution of inquiring with Oskar Miller, whose copy of the *Illinois Staats-Zeitung* confirmed the sad news.

That evening, he handed the paper to his father. "Here. I think you'd better read this."

His father, Niklas, the old warrior, already knew about the March Revolutions in Europe and had read with glee about Prince von Metternich's resignation as chief minister to Emperor Ferdinand I of Austria and his exile in Britain. Calls for a parliament followed, and a new constitution was written: *The Fundamental Rights and Demands of the German People.* The document listed basic rights: freedom of the press, freedom of assembly, written constitutions, arming of the people, universal male suffrage, and a parliament, which was called the National Assembly, now already in place. He followed the progress of the revolution closely as it moved from Austria to the Rhineland in issues of the *Neue Rheinische Zeitung*, published in Cologne and sent to him by Addie Erlinger.

Now he read about the collapse of the revolution with the silent fatalism of so many in Europe. Katrina patted his back. Will stood awkwardly to one side. When the first flood of grief ebbed, his father's face grew dark with anger, and he waved them both away.

"Out!" he said with such ferocity neither dared to stay.

It was over. In Austria, Cologne's own Robert Blum had been executed by firing squad on November 9 despite the immunity that should have been his as a member of the National Assembly. Niklas had shared secrets with Robert Blum in a Cologne tavern years ago, the night before the family boarded *Holsatia* to go down the Rhine, the night before Günter Erlinger was murdered in the woods while driving the Kästner's wagon back to Berleburg.

Prussia's King Frederick William IV had been offered the crown under a new constitutional monarchy and refused, calling it "an offer from the gutter." At this, the National Assembly fell apart. A few men tried to regroup in Stuttgart but were scattered by troops loyal to the king. Armed uprisings in support of the new constitution erupted in Saxony, the Palatinate, and Baden, all short-lived and crushed by Prussian troops. Revolutionists were caught, executed, or imprisoned. The achievements of the March Revolution, including the Basic Rights, were abolished everywhere.

The revolution had failed. The article noted an influx of German patriots to the United States, among them Carl Schurz, Franz Sigel, and Niklas Hecker, known as Forty-Eighters. They swore to honor Blum and remember his last words: "I die for the German liberty I fought for." The day of his death, November 9, was already being called Germany's Schicksalstag, its "Fateful Day." The revolution was in ashes.

Niklas set aside the newspaper. It had taken so many years for a blow to be struck for German freedom and unity, and now it had been beaten back to nothing, the worst monarchies reinstated in power. For years he had worked for the revolution, but in the end, he had not been there. All his efforts for naught, the German Democracy Movement destroyed, the chance for liberty gone, his beloved country lost to a tyrant.

Eventually, Niklas raised his eyes and looked at what was right in front of him. It was a scene of undeniable domestic bliss, the mantelpiece Jakob had carved for them and above it the silver-handled sword he had wielded so long and so well. A cheerful fire crackled away, and soon Katrina stole in and left a pot of tea and a cup and saucer on the table beside him. He heard her in the hallway admonishing a grandchild, "Leave Opa alone. He wants some peace and quiet, and God knows he deserves it."

An idea was already bubbling within him. He could feel it taking shape, and he listened with his heart, waiting, feeling it begin to spin around him in his comfortable house, his comfortable chair, through the warmth and the cheerfulness of home.

He was breathing hard, he realized, dizzy with this new idea even as it was still forming. He tried to seize it, feeling, unreasonably enough, that grief demanded he ignore it. Then, as the idea took shape, the words spun in his ears: "We did the right thing!" The anger, the blank stare melted away, and his pulse ran as if he were once again in the cavalry, sword in hand, victory imminent, laughing with his compatriots.

It was bittersweet, this feeling. He would grieve again, he knew, whenever he thought of Robert Blum, of false kings and their toadies on parade, of patriots festering in distant prisons, of cruelties administered without conscience or humanity, of brave men lined up against a wall and shot.

But he saw beyond anger and grief to a long life ahead, to his children's and grandchildren's lives, safe in a land where kings were no more. He stood, a little uncertain on his feet, reached up and took down the sword, swinging it a little. *Here,* he thought, *we fight for ourselves and for our futures. I did the right thing to bring them here. We were right to escape, in spite of Jakob's almost drowning, in spite of losing Hank to the lure of the Great West, in spite of Izak and the fire. Here, I might lose a son, but not to a king's army. Here, no king has a God-given right to anything. Victory is ours,* he realized, *and its spoils are citizenship and liberty.*

"Niklas? Are you all right?" Katrina was concerned to see the sword in his hands.

"You don't need to worry," he said. "I am my own man in my own country."

He thought of how Will had leapt ahead, making the family comfortable, knowing how to seize opportunities, giving them one beautiful grandchild after another, filling the house with life and possibility. He had fallen into an old man's trap, the child who left idolized, the child who stayed only human and thought less for it. *I must thank Will, clap him on the back, and tell him how much good he has done.*

He started for the doorway, but a commotion at the front door stopped him. A muffled scream, children running and laughing. Will's deep laughter of pleasure. Another voice, somehow familiar.

Katrina was looking down the hallway, and he joined her. At the other end of the hall, around the bend, burst their family, two generations of them, and in the lead was Hank.

"Father! Mother! Your prodigal son has returned!" His pretty young wife was with him, and several children followed them.

But it seemed Hank's sudden appearance had undone all their hopes, for Niklas dropped to his knees, his face ashen, his hand held to his chest. The sword clattered to the floor.

It was hours later, when his sons had carried him to his bed, and the doctor had come and gone, that Niklas held Katrina's hand while he welcomed Hank home properly and told with pride of Will's many accomplishments.

Niklas could have died a happy man at that moment, but he was not about to give Old Scratch the satisfaction. Not yet, and not for many long years to come, not until he had built the solid stone house he wanted and welcomed many more grandchildren. Not until he had taught them about the Old Country, and Napoleon's foolishness, and his own, and war's, with all its obligations and shocks and absurdities.

Only then would he shake his head in joy and amazement at his sons and daughters and the unimaginable success they had made of America.

Only then would he go in peace.

FROM THE AUTHOR

The word "novel" comes from Latin, *novellus*, and means a story that does not rework an ancient myth, folktale, or parable, but instead, is something new, fresh, strange, amusing, and surprising.

1836: Year of Escape, 1837: Love Among Strangers, and the yet-to-be-written *1880: All Our Strength* are examples of this form. How could they be other than new, strange, and surprising when they spring from the true stories of my families? Their actual lives were filled and shaped by their immigration journey, an explosion of the new, fresh, strange, amusing, and surprising.

And yet...fictionalized. For the most important reasons, this fictionalized account depends on speculation about motives, relationships, and beliefs. To tell that kind of story, in all humility, requires fiction.

The Immigration Chronicles are "hard" historical fiction, which adheres to a real timeline, tells stories of real events, and restricts fictionalization to unrecorded, imagined conversations and thoughts. Real people may appear, like Abraham Lincoln in this story. (Yes, he and Allen Gentry really were attacked while taking a flatboat down to New Orleans, and he really did suffer a nasty cut to one ear that left him with a scar for the rest of his life).

Fictionalization allows an author to change names and add the characters and events that make storytelling sing. For example, I kept all the family members' birthdates in line with history, but it is only a guess—suggested by the many years between the first two children—that there could have been a first wife. She is fictional. As another example, the historical records showed an unusually long voyage, but with no hint of what delayed them, I had room for much speculation.

The Immigration Chronicles were inspired by family stories and astounding family documents like the one shown below, a December 1815 safe-passage. It allowed my real great-great-grandfather, Rudolph Sauer, to travel safely home through territory that had been Napoleon's when Rudolph joined the army but had by June 1815 changed hands, and belonged to the victor, the king of Prussia, Frederick William III.

As I worked on the novel, a new tranche of documents was discovered, showing that the family had actually departed from Bremerhaven, landed in Baltimore (with another lost-to-history Sauer family!) and sailed coastwise to New Orleans, arriving as portrayed when many men were returning from the war in Texas. The novel had already taken its present shape by then, so I left their admittedly odd itinerary as it was. Someone's journey could have followed the path I outlined, and that is part of the theme of this book, to explore the very different immigration journeys so many of our ancestors experienced and how these changed over the centuries.

Even today, the dangers of immigration, worries about the effects on children, difficulties of establishing a new home, and shocks of a new culture and language still face immigrants. This is their story, too.

Rose Osterman Kleidon, October 1, 2024

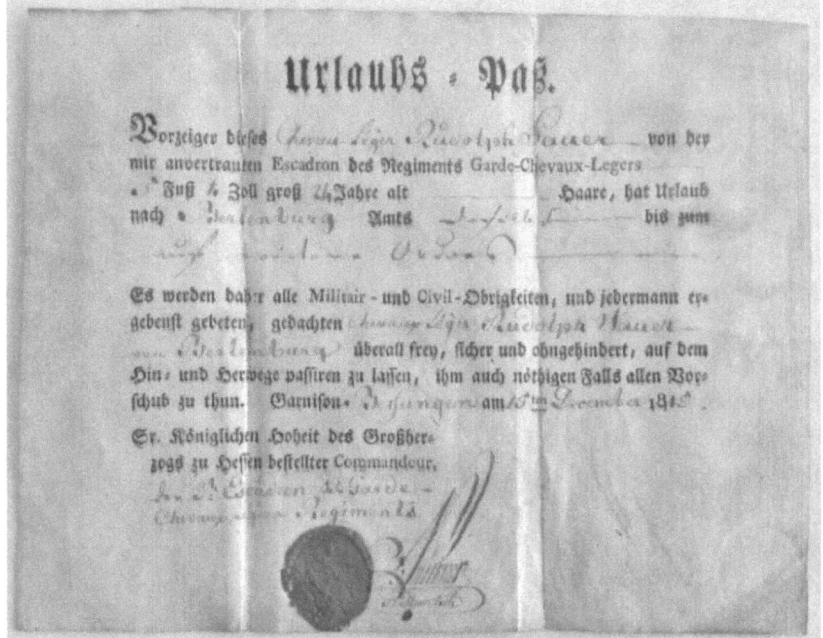

ACKNOWLEDGMENTS, 2024

The week that I wrapped up writing *1837*, I received this email from a friend who was beginning to read my first novel, *1836: Year of Escape.*

> "I'm about eighty pages into *1836* and I'm impressed by the quality of your writing and the knowledge you have of daily life back in the early 1800s. It's almost as if you are recalling something you've experienced—are you sure you haven't been reincarnated?"

That's enough all by itself to inspire any writer! So…first, let me say thank you

- to my many readers for their fabulous endorsements, glowing reviews, and interesting, insightful responses of all kinds, including invitations to speak to book clubs.
- to my family and friends, especially those who served as beta readers. You are always in my heart.
- to my brave ancestors, who walked, rode, and sailed through the premodern world, and who speak to me as they did to Linda Hogan:

"Suddenly all my ancestors are standing beside me. Be still, they say. Watch and listen. You are the result of the love of thousands."
>   — Linda Hogan, *Dwellings: A Spiritual History of the Living World*

For me, as I write, history springs to life, bringing to me my ancestors and those they met, the many weird, annoying, dangerous, kindly, and fascinating people of the premodern world. I find the conditions of their lives and the challenges they faced endlessly interesting, and I hope you can follow me into that forever-gone world, and reap the new awarenesses and amazing insights that result from the armchair time travel that is the glory of good historical fiction.

ACKNOWLEDGMENTS, 2022
REPRINTED WITH EDITS FROM
1836: YEAR OF ESCAPE

First, I thank my students. For years I taught college students to write in various ways—for other classes and for future careers in the sciences or at marketing communications firms. All that time, they were teaching me, too, giving me the courage to take on an extreme writing challenge, historical fiction. Luckily, I had taught how to do reliable research, so when I began telling a story of nineteenth century immigration, I could take delight in the required research.

Writers need a spark of inspiration, and for me, it came from a small, admittedly obscure writing group in the Estancia neighborhood in Surprise, Arizona. Friends, your amazement at whatever I came up with encouraged me to think I might have something of value to say.

Others who kept me on track include Barbara Ellis, a fine editor who became a friend, Jan Kardys, who had confidence in me, agent Emily Kim, and the always friendly, helpful and capable team at River Grove Books. I also thank Christopher Norris, who read with sensitivity to PTSD, sharing his own experiences and those of veterans he had treated; and Steven Ellis, who brought his sailing expertise to bear. Then there were the language experts, including Chris for Spanish, Ewa Kapera for Polish, and Rebecca Barnum for French. My German experts included Dr. Barbara Fischer and Dr. Paul Reidesel, whose unrivaled knowledge of the Berleburg region, its local language and customs, and the politics of the era did much to keep this fictional tale within the strictures of historical accuracy.

I owe a special thanks to Nancy E. Turner, author of *My Name Is Resolute,* the NYT bestselling *These Is My Words,* and all of the Prine family saga. Her encouragement and sensitive, sensible editing suggestions came at just the right time. And to Steve Vogel, a classmate in high school and college and the NYT bestselling author of *Reasonable Doubt* and *The Unforgiven.*

My friends and family read for me, especially Judi Kleidon and Pam Osterman, who said this story deserved readers far beyond the family. My brother John found an amazing cache of documents for me. My deep thanks go to William Zucker, who did brilliant translations of Carl Ewald's stories for children and who was my cheerleader from the beginning. Also on that cheerleading team were good friends Gurinder and Sandy Rana, Mike Kolsky and Barbara Rosen, Rose and John Richardson, Quentin Maguire, Diane and Henry Lynch, Irish genealogist Tom Crowley, Mike and Kathy Lehr, about a thousand Fosseys, and the plant experts among my garden club friends, especially Claire Purdy, Pam Reitz, and Mary Ann Slattery, who also let me borrow her last name.

My Osterman, Hakes, Kleidon, Sauer, Smith, Sandhu, Ballos, Jungknecht, Nishigaya, and Rokusek relatives have watched both the fictional and the genealogical sides develop, offering photos, documents, maps, and much enthusiastic support. Among them are direct descendants of the family who inspired this story, those who knew the family, and kissing cousins. Behind them all are my father and mother, who could tell stories of the family in great and loving detail, speculating on mysteries about who and why and when. This story is for them and for the long-gone grands, great-grands, aunts, uncles, and cousins whose courage, love, loyalty, and wit outlasts them, shared by many and now inspiring this story.

Most of all, I thank my sister, Linda, who read tirelessly, one draft after the other, seeing strengths in each; Joan, with her reliable enthusiasm and kindness; and Steve, who just plain likes the way I write. My son, Kurt; daughter-in-law, Megan; grandchildren; and especially my husband, Dennis, deserve big, solid gold Oscars (or reasonable facsimiles) for keeping the home fires burning while I ignored everything in the twenty-first century. Perhaps most of all, I am thankful to Dennis for his relentless optimism and his masterful methods of encouraging creativity. I thank you all, dearest family and from somewhere in the mists of fiction, so do the Kästners.

www.ingramcontent.com/pod-product-compliance
Lightning Source LLC
Chambersburg PA
CBHW021504110726
47899CB00001BA/284